A
RECKLESS
INDULGENCE

Tides of Pleasure Series: Book 1

in the Fangs With Benefits universe

Aveda Vice

Bad Bite LLC

Also By Aveda Vice

Fangs With Benefits

Hunger Duet
Feed
Yours, Insatiably

Lost Touch Duet
Skin
Inextricably Tied

Wed in the Wild Series
Bound
Vicious Devotion

Tides of Pleasure Series
A Reckless Indulgence

Headless

Fear, and Other Love Languages

Christmas with the Horned God

Dedication

If this is not the life you planned,
if you can't go back to who you were,
if you lost some part of yourself to survive,
you can still have something beautiful.

You still deserve that.

Author's Note

This book contains sexual situations. It is not intended for anyone under the legal age of adulthood. All characters depicted in sexual situations herein are over 18 years of age. This book is not to be used as an informational guide to any type of sex or sexual education.

Some topics within this book may be sensitive or disturbing to some readers. Reader discretion is advised.

For detailed information on the topics addressed, please visit the author's website **or scan the codes below.**

ONE

Cav

Captain Heathen is going to kill him, but at least he'll leave a pretty corpse.

That's what Cav tells himself as he rows toward the *Silver Spoon*, his dragon scales flattening against the wind. From his dinghy, the luxurious restaurant ship looks impressive, a wooden double-decker covered in carvings and candles flickering against the night. The *Spoon*'s path of travel is a meandering circle around the wealthiest island, reminding the rest of the archipelago where the elite reside.

Cav churns the oars and hisses when his shoulder twinges. That old wound seems to flare up when he's doing something he shouldn't. Cypher would say that's a sign, but Cypher says a lot of shit, like —

Cav's fingers tighten around the oars. No distractions. Either he catches the *Spoon* before it passes again, or he has to row all the way back to shore...and he's not leaving without something to show for it.

As he travels, he faces the smaller island where he cast off. How poetic that he's forced to stare at the reminder of where he's supposed to be. Over the tops of the palm trees, he can barely make out the crow's nest of the *Indulgence* bobbing on the sea.

Cav's captain will be pissed once word spreads about what he's done, but Cav's not yet sure what that'll be. All he knows is he's not letting this loose end slip away. He ties his hair up and blows auburn bangs out of his face. Fuck it. He works better without a plan. Once he gets an idea in his mind, his jittery body pays the price until he turns that thought into action. *Hyperactive*, Cypher describes it. *Deficit of attention. Lack of —*

Cav's sharpened teeth grit. Focus. He has to focus. The *Spoon* is here.

The large ship cruises by and casts him further in shadow. Out here, his tiny dinghy is nearly invisible; the rich patrons of the *Spoon* don't notice him bracing on the edge of his boat. When the *Spoon*'s rope ladder passes, he leaps and grunts as his body knocks against the hull before he climbs.

Piano music trickles from the *Spoon*'s open windows, muffled by the clatter of dishware and conversation. Cav clings to the top of the ladder and peers through the slats in the railing. Guards lean against the stern of the ship, rolling cigarettes and grumbling in a cloud of smoke. The rest of the deck is enclosed, except for the grand entryway that stretches before Cav. It's certainly eye-catching, with dozens of lanterns hovering over the ornate host stand...and it's the only way in or out.

Cav cranes his neck to catch a glimpse of the lavish dining room inside it. The dim lighting adds to the ambience, highlighting flashes of jewelry in candlelight. Waiters weave between tables, presenting meals and bottles that would cost

Cav a month's wages.

He scrapes his muddy heel against the ladder, ignoring the hem of his breeches clinging to knees. His entire ensemble is too tight, but it's all he could find in a pinch. If nothing else, it complements the fiery hues of his scales. He'll blend in as long as no one looks too closely.

Ignoring the protests of his shirt, Cav pulls himself over the railing with a distinct ripping sound.

"*Shit.*"

A breeze teases the snag in his waistcoat, but he can't stop for it. It'll have to hold until he's finished. Maybe he can distract the staff with something else…

He reaches for his top button to expose his cleavage before he thinks better of it. This isn't the *Indulgence*; people in these places can be bizarre about that sort of thing. Best not to draw attention to himself.

With a sigh, he positions his hand over the rip and strolls through the entryway.

The host lifts his head, eyes darting to the wet footprints Cav has left across the floor.

Cav blocks them from view, sweeping his tail through the tracks and leaning against the host stand. "Good evening." He drapes on his most charismatic smile, tucking his bangs behind his horns and keeping his shoulders hunched to disguise his chest. "I took a bit of a self-guided tour when we set sail, and I'm afraid I got separated from my companion."

The host smiles mildly. "What's the name?"

Cav fights not to clench his jaw. "Roderick."

While the host checks the reservation list, Cav squints toward the tables behind him. It's like the *Spoon* wants their guests to be unidentifiable. Even if the technology from the continents doesn't function out here, surely this luxury diner can provide more than a couple of candles per table.

It's not until Cav's second sweep that he catches the

bastard. Roderick sits at the furthest row of tables with a ring on every pale finger, his eyes outlined in kohl and a smug grin on his face.

Asshole.

The host clears his throat. "I'm afraid the Roderick reservation is for a party of two."

"Exactly." Cav maintains his smile. "I'll just —"

"And both members are already seated."

Cav flexes his fingers. There's no need to panic. *You're supposed to be rich. Think rich.* Summoning a chuckle, he knocks on the host stand with a playful lift of his brows. "He must have made a *friend* when we boarded. I'll make sure we each have a chair."

The host sputters, but Cav is already slipping away into the dining room.

Lowering his head, he snakes between floral arrangements and serving trays. He rounds on the last row of tables, and Roderick is still oblivious, trailing hungry eyes over his companion. It's no surprise Roderick enticed some unsuspecting ingénue to join him for dinner. Poor girl. She has no idea what she's gotten into.

Cav knows he shouldn't say anything yet. He should play it cool, he should sit at the table, but the fire inside him burns up his better judgment. He opens his mouth to call out —

But something stops him. He can only make out the woman's back, but that's enough to make his mind grind to a halt. Her body is as plump and juicy as peeled lychee, her luxuriously wet hair piled atop her head. Her dress clings to her curves, styled to look like she's dripping in pearls and absolutely nothing else.

Heat surges up Cav's throat, and he swallows to stifle the draconic ember in his chest. He shouldn't stare. He's here to keep an eye on Roderick, and despite what a disappointing subject that is, he has a job to do.

A waiter squeezes past, setting a charcuterie board and drinks on Roderick's table. Roderick doesn't so much as glance his way, gesturing instead to the view out the window. The woman follows the motion, but Cav doesn't. He watches Roderick flip back the gem on one of his rings and tilt it over the woman's glass, dispensing something powdery. Then, Roderick lifts his own drink in a toast.

Cav digs his claws into an empty chair beside him and drags it across the aisle until it's right next to Roderick.

The man recoils at the instruction, but his eyes sharpen when he recognizes Cav.

"Ordered for me already?" Cav asks sweetly, snatching the woman's drink and lifting it toward Roderick in mock-salute. "You know I *hate* when you don't ask."

Roderick's slimy smile stays in place. "I'm entertaining a guest."

Cav reaches past Roderick to dump the woman's drink into a plant. "Then they'll have to forgive me."

Around them, the buzz of conversation falters. Roderick shifts in his seat, but Cav sinks back in his chair, plucking the lemon wedge from Roderick's drink into his mouth.

Roderick straightens his ascot. "I paid for my visit to your ship." He lowers his voice. "In full."

"I'm not here about your *payment*," Cav spits, dragging his finger inside the woman's glass. When he holds his claw to the light, it sparkles with grainy dregs. "I'm here about what you tried to do during your visit. What you tried to do *here*."

"Do you mind?" Over Cav's shoulder, the woman grows impatient. "You're interrupting our evening."

She doesn't realize the danger she's in, but Cav does. He refuses to look away from Roderick. "Trust me, I'm doing you a favor."

"Well, *undo it*."

That voice stirs a chord deep inside Cav. It's hauntingly

familiar, a tune he hasn't heard in so long, but one he's never forgotten. It reverberates inside him, singing through his veins when he turns to face the music.

Everything about Lyx is cool, like splashing into water on the longest day of summer. Strands of soft pinks and purples color her hair like a fuchsia flower. Her milky blue skin glows nearly translucent before it darkens at her hips. Purple scars wind around her arms and chest in thin ropes across her skin.

She looks exactly as he remembers. She is the siren who haunts his dreams, even if the hollows under her eyes are darker. Her brows knit tighter. Her scowl deeper, like it's daring a smile to cross her face.

There's no recognition for him in her eyes; she's as detached as if she were looking at a stain on the tablecloth.

Cav's heart twinges. He can't blame her. The last time she saw him, he was so weak he was hardly recognizable, battered by waves and sun. She doesn't remember the two of them in her grotto. Her frustration butting up against his lazy smile, her hands roaming his skin, her gasps against his mouth...

That's what does it. As if the memories are playing across Cav's face, Lyx's expression changes. She *does* remember him. Her fingers curl into the tablecloth, pupils blowing wide before they shrink to slits of unadulterated hate.

"*You.*"

TWO

Cav

Loathing rolls off of Lyx in waves. She doesn't hesitate, grabbing a cheese knife and slamming it down into Cav's sleeve. The blade tears through the fabric, narrowly missing his arm.

"Lyx —"

Behind Cav, Roderick tries to stand, but Cav and Lyx both grab for him to force him back into his seat.

Whispers ripple through the restaurant. Across the room, the host speaks to a burly man and points in Cav's direction.

He has to wrap this up, but his guilty conscience has him turning back to Lyx. "Listen, I know —"

"You are ruining this!" she seethes, yanking the knife out of the table.

More muscular guards appear behind the host. Cav's grip tightens around Roderick's wrist. Things have gotten out of hand; he needs to get them back under control.

This time, Lyx's knife finds his forearm. He recoils with a hiss, and Roderick seizes the opportunity, knocking over a chair as he flees toward the back of the boat.

Goddammit. Cav knows he has to stop him, but he doesn't want to leave. Something inside him begs to stay with Lyx and all her anger.

He forces himself to his feet. "Stay and take another stab at me. *Please.*" Then he yanks the knife from the table and takes off after Roderick.

There's no use trying to blend in now. The top button of Cav's shirt pops when he picks up the pace. Roderick glances over his shoulder, foot catching on a tablecloth and sending him tumbling into a bar cart. Dinner plates smash to the floor. Guests scream over the sound of shattering glass, splattered with creams and sauces. Cav snatches the back of Roderick's shirt and hauls him to his feet as they crash onto the open deck.

The doorjamb slams into Cav's ribs. He gasps for breath, but Roderick's fist finds his face and cracks his cheek. Teeth grit, Cav coils his tail around Roderick's ankles and hoists him over the railing. There's a thirty-foot drop into nothing but dark ocean, and Cav's shoulder throbs, but it's nothing compared to the adrenaline of dangling Roderick over open air.

Roderick flails. "It won't happen again! It won't!" He grasps for the front of Cav's shirt. "I can get you the drugs for free! Free of charge. You can use them for —"

Cav releases his hold, and Roderick plummets with a scream.

Shouts rise from the restaurant. Cav braces to be tackled by guards, but Lyx appears instead, leaning over the railing and cursing.

Behind them, the restaurant clamors. Cav scans the rest of the deck for lifeboats that hang only a few meters away. If he doesn't make a move, he'll be in chains before the night is through. With a pained grunt, he retrieves the cheese knife from the floor and swipes at the blood dripping from his mouth. "You need a ride?"

Lyx scoffs in disbelief. "*Me*? They're coming for *you*."

In the dining room, the panicked crowd presses against the windows while the guards struggle to push through. Cav shrugs weakly. "I'm sure they'll have some questions for you, too."

Lyx balks, but he doesn't move, not even when the commotion behind her grows. An alarm bell clangs in Cav's head, but it's not as loud as the foolish, hopeful ringing that keeps him here.

He turns the knife in his hand and extends the handle toward her. "I promised you another stab at me."

Her glare is venomous, but it seems she's actually considering it. After a moment, her hand darts toward him, bypassing the knife and shoving him toward the lifeboats. "Arrogant fucking pirate."

A smile breaks across Cav's face, and the two of them race toward the dinghies hanging off the side of the ship. Cav hoists himself over the railing before he extends his hand back toward her.

Her expression darkens. Somehow, this offer is the riskiest thing he's done this evening.

The footsteps behind her grow closer.

Reluctantly, she grabs onto him and yelps when he hoists her into the boat. "Hang on." He clears his throat to stoke the ember in his chest. Fire builds in his mouth, flowing between his lips and catching on the rope that keeps them attached to the *Spoon*.

With the guards hurtling toward them, the dinghy drops out of the sky.

Wind whizzes past and whips Cav's hair into a frenzy. He

braces against the bench as the dinghy splashes into the water, sending him sprawling on his back and knocking against the side of the boat.

He groans under the weight on his torso. Lyx winces and tries to right herself, but their legs are tangled, chests heaving against each other as she stares down at him.

The sounds of the *Silver Spoon* fade in the distance. Moonlight washes over her skin, her breath soft across his face. He remembers this. He remembers having her this close, the two of them in the middle of the ocean, no one else around for miles.

Then she grips his neck and forces his head down into the sea.

The boat nearly capsizes. His fingers close around her wrists, mouth spluttering as he's submerged. "I'm sorry. I'm sorry!"

They're going to flip if she keeps pushing. Water churns around him, soaking through his clothes and over her wrists. Only then does she pull back, jostling to the other side of the boat.

Cav's voice is hoarse. "Lyx —"

"Don't start."

"I need to apol-"

"I don't want to hear it!"

The silence resonates. She doesn't lunge for him again, but most shocking of all, she doesn't dive into the ocean to make her escape. She just keeps her arms crossed, fingernails digging into her skin.

Cav can do nothing but catch his breath and reach for the oars. His shoulder throbs in protest, but he grits his teeth. It's a mile to the wealthy island; he can push through the pain. It's the least he can do.

Carefully, he begins to row. Despite the darkness, the two of them glow like beacons in hazy shades of blue and red. He'd forgotten her body could do that, as bioluminescent as a jellyfish, the light highlighting the tension between them. For a long time, there's nothing but the sound of ocean waves until he can't help but speak. "I didn't mean for it to happen."

"I don't care what you *meant*," she hisses.

"I wasn't trying to send hunters your way."

"Oh, weren't you?" Mockery thickens her voice, but her sharp tongue slices through it. "You washed up in my grotto, and I kept you alive. *Senselessly*. And how do you thank me?" Her fists tighten like she wants another swing at him. "By telling the first port you land in all about your adventure."

Shame creeps Cav's neck. "That's not —"

"Spare no details, *Cavalier*. You certainly didn't then."

The boat drifts on the tide. Cav tries to row again, but he sucks in a breath when his shoulder spasms.

Lyx's gaze jerks toward it.

"It's fine," he insists.

She ignores him, snatching the oars and jamming them into the water. "And I knew better." She puts all her strength into rowing, like it's the only way to escape him. "Of course you sent hunters after us. Of course you told them exactly what to look for. Just like a fucking pirate."

Cav wants to argue, but how can he? No matter what he intended, she's right. The only reason hunters found the siren hive was because Cav made that fucking map. Because he was careless with it. Because he couldn't stop searching.

"Really, it's my fault," Lyx sneers. "Perhaps I was too vague. Should I have sworn you to secrecy? Should I have *specifically requested* that you not pinpoint our location? Silly me. Here I was thinking I'd been clear when I made you promise never to return." Her eyes spark humorlessly. "At least you followed *one* command."

He bites his cheek until it throbs. "What happened to the rest of the sirens?"

"Vanished. Captured. Killed." She slaps the oars into the water. "Take your fucking pick."

Cav rests his elbows on his knees. Sirens have been the mythical monsters of sailing stories for as long as he can remember, but he never wanted to harm them. Hell, he wasn't even sure they were real until he washed ashore in Lyx's cave. Now, he's played a part in their destruction.

"I am truly sorry." He wrings his hands. "For what little it's worth."

"It's not worth little." Lyx shakes her head bitterly. "It's worth *nothing*. You might as well be proud of yourself. At least I could respect that."

Cav's mouth falls open. "I'm not *proud*."

There's no use fighting it. He could never grasp the siren notion that any pain is good, that they would seek discord to their own detriment.

A cloud crosses over the moon. Cav scratches his claws against the side of the boat. "Is that how you ended up with Roderick?"

"That's *right...*" Lyx takes out her renewed fury on the paddles. "Yet another thing you ruined for me."

"He's a bad guy."

"I'm supposed to take your word for it?"

"He spiked your drink!"

"I know!" The oars slice through the water. "I had it under control. Everything was *fine* until you showed up." She leans back, putting her full weight behind the rowing. "Is this what you do now? Sneak onto fancy ships and toss their guests overboard?"

"That *guest* pulled some shit on our pleasure ship." Cav winces when the tender skin under his eye pulls taut. It'll be swollen tomorrow. A small price to pay for how he fucked this up. "I was taking care of business."

The oars stall as Lyx looks up at him. "You work on the

Indulgence? For Heathen?"

It's strange hearing the familiar names from Lyx. Despite the pain, Cav narrows his eyes. "How do you know Heathen?"

Lyx's spine straightens, like she's been forced into civility. "I didn't realize you were acquainted."

"Or you would've been happier to see me?"

Her sour look returns. "Roderick said he had a connection to her. That's why I was meeting him."

"Of course he did," Cav huffs. "But why are *you* looking for Heathen?" He gestures behind her to the wealthy island now looming over them. Light glints off the sleek materials, buildings dotted with contraptions Cav has never even heard of. "If you're meeting with people who run in Roderick's circles, I don't see what Heathen could do for you."

Lyx's jaw clenches. It's so brief, Cav wonders if it was a trick of the light, but whatever it was is replaced with her unflinching expression. "That doesn't concern you."

"But you want my help."

Her eye twitches. No doubt she's itching to be free from Cav and everything he brings with him. Maybe she would rather take her chances with Roderick. Gods, what does that say about Cav?

"Or maybe you don't." Cav holds up his palms. "I shouldn't assume. I'm sure you've got —"

"I do," she interjects, neck straining like it pains her to say. "I do. Need..."

There goes that foolish hope in his chest, refusing to die out.

As the boat floats into the dock, Cav digs into his pocket and holds out a cloth pouch between them. "You see that island?" He points to the smaller shape in the distance, a stark contrast to the opulent one before them. "The *Indulgence* is docked there. Come before sunrise, and you can meet with them."

Skeptically, Lyx opens the pouch and withdraws two coins. "I have to pay my way?"

"No. Consider it a token of atonement." Cav reaches out to brace against the dock, steadying the boat against the waves. "Since I ruined your dinner. Among other things."

There's the barest hint of emotion in her eyes. Maybe Cav imagines it, because he wants it to be true, because he wants to say more, to ask if she'll show up tomorrow, to plead for another moment alone.

As if she senses it, Lyx rises abruptly to her feet. She tips backward, and Cav catches her around the waist to keep her from falling. Her body is solid against his, her eyes clinging to his mouth like it's against her will. Like she hadn't allowed herself to look until this moment.

When his lips part, so do hers. He can almost pretend she remembers this, too, that Cav hasn't been the only one clinging to memories...

Then she clamps her mouth shut, shoving his chest and sending him splashing into the water.

In the Grotto

Lyx

Of all the things washed up in Lyx's grotto, the biggest surprise is a pirate.

At least, one who's still intact. Plenty of bodies litter this place, skulls crushed between rocks while their bones lie ensnared in plants. By the time the corpses make it here, they look very different from the way Lyx left them. All that remains is gold teeth and rotted clothing, but she remembers their faces from the shipwrecks — the hopeful lust in their eyes, the seaweed reaching toward them, the blue tint of their skin as they sank deeper.

This pirate, however, she doesn't recognize. He's pale and sickly from the sea, but there's still a red hue to his skin. The shape of his face is human, but there are horns sprouting through his short hair. Salt clings to his eyelashes and the spiked tail curled limply beside him. Despite the patches of scales on his body, it's clear he's not amphibious. He wasn't made to withstand the ocean as she is.

The tide lifts Lyx onto a rocky ledge. Water drips from her body and takes her siren form with it, her jellyfish tentacles weaving into two legs, fins and webbing shrinking until she looks almost human. This is the body pirates expect when they hunt for sirens. Beautiful. Vulnerable. Intriguing, but always familiar.

Waves splash against the pirate and rock his body closer to deeper water. If Lyx doesn't intervene, he'll drown.

A smile flits across her lips. Good. It will be her gift to the sea.

But the sea doesn't need his trinkets. Kneeling in the shallows, Lyx feels along his body for pockets. Most of his clothing is torn, leaving his skin exposed to the elements. She runs her hand over one muscled thigh and traces up his abdomen.

Her head tilts, wet hair slipping down her back. Where she expects to find flat pectorals, she's met with the curve of two breasts. Across his chest are faded marks, like a strip of fabric had been wound around it. More surprising, the pirate's shoulder bends at an odd angle with muscle pulled taut over the joint.

She hovers over the injury. Feebly, volcanic cracks spread between his scales as if a fire burns beneath the surface. When she leans closer, there's the faintest scent of soot and cinnamon —

"What a...way to go."

Her hand clamps instinctively around his throat. Did he speak? She can't be sure. His mouth doesn't move now, lips chapped and still. She must have imagined it. The waves are so loud, and whatever she thought she heard was as faint as two grains of sand rubbing together.

But then the pirate rasps in a breath.

Her fingers flex around his fragile neck. Any pulse he has is overpowered by her own, amplified when his golden eyes flutter open. This changes nothing. She will do as she always does, holding him underwater until the bubbles stop rising.

She waits for him to fight her. It's better when they do, yet even with her choking him, he doesn't move. Doesn't speak. Doesn't beg. If anything, he looks...serene. Her palm grows warm. Beneath her hand, his skin flickers with light.

She tightens her grip. "You're pathetic for a pirate."

His mouth twitches upward. One of his top teeth is chipped. "Apologies," he wheezes. "Presently, I'm...indisposed."

There's not an ounce of strength in his body. His hands lie feebly at his side, and there's not even a knife in his belt to fend her off with.

Her nose wrinkles. "You didn't bring a weapon?" Insulted, her tongue clucks. "It's always the most arrogant hunters who die in these waters."

"Consider," he pants, flinching when her fingers tighten, "that I'm simply foolish. Not arrogant."

Never has a pirate admitted to his shortcomings, but she won't be tricked. "You truly are a fool if you think I believe that."

"I'm not a hunter," he gasps. "I work...on a ship. I took a boat...to get supplies. A storm blew me off course."

Her fingers flex. She had called upon the sea for a storm...but it doesn't matter. All that matters is that he's here. "Your story won't spare you." Power builds in the base of Lyx's throat as she sets back on her heels. She doesn't have to kill him herself. With her song, he'll destroy himself, and he'll be grateful for it. She opens her mouth and plucks the persuasive strings of her vocal cords —

"I'm not asking," the pirate breathes, "for you to spare me." There's a long pause, like he's used all his strength to speak. "But I hate the thought...of dying...while you think so poorly of me."

Bewildered, Lyx blinks. Surely she misheard him. It's the strangest attempt to save himself that she's ever seen, yet he seems completely at ease.

"Will you give me that...one kindness?" His crusted eyelashes brush his cheeks like he might drift off to sleep. "Think generously of me...before you kill me?"

Lyx scoffs. Why is she entertaining this? Granted, it's the least offensive thing a pirate has asked of her. It's the only thing a pirate has asked; most of them are too busy making demands to realize their fate is sealed.

"Please," he whispers. "If you do it...then I'll...go quietly."

"I don't care how you go," she growls, "all that matters is that you're going."

That should frighten him, but he doesn't respond. Perhaps he can't. His chest rises and falls shallowly, skin more ashen than when she arrived.

Pitiful indeed.

Her eyes roll. This pirate won't last another hour. The faster she gets rid of him, the faster she can comb the shipwrecks for spoils. With some struggle, she searches for the unfamiliar words. "I think — passably of you. Now, drag yourself —"

"What are you thinking?"

Her thoughts slip away like a fish. "What?"

"What passable things..." He breathes slowly, eyes fluttering again. "Are you thinking about me?"

She swallows. They're closer than she meant to be. His expression is familiar, the dreamy look of a hunter under her thrall, but she hasn't yet used her song on him.

He sounds delirious. "Are you thinking, 'He's...adventurous. So brave. Ruggedly —'" A vicious cough overtakes him, water spluttering from his mouth until his voice is rough with salt. "Handsome?"

Her cheeks heat. She's not sure if it's humiliation or

something else. This half-drowned pirate is making a mockery of her, like she doesn't hold his very life in her hands. With gritted teeth, she digs her nails into his broken shoulder. "I could command you to drown!"

A pained noise escapes him.

She tightens her grip. "I wouldn't even have to touch you. My voice alone would send you to the bottom of the sea. If I speak it, then you obey."

He gives another helpless gasp before she jerks her hand away, splashing it clean in the pool of water beside her. The pirate can do little more than pant, grimacing until his face contorts into something else.

Lyx gapes at him. "You're smiling?"

Even in his state, it's undeniable, his mouth tilted up at the corners as if death isn't waiting to greet him. "If that's how I'm gonna go..." With chapped lips, he gives a poor attempt at a whistle. "Kinda...poetic."

Her teeth grind. "Poetic?"

"Pirates 'n sirens..." His words turn to slurry, fading as swiftly as the rest of him. "Tale as old as..."

Finally, the pirate falls silent. Slowly, Lyx rises to her feet, fearing the movement might rouse him into another inane conversation. But the longer she waits, the quieter it grows. Soon, there's nothing but the shush of waves disguising any rise and fall of his chest.

She doesn't even have to kill him. He'll be dead before sunrise.

Still, she should do it herself. Killing him would fuel her, stirring up chaos to bask in like a lizard on a rock. Her siblings wouldn't pass up the chance to feed; they would drown him and eat the remains for fun.

But this pirate is so weak already. He wouldn't even put up a fight. Where's the fun in that?

She watches him down her nose. Such an odd creature.

He's as brazen as a seagull, but placid as a whale. It's...unnerving. Only like this can she tolerate him — when he isn't speaking, isn't saying strange things that no normal person would utter, isn't looking at her with those eyes as warm as wax.

Why does it rattle her? What about this pirate is so confounding?

Her toes curl against the rocks. It doesn't matter. He'll die the same as all the others, and when she returns tomorrow, all that will be left will be a corpse...or nothing at all.

With that, she wades to the edge of the ledge and dives back into the sea.

THREE

Lyx

Killing Cav is always an option.

Lyx jerks to a halt where she's stalking down the beach. The temptation is strong; she could turn back. Cav can't have gotten far from the docks. She'll find a broken bottle along the way and entice him into a dark corner before she drags the jagged edge across his throat.

But killing him isn't *enough*.

Not for all the time she's spent imagining it. For the past two years, *that* vision has hung like a portrait in her mind. It's the backdrop to all her thoughts, a work of art that she pours over day after day. There are always new details to enchant her. What sounds will Cav make when she gets her teeth into him? Which will die first: the ember inside him, or the light in his eyes? Will he fight her off, or will he embrace this urge the same way he welcomed all her others?

A shiver darts through her. *No.* No matter how the

memories try to crawl back into her conscience, she sloughs them off. Killing Cav is too easy. After all these months, she wants to take her time with it. Saliva gathers in the back of her throat. It's not Cav's death that entices her; it's the thought of ripping him apart and devouring the pieces, a torturous end that she can draw out for as long as she pleases. He doesn't deserve a quick death. He deserves the agonizing pain he's caused her. He deserves to have every second of his life invaded the same way he's done to her.

Her foot snags on a clump of seaweed. She kicks to free herself, but the tendrils tangle around her legs until she's forced to tug off her sandals.

For all this time spent imagining Cav, she wasn't prepared for what seeing him again would do to her. He looks different now. His hair is longer, half-covering the slit pupils of his eyes. Even the vibrant color has returned to his skin.

She clamps her lips together, like that will stifle the thoughts. The pearls of her dress clack as she picks her way along the beach. She doesn't know which direction she's headed, but she knows it's the right one; the tugging sensation at the base of her throat tells her that. Eventually, she comes to a shallow inlet where the waves roll deep into the island.

Her shoulders tense. She has to cross here. Wading across would be simple, but her gills flutter anxiously. The ocean is not her home anymore; she lost its favor when she lost everything else. Waves that once created her now roll past with white cap warnings that she doesn't understand, spoken in a language she can no longer decipher.

She dares not even dip her toes in.

Instead, she moves further inland until she finds some jagged rocks poking out of the water. With each step, the sharp edges dig into her feet, but she bites her cheek to keep moving. Past the shrubbery and driftwood, an abandoned cottage comes into view. It can hardly be called a building any longer, vines growing wild over its sides and leaving little more than broken windows and a lamp flickering inside.

Lyx's stomach drops. Tidus beat her back here. Who knows how long he's been waiting? No doubt he's been stewing in the dark, turning his anger over in his hands until it sharpens into something worse.

She has to remind herself that's what she wants. It's what she *needs. Chaos.* That thought alone stirs the hungry pit inside her until it opens its jaws to be fed.

The splintering cottage stairs prick her. She feels for the door, but when she pushes, it doesn't budge. She has to jam her shoulder into it twice before it opens. Its rusty hinges squeal, a grating sound outdone only by the stench of mildew. When Lyx finally squeezes inside, grains of salt and sand dig into her feet.

Across the room, a busted crate hosts an oil lantern that sheds less than a foot of light.

Lyx lingers in the shadows for an entire minute. It's a foolish act of rebellion, but she relishes the small hit of power, like she can control what happens. She's not naive enough to believe that completely. Her defiance will be nothing more than foreplay, but it works for now.

A figure finally leans forward into the light, lips curled back over his teeth. "You lost our fucking mark?"

There's no use denying Roderick is gone, but giving into Tidus does nothing for her. He'll be pissed no matter what she says, and the air is already thick with discord. She might as well get her fill. Without a word, she slinks across the room, bending at the waist to twist the lantern's knob. As the wick grows, so does Tidus's scowl.

He looks different than the day he captured her. He was brutally handsome then, but now, he's just brutal. His teal skin has faded to a sickly gray under strands of seaweed tangling in his hair. Barnacles cling to his face next to sand dollars embedded in his dry gills.

The sea is trying to reclaim him. It's a part of their pact, the agreement all marine species made with the ocean long ago. Whatever they do must embody the powerful allure of the sea. Sirens are given their songs in exchange for inciting chaos. Undines are free to traverse the land, so long as they have a band of loyal followers behind them.

Unfortunately for Tidus, his company has dwindled to only Lyx and a small sloop. When he caught her, he boasted a massive ship and a crew of thirty men, pickpockets and crooks and racketeers. They were all hungry for glory, but Captain Tidus's cruelty and greed drove even them away until he was left with nothing.

Nothing but Lyx.

Yet Tidus refuses to return to the ocean. It's as if he thinks he can outsmart the sea itself, taunting the waves by sailing from one con job to another and upsetting the balance of nature. Most infuriating of all, it works. No matter how many storms they weather, Tidus always finds a way back to land.

The sea always claims its due.

That's what Lyx reminds herself, even if she is powerless to make it happen. Whatever sway she had with the ocean was destroyed the moment she was forced into Tidus's service. She hasn't stepped in the sea in years. If she called out to it, she fears she'd hear only an empty echo in return.

Impatient, Tidus presses his pointer finger down against the table. "You heard me."

The hungry pit inside her takes a long drink. Despite the pandemonium on the *Silver Spoon*, she needs more. With one hand, she plucks a pin from her hair and turns away. "Relax."

Tidus's chair creaks under his weight.

She refuses to flinch, no matter how her skin crawls. Give Tidus an inkling of fear, and he'll hunt it down like a shark with a drop of blood. Placing the pin between her teeth, she unwinds the tendrils of her hair and takes a steadying breath.

Tidus's voice is low and threatening. "I'm sure I didn't hear you correctly."

The scales on the back of her shoulders lift. It's like she can't help herself, her hunger egging her on. She pulls another pin from her hair and slips it between her knuckles. It's a flimsy weapon. She should have kept the cheese knife from the ship, but using that on Tidus would only enrage him.

Which is what she wants, she reminds herself again. Fighting means feeding. Fighting is what she needs.

Her voice is clipped by the pin between her teeth. "I got what you wanted."

Tidus pushes to his feet, and the rotting floorboards groan. "Is that so?"

She hates having him at her back, blocking out the light when he towers over her. With one finger, he twists a lock of her hair until it tugs at her scalp.

She doesn't gasp. Doesn't even breathe.

His teeth scrape her neck, but any tenderness is a mask for his barely-concealed fury. "How could you get what I want," he asks slowly, "if our mark is at the bottom of the *fucking ocean?*"

Her throat constricts. Depths, she wishes she could command him away, but she can't even look at him. That would be an invitation, a strike of the match she was so eager to light moments ago. She thinks of all the sailors she's drowned. Is this how they felt as she pulled them beneath the waves? Is this what it's like to dangle over the mouth of a beast?

Tidus's fingers clamp under her chin to jerk her toward him. She resists, but he wrenches harder, and she bites down a pained gasp when the broken shells that coat his hands dig into her flesh. "You seem distracted, little fish." His saccharine tone curdles in her stomach while his fingers tighten. "Which is odd, because *I'm speaking to you.*"

Her pulse races. She has to remember that this is what she needs, an appetizer for the feast that comes after. The danger is a necessity. It's the drink that fills her, drizzling down her throat until she can't swallow any more. She chokes on it and spits back all the venom she has. "I told you, I *got* what you *want.*"

FOUR

Lyx

Curiosity overtakes Tidus's rage. "You got a meeting with Heathen?"

Pain tingles through Lyx's jaw. She jerks out of his grip. "Turns out your favorite little rat works for them now."

Tidus lifts a puzzled brow.

"*Cavalier*," she reminds him. When Tidus looks at her blankly, her skin prickles. "The one who drew the map!"

"*That's* who threw Roderick overboard?" Tidus balks before he laughs heartily. "Well, I'll be damned; that chatty little dragon keeps coming through for me."

His delight makes Lyx's blood boil. That *chatty dragon* has haunted her for the past two years, yet Tidus can't be bothered to remember his name. She yanks another pin from her hair and curls her fist around it.

With a sigh, Tidus returns to his chair and basks in the glow of a job well done — *Lyx's* job well done. "You know…"

His voice shifts lower than before. "Heathen doesn't give meetings to just anyone."

Lyx doesn't like the way he looks at her, gaze traversing the pearls that cling to her thick frame and curve over her breasts. It was Tidus who dressed her. She had to look the part for the *Silver Spoon*, draped in her last remaining piece of finery. Tidus likes when she wears it. It reminds him of when he was on top of the world, flush with gold and jewels and parading Lyx to distant ports to show off his siren catch. A reminder that he had her, and no one else could.

"You must have looked like quite the damsel in distress." Tidus props his elbow on the table and opens his palm toward her. "Maybe we can use that to our advantage."

Her jaw twitches. A new plan is brewing in his mind, leaving the room as heavy and humid as a storm cloud.

He opens his legs to make space for her. It's an instruction, not an offer. She knows it well. Just like she knows the best way to weather Tidus's schemes is to grin and bear it, but still, her feet stay rooted in place.

For a moment, she allows herself the fantasy of resisting. In another world, she would tell him no. She would spit in his face and smack him until her hand burned with pain...but that isn't this world. In this world, she lowers her lashes and sways toward him.

His eyes follow the motion of her hips like a pendulum. She comes to a stop in front of him and flicks a loose scallop shell off his shoulder. "What is it you're asking?"

His fingers skim the backs of her thighs. "I'm not asking."

Her hands curl into fists. Of course he isn't. Why request anything when he has the power to command? The screech building in her throat turns into a smile. "What would you have me do?"

Her body jerks when he pulls her into his lap and presses her back to his chest. "Take that meeting with Heathen." His breath is hot against her ear, his hands wandering her ample waist. "Give her some sob story. Say you've always dreamed of working on that pleasure ship." His smile stretches against her cheek. "Tell her you're running from your captor. That you're trapped. That you need safe passage."

She digs her nails into his arms, but they tighten around her. A leaden weight fills her stomach until she can barely breathe. This is what life with Tidus has always been like: a drowning, suffocating well of chaos with no end.

Exactly what she needs.

"Make up something pathetic." He squeezes her hips. "Something that'll get you on board. We're gonna take down that bitch's business from the inside."

Lyx squirms, but her body is heavy and drunk from feeding. There's no use trying to fight her way free, so she settles back against him until his grip loosens. "Why?"

Tidus's lips skim her throat. "Heathen has plenty of followers. Once we destroy her livelihood, the crew will be looking for a new captain to serve."

"But why this ship?" Her heavy eyelids struggle to stay open. "What's your obsession with her?"

Tidus tenses.

Lyx tries to remain still, fighting not to flinch as his heart picks up its pace against her. When Tidus gets quiet is when he's the most dangerous. Her throat goes dry. She wasn't thinking. She shouldn't have said anything. Her mouth opens to pre-empt his anger, but then, he laughs loud and long.

"The *Indulgence* is an easy mark. Running a pleasure ship is simple." He buries a chuckle against her hair. "Loyal followers come with the territory."

Shakily, Lyx exhales. She should be grateful for his unexpected pleasantness, even though she's waiting for lightning to strike. Still, his good moods are few and far between. She can't help but push her luck. "And if I do this for you, what do I get?"

Tidus laughs again. It's a joke, but she never finds humor in it. It's easier for him to give her *something* if he wants the job done without a fight. If he wants her to do it well.

Easing off his chest, she lifts her hair and looks at him over her shoulder. "Unclasp me?"

His eyes narrow, but she knows him; he can't resist temptation. Sex always manages to distract him. He brings his hands to her neck, unhooking her dress before he drags his roughened palms down the bare skin of her back. He hums in his throat, leaning forward to press his lips to her hairline. "If you do this for me," he murmurs leisurely, "I'll return your song."

The pins drop from her hand and clatter to the floor. She grabs the table to stay upright, her body thrumming like the hammered strings of a piano. Tidus has never offered that. Surely she heard him wrong. She has no doubt that if she turns, she'll be met with his merciless smile and the crushing truth, so she doesn't move. She doesn't even speak.

"You want it that bad, huh?" He traces the tense muscles of her shoulders that wind down her spine. "I'm starting to think this song controls *you*, not the other way around." Pityingly, he clicks his tongue. "You're never gonna free yourself like that."

Fuck him. He doesn't want her to be free at all. He enjoys this too much, dangling her song in front of her like a worm on a hook.

Acid swells on her tongue, but she bites it until it bleeds. "Why would you give me that?"

"What use is it to me?" Two years of irritation seep into his tone. "I can't get it to work. You can't use it for me." He curls his arms around her. "The only thing it's good for is keeping you *close*."

She waits for him to change his mind, but it doesn't

happen. He's serious. Foolish hope darts through her chest, and she turns to push open his shirt.

Scar tissue grows around the spiral shell embedded in his left pectoral. When she hovers her hand over it, it glows, like her song is a living thing trapped inside. The light's not as strong as it used to be. Over time, its sheen has faded, returning only when she craves something to desperation. These days, it only shines when she imagines her freedom.

There's no stealing it from Tidus. Depths know she's tried. There's no running from him, either; she aches when she's apart from it, a pain so deep that she swore it would kill her. Her song is so frail now. She fears it needs a host, that Tidus is the only thing keeping it alive outside of her body. As much as she hates him, she dreads what would happen to her song if he dies.

He snags her wrist to pull her focus back toward his face. "See? I'm not as bad as you tell yourself am."

Her fingers flex. She wants to drag her nails into his face, but she lifts her other arm to watch her song react to her presence. It casts light into her hand, a soothing reminder that she's not alone.

"To think I almost caught *two* sirens." Tidus sighs and leans back in his chair. "That would've made shit so much easier. I'd have an entire fleet of ships by now."

The memory blisters in Lyx's mind. *Mollo*. It's so easy for Tidus to recount the day Lyx's own sister betrayed her. Lyx still doesn't know how she did it, using magic to snatch Lyx's song and trap it inside that shell.

Just like a siren to betray one of her own. It fills Lyx with a concoction of emotion. Fury. Pride. Hunger. She wants to smash Mollo's head in. She wants to see what Mollo does next. She wants to get her revenge again and again until it kills one of them.

But right now, Lyx is powerless to do anything. Without

the sway of the ocean or the swell of her song, she might as well be a ghost. Impotent. Unreal. So transparent that she can only wail against the walls of her prison.

"Tell me again," she breathes, reaching for the buckle of Tidus's pants. "Tell me you'll return my song."

He lets her dress fall away, cupping her breasts when he meets her eyes. "Once you get me Heathen's secrets, this song? Your freedom?" He drags his thumbs against her nipples until they peak. "It's all yours."

Her mouth collides with his, hips grinding into his lap. The promise fuels her almost as much as her hatred for Tidus, for Mollo...

For Cav.

Her teeth sink into Tidus's lip. He curses when she draws blood, gripping her ass to draw her closer. He meets her fervor, pearls scattering to the ground as he drags his mouth down her body.

The image of Cav burns behind her eyes. She'll take her time destroying him. She'll savor his pain and draw out his suffering, swallowing him until there's nothing left.

When she pictures it, the shell in Tidus's chest glows.

In the Grotto

Cav

Of all the ways to die, this is the one Cav would choose.

Being dragged into sleep requires so little from him, his mind drifting lazily. There's no fighting it. His body is heavy, submerged in dreams that cling to him like syrup. By the time he reaches the surface, fatigue wraps around his ankles and pulls him under again.

At least the hallucinations are nice. He eats delicious feasts and laughs at silly jokes and feels the wind on his face. The siren is his favorite reverie. It makes sense she would appear when he's swallowed half his weight in saltwater; everyone's heard tales, but sirens don't really exist. Any pirate who searches for one might as well be digging for fool's gold.

Still, she feels real. While Cav's other delusions are soft and nebulous, her hands around his throat were cool and slick, as refreshing as the first drink of an oasis.

He almost forgets she was trying to kill him. Now that

would have been the best way to go.

He didn't get a good look at her, his eyelids to heavy from sunlight glinting off the water, but her voice...he clings to that. It was hypnotic, dissonant, pulling him out like the receding tide.

In his dreams, she is a dark shape beneath the water and always out of reach. If he had any sense, he'd be frightened — but who cares? He's dying anyway, and her menacing presence makes him feel less alone.

Like now, when she stands over him and casts a shadow across his face. It's a relief from the morning light, allowing his mind to return fully to his body. The water around him has grown deeper, his lower half floating weightlessly. From above, cool water drips onto his face. He wants to drink it, but his forked tongue is thick and stiff. An aching pit gnaws at his stomach, and his shoulder throbs and twinges. He can hardly move his mouth, his inhales fading, the gaps between breaths growing longer and longer.

"You're still not dead." The siren's voice is rife with disappointment. Despite the pain, Cav's mouth twitches. He means to smile, but from the disgusted sound she makes, he's not sure what his body is doing.

"Y..." His voice is as fragile as wet parchment. He can't even try to clear his throat, lips cracking around the words. "Came...back?"

He has no concept of time. In truth, he's still not convinced this is reality. Maybe it isn't. Maybe his withering consciousness has crafted a companion to carry him into death. His smile spreads wider. If she's the one to accompany him, he'll go gladly.

Beside him, glass bottles clatter against the sand. The siren's closer than before, but Cav can't pry his salt-crusted eyes open to see her. Something grips his shirt, and Cav hisses when his shoulder spasms. A shredding sound echoes off the cave walls before a breeze tickles the bare skin of his chest.

When the siren's hands move to his pants, he coughs a laugh. "What're...you..."

"Your clothes are in tatters." There's another ripping noise before his legs are exposed to the air. "They're soaked. You'll be infected before long."

He doesn't argue. It's nice to be free of his sopping clothes, and nicer still to be under her hands again. This time, she tugs on his good arm, hoisting him onto something flat and waxy with a long stem pressed along his spine.

It's slow work, but eventually, the siren tugs the massive leaf (and Cav atop it) out of the water. The smooth rocks beneath him change to grains of sand and clumps of soil. The scent of the sea is dampened by flora. Fronds brush his body while leafy shadows bob across the backs of his eyelids.

Another huge leaf drapes across his body, preserving whatever modesty he has left. "'M not...shy," he manages. The siren doesn't reply, but he hears liquid sloshing inside the clinking bottles. It's a reminder of how tight and dry his skin is, stretched uncomfortably over his bones like a strip of leather.

Something pours onto his wounded shoulder, making him hiss and clench. It doesn't deter the siren. Her motions are sloppy, heaping on gobs of cream that drip down his body. It's clear she doesn't understand exactly what she's doing, but she finds every scratch on him and coats them with different fluids.

After a few minutes, the burning pain subsides. His injuries feel cleaner, if nothing else, and that allows him to unclench his body.

Is she tending to him? Surely not. More likely she's preparing him to be eaten, although the ointments smell more medicinal than savory. He tries to listen for her, but all *he can make out are the distant ocean sounds. Waves crashing, gulls calling, breeze whistling through the cavern above him.*

His heartbeat picks up for the first time in days. What if she left? He fights to open his eyes, but his crusted eyelashes tug against each other. "What's — your name?" he rasps.

There's no reply.

His voice isn't strong enough. He tries again. "I'm — Cav. Short for — Cavalier."

After a long moment, there's a scoff. It's further away now, followed by a disparaging remark about pirates. Cav's laughter nearly strangles him. He can do little more than gasp, drowning in whatever seawater is left inside him.

Unhurried footsteps approach him before a bitter liquid drizzles into his mouth. He gags, but the siren grips his chin and forces him to swallow. He splutters against her slick fingers.

Maybe she'll suffocate him. Maybe he would like that.

But then she pulls her hand away, and when he gasps for air, he's surprised at how deeply he can breathe. "Thank you."

She grumbles. "Thank whomever gave you that dreadful name."

"I did."

"Why in the Depths would you choose that?"

His mouth quirks. In truth, he chose a name that could toe both sides of the gendered line. He wanted something true that could also find the path of least resistance. Living as a man makes it easier to secure spots on working ships, to find adventure on the open seas, to keep people's hands from wandering. Over the years, Cav has grown accustomed to it, but it's never been the whole story. He loves this part of himself, but there's another half that's been left to wither, as stifled as his ribs when he binds his chest.

Despite the lingering pain, he stretches like a cat and arches his breasts against the leaf with a long, deep breath. "I like to keep people guessing." There's no telling if Lyx is looking his way. Gods, he must be delusional from dehydration. Why is he trying to entice her, anyway?

Right: her name.

"What's yours?" He craves to hear her voice again. He knows she's still there, rustling through the bottles, but she doesn't say anything. The silence goes on for so long that he doesn't think she'll answer, but then a wave recedes, and he swears he hears one syllable.

He tilts his ear toward her. "What was that?"

She doesn't speak again. He scrambles to decipher the sound.

"Lyx," he repeats. Her name is fresh water over his tongue, like it could heal the dry cracks of his lips. "Is that short for something?"

She sighs.

His smile grows. "Tell me."

Her fingernails tick against a bottle. "Only the ocean can pronounce it."

"Tell me anyway."

There's a long stretch of silence again, and then the sharp tip of her finger presses to his bare chest. "I've kept you alive, pirate, and still, you ask for more."

There's venom in her tone, but beneath that, Cav swears there's a hint of amusement. He wonders if it shows up in her eyes, but there's no telling when his own are sealed shut. "Then let me repay you," he tries. "Whatever you want, I'll give it to you."

Lyx's laugh is a delicious sound in the back of her throat. "Look at the state of you. There's nothing you could give me, Cavalier." Her cool breath gusts across his face when she leans closer. "There's even less that you could stop me from taking."

It's clearly a threat, yet his body's reaction is the faint stirring of the ember in his chest. His tongue slips over his lips and brushes against something even softer.

She inhales sharply. He can feel it across his face. His stomach clenches. She must be close. He lifts his hand to pry the crust from his eyes, but she snatches his wrist and pins it to the ground. They stay like that, breaths heaving and hearts racing. He still can't see her. Danger prickles beneath his scales, but Cav wants to push it further. Wants to feel her entire body against him. Wants to drag his tongue against her lips again. "Are you sure there's...nothing I could give you?"

Her nails dig into his skin. He imagines her glaring down at him, teeth grit with frustration. "Don't mistake me, pirate. Your death is still coming, and it's mine to deliver."

He hates that she releases him. His fingers flex at the loss, but she's already splashing through the shallows. He calls after her, like that might incite her to stay. To punish his insolence. "Is that why you healed me?"

She pauses, but then, she continues away. All he gets is her voice tossed over her shoulder. "It's not as fun to kill you when you're halfway dead already."

FIVE

Cav

No one can say Cav doesn't pay for his indiscretions.

He waits at the docks for hours before the ferry master takes pity on him. With Cav's black eye and bloody sleeve, he's surprised that anyone offers him a ride, but he won't look a gift fish in the mouth.

The sun hasn't yet begun to rise. He still has time to get back to the *Indulgence*, but he hasn't slept in twenty-four hours, and a cramp is spreading through his shoulder. Despite that, the only thing occupying his mind is Lyx. He leans back in his seat on the ferry and watches the wealthy island fade into the fog.

Seeing Lyx again was...

Every word that comes to mind is foolishly sentimental. Did he learn nothing from the night before? She'd rather see him dead than take him up on his offer to meet Heathen, but maybe that can work in his favor. Maybe she'll show up today just to try and kill him again. Or maybe he thinks too highly of himself; it's possible she's just glad to be rid of him, but the way she lunged at him last night…

Heat coils in his stomach. Lyx may hate him, but that means she feels *something*. Hate isn't apathy. Hate, he can work with.

The ferry bumps against the dock as they arrive. Compared to the glimmering wealth behind them, this island looks like a makeshift stand on the side of the road. Cav slips the driver a few coins and stretches out his shoulder.

Just seeing the *Indulgence* makes him breathe easier. The ship takes up a good portion of the small port, the deep magenta and emerald sails creating a perfect backdrop for the sensual golden sigil. Tableaus are carved into the sides of the ship. Even the prow is meant to tempt passerby, a figurehead of three creatures entwined in bliss.

It's a shame the ship's exterior is the most salacious thing about it. With a huff, Cav crosses the dock and climbs the *Indulgence*'s rope ladder.

The ship is barely awake. Below deck, the crew begins to stir, but no one appears from the hatchway. If Cav hurries, he can get cleaned up before Heathen catches him. If he lays low for the next few days, his face can heal, and —

"Heathen's not gonna be happy about that."

Cav's jaw clenches. When he lifts his eyes to the forecastle, he sees Cypher scrawling in a tattered journal. She looks like a piece of parchment, light skin covered in tattoos that morph and shift. Black markings linger on her cheek like a spilled inkwell. Her pet crow sits on her shoulder, blinking its beady eyes and nuzzling the stubble of Cypher's shaved head. Her entire being screams to *stay away*. Cav wonders if she's always been this way, or if it's a side effect of her curse. He doesn't dare ask; she's already hostile enough as it is.

She doesn't bother to look at him, tapping the quill beside her eye until the ink in her skin morphs to match Cav's bruising.

Asshole.

He hoists himself aboard and grabs a clean rag from the clothesline. "Heathen doesn't need to know."

"She already does." Cypher's quill twitches toward the captain's quarters. "You're late to your meeting."

"What meeting?"

"The one Heathen called five minutes ago." She yawns. "When they stormed across the deck cursing your name."

Cav dips the rag into a barrel of rainwater. Of course Heathen found out about his extracurricular activities. Granted, he wasn't inconspicuous, but he didn't think word of his misdeeds would get back to the *Indulgence* before he did. He scrubs at the crusted blood on his knuckles. That means someone told Heathen. Someone went out of their way to point it out to her, interrupting her morning routine when they all know she hates any disturbance to her schedule.

"Did *you* tell them?" he accuses.

Cypher sighs. "Stalling for time, huh?"

"Was it a tattoo?"

"I don't need magic to stay informed of your activities." Boredly, she twirls her quill, never looking up from the page. "Your unpredictability has become predictable."

"So that's a yes?" He finds an oversized vest on the line and tugs it over his ripped clothing. "Some new ink showed up on you, and you went running to Heathen?"

For the first time, Cypher's chilly gaze meets his. Her bird stops preening to give Cav a disapproving glare.

"Or maybe you have all the subtlety of cannon fire," Cypher snaps. "Maybe everyone on this ship knows what you do as soon as it happens — sometimes before." Her head shakes, tension knotting through her shoulders. All this bickering belies the root of the problem, but now, it's cracking through the surface. "Why would you go after Roderick on your own? That was senseless. He's *dangerous*, Cav."

"Not anymore," Cav grumbles.

Cypher doesn't laugh.

Loathe as he is to admit it, the answer is very simple. "He tried to hurt Briar. He tried to hurt *you*."

Cypher shifts uncomfortably. She won't look at him now, still shaking her head and hunching deeper over her notebook. "You shouldn't have done it."

There's no use arguing. From what little he knows of Cypher's hex, she keeps everyone at a strict distance. It wouldn't matter either way; the two of them would be at odds regardless of her curse. They never see eye-to-eye. Even this brief conversation has put a strain on the meager camaraderie they have.

Without another word, Cav tosses the wet rag aside and crosses toward the captain's quarters.

The curtains are drawn tight, blocking out any clues as to what's waiting for him. He sidles up to the window, pressing his ear to the glass and straining to hear.

Nothing. That's telling. He knows exactly what's going on behind that door; Heathen, sitting rigidly at their desk, glaring into the distance as they stew over what to do with Cav.

He tilts his neck and groans when it cracks. Gods, his body's fucking sore. Every part of him yearns for his bed, but there's no avoiding Heathen. As soon as she hears he's onboard, she'll be rapping on his door.

Another crew member emerges from below deck. "Cavalier!" Sweeney gasps, drinks sloshing in surprise when she sees his face. "What happened?"

Cav only smiles, wincing when the wound in his lip reopens, and tilts his head toward the coffees. "Who's that second one for?"

Sweeney's blinks are thick with sleep. "Uh — Cypher?"

Perfect. An opportunity for Cav to reestablish the barbed

wire between them. "She prefers tea." He reaches for one of the cups. "I'll take this off your hands."

Blearily, Sweeney nods, and Cav plucks the drink before he pushes through the captain's door behind him.

Much like everything about Heathen, her quarters are meticulous. Nothing is out of place. The furniture is built-in or bolted down, and the sparse decor gives little insight to the captain themself. A large window spans the back of the room and looks out across the ocean. On the left wall, a bookshelf is arranged by size and topic with a smattering of glass jars along one shelf. A large curtain hangs on the opposite side, obscuring the captain's bed from view.

At the center of the room, Heathen sits behind a wooden desk. In the dawn light, their banshee appearance is even more intimidating. Bones press up through the fat and muscle of her body, her skin a mixture of white skeleton and darker shading. Her dark hair is cut short, bangs obscuring her opalescent eyes and the displeasure honed directly at Cav.

He forces his smile wider. "You're up early."

Heathen points toward one of the chairs facing her desk.

Cav moseys across the floor with his tail swishing behind him. He deposits the mug onto a coaster and eases down into one of the seats, inching the proffered coffee toward her.

If he acts like nothing's wrong, then nothing is, right? Never mind the bruises blooming on his face. He prays there's no remaining blood on his teeth when he beams. "How was your night, Captain?"

"Not nearly as exciting as yours."

SIX

Cav

Cav's smile falters. "Straight to business, huh?"

"Why did you go after Roderick?"

"Because he went after the crew!" Cav's facade falls away as he leans forward in his seat. "You were right; he *did* try to drug some of the girls the other night. I couldn't sit there while he sailed off and got away with it. Someone had to stop him!"

"Someone would have."

"Not fast enough."

"Not *publicly*." Heathen's voice lowers between her teeth. "Colt was already on the *Silver Spoon* waiting in the bathroom. He was going to deal with Roderick quietly, but instead, the entirety of the ship got a front row seat to your performance."

Cav flinches. It's like he's back in school, reprimanded with the dull *thwack* of a ruler. Of course there was a tail on Roderick. Of course Heathen had a plan for him. Why the fuck hadn't that thought occurred to Cav?

He sinks lower in his chair, but there's no escaping this. Goddamn his restless brain and how it itches with ideas until he scratches them. "I didn't want him to hurt anyone else."

Heathen flattens their palms to ease the tension from their body. "You don't hunt down bad actors anymore, Cav. That's not your job."

"It used to be."

"Yes: *used to.*"

The reminder stings like saltwater in his eyes. He knows Heathen's right, but sometimes, Cav lets himself forget that things have changed. That he can't do all the things he used to. That he's not living the same life he was before.

Morning duties begin outside Heathen's quarters. She glances toward the sound before her tone softens a fraction. "What's going on with you? The past few weeks, you've been more...erratic than usual."

She tries not to make the word sound like an insult, but Cav knows better. His spontaneity makes her skin crawl. The two of them may see the same big picture, but their methodology is completely different. While Heathen sketches a detailed outline, Cav is already splashing paint across the canvas.

He gives a halfhearted shrug. Outside, metal pots clang above the din of the crew. It's a stark contrast to the silence that drags on in Heathen's office. She's deep in thought, fingers steepled on her desk. Cav's foot begins to bounce. Only once the quiet starts to chafe does Heathen finally speak.

"You have to find something to guide you besides your whims." As a peace offering, Heathen takes the mug of coffee and settles it closer to her. "You can't dive headfirst into everything and damn the consequences. You need purpose. You need an outlet. You need *something.*"

Cav tugs at a loose thread on the chair. Maybe it'll unravel as easily as he does. Maybe it'll explain why he can't keep things together like Heathen and Cypher can. Maybe it'll help him understand why, no matter how much he cares for the people on this ship, he always feels restless and aimless.

Heathen stares at the fraying fabric. "Stop picking at it."

Cav releases the thread and fights the twitch of his fingers.

Heathen nods. "Now, tell me what you're thinking."

With a sigh, he scrubs a hand down his face. "I don't know. It's like I'm...some alley cat you brought inside. I'm clawing up the curtains, knocking over glasses, fucking everything up."

Reckless. Impetuous. Impulsive. He's heard all the descriptors before, but these days, it's getting worse. It's like he's spinning in a circle, desperate for the momentum to carry him toward something that will hold his attention.

"Working on the convoy was so different," he tries. "When I was a guardian, I got my hands dirty. I did the physical labor. I got rid of the people causing problems. I had an impact, but on the *Indulgence*, I'm just...here." He turns his hands up helplessly. "Everything is routine. It's..."

Boring.

He doesn't say the word aloud, but from Heathen's pursed lips, it's clear she hears it. "Regularity is a sign of things functioning as they should be."

"I don't want things to go *wrong*." He tips his head back toward the ceiling. How can he express it? "Everything's restricted nowadays. We visit the same ports, keep pleasure 'recreation' to the cabins, offer only the most basic services..." His fingers flit to the loose thread again, but he grips the arm of the chair instead. "I'm just saying, it's gotten stale."

Heathen's brow quirks. Cav knows he shouldn't speak so freely, but she asked.

"And I don't think it's a coincidence that things locked

down after Prodeus took off with the convoy."

Heathen bristles. Even years later, the former co-commander is a sore subject. Cav can't blame her. He served on the guardian ship hired to escort the *Indulgence* from port to port. On the last night the two ships were together, Heathen and Prodeus argued until the wooden walls couldn't contain it. Rumors ran wild. *Heathen denied him a larger stake in the business. She refused him a bigger crew. She spurned his sexual advances.* It always came back to what Prodeus felt he was owed.

Maybe Cav should have seen the signs. On the final morning, Prodeus was uncharacteristically cheery, clapping Cav on the back when he disembarked to make some trades. By the time Cav returned to the docks, Prodeus had sailed away with the guardian ship and its crew, leaving Heathen and the rest of the *Indulgence* to fend for themselves.

Somehow, they made it work. Cav joined the *Indulgence.* They cut out visits to the most lucrative ports, limiting their routes to the safest waters. Heathen laid out strict new rules for the pleasure ship to follow and removed any opportunity for surprises.

Funny how the person who cornered the market on pleasure can be so clinical. It's as if Heathen thinks loosening their grip will send the *Indulgence* crashing straight into the rocks.

"I know you want things to run smoothly," Cav acknowledges, "but this is not the crumbling business Prodeus left you with. You rebuilt it from the ground up. Now, it needs room to grow." He counts on his fingers. "The ship is too small. The route is too stale. You resist any new idea that comes along. We can't keep up with demand; that's how Roderick slipped through the cracks."

Heathen's mouth twists. Cav's lips tingle to amend himself, to fill the empty space, to say *something*, but Heathen always takes her time answering. *Processing*, she says. Finally, her fingers flex over the map on her desk. "You've certainly got a lot of *opinions*." The word is sharp, but it falls away as her fingers trace the *Indulgence*'s familiar route. "But perhaps I have been playing it safe."

Cav blinks. It's not what he expected, even if it is true. "I only say it because we're capable of more; *you're* capable of more. I watched it first-hand. And I know a way it can happen again."

Heathen sighs when she realizes where he's headed. "We've been over this —"

"You don't have to do anything," he insists. "Let me prove it to you. The only way to be certain is with a good, old-fashioned experiment, right?"

Heathen's eyes narrow. They didn't expect him to use their own words against them, but they don't give in so easily. "We don't need an experiment. The *Indulgence* is popular because people know what to expect." She spreads her hands. "Excellence."

Cav shakes his head. "The *Indulgence* is popular because people want something provocative. An adrenaline rush. A risk."

Both of them lean back in their seats. Heathen drums their fingers on the logbook and mulls over their rebuttal. "Despite my initial misgivings, Cav, I know you can perform. Your transition from guarding to sex work has been impressive. You're a natural. Clients adore you, the crew respects you —"

Cav smirks. "You're making my case for me."

"However, I question your dedication."

His mouth clamps shut.

Heathen continues. "No one can say that you don't have creative ideas, but I've yet to see one come to fruition. You lose interest. You may be easily inspired, but you're just as easily diverted."

He averts his gaze. What Heathen says is true. He knows she doesn't say it to be cruel, but it's like she's shining a spotlight on his biggest faults.

Maybe Heathen understands him more than he wants to admit. Maybe he is chasing a feeling more than any real result. Maybe he's searching for something to make him feel alive again. Maybe this experiment would be another in a string of failures, but he *needs it.* He needs to pour himself into something. He needs something to pull his mind back on track, or he's going to end up beaten and bloodied on another *Silver Spoon.*

"Please —" His voice is dry. He clears his throat. "If you give me a chance —"

A sharp knock comes at the door.

Cav keeps his back turned, desperate to see this conversation through — but the visitor doesn't wait for an invitation.

Cav grits his teeth when he turns in his chair. "We're in the middle of —"

Cypher's expression throws him off. She looks stunned, her motions slow as she closes the door behind her. Even her crow looks disturbed, shifting back and forth on its feet.

Heathen prods her to speak. "Yes, Quartermaster?"

Cypher wets her lips. "There's a woman here to see you. She mentioned Cav. I think she's..." Her hand tightens around the doorknob. "The siren."

Cav is standing before he realizes. "She showed up?"

Heathen balks. "She's *real?*"

Since the day Cav returned from his shipwreck, Lyx has been a myth on the *Indulgence.* No one believed he'd actually been saved by a siren. It's been the crew's favorite joke for years. When they spot a dead fish in the ocean, they say it's a gift from Cav's mysterious lover. When the wind howls in the distance, it's the siren calling his name.

Slowly, Heathen rises from their chair. "Why would she come here?"

Cav clears his throat. "I may have run into her last night. On the *Silver Spoon*."

"And you invited her to the ship?"

Cav doesn't miss the way Heathen's eye twitches when he follows her toward the door. "She wanted to meet with you. And since our reunion was a little rocky…"

Cypher's brow lifts, but Cav pushes past her.

On the deck, the morning duties have halted. Everyone is staring at the top of the gangplank where Lyx stands, distrustful and beautiful as ever. Her gaze slides from one face to the next while a chorus of whispers spreads through the crowd.

It's hard enough to believe that sirens exist, but *Cav's* siren? That's more shocking than anything else.

"I'll be damned," Heathen murmurs. "She *is* real."

SEVEN

Lyx

The stares are unsettling.

Not that they're anything new. Lyx is used to thinly-veiled glances, an audience that can't determine why it's intrigued by her. People never realize they're looking at a siren, the creature of myths and stories relegated to the stormy depths of the sea. What would a siren be doing *here*? She's out of place on land, walking on two legs without a song spilling from her mouth.

Yet the ogling from the *Indulgence* is stranger still. The crew members don't look captivated or entranced; they gawk like she's some delusion made flesh. Even Cav looks surprised to see her.

In the daylight, she can get a better look at him. His black eye looks more painful now, but that's not the only difference from the grotto. The chipped tooth she remembers has been replaced by glinting gold. He's still half-a-head shorter than her, but his shoulders and hips are broader. Everything about him is more vibrant, skin and scales morphing from red to orange in the sun.

He's striking. It's irritating, so she turns to the people beside him. One is the tattooed woman who stopped Lyx at the gangplank. The other looks like a fleshed-out skeleton, tipping back their rugged captain's hat to get a better look at Lyx.

So this is the infamous Heathen. Lyx was expecting...more. Someone louder, crueler, a rival to Tidus's arrogance, but Heathen doesn't make a sound. There's something powerful about that. Heathen's stature is small, but there's a potency in their expression, their mind cataloguing everything that happens. Lyx waits for Heathen's gaze to dip down the curves of her body, but the captain's eyes stay on her face.

Lyx keeps still. Let them get a good look. Tidus dressed her in the most bedraggled clothing he could find, a corseted dress in varying shades of brown.

"You need to look helpless," he said, ripping a jagged slit up the side. "Wanton. Willing."

Lyx is anything but. Her eyes flick to the barest speck of Tidus's ship on the horizon. Everything inside her reaches for her song. This is truly a test of how far away from it she can be, and it shortens her already-diminished temper. "I'm here for a meeting."

The tattooed woman's eyebrow twitches. It's clear she wants to say something, but after a moment, Heathen steps back and gestures toward the room behind her.

Lyx expected more of a fight, but she won't waste this opportunity. Shoulders back, she pads across the deck with her bare feet.

Cav skirts in front of her to open the door. "I didn't think you'd show."

She wants to scrape her heel against his shin. "Pretend I didn't."

It's the smallest captain's quarters she's ever seen. Even in Tidus's little sloop, he takes up most of the space below deck. On the contrary, Heathen's room is sparsely decorated with a ship wheel framed by a rope hanging on above the bookshelf. There are no papers or clothing strewn across the floor, no day-old ale crusting in the corner, no smoking pipe out of place. When the ship rocks, the books hardly move in their perfectly-fitted shelving.

The door shuts behind her. Heathen circles to her desk. She doesn't sit, folding her arms and inspecting Lyx like she's a specimen in a jar. It's...disconcerting, like Heathen can see past her ratty clothes and down to some deeper part of her.

There's a shuffling behind her. Lyx catches red in the corner of her eye and realizes Cav is leaning against the wall. Watching her.

Her teeth grit. "Does he have to be here?"

Cav's hand moves for the knob like he might leave, but Heathen stops him. "Cavalier is the reason I'm taking this meeting, Ms...Lyx?" Heathen gestures to one of the chairs before her. "Is that correct?"

Lyx bites back a curse. Sitting would give up what little power Lyx has, so she doesn't move. She's tempted to ask outright for what she's after, but with Tidus it always requires flattery. Flirtation. Some clever quip to weasel her way in. "Interesting name, Heathen." Lyx can't help the quirk of her brow. "Little on the nose for the captain of a pleasure ship."

Heathen's expression shifts before it settles again. She rolls the cuffs of her sleeves up to her elbow, and Lyx can't help but follow the motion. She expected the captain's sexuality to be far more straightforward, a short skirt and ample cleavage to draw in customers, but Heathen is nearly completely covered. Her clothing is tailored. Her sensuality is controlled.

Lyx's toes curl.

"I'm surprised you wanted to meet," Heathen says. "I thought sirens preferred to *sing* to pirates, not talk with them."

The reminder makes Lyx's throat ache. "If only those pirates stayed out of our waters."

"If only you stayed in them."

Lyx's teeth click. So Heathen knows more than surface-level myths. Siren territory was always a nebulous thing — at least, to sirens. Perhaps they dipped outside of their established boundaries from time to time. Perhaps a few innocent ships were caught in the crossfire. It wouldn't have mattered, anyway. Even if the sirens built a home beyond the reaches of man, the hunters would have still come chased after them.

Clearly, Heathen doesn't care for beating around the bush. She braces one hand on her hip. "You're here to ask for something."

There's no point denying it. Lyx lifts her chin. "I'd like a job."

"What use would a siren have for a job?" Heathen wonders. "Surely you can demand anything you want from any number of people."

Lyx swallows roughly. Admitting the truth is suicide; if she confirms she has no song, that a siren's power can be snatched away... She won't risk that.

"In any case..." Heathen waves the thought away. "My payroll is full. We have no need for you."

Lyx digs her nails into her palm, like that might keep this conversation from slipping away. "A siren is a novelty. On a pleasure ship?" She forces the words through her teeth. "Customers would come from far and wide to bed one."

A dark look crosses Heathen's face, and she lifts her hand

toward the door in dismissal. "That is not how I run my business."

Lyx's heart clenches. This isn't working; it *has* to work. She has to get onto this ship. She has to get her song back. She has to get away from Tidus, and free herself, and —

"Someone's looking for me. I need safe passage."

The words escape her in a rush. She hadn't meant to sound so distressed, but her voice wobbles. It gives Heathen pause. "You owe someone?"

Lyx shakes her head. The lie comes far more easily than it should, like she's pulling from some well of truth inside her. "It's an ex. I need to get him off my trail. If I lay low and sail to a few different ports..."

Behind her, the floorboards creak. She can feel Cav's eyes on her, searching her face for answers. She keeps her eyes locked on Heathen. Heathen does the same.

"Why not return to the ocean?" Heathen asks. "Surely he couldn't follow you there."

The hollow place in Lyx's throat burns. She can do nothing without her song. This conversation is just a reminder of how helpless she is, a drum struck again and again until Lyx can hear nothing else.

"Do you think..." Lyx clenches her eyes shut. "That I would ask for this if I could help myself?" The words boil in her mouth. She knows she should swallow them down, but it's too late. They flow past her lips and spill between them. "Do you think I enjoy this? Debasing myself? Begging and pleading for charity?" Shame heats her cheeks. Depths, she sounds absolutely pathetic. "I wouldn't be here if I had a choice. There is no other option. I need help. I need *your* help."

The air goes still.

For a foolish moment, Lyx wonders if she can feel Heathen's mercy. If the captain possesses that sentimental lenience Lyx has never experienced herself. But when she opens her eyes, Heathen's posture straightens. "I'm sorry. We have no room for you."

EIGHT

Lyx

The hope Lyx was holding onto slips through her fingers and shatters against the ground.

Cav appears beside her. "Come on, Captain, there has to be —"

"*Don't*," Lyx hisses. She doesn't want Cav anywhere near this. She turns back to Heathen and fights to keep her voice level. "*Please*. I'll work for free. I can make you more money than —"

"It's not about money." Heathen's mouth sets in a thin line. "There are no spare rooms. You are an unknown variable; I can't set you loose on my customers. Now, Cavalier, please see your guest out."

Lyx's head swims. How could she have prepared for this? What brothel owner doesn't put a siren straight to work? Tidus will be furious if Lyx returns empty-handed. He'll be furious if she returns at *all*, squandering the one opportunity to get on this ship.

She cannot go back. She cannot lose her song.

"What if she takes my room?" Cav asks. For once, there isn't a hint of humor on his face. "I'll sleep in my hammock on the deck."

Heathen's jaw tightens. "Cav..."

"If it doesn't work out, you can drop her off at the next port."

"*Cav.*"

"Playing it safe?"

Lyx's eyes widen. She's never seen someone question their captain so brazenly, especially in front of an outsider. Tidus took people's tongue for that, but Heathen doesn't call for her guards. Her eyes lock on Cav's in some conversation Lyx isn't privy to.

"*Please,*" Cav whispers. That one word is threaded with so much desperation, Lyx wonders if this isn't about her spot on the ship at all.

Heathen looks like she wants to reject him – but then, the corners of her eyes soften. That tenderness makes Lyx recoil before Heathen turns back to her with a staid expression. "If you accept passage on this ship, you agree to assist Cavalier with his endeavor."

Lyx is distracted from her relief by bewilderment. "Endeavor?"

"Let's call it a project," Heathen corrects. "That sounds structured." Clearly, Heathen is grasping for some comfort. "Cavalier has some...*unique* ideas for the pleasure ship, and you will aid him in bringing those to life."

Lyx's eyes narrow. "What ideas?"

"A broader introduction of kinks." Heathen opens their hands as if they were commenting on the weather. "Our current system is much more fixed, and Cav would like to play with the bounds of that. He requires a partner willing to explore the terrain with him."

Despite Heathen's delivery, the revelation is jarring. "The condition of my stay is me *fucking him*?"

Cav blanches. "That's not —"

"Whatever his venture requires," Heathen clarifies. "You two can determine your boundaries. In return, he will be your sponsor on the ship, responsible for anything that happens to you, and anything *you* happen to. Do we have a deal?"

Lyx's hands curl into fists. How quickly Heathen's change of heart has changed Lyx's mind. It was bad enough seeing Cav again, but now she'll have to share a ship with him? Share a bed? Share her *pleasure*?

She hasn't forgotten what that's like. Traitorous arousal trickles down her spine. It only happened once. It *barely* happened, but she recalls her last hour with Cav in excruciating, exquisite detail. That night comes back to her when she can't sleep, when she lies next to Tidus and tries to drown out the sound of his breathing. She closes her eyes and returns to the grotto to feel Cav's hands on her again, that sticky heat between both their legs, his breath against hers...

Her head jerks to scatter the thoughts. The memory doesn't matter. It's something she uses to cope, not something with any real meaning. Not something she actually *desires*. All she wants is her freedom and to ruin Cav. If this will give her the opportunity for both...

"*Fine*," she snaps. "At least it'll be over quickly."

Cav's mouth twitches up at the insult. Lyx refuses to look at him.

Heathen steps toward her bookshelf to retrieve an empty jar. "The *Indulgence* has magical wards in place, meaning there's no risk of pregnancy or sexually-transmitted infections." She returns to Lyx, unclamping the jar and flipping the lid open. "It also means any coercive abilities you have won't work on board. Consider them forbidden until you leave this ship for good."

Lyx's mouth twists. No siren would agree to that so easily. Even if Lyx has no power of her own, she has to act like she does. Her head tilts coyly. "What if there's an emergency?"

"*Forbidden*," Heathen enunciates.

The two of them watch each other in a silent standoff. Heathen barely blinks. Eventually, Lyx rolls her eyes in agreement.

That's enough for Heathen. "By every third day, you will assist Cav in his venture. There are no extensions or payment plans; that is your schedule. If you agree to these terms, you can make your deposit." She taps the jar and extends it toward Lyx. "You can use whatever you like: a few strands of hair, fingernail clippings, loose scales."

Warily, Lyx eyes the glass. "Why do you need that?"

"Your deposit is like your signature on a contract." When Lyx doesn't respond, Heathen purses their lips. It's clear they don't wish to elaborate, but Lyx doesn't move. Finally, they straighten their posture. "While you're aboard the *Indulgence*, any pleasure you experience will be collected."

"Collected?"

"It will have no effect on your experience. You won't notice a difference." Heathen sets the empty jar on her desk to put some space between them. "When anyone comes aboard, they make a deposit, regardless if they're customers or crew. The deposit has no negative effects; I've spent a lot of time ensuring that. It's only used to compile pleasure."

Lyx scoffs. "How can you measure something like that? How can you *collect* it?"

That, Heathen doesn't answer. "I understand this is unorthodox, but it's the way our ship operates. If that's not agreeable to you, then you're free to go."

Lyx bites her cheek. Why does the thought of giving up some part of herself make her skin crawl? She can still remember the feeling of losing her song, the strands slipping out of her mouth, and her helpless to stop them. But this is unlike any deal Tidus ever made. He took payments in wealth alone, dealing in threats and fear. People signed away ships and jewels and their lives, but never anything as inconsequential as nail clippings.

Lyx has spent the past two years surrounded by liars and thieves. She's gotten good at knowing when someone's trying to rip her off, and Heathen doesn't send up any red flags. Besides, they didn't want Lyx on the ship at all. This can't be part of some bigger conspiracy to crush her — can it?

Cav moves in front of her to shield her from Heathen's sight. "You don't have to do this." His voice is low between them, his tail curling beside her feet. "I could help you find something else."

Great Abyss, she *hates* his gentleness. He acts like he's on her side, but she knows better. She's alone. Her lip curls into a snarl.

He gives her a lingering look before he settles back beside her. "If it helps, I've given my scales for a while now. Never had any problems."

It doesn't help. It *shouldn't*, because Lyx would never seek comfort from *Cavalier*. But...fuck it. This is her way onto the ship. Once she gets onboard, she'll figure out how Heathen's business works. She'll get Tidus the information he wants. She'll destroy Cav and the life he's made here. At the end of this, she'll escape the past once and for all.

That's all she can do.

Resolutely, she pushes past Cav and holds out her wrist. Her loose scales wink and shimmer as they fall, and Lyx tries not to imagine the shell glowing in Tidus's chest.

Heathen flips the lid of the jar closed. "Looks like we have a deal."

NINE

Cav

"Give Cav a physical description of your ex." Heathen flips the clamp to seal the jar. "We set sail in ten minutes."

Lyx looks wary as Cav leads her away, but Heathen calls after them.

"Cavalier. Stay back a moment."

Despite her even tone, it isn't a request. Cav tenses as he pulls open the door, and Lyx pauses at the exit, tongue slipping over her lips like she can taste the chaos. "I think I'd prefer to watch you get chewed out."

No doubt his suffering is a delicacy she's been waiting years to savor. He presses a hand to the small of her back. "Don't want to overload you with pleasure on the first day, do we?"

She swats him away, and the door shuts behind her.

At her desk, Heathen holds the jar to the light to inspect the scales. It's impossible to read her expression, but the stern line of their brow isn't promising. Cav releases a breath. Whatever dressing down Heathen has planned for him is well-deserved. He didn't play fair when he asked for this arrangement, mixing business with personal in a way that Heathen hates...but they didn't deny him. That has to mean something, right?"

He scratches his claws against his neck. "Look, I'm sorry —"

"Why do you want Lyx here so badly?"

His expression goes slack. This is not the conversation he expected. He was prepared for a reprimand, not a question. It makes his answer feel more significant. He drops his hands back to his side. "Because I owe her. For saving me, and for what happened after."

"And no other reason?"

Her knowing stare makes him feel as flimsy as his excuse. He *does* want to make this right, to repay Lyx for her mercy and the misery he caused, but that's not the *only* reason. Something far more sentimental tugs on his heart like a fishing hook. He finds the easiest smile he can. "People have lots of reasons for the things we do."

Heathen lifts a singular brow and sets the jar aside. "I hope you approach this agreement as a professional endeavor, not a personal one. Especially given a siren's...proclivities when it comes to emotion."

Everyone knows the stories. Cav heard the words straight from the source, and they've lived in his head since the grotto.

Sirens don't feel sentimental emotions. We cannot love.

Shame heats his cheeks. Of course, he isn't in love with Lyx. Whatever residual feelings he has are just a void of something left unfinished. This deal they've made is a search for closure, brought on by simple physical attraction. Even Cav, in all his recklessness, understands there can't be anything more. He curls his hands around the back of the chair. "You seem to know a lot about sirens."

"I've done my research." Heathen traces the carvings on the edges of their desk. "Even if the prevailing thought was that they were myths, I like to be prepared, especially after your shipwreck." They fold their hands behind their back. "Truth be told, I didn't expect her to accept the deal."

Neither did Cav. Moreover, he never expected Heathen to propose it. "Why *did* you offer?" He asks before he thinks better of it. He shouldn't inspect this too closely, but he's never known how to quit while he's ahead. "Don't get me wrong, I'm grateful, but I was prepared for a much different reaction."

"And that was?"

Scolding. Punishment. Dismissal. "I'd rather not say. Don't want to give you any ideas."

The corner of Heathen's lip quirks. It's a rare sight. "I want to see what comes of your venture. It's innovative, even if it is uncharted territory. The *Indulgence* has never been the most experimental place."

Cav's brows lift. "So you think it's a good idea?"

"Innovative," Heathen repeats.

It doesn't dissolve Cav's pride. As careful as Heathen is with their words, they wouldn't say something they didn't mean. "Innovative" might as well be a full adulation coming from them.

"There are a few parameters," Heathen adds. "On this ship, safety is the top priority; I expect your venture to be the same. No harm should come to anyone."

"Without consent."

Heathen's eyes narrow. "Without consent."

"Are we limited to my cabin?"

Heathen's mouth twists as they consider it, sinking down into their chair. "No. But you are limited to each other. No one else should take part except for you and Lyx."

"*Physically* take part, you mean?"

Heathen settles back to take him in fully. Mischievously, Cav's tail flicks. He knows he's testing his luck, but if there's one thing Heathen loves, it's clarity.

"No physical contact with any third party," Heathen confirms. "In fact, I'd prefer you stay ten feet away from anyone else during your...entanglements."

"Can do."

Heathen straightens somberly. "I also hope this experiment keeps you busy. Keeps you out of trouble." She levels her gaze, and Cav resists the urge to flinch. It's uncommon to get such direct eye contact from Heathen. It feels heavy and intentional. "I want you somewhere I can keep an eye on you. Where your risks are taken in a controlled environment and not on a high-class dining ship."

He winces.

"This endeavor needs to work, Cav. Even if it doesn't become a permanent fixture, you have to think it through. Be deliberate. Spontaneity is all fine and good, but not at the cost of well-being." Heathen leans forward in their chair and picks up a roll of parchment. "If you aren't vigilant about this, we'll have a different conversation. One more like the kind you expected."

Cav swallows. Careless as he's been, losing his place on this ship is not the goal. He has to take this seriously. He *will*. It's the most flexibility Heathen has given him, and he won't squander it. Curtly, he nods.

Heathen jabs the roll of parchment toward him. "Don't make me regret this."

He backs toward the door, holding up his pinched fingers. "Only a little."

He leaves before Heathen reconsiders. Lyx is waiting outside, her back to the windows of Heathen's quarters.

"Eavesdropping?" Cav teases.

She doesn't laugh, her gaze trained across the deck. "They certainly like to stare."

By now, the crew of the *Indulgence* has come to life, finishing breakfast and preparing to set sail. Swabbies lug crates of food onboard as others untether ropes and lower the sails. Nearly all of them have their eyes trained on Lyx.

Cav plucks an orange from the nearest barrel and holds it out to her. "Until ten minutes ago, they thought you were a figment of my imagination."

"Drop the act."

His brows knit. He checks the orange for mold or some other offense before he rubs it clean on his vest. "What act?"

"This nicety shit. You got what you wanted; I'm stuck with you. You don't have to play it up."

He chuckles, but Lyx's eyes are cold. He offers the orange again. "You know, most people would say, *'Thank you, Cav, for helping me get a spot on this ship that I so desperately wanted.'*"

She folds her arms.

He retracts the fruit. "You didn't tell me someone was following you."

Her *ex*. Why didn't she mention it last night? Cav could have helped her. He certainly wouldn't have left her on her own. Perhaps that's exactly why she said nothing; she'd rather fend for herself than deal with Cav.

His face burns. The fact that she has an ex at all is surprising. He thought sirens didn't form such intimate relationships — hell, Lyx told him as much in the grotto.

So what is Cav to her? A fling? A failed victim?

His fingers tighten around the orange. No matter how short their time together, no matter how waterlogged his mind was, there was something between them. There had to be *something*. Or was Cav imagining it all, prescribing some draw that she never felt?

And what is it about this other person that was enough for her to stay?

That thought gnaws a hole in Cav's chest. He'd accepted that she didn't want anyone close, that no one was good enough to disturb her solitude, but someone *else* was.

When Cav looks at her, she's glaring, like his sappy emotions are poisoning the air. He pushes off the wall to rid himself of the thoughts. None of it matters; that's not why they're here.

He digs a claw into the orange and peels off the rind. "Shall we give you the tour?"

TEN

Lyx

"You've met Cypher." Cav gestures to the tattooed woman standing above the captain's quarters. "She's serving double-duty right now, overseeing the crew and the ship."

The ink on Cypher's skin undulates as she watches them down her nose. Of all the looks Lyx has received today, only Cypher's is openly hostile. It's as if she has a sense about Lyx, like she knows the real reason Lyx is here.

Lyx's scales prickle. There's no way Cypher could know anything; she's just suspicious of a siren. When Cypher keeps staring, Lyx lifts her brow in a challenge.

Cypher's scowl deepens.

Cav places his hands on Lyx's shoulders. "There'll be plenty of time to make enemies later. Let's not start with the second-in-command."

As he turns her, his claws brush her collarbone. It sends her mind down a familiar path overgrown with memories that reach out and cling to her. It's the same way Cav's talons dug into her hips, scraping down her back and teasing her —

She shudders out of his grip, but it puts little space between them. The deck is crowded, filling her with a familiar unease when she's forced to recognize that she's surrounded by pirates.

A couple leans over the forecastle railing with devious grins. The woman hooks her arm over the man's shoulder and whispers in his ear. Both of them keep their eyes on Lyx. It's clear the two of them are some magical species; each of their skin is vibrant, but they have their own color schemes. Seeds and leaves and berries dot their bodies, as if they're both descended from different fruits.

"There go all my customers," the man murmurs. His voice is so sultry it's like he's speaking against Lyx's skin.

Cav picks up a wicker bowl and tosses some salted pork inside. "Lyx isn't serving customers. She's working with me." He reaches for a block of cheese and lowers his voice to Lyx. "He's Lace, she's Briar. Never see one without the other."

"In that case..." Briar rests her chin in one hand. "Maybe she wants to *be* my customer."

"Are the stories true?" Lace asks, eyes sparkling. "They say sex with a siren is like fucking a black widow."

Cav scoffs. "That's enough from the welcoming committee."

Hunger gnaws at Lyx's stomach. Briar and Lace are brimming with discord, their natural magnetism something Lyx hasn't felt since she was snatched from the other sirens. The two of them are a tempting invitation for trouble, but Cav maneuvers her toward the hatchway.

Briar reaches down to tousle his hair. "If you get bored with Cavvy, we're always close by."

Cav grabs her hand to pull it away, but the touch reminds him of something. Soberly, he meets her eyes, and his voice softens. "Roderick's gone."

The mood shifts. Briar's eyes widen. Lace's face swarms with disgust, nose wrinkling at some nasty memory. Almost imperceptibly, Briar squeezes Cav's hand before she sets a smirk back onto her face. "I knew you were good for something."

When Cav releases her, she and Lace dive into animated conversation while Cav and Lyx descend below deck.

The stairs are steep, opening into a tight corridor lined with doors on either side. Crew members mill about in stages of undress, leaning into the hallway to converse or argue. Cav carries the bowl through the narrow gaps and chews a piece of cinnamon bark between his teeth.

The scent smacks Lyx in the face. "Straight cinnamon?"

He smiles around it. "I like spicy."

Her eyes roll, until she realizes they aren't passing any barracks. Everyone has their own rooms. When Cav offered his cabin, she'd thought he was exaggerating. On all the ships she's boarded, she's never seen so much space. Even in Tidus's heyday, the crew slept in a shared room while he kept Lyx in his massive captain's quarters.

"Heathen's been working on it a long time." Cav squeezes past her, hands ghosting over her hips. He holds a low-hanging rope out of the way. "Each room can only fit a bed. The walls are thin, but it's better than nothing. At least, until we get a new convoy."

"Isn't that where you're supposed to be?"

Dammit. Her teeth grit. The thought slipped out before she thought better of it. She's not supposed to remember that; she's not supposed to remember any details from the grotto.

Cav's expression muddies into some strange mix of delight and disappointment. Lyx isn't sure what that means, but all he says is, "If only," before he pushes open the door at the end of the corridor.

This room is nestled into the bow, running parallel to the ship. Sunlight shines through a round window on one wall and casts across the bed on the opposite side. The floor space is limited, leaving most of Cav's things strewn across his sheets or tucked into cabinets and the hanging desk on the wall. The bed is half-made, the drawers beneath it closed haphazardly around paintbrushes, clay beads, and spools of thread.

Lyx tries to dull any curiosity in her voice. "Never pegged you as an artist."

"I like to pick things up: crafts, hobbies." He leaves the door open behind them and stuffs a skein of yarn back into place. "Keeps my mind busy. Gives my hands something to do."

Lyx wanders toward another drawer and tugs on a loop of rope until an entire bundle emerges. It's different from the yarn, not scratchy and frayed like the lines used for sails and cargo. This rope is smooth and black, mysterious enough to be intimidating. When she tugs, the knot holding it in place slips.

The heat from Cav's body spreads across her back. He's close now, hovering over her shoulder until there's an inch of space between them. His face hovers in her periphery. They're alone, like last night on the dinghy. Like last night on the docks.

The air in the room crackles, like even the atmosphere forgets what it's meant to do when it's just the two of them. Lyx turns to face him. She braces against the rocking of the ship. When Cav reaches for the rope, she pulls it away.

His golden eyes flicker.

She doesn't know why she provokes him. Maybe for chaos. Irritation. A little opportunity for revenge. Whatever the reason, she keeps the bundle behind her back, even when Cav leans toward her. Even when he reaches behind her, skimming his hand down her forearm to reach her fist.

She doesn't give. "What's it for?"

He keeps his eyes on her face, slipping his digits between hers to pry her fingers open one by one. "Play your cards right..." Once he has the rope again, he taps it on the underside of her chin. "You might find out." Then he tosses it into a bag in the corner.

The room is suddenly stifling. She lifts her hair off her neck, but it does nothing to soothe her.

Cav leans back against the opposite wall. "We need to establish some rules. Before we start this...journey of ours."

Hearing him speak about it makes her skin tight. She releases her hair and folds her arms across her chest. They might as well be negotiating a hostage situation rather than intercourse. Maybe a hostage situation would be easier.

Cav must sense it, too. He relaxes his shoulders, tail curling non-threateningly around his leg. "This'll be easier if you act like you can tolerate me."

"I'm tolerating enough already."

"What would make you feel more cooperative?" Depths, he sounds earnest. "What sort of things do you want to try? What do you like?"

"Nothing you could give me."

He exhales sharply, ruffling the hair across his forehead. "Fine. We need to choose a safeword. Something either of us can use if we want to stop at any time."

Lyx shakes out the waves of her hair. "Nothing you do will surprise me enough for that."

"You don't even know what the rope is for."

Her lips feel dry. She drags her tongue across them and ignores the way his gaze follows. "I can guess."

"Yeah? Guess, then." He stretches his arms overhead, then brings them across his chest to match hers. "I'd *love* to hear what it makes you think of."

He looks more like a pirate than she's ever seen him. Easy and unbothered, reclining with his foot against the wall. His knee tilts outward as if he's making space for her.

So fucking nonchalant.

Her fingernails dig half-moons into her palm. She wants to upend that smirk on his face, to step between his legs and —

"*Parley*," she finally snaps. "That's the word. Are we done?"

He scrutinizes her for a long moment before he drops his foot back to the floor. "Not quite. See, you can put on a show for everyone out there. Act like this agreement is testing you. Like it doesn't turn you on…" He wanders closer. Even when he's looking up to meet her gaze, something about him engulfs her. "But when it's just us, I want the truth."

Her body thrums like a compass finding magnetic north. She refuses to look anywhere but his eyes. "I agreed to be an active participant. I'll help you with your little project. I'll *fuck you*."

He sucks a breath through his teeth. "Careful…" It fans the flame in his chest. "Or I might start thinking you're into me."

She glances toward the open door, but it doesn't concern him. He isn't threatened by the thought that anyone could pass by. He acts like this is a game, just foreplay to something bigger. That thread of chaos weaves inside her. She swallows it down, too proud to feel the heat. If he's not worried someone might overhear, then fine; she'll use it to her advantage.

"You couldn't even get out of your pants last time." Her head tilts, unimpressed. "It should be easy to finish you off."

His teeth flash in a smile that makes her toes curl. "Are we rewriting history?" He eases toward her, voice low as a chain dragged across the floor. "Because there are some other things I'd like to revise."

Smoke drifts between his lips. That's the only reason her gaze is drawn to his mouth, her eyelids suddenly heavy. The wisp outlines his jaw.

"You're paying in pleasure, right? So let's give it to you."

Her body could melt right here, but then Cav turns away, dispersing the smoke and peeling off his oversized vest.

"If you don't feel like telling me what you want, then we'll have some trial and error."

Now she can see his attire from last night. It's bloody and ripped, but worst of all, the pants cling to his ass. The waistcoat molds to the muscles in his back as he undoes the buttons one by one.

"I'll figure out what gets you hot. I'll make you come. I'll tailor this entire experiment to getting you off, and I'll give you everything you want — except for me."

It takes a moment too long for her to scoff. "I don't want *you*."

He strips off the waistcoat and reaches for the collar of his shirt. "Then you won't miss out on anything."

He tugs it overhead, exposing the bare scales of his back. His skin glows molten between them, magma threatening to break through the crust of the earth. Freed of the fabric, the spikes along his spine lift on end, trailing down between the dimples above his hips. There are bandages wrapped around his torso, but these wraps don't flatten his physique. In fact, the binding seems to enunciate his chest, lifting his breasts until they sit perfectly in place.

Only now does Lyx realize he's turned back to face her. That he can see everywhere her eyes go. Her face heats, and his smirk grows. "If you do change your mind about wanting me —"

"I won't," she grits.

"But if you do. If you want more. If you want me to give

you *everything*…" His thick eyelashes dip as he watches her mouth.

Something inside her tightens. She tries to remind herself of her purpose; she is here to ruin Cav's life and get Tidus what he wants. That's it. There's nothing else. Yet when Cav leans closer, she remembers the feel of his lips, the drag of his teeth, the hot slide of his tongue. She wants to see if it still feels the same. She wants to bite him and lick the blood out of his mouth. She wants to hurt him, and she wants to taste it.

But when her lips part beneath his, Cav tilts away. Just so. "You have to be honest. It has to be real." He reaches for the shirt at the end of his bed. "Show me more than this facade, and I won't hold anything back."

Her throat is tight. "Is this revenge –" She tries to clear it. "Because I didn't give you everything last time?"

He hums. "Consider it an exchange of vulnerability."

Lyx refuses to give in. She doesn't cave to the tingling in her fingers or the twinge between her legs. She feels nothing; she assures herself of that. "That's never going to happen."

"We'll see, *partner*." Cav scoops up his satchel from the corner and slings it over his shoulder. "Be back in three days."

In the Grotto

Cav

Lyx doesn't return the next morning.

If Cav were smarter, he would be saying his goodbyes. She said herself that she's nursing him back to health just to have the thrill of killing him, but Cav has never let good sense get in the way of good faith. Lyx will return. Of that, he is certain.

His stomach groans. How many days has it been since he's eaten? Time is impossible to keep track of with his eyes shut. Worst of all, he still hasn't seen Lyx in all her glory, and he refuses to die without at least a glimpse.

With one arm, he reaches out beside him. Glass bottles jostle under his fingertips, an algae net clinging to his palm. He works by sound and touch alone, tugging Lyx's bag closer to rifle through it. One by one, he uncorks the bottles and holds them to his nose. His nostrils flare at the sting of alcohol. The next scent makes him gag, but finally, he finds one that seems tepid enough.

He presses his thumb to the mouth of the bottle and pours it onto his eyelids. Slowly, the crust dissolves until he can crack his eyes open. It's so bright with the sunlight reflecting off the water that it takes five full minutes before he adjusts.

This grotto is much like a cave. Foliage grows around him in large fronds stretching over the mossy bank. At his feet, a pool of ocean water has collected on a ledge. It must be low tide now. No waves splash against the rocks; instead, he hears the ocean moving gently beneath the drop-off. That water flows out of the cave entrance and continues into the sea.

His head tilts back. Above him, the rocky ceiling is solid, but light leaks through the natural holes worn into it. One beam shines a few feet from him and glints off the glass bottles. The vials are a variety of shapes and colors with faded labels, but he recognizes them, classic medicines and potions found on nearly every ship.

Behind the bottles is a jug of fresh water. His tongue scrapes his lips like sandpaper. It takes some maneuvering, but once he reaches it, he has to restrain himself from downing the whole thing.

Lyx doesn't return all day. Eventually, the air around him grows chilly, forcing him to burrow beneath a few massive leaves. He wants to be awake when she arrives. He fights sleep like a child, but eventually, the soothing sounds of the ocean send him off.

In his dreams, he assembles Lyx with what pieces he knows. Her skin is slippery like a jellyfish. There's a solid weight to her, her body far from frail when she sat atop of him and threatened to strangle him.

His fingers flex. His dream changes. This time when she pins him down, his hands move to her thighs. She lets him touch her until he reaches the width of her hips, and then, she closes her hands around his throat once more.

Beside Cav, something splashes. He ignores it and tries to sink back into the dream, but the splashing continues. It takes a while to realize what he hears are footsteps drawing closer and stopping next to his head.

He doesn't want to wake up. He wants to keep dreaming about Lyx, but when his eyes flutter open, he half-believes he's still asleep. The woman standing over him looks like an illusion. Her hair falls in wavy ribbons, colors shifting in the light. The milky skin of her torso glows nearly translucent, darkening to blue and purple at her hips. Scars wind around her arms and chest like thin ropes raised beneath her skin.

So this is a siren. She looks as divine as the stories say, but it's strange seeing her walk on two legs. All the tales depict sirens with tails that restrict them to water. Is that a lie created for comfort, an assurance that some place is safe from sirens? Or did sirens spread the fiction themselves, an easy way to move about unnoticed?

The siren watches him with a look that could almost be concern — until she catches him staring. Instantly, her expression shifts back to distaste. "You're still alive."

He can't help but smile. It is Lyx. He knows that voice, the one that kept his mind afloat when his body tried to give up. "As long as you will it."

She rolls her eyes and turns back to the ledge. Her skin has dried impossibly fast, leaving only traces of water behind. That's when Cav realizes she's as naked as him. He watches her movement, following every curve and ripple of her flesh. He wants to take in all of her, but when she turns back to face him, he forces his gaze to the ceiling.

She dumps out a new bag of supplies before she notes the bottles beside him. Her lip curls. "I see you've helped yourself to my bag." She pulls a rag from the pile and sits to clean each bottle's rim.

His laugh is rough. "Afraid you might catch something from me?"

"I'm not afraid of you," she spits. "Next to me, you're an anchovy. You're chum." Indignantly, she reaches into her pile and tosses something toward him. "Here, you little fucking plankton."

It lands with a wet slap beside him. He has to roll over to reach it, but the string of small fish is a welcome sight.

"You gutted them for me?" He doesn't concern himself with eating politely, using his sharp teeth to rip meat from the bones. Raw fish wouldn't normally be his first choice, but he's ravenous. Before long, he's polished them off, wiping his mouth on the back of his hand with a long drink of water. "Thank you."

Lyx continues cleaning the bottles, monitoring him from the corner of her eye. "Are you a dragon?"

For the first time, there's no threat coming from her, besides the steely sheen of her eyes. "Half," he answers.

"Half-what?"

"Half-dragon, half-human."

"Are you half-man and woman, too?"

A laugh startles out of him, but Lyx's expression doesn't change. Her words are neither a joke nor an insult. Most people prefer to see him as one or the other, but Cav has never done well with constraints. No one's ever put it as concisely as she does. Slowly, he nods. "Yeah. Something like that."

"Do you breathe fire?"

He clears his throat to stir the weakened ember in his chest. "Not when I've swallowed two gallons of sea water."

She lifts her chin to scrutinize him. "You don't have wings."

"And you don't have a fishtail."

Her eyes simmer, but then his stomach rumbles loud

enough that it can't be ignored. Without a word, Lyx rises to her feet and moves away. He wonders if he's offended her, if she's leaving already, but she returns moments later with a bundle of flora picked from the bank. Cav relishes the sea peas and samphire, and when he finishes them off, his stomach remembers what it's like to be satisfied.

The whole time, Lyx watches him, repolishing the same bottles over and over. "You say you don't hunt sirens." She speaks like she doesn't believe it, eyes following him like a hawk. "So what do you do?"

"Curious about me?"

That gets under her skin. She pushes to her feet, leaving Cav scrambling to answer.

"I work on an escort vessel. We convoy another ship to guarantee its safe passage."

Lyx remains standing, but she doesn't leave. It's the best he could hope for. Finally, she corrects him. "You worked on an escort vessel. Don't forget you're dying here, pirate."

The corner of Cav's lip lifts. "My mistake."

They remain in silence for a few minutes before Lyx speaks again. "Will the rest of your ship come looking for you?"

There's something chilling in her voice, a reminder that Cav is trapped here. That there is no one to save him. That his fate is in her hands alone.

He should say yes. He should insist that he's invaluable, that Captain Prodeus and his crew will sail the entire ocean looking for him, but Cav rests on his uninjured shoulder. "Honestly?" He blows out a breath. "I've only been with them a few months. I doubt my captain knows I'm missing; I don't even think he knows my name."

It's foolish to admit, but maybe he wants Lyx to know they're alone. Maybe he wants her to have free reign of him. Maybe he wants her to take him apart in any way she desires. When he shifts the leaf blanket lower, Lyx's eyes flick toward his chest.

His heart hammers. He's pinned beneath the gaze of a predator, but he doesn't want to run. He wants something else. He takes a deep breath in and lets his breasts rise and fall.

She follows the motion. There's a glassy look in her eyes, a hunger that Cav wants to feed, but Lyx rises abruptly to her feet. "I won't be back for a while. Maybe never." Her voice is clipped as she tosses a heap of wet fabric toward him. "You can keep these." Then she hurries toward the ledge.

"Wait!" Cav scrambles to sit up and grunts as his shoulder spasms. His heart keeps up its rapid pace. He barely notices the clothing she's thrown at him. It's not Cav's survival he fears for if she never returns; it's this feeling inside him, like a wick has been lit and he needs to see it explode. He searches for any reason to keep her here even a moment longer. "If you lay those clothes out in the sun, they can dry. Maybe some driftwood, too. Then I can show you my fire."

Lyx stops in her tracks. The air around her bristles like she's warring with some part of herself. Slowly, she looks at him over her shoulder. "Don't instruct me."

It shivers through him. His tongue sweeps over his lips. They're wet for the first time in days, and Lyx notices it, too. Her gaze jumps from his mouth to his eyes and back, drawn in despite herself.

Heat flares through his body. As cautiously as he can, he pushes up to sit. Any sudden motion might frighten her away. "My most tolerant captor..." His voice is raspy with salt and something else, scratching low in his throat. "Will you set my clothes out in the sun? Please? Or should I wait for you like this?"

Something slick and dangerous twists in his gut. He lets

the leaf fall away, exposing his naked body to her. He leans back against the rocks, hand wandering between his breasts and raking through the soft scales trailing the lower part of his stomach.

What is he thinking? Why is he playing this game? Why is he risking his life for a thrill? But it's not just that. He wants more.

From the look in Lyx's eyes, so does she.

Her eyes are hot and angry, doing everything they can to remain on his face. He might even believe she hates him if the light didn't reflect off her supple thighs clenching together.

The needy sound in the back of his throat makes her grit her teeth and storm back to him.

He isn't sure if she'll fuck him or kill him. He isn't sure he'd say no to either, and he knows he should be afraid, but his body hums when she presses her wet foot to his sternum.

It shoves him back against the wall. A rivulet of water trails up the inside of her thigh, following gravity's course between her legs. She knows where his gaze goes. The sight of her cunt makes his mouth water. He wants to drag his tongue between her lips, he wants to delve his tongue inside her, he wants to make her come against his mouth —

She leans down closer to him. "I'm keeping you alive for my amusement. Be careful how you entertain me."

With every beat of his heart, his chest glows and spreads heat where their bodies connect. She watches light spread between his scales before she moves back and disappears off the ledge.

The droplets on Cav's chest sizzle long after she's gone, and no amount of water can quench his thirst.

ELEVEN

Lyx

Lyx shakes a scorpion from her boot. "I only have until sunset."

This is the first port the *Indulgence* has docked in since Lyx boarded three days ago. Out here, the terrain is rough and dense. It's nothing like the streets and shops of the town proper, but of course, Tidus expected her to find him in the overgrowth. His sloop is moored in a tiny cove hidden from the rest of the island, the boat's ragged blue flag growing more bleached in the sun.

Tidus reclines beneath a tree and tips back his dented tankard. "Don't rush me." As if he didn't expect *her* prompt appearance. As if he wouldn't be furious if she lost her spot on the ship. Lazily, he swirls the drink in his cup. "Were you followed?"

"What do you think?"

His eyes cut toward her. It's risky mouthing off to him,

but she's walked for nearly half an hour to reach this spot, tripping through mud and bramble bushes. Sunlight sears across her bare arms and bakes in the dirt and scratches. Tidus can handle a little bit of fucking attitude.

Not to mention she's parched, and not just from the heat. It's been days since she's been this close to her song; the shell in Tidus's chest glows like it's straining to reach her. Being near it is enough to loosen the knot in her chest, but that relief is forgotten as soon as Tidus touches her wrist.

"You look faded." He runs his jagged thumb over her skin and digs his fingernail under a loose scale. "Don't they feed you on that boat?"

She jerks away. It's not food he means. Given the *Indulgence*'s area of expertise, she expected far more disorder, but the ship runs like a well-oiled machine. Racy sounds pitch through the walls, but nothing juicy. When there's a disagreement, it's only mild bickering. Where's the cheating? The threats? The brawling? Without them, Lyx's coloring has faded and dulled.

That was never an issue on Tidus's ship.

"Didn't Heathen put you to work in her whore ship?" Tidus toys with the slit in Lyx's long skirt and pulls her down into his lap. "How many customers have had the pleasure of siren pussy?"

It sounds like the idea thrills him, but she knows better. He only likes the thought of tormenting her; he hates the idea of "sharing." If she confessed to providing her services, Tidus's entire demeanor would change. "I'm not servicing customers. I'm working with Cavalier."

Tidus's brow quirks unremarkably.

Her jaw clicks. Three days, and he still can't remember Cav's name. "Your *chatty dragon.*"

Tidus tips back his head and laughs. "That's what Heathen wanted you for? To keep her cabin boy's dick wet?"

"He's not —" Lyx blows out a breath. Why bother explaining intricacies when Tidus clearly doesn't care? "No. Heathen's collecting something else from me."

Tidus skims his palm up her thigh. "I'm not giving you any money."

"It's not money. It's pleasure."

"*Pleasure?*" His lip curls. He gropes the meat of her hip. "What the fuck does that mean?"

"I don't know." Great Abyss, these constant questions are getting to her. Even in the shade, her skin is dry and tight, made more stifling by Tidus's insistent touching. Her blouse slips off her shoulders. A fly buzzes near her ear, and she swats it away.

Tidus grabs her chin. "Answer me." His grip tightens to bruising. "Is Heathen fucking you? Is that what it is?"

"*No!*" she splutters, fighting his grip. "Depths, *what* is your obsession with her?" She can't escape Tidus's hold, but she needs to temper both their fury. Fingers flexing, she snatches the tankard from his hand. She'd like to slam it into the side of his head, but that wouldn't be enough to stop him. She lifts the mug to her nose and gags at the heavy scent. Of course it's ale. It's the only drink he keeps on his boat, despite how much she hates it. It doesn't matter; her throat is aching. With a grim look, she drains the cup and tosses the tankard to the ground.

Tidus's eyes flash. He releases his hold on her face, but when she wrenches away, he jerks her back by her bodice instead. His gnarled fingernails tear through the fabric, his ale-stained breath hot on her face. "That's not an answer."

The laces constrict her lungs. "What do you *want?*" Her mind is a rabid creature, searching for whatever words will make him stop. "I don't know how they collect pleasure! When I got onboard, Heathen took some of my scales for the contract. I don't know what happens after that."

The bodice crushes her ribcage. His nails dig into her skin. He doesn't release her. Not until she gets a good look at the warning in his eyes – then, he shoves her away. "Get back to the ship, then. Find out how the fuck she's doing it."

Her sudden breath and chaos leave her head spinning. This sudden feeding is enough to make her sick, but she swallows down the urge to vomit. No matter how she suffers, Tidus's unpredictability always gives her what she needs. A brilliant purple color seeps across her legs, but Tidus doesn't look at her when she leaves.

By the time she reaches the port, it's late. The sun has dipped below the horizon, leaving the *Indulgence*'s lanterns shining like beacons. The deck of the ship jostles with a party in full swing. On the docks, a crowd has gathered, craning their necks while they wait for their turn to board.

No one is looking for Lyx. Her brows lift in surprise. She'd expected Captain Heathen to go back on their word and advertise the prized siren, but instead, only a few customers glance at her as she elbows her way up the gangplank.

Crew members wait at the top, collecting coins or holding out glass jars. The guests pluck their eyelashes or feathers and drop them inside. Lyx needs to see where those jars go. With a grunt, she squeezes onto the ship and follows a tray of full jars across the deck — until a tattooed arm blocks her way.

Cypher glares down at her, the bird on her shoulder tilting its head in indictment. "Where have you been?"

Lyx lifts on her toes, but the jars are already disappearing below deck. With a hiss, she shoves Cypher's arm away.

Cypher's jaw ticks above her black neckerchief. For fuck's sake, it's hot enough already; is that why she's so pissy? "Sunset was the cutoff," Cypher emphasizes. "You're late."

"And I'm here now." If Cypher won't budge, neither will Lyx. She plants her feet, glaring up at Cypher until the woman presses her mouth into a thin line. Cypher's not going do shit, even if she *wants* to. That's a flaw Lyx can work with.

Smugly, Lyx turns toward the hatchway to make her way below deck.

"Has Cav collected your pleasure payment?"

Lyx's eye twitches. She keeps her back turned when she responds, "Yes."

"You're lying."

Lyx's body bristles. The air is sweltering. Everyone who speaks to her is an asshole. She lost her first lead on this ship, and the gaping absence of her song has opened up again. How much more can she take?

When she turns back to Cypher, Lyx's smile is sharp. "Nosy bitch, aren't you?"

Cypher's nostrils flare. The crow flaps in alarm, but Lyx isn't deterred. She lunges, but then, two warm hands curl around her shoulders from behind.

"Just the person I was looking for." Despite Cav's breezy voice, he's purposeful as he leads her away from the fight. Only once they're out of Cypher's line of sight does he stop moving Lyx along. "I see you've found the time to make enemies."

Lyx pries away from him, snatching a drink from the nearest tray. "It's not like I'm going to make *friends*." She takes a long swig, but it lacks the burn of liquor. She scowls.

"One of Heathen's recipes," Cav confirms. "Strong enough to loosen inhibitions, but not enough to get you drunk. Important distinction for a pleasure house."

Yet another way to stave off chaos. With a roll of her eyes, Lyx sets the drink on a barrel and moves toward the railing.

Cav picks up her abandoned drink. "You know, if you were trying to get drunk, you could have done it at the pub."

"I didn't need a drink until I got back here."

He sidles up next to her. "Then what have you been doing since we made port?"

His words aren't as hostile as Cypher's, but it's not an innocent question. Cav is looking for something. Lyx narrows her eyes. There's no way he can suspect what she's up to. She won't incriminate herself. Let him throw out the allegation if he wants.

But when he speaks, it's not an accusation. "If your ex is chasing you, you need to be careful. You shouldn't go off on your own."

So that's what this is about. With a sigh, she leans her elbows back against the railing. "As much as you relish interfering in what I do, I only have to deal with you during the experiment. I can handle the rest of my time. *Alone.*"

"Is that how your dress got ripped?"

Only now does she recognize the breeze against her stomach. The hole from Tidus is bigger than she realized, uneven and jagged. Cav watches her expression closely. She's missed her opportunity to pretend to be surprised, so instead, she flexes her fingers and looks out across the deck. "Must have caught on a loose nail."

It's obvious she's lying. It's pathetic attempt, but Cav doesn't call her out. He lifts his hand to the damage, slipping past the fabric to brush the marks Tidus left on her skin.

Despite herself, she shivers.

Cav outlines the hole with the tip of his claw. "Doesn't look like a snag."

His voice is dangerously soft. She has to pull away, still tingling when bumps prickle along her arms. She needs to think about something else — anything else – so she scans the rest of the ship.

It's clear the *Indulgence* is built for show, its sails and decor more opulent than any normal vessel. Along the taffrail, an assortment of carved creatures drape around closed clamshells. The atmosphere and dim lighting add an air of sensuality, but aside from the decor, the rest of the party is tame. Everyone chats and laughs, but there's hardly any physical contact. Most of the crew remains standing, as if their flirtation is constrained to glances alone. It's unlike any of the brothels Lyx has been to. Everyone seems comfortable, but they're almost...hesitant.

"Why do customers come here?" she asks.

"What do you mean?"

"Why don't they visit a pleasure house on the island? Surely the experience isn't that different."

"They can't." Cav finishes off the drink and sets it aside. "We visit ports that don't have their own brothels. Either the government blocks them, or the population's too small, or some other reason. That's why people come to the *Indulgence*."

Lyx tugs out a cord from her belt and gathers her curls atop her head. Finally, the night breeze begins to cool her neck. "Nothing about this looks very *indulgent*."

Cav sighs and leans back against the railing. "You're not wrong." Then a mischievous smile flashes across his lips. "Maybe it's time we spice things up."

Heat coils in her gut. She hasn't forgotten that time is ticking on this venture they agreed to. In truth, she's been thinking about it since the morning she boarded. Remembering how close he was, how his body looked beneath his clothes...

How he refused to fuck her.

Not that she cares. Not that it matters, because he won't be able to stick to it. Of the two of them, it's *Cav* who'll be begging to give her everything.

Nerves flutter in her stomach, but she resists them, keeping her face passive as she looks across the party again. This will be simple and fast. She's a siren; she knows how to wrap things up quickly. With a heavy sigh, she pushes off the railing and moves toward the hatchway. "Let's get it over with, then."

She makes it down the third step before he calls after her, "Not down there."

When she turns back, he looks positively pleased with himself. His tail weaves behind him in a hypnotizing motion she tries not to follow. Why does she feel off-balance? She grips the banister to keep from slipping, like it's her first day on land.

Cav tilts his head toward the center mast. "We're going up."

TWELVE

Lyx

Lyx's gaze trails up the main mast, past the ropes and ladders to the crow's nest set against a backdrop of stars. "Funny," she says dryly.

"You need convincing?" Cav wanders closer. "I thought the prospect of chaos would be enough, but maybe you need more incentive." He stops at the top of the stairs, bending at the waist to meet her eyes. "I dare you to climb the crow's nest."

She looks toward it again. She hates how he can sense her hunger sparking like steel on flint. She's too proud to tell him that he's right, but she's also too proud to turn down a challenge. Jaw clenched, she pushes past him and grasps the first rung of the rope ladder.

It digs into her palms with a satisfying sting that keeps her climbing. She's calling Cav's bluff. There's no chance he truly has a plan. Once they're in the crow's nest, he'll stumble over his words and be forced to admit he wasn't prepared for her to match him. He wasn't prepared for *her*.

When she's halfway up, murmurs rise from the crowd. She never glances back to check if Cav is behind her. At the top, she pulls herself through the trap door and rises to her feet. The crown's nest is larger than she expected, a wooden bucket with the mast piercing straight through the middle. Up here, the sound and light from the party are dim. At the far side of the island, she can just make out the tip of Tidus's ship, its flag flapping in the wind.

She turns her back on it and faces out toward the sea. Her hands curl around the railing, and she inhales the beautiful sting of salt. All she can see is the ocean, but this is only a fraction of it. Its true size is beyond comprehension. She watches the waves roll in and rock the boat beneath her. The water is constantly in flux, always moving, never the same, but she bets every drop would remember her. All she'd have to do is dip a toe in...

"It really is a wonder." Cav moves to stand beside her and stares out across the waves with earnest admiration. Stars reflect in his eyes. "Constant, but uncertain. Calculable, but volatile. Intimidating. Beautiful. Powerful."

It strikes a chord deep inside her. They are words she's never spoken, but she recognizes their echo through the emptiness inside her. It's the same longing she has. When she looks at Cav, she realizes he's staring at her, like his fondness isn't *just* reserved for the ocean. She jerks her gaze away and lifts her chin. "You speak about the ocean like you would a lover."

"I speak far more highly of my lovers."

Her skin prickles, but she turns her back to the horizon. She can't allow herself to be distracted. She can't return to the sea. Not yet. "Why are we up here? Because I'm sure it's not to chat."

He watches her for another moment before he bends to seal the trapdoor. "We're here to feed your appetites."

Bitterly, she laughs. What does Cav know about meeting her needs? "I thought this was about your little project."

"The project is the vehicle." He digs into his pocket, eyeing some point further up the mast. "Your pleasure is the destination."

Her eyes roll. "What, are you going to bend me over the railing in front of the crowd?"

Cav holds onto the mast and swings to her other side, eyes glowing in the dark. "Are you asking me to?"

She swallows. The thought alone makes her hot, but he acts like he's hanging on her every word, ready for her answer.

When she doesn't, he holds out something between them. "Then no. We'll try something else."

It's the bundle of dark rope from the cabin. She takes it, running her fingers over its smooth surface.

"Or you could push me off." He sits back against the railing, unafraid to tempt fate. Unafraid to tempt *Lyx*. "The choice is yours."

Her fingers curl around the rope. When she steps closer, Cav doesn't brace himself. He just makes space for her, not a hint of arrogance in his body. If anything, he looks like he's made peace with the fact that this could be his final breath. She eyes the drop below. Every pirate she's known has believed themself invincible, like no sea or siren could fell them. Cav, on the other hand, wears his mortality like a cloak. Like he knows how easily Lyx could destroy him, and still, he takes the risk, dangling by a thread and handing her the knife.

That knowledge stirs inside her. She steps between his open knees, their gazes locked before she presses the rope to his chest. His balance wavers. She could do it. She could push him. But his fingers splay across the back of her hand, like the only thing he wants is to touch her, even if it means meeting his end.

Arousal clenches deep in her gut. "Fine."

His eyes flare, but he doesn't reach for her. Instead, he begins to unwind the rope. "You remember the safeword?"

Her brows knit. Never has someone *taken their time* when she's standing before them and offering everything. It chips away at the armor of her pride. She reaches for the rope. "Don't need it."

"But you remember it." His hands close around her wrists. "Just in case."

His calluses are stark against her smooth skin. It's strangely appealing, like a pumice stone wearing away at her. He could use that rough touch on all of her other soft places, too: the small of her back, the inside of her cheeks, the juncture of her thighs...

He doesn't loosen his grip. Not until she finds her voice. "Parley."

Finally, he nods and loops the rope around her wrists.

She's never seen a knot like this before. It's firm but not tight, allowing enough room for a finger to slip between the rope and her arms. He takes his time with it, and she has no choice but to look at his face hovering before her. Scales fan out around his eyes and across his cheekbones, trailing down his jaw. They're smaller than the rugged scales of his hands. They feel different, too.

She remembers.

He stands suddenly, turning her toward the mast to press her chest against it. He lifts her bound hands over her head where he notches them on a hook, leaving her swaying on her toes. She tugs on the restraints. They don't budge.

Her heart trips over itself. When's the last time she was this helpless, hoisted up at the whims of some pirate?

Cav's warm body presses against her back. "Is that good?"

Her fingernails dig into her palms. It's dizzying being this high, her hands tied, Cav's sturdy frame behind her. "Is that all you have?" She fights the urge to rock back against him. "This isn't chaos; it's barely disarray."

He hums knowingly before something covers her eyes. Fabric pulls tight against her temples and blocks out all of the light. She clenches her fists to keep from shivering, but then his breath teases her ear. "What do you think of this?"

"A blindfold?" Her voice sounds foreign to her ears. Breathy. Tight. *Needy.*

His fist keeps the bandana in place. "I think it's better for the chaos if you don't know what's coming."

Cav's teeth nick her earlobe before he pulls away. She leans back, trying to place him in the dark, but she can barely bite back a gasp when his mouth presses to her other ear.

"If you can't predict it."

Hunger coils inside her like a snake. It's not the aching hollow that she's used to, the one she knows from Tidus. This hunger is sharp, carnal, animal, desperate to sink in its fangs.

Cav speaks again. "I dare you to trust me."

She shudders, trying to hide the need in her voice. "Stop asking. Just do it."

"As you wish." Cav knots the fabric behind her head. "I won't ask if it's comfortable."

"Better than looking at you."

His laughter sounds different when she can't see him, a dark chuckle that makes her toes curl. The heat of his body vanishes, and she grits her teeth to keep them from chattering. It can't all be blamed on the cold.

Far below, the party buzzes. The boat sways. Boards creak beneath her, and she knows he's moving, circling the mast to inspect her.

Everything is heightened like this. When his fingertips brush the skin of her shoulders, she twitches and bites down on the curse in her mouth. It's bad enough that she can't see or free herself, but her body reacts to the slightest touch…and Cav can see all of it.

She arches and tugs on the restraints. "Why are you going so *slow*?"

Nothing she says spurs him on. If anything, he moves slower, dipping one finger beneath the waistband of her skirt. "Do you ever get fixated on something?" His voice sounds dreamy, as if his mind is lost on where his hands are wandering. "You can't think past it. You want to spend all your time on it. Get lost in it."

His fingers drift lower, tracing the juncture of her thigh. She fights not to roll her hips, not to admit that her thoughts of ruining Cav have been her obsession for the last two years. "I don't have that problem."

Cav's touch is so light between her legs that she nearly spasms. His lips are hot on her neck. "One track mind, I guess."

Depths, she *hates* him. Hates how she can't keep herself still, how the words and his breath make her tremble.

"And the one track I've been stuck on…" He withdraws his hand from beneath her clothes and slides his palms down her thighs. "Is the last time we were this close."

The scales on his shoulders drag against the bare skin of her back as he gathers the front of her skirt and tucks it into her waistband. Goosebumps spread along her thighs when they clench together. "That was years ago." Her voice isn't as strong as she wants it to be. "Forget it. Move on."

"Have you forgotten it?" His tail curls pointedly around her ankle, spikes teasing up her calf. "Have you moved on?"

The question burrows under her skin. She tries to convince herself that Cav doesn't know the truth. That he can't see through her. That he can't tell how she's revisited their last hour together a thousand times. That she replays it to get her through any emotion: anger, sadness, desperation.

She can't tell him any of that. She can hardly tell herself. Being impaired makes her venomous, a cornered creature lashing out. Her voice makes a mockery of him. "The only thing I remember is how pathetic you were. Too sick to stand. Washed ashore like a piece of driftwood."

Her knees threaten to give when he laughs against her hair. "Do you grind yourself against every piece of driftwood you come across, or was I just special?"

THIRTEEN

Cav

Cav knows Lyx remembers that final night. She *has* to, because it's consumed Cav for the last two years. It doesn't matter that they barely touched; the memory stays buried in the back of his mind, like seeds that never got a chance to grow. He's craved to see them bloom ever since.

He lifts his fingers to Lyx's mouth. She flinches, but she doesn't pull away. She doesn't move at all, save for the breath passing between her lips. It gusts over his skin so lightly that he can hardly believe it's real. After a moment, he traces a claw around the bow of her top lip. He could stay like this for hours, memorizing the intricacies of her face when she isn't hiding them. It's like the blindfold covers her eyes and exposes everything else, like her expression is no longer being guarded by a firing squad.

The thought makes him reckless, his head inclining until their noses brush. "Can I kiss you?"

Her tongue slides over her lips, so close that he can almost feel it. Her voice is hoarse. "Why?"

It's not disgust. It's not an outright *no*. His taste buds prickle. "To see if you still taste as sour as you look."

Tangy and sharp as a lemon. Deep purple blooms in Lyx's cheeks, but she rushes forward, colliding with his mouth until he whines. It's not a kiss. Not quite, with its teeth and seething hatred and sounds she tries to hide.

Blood trickles into his mouth. It stings when her saliva fills the wound. He groans, but it doesn't hurt enough to pull away. Her teeth scrape his lip again, like she's as hungry for it as he is. The burn is a delicacy, heat throbbing between his legs when he eases forward.

Her teeth release. He sucks in a breath, but it's not quite relief. He doesn't want to disrupt this. He fears she'll pull away, but her tongue glides over the damage to his lip instead.

Cav braces a hand against the mast. He doesn't move. He doesn't even breathe.

Cautiously, she licks into his mouth, like the taste of his blood is a treasure she thought she'd lost. She plunders him like she's in a trance, tongue probing the cut until Cav shivers at the raw, delicious feeling.

Her mouth stills like she's been drawn out of a dream. She doesn't pull back. Doesn't move her head. Doesn't turn away from both of their heavy breathing.

"You never know when to quit," she pants. He wishes he could see her eyes. He hopes they're as glassy as his feel. "It's always going to come back to bite you."

He runs his tongue over his wound, savoring it the way leather hugs a brand. "Maybe I like being taught a lesson, even if I don't learn it."

Her fingers curl in the restraints. He has the sudden urge to untie her, to place her hands on his chest and let her grab onto *him*, but her voice cuts through the vision. "You need to get back to putting on your little show. Your audience is waiting."

The hum of the partygoers fades back in. He'd forgotten about them; he'd like to forget them again, but he has to remember what this is for. He's here to give Lyx chaos. He's here to feed her. With great restraint, he pushes back from her. "I told you, it's not for *them*."

He allows himself one last, lingering look at her. Purple scars rope around the thick swells of her body, fuchsia hair slipping from where it's piled atop her head. Even tied to the mast, she's lost none of her ferocity.

Cav runs his fingers over the soft glow of her bare shoulders. "Down there, they can only see outlines. They can only guess what the two of us are doing — even if one of us is bioluminescent."

Lyx's thighs clench together. Cav locates the eyelets on the back of her corset and unhooks them until it falls away. Her back curves at the newfound freedom, pressing her full breasts to the front of her blouse.

"What do you think they'll see?" Cav lowers his mouth between her shoulder blades. "You, trying to keep your composure?"

She scoffs, but she can barely choke it out.

"What, then?" he asks. "You, failing? You, begging me to finish you off?" He drags his forked tongue up the nape of her neck. "You, whimpering pitiful little sounds on the tip of my tongue?"

Lyx shuts down a shiver. "They can't hear anything down there."

Cav smirks. He reaches for the speaking trumpet that's secured to the railing and angles it down toward the crowd. With his other hand, he finds one of Lyx's nipples through the fabric and settles his fingers around it, tightening and tugging until she cries out.

Below them, a hush falls over the crowd.

"Something tells me they can," Cav whispers, "if you get loud enough. But like I said, it's not about them. It's about *you*."

His hands lower to brush her skirt out of the way. Now he can *see* her bare skin, the plush curve of her ass situated perfectly against his hips. That sight alone makes his mouth water, heightened when she winds back into him.

"No one down there gets to see you," he murmurs. "They only get a glimpse. Only enough to leave them wondering. Only enough to feed you."

He swears it's already working. Her skin glows the more he speaks. Despite the grit of her teeth, her body keeps moving against him, following the slow circles he makes. Fuck, he could give her everything right now. He could shove every piece of fabric aside and slot their legs together and let her ride him until she has her fill — but that's exactly what she wants. That's exactly what she expects.

It's a struggle for him to pull away, but watching her arch back to find him is worth it. When she realizes the heat of his body is gone, her head whips over her shoulder.

"The crowd doesn't get everything," he reminds her, "but you don't, either."

Her arms jerk against the restraints. Gods, she looks absolutely edible, strung-up and wanton. Her voice is a low hiss of fury and desperation. "You *cannot* leave me like this."

"It's better for your feeding if I deny you, isn't it? Make you work for it?"

Her jaw clenches, a curse spiking between her lips, loud enough for the crowd to hear.

"You won't be completely helpless," Cav reassures her. "You're gonna come tonight. You'll get that little reward, but you'll have to do the work yourself."

"*Fuck you*," she spits. She tries to retain some form of

control, but her forehead knocks against the mast as she sways on her toes. It's pitiful. It's so fucking *hot*.

"Aww..." Cav lifts his hands to outline her curves, her intensity rising off of her like a haze. "How about I give you something? Something to help you get there. Something you can use however you want."

"What the fuck am I supposed to use?" she snaps. The soft muscles in her back flex. For once, it's not Cav's presence winding her up; it's his absence. Finally, he's withholding something she craves.

He sinks to his knees behind her.

Once she realizes where he's gone, she tenses and tilts her face down toward him. He smooths his hands over the backs of her legs. "I remember this." Last time, she barely let him close enough to touch her. This time, however, he sets his mouth against one thigh and sucks a mark against her skin. He pulls back, breathing over the wet spot he left until she trembles.

He eases her knees apart and crawls between them to settle his back against the mast. The back of her skirt falls into place, draping a semi-circle of fabric around him.

Goddamn, he's imagined this moment for two years, and now, he's inches away from the slick desire between her legs. His hand splays across her pubic bone and brushes the scar on her hip. He smooths his pinky over it before he realizes what it is. This scar is different than the others, an angry burn faded with time. He can't help himself. He pushes up, pressing his lips gently against it until she makes a helpless sound in the back of her throat.

He wants to linger, but he doesn't. He moves lower until his nose drags between the juncture of one thigh. It's the first time he's been this close, and he wants to savor every detail. Aside from the radiance of her skin, she looks almost human. With two fingers, he traces around her clit, skimming her folds where she's soft and slippery.

Her hips buck.

"Do you always look like this?" He breathes against her. "In the water?"

The question seems to surprise her, but his voice is low enough that no one below them will hear.

"No," she finally mutters. "Only on land to fool pirates." She shifts against his claws like she's a fish strung up to be gutted. "Give you a hole to fuck, and you'll fall for anything."

He's not sure why his chest twinges. This is the only form he's seen her in. When he was shipwrecked, she never let him see her in the water, but he always wanted to. He still does.

Longing stirs inside him. With his fingers, he circles her clit and presses against her slick entrance. "Is it all for show?" He leans his head back to look up at her. She's a mess of tense arms, parted lips, and heaving breasts. He leans forward to scrape his teeth against her thigh. "Or can you still feel everything?"

"You know I can," she bites out. "So stop fucking *teasing*."

His smile flutters. "Make me." He settles his mouth above her clit, suctioning his lips just north of where she wants them. "If you want to come, you have to use me. Every part of me is yours for the taking." He drags his lips against her. "You speak it, and I obey. Tell me where to go. Direct me."

The forks of his tongue settle on either side of her clit. She twitches and groans at the contact, and murmurs ripple through the crowd below. Cav doesn't spare a thought for them. His mind and body are hungry for a taste of Lyx, thrumming at the prospect of following her every command.

He speaks slowly against her, honing all his attention on where they connect. "*Wield me.*"

FOURTEEN

Lyx

Lyx tries to tug herself free, but she only rocks in the restraints. Damn her for being so proud. Damn her for insisting she didn't need Cav, because now she's slick and desperate and incapable of taking care of herself.

Depths, she's a fool. How did she let herself get here? Climbing the crow's nest, binding her hands and eyes, letting Cav whisper in her ear. She tries to drag her clit against his lips, but he keeps them out of reach. "Is this your plan?" she snaps, breathless. "Subdue me so that I need you?"

His voice rumbles against her leg. "Thought it might be easier for you. Create chaos, tie you up, get you hot and bothered..." He traces her cunt with his claw before there's the *snick* of it retracting. "Then you don't have to admit that you want me."

Her cheeks flush. "I *don't* want you."

"Exactly. Just like that." He acts like he's playing along

with some lie. "You can pretend using me is your only option." He glides the soft pad of his finger between her legs. "Because that safeword's still waiting for you to use it."

She grits her teeth. If she had any sense, she'd say the word just to prove him wrong. She'd say it to spite him, but the problem is, he wouldn't be the only one left suffering. Abyss, she hates how he knows that. She hates how he uses it against her, finding ways to both wound and preserve her pride. It coils lusciously inside her.

"All you do," she seethes and sways, "is run your fucking mouth."

"If you hate it so much, then ride it."

Warm air rolls across her hips like smoke is spilling from that very mouth. Cav's desire burns so hot that it can't be contained by his body, his palms roving her thighs and spreading warmth wherever he touches.

Desire rolls like a storm inside her. Her mind is the last holdout, searching for any way to deny him. Her pathetic voice sounds more like a choked sob when she speaks. "I can't stand you."

"Then sit," he growls, gripping her ass and nudging her forward. "Show me how much you hate it. Give my mouth something else to do."

She can't see anything, but she can *feel* it, his breath cascading over the wetness between her legs. *Fuck*, she hates these restraints. Only her hips are free to move, and that leaves every twitch and shiver on display for him.

"I've got all night," he murmurs, "so if you —"

Lyx drags her cunt across his mouth.

They both groan at the contact. Mercifully, finally, Cav is quiet. His lips mold to her clit, sucking like he's been deprived for years. She tilts and shifts away from his mouth, and he makes a sound of protest, but it's quickly replaced by a moan when her pussy slides over his forked tongue.

He delves inside her, teasing the walls of her cunt until her thighs clench against his cheeks. Only then does he pull away. "Are you acidic?" he gasps.

It's been so long since anyone put their mouth on her that she's forgotten her cunt has its own deterrents. "It's a warning," she pants, "that you're doing something you shouldn't."

Not that it's ever dissuaded a pirate. They're too busy chasing their prize that none of them notice the burn. At least, not enough to say anything. Not enough to wonder why.

Cav stays silent. For the first time, a strange fear prickles up Lyx's spine. She can't place it. She isn't sure she's felt it before, but it scratches the nerves inside her. She needs to see Cav's face. To monitor his expression. To read his reaction, but there's nothing but darkness and the weight of her breathing.

She stings with humiliation. She should have known this would be too far for Cav, that he can't handle —

She nearly squeals when he buries his face against her, nose nudging her clit when his tongue fucks deeper, sloppy, and wet. His claws grip her hips, scraping the back of her thigh as he lifts one leg onto his shoulder. Her cunt smears against his jaw and makes a mess of his mouth. The back of her knee tightens against his shoulder, pulling him closer until he groans.

"*Sit.*" He presses the back of her other leg, diving ravenously into her. "Put all your weight on me."

She almost does. She can't think with the way he devours her, so she grinds against his mouth until his head rests back against the mast. She wants to give into it, to feel him fully, to ride his fucking tongue for all it's worth, but he winces when she presses forward.

He doesn't notice. He doesn't care, but she remembers the other night in the dinghy when he sucked in a breath every time he rowed. She remembers the twist of his shoulder when he landed in her grotto.

Cav's too lost in her pussy to care what pain it might cause him. He still tries to bring her closer, making a grunt of dissatisfaction when she keeps her toes on the ground.

"Put your claws away," she gasps instead. "Fuck me with your fingers."

His claws scrape her gently before they retract and slip between her legs. His mouth stays curled around her clit as one finger circles her entrance. Lyx's breath hitches, but Cav doesn't go deeper. He gives her only the first knuckle, pumping an inch inside her. Taunting. *Teasing.*

Lyx tightens her leg against his strong shoulder, rocking down against his mouth until she sinks completely over his finger.

Both of them groan, loud enough that the gasps of the party below are lost. Everywhere he touches her is warm, blood rushing through her as the split in his tongue flutters against her clit. He doesn't move his hand. He makes her work for it, rotating her hips so she rides his finger and mouth in one motion. With every stroke, her walls tighten, but it's not enough. He knows that.

She whines behind the press of her lips. "I fucking *hate* you."

"Better than nothing," he pants against her. "Better than you forgetting." With a second finger, he teases her entrance, words obscured against her cunt. "*Hate me.* Hate me forever. Hold onto it."

She buries her face against her arms, but there's no hiding her need now. He's seen it; it's dripping down his chin. She swirls her hips around his fingers, but she needs more. Chaos slides down her throat like honey, a gateway drug that makes her chase a stronger high. "Give me your tail."

Surprised, his fingers slip in deeper until she moans. Her

throat aches to command him with her song, but she doesn't have to. He retracts, sucking sharply on her clit until he pulls back with a gasp. "If you will it."

The words ring in her ears. She hasn't heard them in years. No one has offered her that since Cav was in the grotto, but now, his scaled tail coils up around her thigh and settles at her entrance.

Her pulse thrums. It was ridiculous to ask. She's never done anything like this, but her craving has made her delirious. She eases back against the tip and stretches over the smooth scales. Stars burst behind her eyes. When she gasps, his tail twitches, pressing his malleable spines against an exquisite place inside her.

Somehow, it seems wrong, but that only melts desire over every other thought until she's sticky with want. Now she has Cav from both ends. She swivels her hips back and forth, fucking over his tail before she grinds against the heat of his mouth. It's impossibly good, enough to make her toes curl behind his back. When she sets a rhythm, Cav is all too eager to follow. She's used people before, but never like this. Never someone who wasn't trying to use *her*. Never someone so willing, giving everything and taking nothing.

Nothing except her sanity. He waits until her thighs start to tremble, her leg tugging him closer, an orgasm clawing to escape. That's when he grips her hips and forces her still. She struggles to grind against his mouth, to sink back over his tail, but he holds her in purgatory.

She snarls and jerks against the restraints. "I'm going to fucking *kill you*. I'm going to *destroy* you. I'm going to rip you apart —"

Only then does he free her, returning his torturous mouth to her cunt. "Say it again," he groans. "It tastes so fucking good."

Her skin glows brighter against the blindfold. Lyx tries to

sprint to the finish line, but the path Cav leads her down forces her to slow and stumble and stop. Everything he does comes with a question, assurance, or confirmation. She hates it. She hates *him*.

Her moans cut through the night air. There's no disguising them. Below, the party grows more frantic, but Lyx can't spare a thought for them when Cav is honed on her clit. With the rock of her hips, his movements grow insistent, hunting her release as eagerly as others have hunted the rest of her.

Then he twists his tail inside her, a new stroke that sears white-hot down her spine. He never switches his pace on her clit. Not when her hips stutter, when she curses, when her fingers curl in the restraints.

She's past the point of no return, boiling over, and Cav keeps up with her when he growls, "I dare you to come."

She tries to hide it from him. As if his tail isn't buried in her cunt, his mouth suctioned to her clit, his hands trying to wrangle her bucking hips. Her lips clamp shut to swallow the noises, but her cunt clenches around him in shockwaves of her release.

His tongue keeps moving. He might stay there all night mouthing at her if she didn't squirm, lightheaded with renewed arousal budding between her legs.

That's a horrifying thought. The post-orgasm clarity falls over her like a veil and stifles her with shame. This is not what she's meant to be doing. She's supposed to destroy him, not come apart the first time he fucks with her.

She uses her knee to push his head back and pry him off her clit. "I meant what I said." Her voice is so pathetically weak, but by some miracle, Cav doesn't mention it. "About killing you."

"I know you did." He eases out from between her legs, boards creaking when he rises, and then, his mouth is against her ear. "I could taste it."

She tries not to shudder. She can smell herself on him. His hands find her wrists to unwind her slowly from the bindings, and she hisses when her arms drop free, pins and needles prickling beneath her skin. She sags back against the mast. Heat spreads through Cav's palms as he rubs up and down the length of her arms.

Only then does she remember the blindfold. Embarrassment streaks through her as she pushes the bandana off her eyes, blinking against the dim light. His face comes into focus, lit by the flickering firelight in his chest. His cheeks and chin are a mess of her desire, but he doesn't look ashamed as he massages the sore muscles around her wrists. His smile is soft, as decadent and inviting as a warm bath.

Her throat cinches closed. It throbs like her song is being pulled away from her, like she's yearning for something out of reach. Did Tidus sail away? Did he take her song and leave her behind? She scans the dark island, but his blue flag is still fluttering behind some trees.

She swallows the discomfort. There's nothing to fear. Her song is still close by.

Below them, the crowd whistles and cheers. She'd forgotten about them. Cav still pays them no mind when his eyes search hers. "Are you ok?"

Lyx doesn't answer. She tries to stand fully, but her legs wobble beneath her. It's a long-forgotten feeling, the same one as climbing onto shore after weeks in the sea.

"Easy..." Cav catches her around the waist and supports her full weight against him. "There's no rush. We can stay up here until you can climb down."

His body radiates warmth, keeping the cool breeze at bay. Her fingers curl into his shirt before she thinks better of it, and she forces herself to step away.

"Don't flatter yourself. I'm fine." Perhaps she doesn't

trust herself to make it down the ladder, but she certainly won't admit that aloud. Instead, she focuses on bracing against the railing and pushing back any curls that have fallen out of place. "Your mouth didn't have that much of an effect."

"No?" His lip quirks, eyes flicking to where her arm is quivering. "What about my tail, then?"

That devilish appendage sways cheekily behind him. Arousal swarms her at the memory of his scales, the perfect stretch, the muscle control when he twisted inside her. She drops her hand, shaking her head and willing her trembling legs to still. She refuses to look at the devilish glint in his eyes.

"Guess I'll have to try harder next time."

FIFTEEN

Cav

After a few minutes, Lyx manages to climb down from the crow's nest. It's a shame, really; Cav was more than willing to stay up there all night. Surely the two of them could find some way to occupy their time. But Cav descends first, keeping an eye on Lyx above him until they reach the bottom.

Her skirt catches underfoot on the final rung. She stumbles off the ladder into his chest, and he keeps them both upright, grinning against her ear. "You sure my mouth didn't have an effect?"

She twists out of his arms with a venomous look. "Three days. Don't bother me until then." Then she squeezes through that crowd that's begun to gather around the bottom of the mast.

A crew member claps Cav on the back. "I always did peg you as an exhibitionist."

Cav's eyes are still following Lyx. "Peg me, hm?"

A guest hands Cav a drink and clinks their glasses together. "I'd pay to watch *that*, too."

Another guest sidles up to Cav, twirling one of the laces on his shirt. "Are you available for the rest of the evening?"

Cav keeps a smile on his face, but it falls flat. All this adrenaline courses through him with nowhere to go. He knows where he *wants* to use it, but she's disappearing below deck without a glance back. After being with her again, no one at this party can hold his attention.

"Unfortunately not." Cav loops his arm through another member of the crew and tugs her toward him. "But Angélique here puts on a better show than *that* every night."

Startled, Angélique pinches his bicep before she extends her hand to the guest. Cav takes the opportunity to slip away. His face still stings from Lyx's acid, but he craves more. Every minute with her was worth the pain. The pain made it *better*, unraveling some desire in him that hasn't been allowed to stretch out for years.

He lifts his gaze to find Captain Heathen watching him from the wheel of the ship. Cypher stands behind her, lip curled sullenly. Cav swallows, lifting his glass toward them before he turns back to the party. Better to ask forgiveness than permission, right?

"If it isn't the star of the evening," Briar purrs. She sits on the forecastle stairs, her legs draped across the lap of a male guest.

On his other side, Lace scratches the man's beard and grabs his chin with a wily look in his eye. "And what did *you* think of that performance?"

Briar twirls a finger in the man's hair, coiling it around her finger and tugging. "We want to make sure our guest is entertained."

Somehow, the man appears at ease between the two of them, gazing directly into Briar's eyes. "I believe you know I'm well-entertained."

Briar and Lace's grins widen as they loosen their grips.

The man turns back to Cav. "But the show was a nice addition. You should perform on the deck next time."

"Yes, *Cavvy*." Lace walks his fingers up the man's thigh. "It was cruel of you to tease us. We could barely see anything from down here."

"Or hear anything." Briar rises to her feet, pulling the man and Lace up behind her. "Though I'm suddenly inspired for a little roleplay." She slinks past Cav, voice pitching into a breathy mockery of Lyx's. "'I hate you. I *hate* you.'"

Cav swats her away. "You know it's only two people per room. One host, one guest."

As the three of them pass, Lace shoves Cav's chest with two fingers. "Don't you have your *own* rule-breaking to worry about?"

They slip away, leaving Cav alone with his drink. He takes a hefty swig, savoring the liquid dribbling down his chin. Just like Lyx did when she tightened around his tail and told him how much she despised him.

That loathing did nothing to hinder her riding his face, though.

His fingers tighten around the cup as he takes a seat on the stairs. It doesn't matter that he's just had Lyx; he wants her again. There's still so much he needs, so many moments he's dreamt about. He wants to know how she'll say his name when he's fucking her. Will it be bitten between her teeth, or buried in his neck, or swallowed by his mouth? How will she look when she's completely naked and stripped of every barrier? Not just when she sheds her clothing, but when she sheds everything else. Every pretense. Every lie. Every excuse.

Normally, his nights working the *Indulgence* are the same. He gives a charismatic smile and a practiced line before he reels customers back to his cabin. It doesn't take much to get them off. They all fall for his charm, but with Lyx, it's a fight, a battle, an excavation of pleasure she tries to deny herself.

Is that what sirens do? Forgo their own pleasure in the search for chaos? Suffer so they can feast? Cav supposes it would make sense, but he's too hungry to feed every part of her to let that slide.

"Cavalier." Heathen's boots come to a halt a few feet away. She clasps her hands behind her back. "Join me in my office."

Only now does Cav realize the party is nearly over. He'd gotten so lost in thoughts of Lyx, he hadn't realized. A few stragglers mingle on the deck as the final guests trickle downstairs with their hosts. Cav rises to follow, grabbing a rag to wipe at his face and tail. It's clear his time with Lyx was a hit. The guests loved it, and the crow's nest had the captive attention of the ship for nearly an hour. Surely Heathen can't be upset about that.

But when she opens the door to her room, Cypher is already inside, leaning against the bookshelf with her arms crossed.

Cav's face falls.

Heathen crosses to their desk at the end of the room, oblivious or unwilling to acknowledge the tension. "Quite a show you put on tonight."

Right. Tonight was supposed to be part of his experiment, not a preoccupation with making Lyx come. He toes the door closed behind him. "The crowd seemed to think so."

"The crowd couldn't see anything." There Cypher goes, pouring rain on his parade. Her nose wrinkles with distaste. "It wasn't the proper setup. The crow's nest is too high for something like that, especially at night."

Cav shrugs. "If our guests enjoyed tonight's conditions, imagine how good it could be in plain sight."

Cypher glares in response.

Heathen stares at a place over Cav's shoulder. "Tonight's…performance was a surprise. You know how I feel about surprises."

A smug look flits across Cypher's face.

Cav resists the urge to flip her off. "There was no physical contact with anyone else," he points out. "And we were more than ten feet away, like you said."

A smile tugs on Heathen's lips. "I appreciate your strict adherence to the rules. I have to say, I'm impressed."

Triumphantly, Cav scratches his temple with his middle finger.

The muscle in Cypher's jaw twitches.

"I gave you permission," Heathen continues, "and you made something happen. Moreover, you prepared for it. I noticed you scoping out the crow's nest the last few days, but I never imagined it was for *that*." Heathen circles their desk to rest back against it. "It wasn't the most visible or audible, but you took precaution. It was a perfect icebreaker, and it set the tone for the evening. Not to mention the impact on our profits."

Cav's tail perks. In truth, he'd only managed to prepare the safety precautions before he got distracted, but no one else needs to know that.

When Heathen looks toward Cypher, she mumbles begrudgingly.

"Can you speak up?" Cav asks.

"There was an increase in private rooms," Cypher snaps. "Longer time slots."

Heathen clears their throat.

"And, apparently," Cypher's teeth grit, "a lot of requests similar to the show you put on."

Cav's chest swells with pride. "So you're saying I'm a success."

"I'm not saying that."

"The money is," Heathen cuts in. "From a cursory glance, our pleasure collection increased tonight as well."

A grin splits Cav's face. "Sounds like we have a hit on our hands."

"That's premature." Cypher's foot drops to the floor like she needs her full weight behind her. "It's been one night; that's not a pattern. I understand this experiment is Cav's *thing —*"

He presses a mocking hand to his chest. "Well, when you put it like that —"

"But the siren is an unknown variable." Tersely, Cypher turns toward Heathen and blocks Cav behind her. "She doesn't need to be involved. She doesn't need to be here at all."

"Her name is Lyx," Cav enunciates, brushing past Cypher to get in Heathen's line of sight again. "And she *is* involved. That's the agreement. She helps me with this venture, and she gets a room on the ship."

Cypher's face is a stone wall. "Then make a new agreement."

"What is your *problem*?" Cav laughs. It crackles with an anger he tries to contain. "You're obsessed with her. You don't —"

"*Enough*," Heathen bellows. The two of them fall into simmering silence, and after a pointed pause, Heathen turns to Cypher. "Is there a reason you're so concerned about Lyx?"

Cypher's fists clench. "I don't trust her. She's up to something."

"You don't trust anyone," Cav sighs.

Cypher starts to give a nasty retort before she clamps her mouth shut. For a while, she only glares at Cav, like she's torn between two ideas. Eventually, she reaches for the bandana around her neck. The knot is drawn tight, forcing her to pick it free before she yanks the fabric away and tilts her head back.

A black tattoo sits on her throat. It shimmers and shifts like all the others, but Cav can't make out the ink from here. Only when Heathen moves in does he take a step closer, and his stomach turns.

On Cypher's throat sits the *Indulgence* engulfed in flames. Fire eats away at the hulls and masts, burning the figureheads to ash. The sails are little more than blazing holes in the sky. The fire rages, not slowed by anything. There's no sign of anyone alive onboard.

A cold chill crawls up Cav's spine.

Heathen sucks in a breath. "When did that appear?"

Cypher lowers her chin. "The day she came aboard."

"Why didn't you say anything?"

"I wanted to be sure." Roughly, Cypher ties the scarf back into place. "I wanted to have evidence. I wanted to avoid this exact conversation where you're questioning my motives."

It's haunting watching the *Indulgence* burn, but it doesn't have to mean anything, does it? It must be a mistake. Cav's voice is hoarse. "Your tattoos have been wrong before."

"They aren't *wrong*." Cypher twists the bandana like it's Cav's neck. "A tattoo forms to show what path we're on. What we're headed toward. If we change course, so does the mark."

"What does that even mean?"

Cypher's teeth grit. "I am *trying* to look out for you. For all of us."

Cav's voice grows stronger over the thud of his heart. "When exactly did the tattoo show up? What time of day?"

Cypher rolls her eyes, but she doesn't return them to Cav's. "It must have been as soon as she got here. Right after I did my morning check."

"So you don't know for sure." Cav's voice is level, despite the uncertain twist in his gut. "It could have been any time that day. You don't know that it popped up the second Lyx walked up the gangplank."

Surely someone would have noticed, wouldn't they? Surely Cav would have been staring straight at the image, but her tattoos are always changing. All Cav remembers about her ink that day is a vague blur.

Cypher's fingers flex. "I can't give an exact time," she finally cedes, "but I *know* it's from her."

That's all the encouragement Cav needs. "Plenty of other shit happened that day. We left port. Colt got food poisoning. I mean, shit, I came back from the *Silver Spoon*; you might as well kick me off the ship, too."

The ink blot around Cypher's eye sharpens. "Works for me."

"Please!" Heathen hisses, fingers pressed to her temples. Slowly, Heathen inhales through their nose before they drop their hands and look pointedly at Cypher. "I want the facts. *Only* the facts. The tattoo appeared between your morning and evening checks the day we left the last port, correct? What else do you know about it?"

"It's on my throat." Cypher's lips purse. "Over my vocal cords. Perfect place for a siren song. That's not a coincidence."

"It very well could be." Heathen runs a hand through her hair. "It could be related to eating, drinking, breathing, screaming...and sometimes the placement doesn't mean anything, right? Your tattoos take up whatever space is available?"

After a moment, Cypher's forced to nod.

Heathen mirrors her. "Then we can't hang anything on that."

"But we can't just —"

"If our focus is too narrow..." Heathen lowers their voice sternly. "We could miss a credible threat. We can't get fixated on Lyx. We need to prepare for a fire, regardless of the cause."

An angry flush creeps up Cypher's neck.

Heathen steps back. "Keep the tattoo hidden. I don't want to send the crew into a frenzy when we don't know anything else." Her spine is rigid as she moves back toward her desk. "Before you turn in for the night, tighten up guard duty. I'll quiz the crew on the fire plan. We'll have to be vigilant for the foreseeable future."

Cypher's jaw clenches. After a moment, she moves toward the door.

"And keep me informed of your tattoos," Heathen calls after her. There's a meaningful edge in their voice. "Changes, new appearances, anything, I want to know about them. Immediately."

Cypher's hand rests on the knob, but she doesn't look back toward them. Her shoulders twitch like she might speak, but she tugs the door open and slams it behind her.

Cav swears Heathen's head shakes as she sits. His presence now seems like an intrusion, but before he can back away, Heathen speaks to him. "Keep an eye on Lyx." When she lifts her face, there's a suspicion she didn't wear before.

Cav's bravado falters. He tries to find an easy smile. "Thought you didn't care about speculation. Only facts."

"I care about this ship and the people on it." Heathen leans back in her chair. "And I believe in Cypher. Her interpretations are rarely wrong. Despite your bickering, you know that."

Cav presses his tongue against a pointed tooth. As much as he hates to admit what Heathen says, it's true. He can't admit that now. He can't give Cypher's campaign any more fuel. "That doesn't mean she's right this time."

"It also doesn't mean she's wrong."

"She's wrong about Lyx."

"And that's your unbiased opinion?"

The spikes on Cav's back flinch. He hasn't forgotten Heathen's warning from the first day, but it's hard to stand up to scrutiny when he fucked Lyx in front of the entire ship.

It doesn't matter. That was work. That was fun. He knows better than to expect — to hope — for anything more than that. "I will keep Lyx out of trouble," Cav assures her with as much confidence as he can muster. "You don't have to worry."

There's a flicker in Heathen's eyes like she knows Cav has gotten in deeper than he can handle, but then, they press their mouth into a thin line and turn back to their parchment. "Yet I always do."

In the Grotto

Lyx

Lyx almost doesn't return to the grotto.

It's clear Cav is playing some game. She turns the memory over in her mind until it's as smooth as sea glass. No matter how sharp the image of Cav is, her brain grows foggy when she remembers the leaf falling away, the dip in his voice, the look in his eye that makes her entire body clench.

She digs her fingernails into her arms. Focus. He's doing this for a reason. What is he trying to accomplish? To confuse her enough to keep him alive?

It won't make a difference. She resolves herself to that, but she still needs somewhere to take out this frustration. Fortunately, the perfect target sails into her territory.

A ship of hunters floats past with harpoon guns at the ready. Lyx makes quick work of them. They're so easy to fool when she lounges on a rock, pressing her breasts together and kicking up her feet. None of them are prepared for her. There is no wax stuffed in their ears, no chewed plant to make them immune to her song. It's almost insulting when they succumb to her, leaving behind a spreading stain of blood in the water.

They all taste the same. She can't convince herself to take more than a few bites of their gamy, stale flesh, so instead, she follows the spoils of their shipwreck to a nearby island. There's a trunk of dry clothing, an assortment of bottles, soggy books and gold coins, so she dumps what she wants into a bucket and leaves the rest behind.

When she arrives in the grotto, Cav smiles like he's been waiting for her.

Only her eyes peek above the water. She blows a stream of irritated bubbles and swims closer until she's obscured by the rocky ledge. She raises her mouth of sharp teeth. "Turn around."

Damn pirate. It's like he can't help himself, leaning forward to get a closer look.

"I said, turn around!" She darts closer to the ledge, heart tumbling like she's not the predator here. "And shut your eyes, since you can't follow the rules."

Sheepishly, he does as he's told. She wonders if the words, Don't instruct me, are dancing on his tongue, but he doesn't say them, so she grabs the bucket floating behind her and climbs out of the waves.

The water droplets on her skin fade along with her siren form. Her most vicious parts retract, leaving behind a palatable human figure. It surprises her that she's almost relieved that he has only seen her like this. It's something she's never felt before, but she can't begin to examine that. She has work to do.

She deposits the bucket on the bank and stands behind Cav. His eyes are still closed, but he tilts his head back like he's enjoying the sun. It bares his throat to the wall, delicate and fragile. She could kill him now. One broken shell would *be all it would take...*

But there's a more tempting offer. Her skin grows hot, but it doesn't stop her from running her eyes over him. She likes him like this. When she can almost pretend he's asleep. When he's silent. When he can't see her. When she can look her fill.

Color has returned to his fiery skin, light playing like flames beneath his scales. His eyes crinkle at the corners, but his mouth is no longer caked and dry. His lips glisten softly, barely parting when he speaks. "May I open my eyes now?"

Her stomach flips. She tears herself away to ward off the shaky feeling in her legs. "You live to see another day."

"As long as you will it."

He turns to face her and reclines back against the wall. It's too reminiscent of the last time she was here. This little bastard is trying to fuck with her, and she refuses to give him the satisfaction.

Even when she refuses to look at him, he keeps speaking. "Why don't you let me see you in the water?"

Great Abyss, this pirate has never met a silence he enjoys. She tries to remember why she came, returning to the bucket to pull out her netting bag. It snags on a thick splinter and unravels one of the knots. She makes a sound of frustration. "It would be the last thing you'd ever see." With her teeth, she holds one strand of the net as she works. "No pirate sees a siren's true form and lives to tell the tale."

"Well, if I'm dying anyway —"

"You are."

"Sounds like it'd be worth it."

Her fingers slip past each other, and the knot falls open again. Cursing, she tosses the bag to the ground. She can't focus like this. Cav's voice is a song she can't get out of her head, repeating through her thoughts.

"No pirate actually wants a siren," she snaps. "They

want a pretty girl with fins. They want a story to take home, the fantasy without the legend." She doesn't like how her voice sounds, brimming with some emotion she can't place. Slowly, she exhales. She is in control. She holds Cav's fate in her hands. Cooly, she turns back to him, never letting her eyes wander from his. "But if that's your dying wish, I'm happy to drag you down and show you."

What she expects is another one of his grins, but he looks almost sad. When he speaks, it's as soft as the way he's looking at her. "If you will it."

Her chest tightens. She bends for the bucket again, desperate for somewhere else to look besides Cav's face. Her fumbling fingers finally close around a shirt and trousers, and she extends the pile toward him.

Once he takes it, she busies herself with the string of fish in her bucket, but her ears perk at every sound Cav makes. She hears the waxy slip of the leaf falling to the ground, the rustle of fabric unfurling, the grunt as he works the clothes over his limbs.

"I need help with this sleeve."

She nearly jumps when he speaks to her. Her head whips over her shoulder to where his shirt is halfway on, hung like a sash across his chest.

Despite his labored breathing, he gives her a smile. "Please, my vicious captor?"

It's clear that simply dressing has exhausted him. No matter how he acts like this is a breeze, his health is precarious. He's still weak. There will be no way to fight her off when she finally turns on him. They both need to remember that.

Lyx moves toward him, taking the empty sleeve between her fingers. She's worn clothing during brief trips to nearby islands, but clothing someone else is hardly second-nature. Her eyes narrow as she inspects the garment from a distance.

He huffs a laugh. "Promise I won't bite."

Her glare slices into him. She extends the sleeve, forced to move in closer to aid him. He shifts his wounded shoulder and winces as his arm struggles to find the hole. Lyx reaches under the hem of the shirt, searching for his hand to guide him, but instead, she finds the bare skin of his rib cage. Above that, her fingers brush the curve of his breasts.

The scales on his side twitch.

His breathing slows. Hers stops altogether. Her traitorous fingers flex with temptation, desperate to trace his curves, the muscles in his stomach, the patch of softer scales that leads down...

His skin glows beneath her touch, casting a shadow of her hand through the fabric. She swallows, finding his wrist to guide through the sleeve before she withdraws.

Her head swims. She turns her back on him, fumbling with the fish like she's never seen them before. What is she meant to be doing? She pulls a knife from her bucket to gut them, but her hands are still trembling.

"How did you get those?" he asks. It takes too long for her to understand what he means, to realize his gaze is following the raised scars wrapped around her torso.

It's been so long since she gave herself one that she'd nearly forgotten them. The scars are perfect impressions of her tentacles, curls and whorls embedded in her skin. "As a child." She lifts the fin of one fish and begins to cut. "Before I knew my own strength."

It would be a warning to anyone else. See what I've done to myself? Imagine what I can do to you.

But Cav doesn't sound frightened. "Nobody taught you how to use them? Your tentacles?"

Her nose wrinkles. "Who would teach me?"

"Your parents."

Her knife moves easily through the fish now. "That's not how we're born. There are no progenitors. There's just a collision of sea foam and chaos, a bolt of lightning, a hurricane…"

She doesn't realize how much she's told him until the silence that comes after. It's the first time Cav has been quiet, carefully considering her words. Her skin is tight. No one else knows how sirens come to be, and here she is, foolishly spilling secrets like it's the easiest thing in the world.

It doesn't matter. He won't get a chance to share anything she tells him.

Resolutely, she rises to her feet and moves further down the bank. A strand of dead vines climbs toward the top of the cave, straining toward the sun. She cuts them down and returns to the shore, dumping the leaves onto the bundle of sticks like she's seen land dwellers do. Expectantly, she looks at Cav.

He looks confused.

"You promised me fire," she reminds him.

Another smile cracks across his face. "I did, didn't I?" He lowers his chest to the ground, packing dead leaves between the sticks. Once it suffices, he curls his hands around the base and curves his mouth to blow. At first, nothing happens. His brows knit before he tries again, producing a faint wisp of smoke.

"That's fire?" Lyx snorts.

Cav grits his teeth and shuffles lower. "Are you the expert now?"

Something about his taunting makes her teeth drag into her lip. She can't tear herself away from the focus in his eyes, the pucker of his lips, the steady breath that finally bursts into flame. It's short-lived, but it's enough. The dead leaves catch and spread to the sticks, leaving Cav with a smug smirk aimed directly at her.

Her nose tingles at the foreign scent, and she stuffs a stick into each fish to lean them into the fire.

Cav leans back against the wall, eyelids heavy from exertion. Now Lyx smirks. Perhaps this is the secret to keeping a captive. Give him enough work to exhaust him. Make him compliant. Enjoy how easily his guard slips —

"Are you lonely out here?"

His question lands like a slap. It's unexpected and debilitating, worse than the first plunge into icy water after a night hunting on land. Her chest tightens in surprise. "Why would – where did –"

"You don't have parents." His voice is dreamy, as comfortable as if he were sprawled out in the sun. "You never talk about anyone else. Do you have anyone?"

Lonely.

She's seen it on young sailor's faces when they take their first watch alone. She's seen it in the old pirates' eyes when they recount their glory days to empty pubs. Loneliness, she imagines, is emptiness and impossible weight all at once.

Has she ever felt that? When she looks inside herself, she finds something raw and ragged buried deep in her chest. She doesn't want to reach for it. Sirens are solitary creatures. No matter what habitat they share, they can't spend their lives together; they are a garden of hostile plants sucking the life from each other.

She is meant to be alone. All of them are.

"Sirens don't feel sentimental emotions," she manages. "We don't understand the things you sing about: loneliness, remorse, grief —"

"Love?"

The fire pops between them. Of course she's heard the word. Sirens use it mockingly, picking their teeth clean of their latest paramours or scavenging shipwrecks. She's heard it a thousand times from hypnotized pirates as she drags them beneath the waves.

I love you. I love you. I love you.

"We cannot love." The word tastes as slimy as the freshly-gutted fish. "It doesn't exist."

"You don't believe in it? You've never loved anything?" Cav's eyes spark like the fire. "Anyone?"

The look he gives her makes her skin crawl, but not in the way she's used to. Less like revulsion, and more like...appetite.

Humming, she settles her weight onto one palm. She's playing with her food, but when doesn't she? His eyes flicker when she leans toward him and forms her lips around a single word. "Never."

The firelight turns his eyes a warm shade of honey. "You've never desired anything? Craved something? Ached for what you can't have?"

Her fingers curl in the sand beside his tail. "That sounds like something you're familiar with."

He looks caught off guard. Finally, she has the upper-hand again. No emotion he describes can shake her. She doesn't feel them. She doesn't need them. But she can read his.

She eases closer, watching Cav's eyes follow her. "You've been flaunting yourself since you landed here. You didn't care when your clothes were ruined. You hardly wanted to cover yourself at all. Why is that?"

She expects the desire in Cav's eyes, but she's surprised by what else appears. There's something heavier, more consequential, weighing down the corners of his eyes. "Getting shipwrecked kind of throws out convention. Strange as it sounds, I like that." A grin twitches on his mouth. "You'll kill me no matter who I am. There's something nice about that. There's no reason to hide."

"Why would you hide?" Depths, why is she asking? She

should feel nothing for this conversation, nothing for anything Cav says, but she's so close to him now. It's like the earth beneath her is slipping, the force of gravity pulling her closer to him.

His tongue trails over his lips. "Have you ever wanted to be two things at once? Have you ever been tired of staying in one box, acting one way, fitting one mold? You don't want to be limited. You want to be everything that you are. Everything you can be."

Something inside her claws to get out, a bowstring pulled taut in her chest. She can't set it free. It's impossible to imagine shedding this skin, this role, this thing she's always been. She is a siren. Her purpose and emotions and desires were laid out before she was born. That is what she knows. That is who she is, and no strange creature washed ashore in her grotto will change that.

Her throat feels like a vise. "I've never felt like that."

"Never?"

He knows she's lying. She refuses to admit it. "What else would I want to be?"

She is powerful. That, she knows. It makes it easy to lean into Cav's space. No matter what else he says, he doesn't resist her. Their mouths drift closer.

"I'm attached to nothing," she hums. "My song brings me whatever I want. And the only thing I want? The only thing I care about?"

Their noses brush. His breath is warm.

She whispers the final word against his mouth. "Chaos."

She doesn't kiss him. It's more satisfying to see him give in, sucked into her orbit, proving her right. He exhales slowly. She can't help but smirk. The bowstring inside her notches tighter, pulling her toward him, but he doesn't move. Only now does she realize she's the one chasing his mouth, her head inclined, her body angled.

Like he's the siren. Like she can't resist him.

His smile is lazy. "Then what are you still doing here with me?"

Stinging pain shoots through her leg. With a hiss, she scrambles back and sees a glowing stick knocked free of the fire. Her hip throbs from the burn. Cav reaches for her, but she rises to her feet and scrambles toward the rocky ledge.

She knew better. She'd been distracted, and for that, she's branded herself with a new scar. A reminder of exactly what she shouldn't be doing. A reminder of exactly what she has to do to him.

SIXTEEN

Lyx

The crow's nest is taunting Lyx.

Not because she could *see* anything the night Cav took her up there, but fuck if she doesn't remember every single feeling. Perhaps that's why it lingers. Perhaps Cav found a way to embed himself in all her other senses. The taste of his blood. The sound of his moans. The scent of his sweat.

She can smell him now, his sheets tangled around her legs when she wakes in his cabin. She holds her breath and lifts her head from the pillow, like that might spare her from the memories, but no. Her clit throbs like his tongue is still branded across it, his tail twisting in her mind, his grin scraping a shiver up the back of her neck.

She's used to the restless sleep of sirens, but it's made worse by the constant ache between her legs. Maybe she could rest if she found some release, but she refuses. She won't touch herself on principle. She will not orgasm to the thought of Cav – again — which means suffering in silence.

Unfortunately, not everyone has taken the same vow, which Lyx learns when Briar and Lace whistle as she climbs onto the deck the next day.

"Surprised you're walking." Briar lifts a cheeky brow. "Thought your legs would still be jelly."

"It wasn't that good," Lyx grumbles.

Lace drags his eyes up her body. "It *sounded* that good."

Lyx's glare deepens. It's clear the show she and Cav put on didn't go unnoticed. Already, the stares and whispers from the crew have started, and that won't do for what she has planned.

She retreats to her cabin until evening. If she's going to sneak around for Tidus, she needs to keep hidden. Easier said than done when the *Indulgence* is at sea for days with no customers to distract them, so she waits until nightfall. Once the ship is quiet, she creeps out of her cabin and trips over a tray of food.

The clatter makes her freeze. Her eyes whip down the corridor, but no one emerges. With a huff, she slides the tray back inside her room before she slips away. There's only the light of the moon shining below deck. Most of the other cabin doors are open, their occupants snoring or drooling as the ship rocks on the waves. Lyx peers inside each one, stepping over piles of clothing and squinting to find the glint of a glass jar.

There's nothing. She passes all the cabins, feeling along the walls until she can't make out anything in the dark. If she wants to go further, she'll need a lantern, but that will draw attention.

Something rustles behind her. She presses back into the shadows as one of the crew members shuffles out of their cabin. Their eyes are bleary and half-asleep, blinking toward her without recognition. Her heart thuds. The crew member begins to climb the stairs, and she waits until they're out of sight before she darts back toward her cabin and shuts the door.

She almost trips over the tray again. Cursing, she sets it on the bed and flops down next to it. If she's going to investigate the *Indulgence* further, she'll need better preparation. A light, at least. Unfortunately, the ship is full of people who could stumble upon her at any moment.

With a sigh, she rolls onto her side and inspects the food selection. Bread, an apple, some other vegetable she doesn't recognize. It's better than nothing. Avoiding the other crew members means missing meals, and her stomach is growling.

Over the next few days, she gets deeper into the ship with a handful of close calls. At one point, she's forced to turn off her lantern and climb onto a barrel to avoid Cypher and her crow. None of it gets her any closer to answers. She may know where the excess storage is, where the bilge pumps and bulkheads are located, but she finds no glass jars.

The meals continue to appear outside her cabin. She knows exactly who's leaving them. Begrudgingly, she eats, ignoring how the food is arranged into melodramatic vignettes. Greens sprouting like trees from mashed potatoes, carrot people on a bread roll ship, dried jerky swept away in a sea of gravy.

It's tiny world of disorder. Obviously, Cav's search for a hobby extends to food preparation as well.

On the third day, she expects him to show up. He wouldn't pass up an opportunity to irritate her. The trays of food continue to arrive, but Cav doesn't. She waits in the cabin all evening, imagining what he could have planned this time. A bar locked between her ankles? Ropes suspending her above the deck? Or, worst of all, the two of them alone with nothing to distract them?

It makes every part of her clench.

But Cav never shows. Her teeth grit together, body tight with unfulfilled desire. He's playing games. He's tormenting her. Is he trying to make her desperate enough that she goes to him? That she gives him whatever "honesty" he believes she has? It won't happen. Her only course of revenge is to furiously get herself off and pretend she doesn't imagine a pair of horns between her legs.

It must be cabin fever. She's been cooped up too long. She needs fresh air. She needs to feed. She needs to get her mind off what a failure her snooping has been.

When the *Indulgence* pulls into the next port, Lyx climbs onto the deck. The dreaded crow's nest is still staring down at her, but she keeps her gaze level. In the fading sun, the ship looks almost golden. Inlaid clams glow yellow and orange around the crew furling the deep, luscious sails.

The scene is spoiled by Cypher standing on the main yard. As soon as she sees Lyx, her hand darts to scratch at the bandana around her neck. Her bird pecks at her fingers. "We don't need another show tonight," she calls down.

"Can't get your mind off it, hm?" Lyx shouts back.

With a hardened look, Cypher grabs a hoisting rope and slides down it to the deck. Lyx's teeth flash. A fight will get her what she needs. But when Cypher approaches, Cav slips between them and braces a hand on Cypher's arm. "Save that spunk for the customers."

She rolls her shoulder out of his grip. "It's been three days. Has she made her payment?" Her eyes never leave Lyx. "Since apparently her presence on this ship is so *essential*."

Lyx presses forward, but Cav loops an arm around her waist. "I've got it under control." His smile is tight, like they've had this conversation before, but he smooths it into something almost believable. "Unless you'd like to supervise?"

It has the desired effect. Cypher's lip curls in disgust, and with one last glare, she stalks toward the forecastle.

That's one aggravation dealt with, but Cav is another entirely. Lyx turns to him, prepared to dismiss him before all her thoughts evaporate.

He's wearing all-black. She's never seen him like this, sleek and polished, ruffles and leather emphasizing his vibrant skin. Pants cling to his muscled thighs beneath an array of low-slung belts and straps. The sleeves of his top billow around his wrists in contrast to the vest cinched at his waist. Bracelets and rings adorn his arms and hands, but the most striking detail is a layer of necklaces that fall across his chest. It draws her eyes to his scales, patches on his shoulders and clavicle that sprinkle around the curve of his breasts.

She's staring. She realizes it when she finally meets his gaze again, and his smirk is absolutely audacious. Leaning back on his palms against a crate, he draws out the lines and curves of his body. "Don't stop on my account."

Her jaw tightens. She refuses to look anywhere but his face.

With a shrug, he pushes off the crate. "Or you can look your fill on the island."

Her eyes dart to the gangplank. A crowd is forming below, and soon, the ship will be crowded with customers again. As with all things involving Cav, Lyx has the stifling urge to be contrary. "I'm not disembarking."

He clicks his tongue, clearly unimpressed with the lie. "You need to get off this ship. I know you must be bored down there. There are only so many card games you can play alone." His hand lifts to her neck, but his fingers flex before he pulls away. "Besides, you look a little...green around the gills. Do you want to go for a swim?"

Her scales prickle. "No." Unfortunately, he is right about one thing; days without feeding have left her sickly again. Spending all this time on her own is catching up with her.

He offers his elbow. "Come with me, then. We'll find some other trouble to get into."

The hollow in her throat stretches hungrily. Dammit. With a heavy sigh, she grabs his arm and follows him off of the ship.

On the island, there isn't a shop in sight. There are hardly any buildings at all, only piles of broken beams and the remnants of foundations. "Horrible hurricane season last year." Cav gestures down the beach to the rest of the destruction. "Most of their buildings got blown away or swept out. They're only just starting to rebuild the taverns, so the *Indulgence* stops by to give them a place to unwind."

Lyx quirks a brow. "How generous of you to offer your loins in these trying times." Thinking of his loins is a mistake. She keeps her expression plain and her gaze ahead as she speaks. "Yesterday was the third day since the crow's nest."

Cav hums. Nothing more.

Bastard.

If she were smart, she wouldn't ask anything more. She would enjoy her freedom and let the chips fall where they may, yet something keeps nagging at her. "Do you no longer require my assistance?"

In the corner of her eye, she can make out the wolfish curve of his mouth. "Would that disappoint you?"

She scoffs. "Of course not."

Her answer is too quick, but Cav doesn't mention it. Instead, he leads her off the beach toward the foliage. It looks like they're walking straight into a jungle, but when they round a corner, the bushes and plants recede. A canopy of trees hangs over an open area scattered with mismatched chairs and tables. A dozen people congregate in groups or couples, chatting and drinking while they watch Cav and Lyx with intrigued bemusement. In the back of the space sits a ramshackle shed, barely big enough to contain a barrel of ale and the man wiping down the counter.

It's an outdoor tavern scraped together from the remnants of the island. Unfortunately, it's calmer than the other pubs she's used to, no aggravated drunks or slippery thieves to stir up agitation. Her nose wrinkles.

Cav meanders toward a dartboard nailed to a tree and plucks the red and blue darts from its center. "Do you know how to play Cat and Mouse?"

"Enough to embarrass you."

"How about a little competition, then?" He sidles up next to her and holds out the feathered ends. "If I win, we play out one of *your* fantasies for the next experiment."

"You won't win."

When she reaches for the darts, he retracts them, lowering his voice until she can feel it scraping the hot pit of her stomach. "But if I do, it means you have to tell me what you want. What you like. What you think about when you're alone."

Her toes curl. What would she tell him? That her fantasies consist of making him suffer? Drowning him in the grotto? Prying her song from Tidus's chest just to command Cav for the rest of his days.

A knot twists deep inside her. Or maybe she should tell where her thoughts go when she doesn't corral them, the dark place where desire and frustration collide. Where she fucks Cav until he can't move. Where she drags him into the water and takes on her true form. Where he's forced to see her as she truly is in a place where he can't run away, a place where he has to stay, a place where she can burrow into his skin.

She snatches the red darts from his hand. "*When* I win, I want a tour of the *Indulgence*."

His brows furrow as he backs toward the bar, trading coins for two tankards from the barrel. "I can show you around any time. You don't have to win for that."

"A full tour. With Heathen. I want to see how everything works."

His eyes narrow skeptically, but after a moment, he sets the drinks on a high-top table littered with debris from the trees. "Alright, deal. Now, do you want to be the cat or mouse?"

She considers it with an exhale. "You seem to adore being helpless prey. Why stop now?"

Cav grins. "It's about time you started chasing me."

SEVENTEEN

Lyx

When Cav begins, he doesn't look away from Lyx. He tosses a blue dart and lands it easily in the triple ring. The next dart sticks, and so does the final one, until there's a perfect arc moving clockwise around the board.

Through it all, he's still staring at her. "Normally, I'd give you a chance, but I *really* want this prize."

The dip in his voice makes her stomach clench, but she does not waver, no matter how her confidence has nosedived. She can do this. She's played this game in countless ports with Tidus breathing down her neck; she can handle a cocksure dragon with trick shots.

Her first dart lands next to his. Cav whistles, but Lyx keeps her focus and manages to match all of his throws. For once, Cav has no commentary. He's silent while he admires the board before he moves to collect the darts again. When he returns, there's a proud glint in his eye. "I see you don't like to be underestimated."

They keep throwing back and forth, Cav running around the board and Lyx following after. When he misses, she smirks. When she misses, he praises her anyway, and that makes her grit her teeth and fumble the rest of her turn.

When they're nearly done, he leans against the high-top table and takes a drink. "What do you say, best two out of three?"

She wants to reject him. Surely she could catch him in time, but the promise of competition swirls inside her. Besides, she has a sneaking suspicion he's *letting* her keep up as some excuse to keep this going. In any case, she agrees.

He wins the first round. Halfway through the second, it's clear he's pulling away, and that sets a smile on his face. "Probably a good time for you to start thinking about that fantasy."

"You're not going to win."

"Humor me, then." When she misses and curses, he takes the familiar path to the board and returns with the darts, but he doesn't throw them. He turns back to her. "What do you dream about? What's one thing you wish for?"

Mockingly, she tilts her head. "Killing you. What my life would be like if I had."

He pricks the end of a dart against his finger. "Sounds like you should let me win so you can play that out."

"Just take your turn."

He takes his time instead, tipping back his ale and glancing toward her mug. It's still full, the liquid warm from the evening. Surprised, he sets down his own drink. "You don't like it?"

Surely this is an attempt at distraction, but Cav looks genuinely perturbed. Her skin prickles under the sudden attention. "It's not to my taste." She jerks her chin toward the board. "Now, throw."

But the game is all but forgotten by Cav, his darts discarded on the table. "Why didn't you say something? I'll get you something else."

Lyx eyes the lean-to bar. "They don't *have* anything else."

That doesn't stop Cav. He moseys toward the bartender, a gnarled and sullen man who shakes his head before Cav finishes speaking. Cav leans against the bar, withdrawing more coins from his pouch and tilting his head knowingly.

After a moment, the bartender grumbles and crouches behind the bar. When he stands, he slides a bottle of yellow liquid into Cav's hand. Grinning, Cav snags the bottle and returns to Lyx with a proud sway of his hips.

"He's not a fan of ale either. I thought I remembered that." With his teeth, Cav tugs the cork loose and presents the bottle to her. "From his personal stash."

Lyx blinks. The smell of citrus makes her mouth water. She isn't sure what to do. The action is so small, but it hits her like an anchor. No one else would have gotten her this; she wouldn't have even done it for herself. Depths know Tidus wouldn't have even noticed, just happy she left more ale for him.

A word she's never used springs to the end of her tongue, buzzing against her lips like a trapped bee.

Cav raises his brows at her silence. "You don't like lemon?"

"*Thanks,*" she blurts.

It's foreign and unfamiliar, a language she's never spoken. Her emphasis is so off that it might as well be sarcasm, but Cav's nose wrinkles when he grins. "Does it pain you to say that?"

Her entire body feels hot under his gaze. She busies herself grabbing the darts and shoving them back into his hands. "I won't make a habit of it."

His gold tooth glints. "No, we couldn't have that."

Once Cav lines up to throw, Lyx steals a drink from the bottle. Her eyes slip shut as soon as she tastes it. It's fresh and crisp, so refreshing she drinks nearly a quarter of it before she realizes. When she opens her eyes again, Cav is watching her. She nearly chokes, dabbing at her mouth to disguise it.

"You know, you don't smile much," Cav notes. "It's nice when you do."

A sickly feeling swarms in her stomach. It's oddly nauseating, but almost...nice. She doesn't know what to make of that. All she knows is the feeling grows stronger every time he looks at her. She needs to turn his attention elsewhere, or the thoughts in her head will continue to spin. Stepping beside him, she keeps her eyes on the dartboard. "What about you?"

"What about me?"

She shouldn't ask. She doesn't care, but it's better to know her enemy. It'll make all of this easier. "What's *your* fantasy?" With a fingernail, she traces the rim of her bottle. "It must be rather shocking if you've dedicated an entire experiment to it."

Cav finishes his turn in contemplation. Only then does he speak. "What *isn't* my fantasy?"

She hates to imagine that. Hates picturing Cav in a thousand positions, a thousand scenarios, a thousand kinks. It makes her knees weak. She throws a dart that completely misses the board.

Cav doesn't taunt her. "I like the thought of being useful. Being bossed around. Acting up, driving someone mad, testing the limits."

Lyx finishes her lackluster turn. "No surprise there."

Cav's lip twitches as he retrieves the darts from the board. "Truth be told, I enjoy most things. I like giving other people what they need." He lines himself up, but his eyes slide to hers. "I like intensity."

Thud. She's not sure if the sound is the dart or her pulse.

His bicep flexes when he throws. Hunger stretches within her. She wants to hear more, to know why, to dig her teeth into his muscle until he continues.

"I like to be consumed by the experience." *Thud*. "To be consumed by someone else." *Thud*. "But my biggest fantasy is the most boring thing you can imagine."

It's so hard to breathe with him next to her, but it's worse when she realizes he missed all three of his shots.

He returns from the board with the darts in hand. "You'll laugh if I tell you."

She swallows roughly. "From the sound of things, you'd get off on that."

His lips twitch upward. He keeps her in suspense when he steps away for her to play her turn. She hadn't realized the game is almost over. It takes all her focus to land her throws, but she manages to catch up to him. It hardly feels like a victory. Cav retrieves the darts without complaint, and she wonders if there's more than one game going on here.

Twilight settles around them. Creatures whir and call in the trees, surrounding them in a dull hum that seems to preempt something. It vibrates through her toes and the tips of her fingers, a reminder of the secret Cav still hasn't shared.

She can't ask again. She can't show him how curious it's made her, how desperately she wants to know the singular, dullest fantasy that occupies his mind. It's as if he knows it, lifting his tankard and taking a long drink. His throat bobs when he swallows, and then, he licks his lips, like he's waiting to see how long she'll wait. Did he take his turn already? She can't be sure.

Perhaps he's taking mercy on her. Perhaps that's why he finally speaks. "I dream about things you don't believe in."

Her body buzzes like she's strung up over the Great Abyss, preparing to take the deepest plunge. Cav is still, like watching her is enough to sate him. Anticipation coils inside her, a screaming need that threatens to shriek out of her. She wants to know more, she wants to hear it, she wants —

"I dream about love."

The word jolts through her. She doesn't speak. It's too risky when her throat is this tight, like a pitiful sound might slip through if she opens her mouth.

Cav presses her darts into her palm with a heavy look in his eyes that drag her in deeper. "I dream about knowing someone fully. Every intricacy. Every secret. Every regret. I dream about giving myself to someone, and trusting what they'll do with me."

His palm is hot over hers, warming the metal between them.

"I dream about fucking like that. Slow. Deep. Languid. Staring into each other's eyes so that we see *everything.*"

The word is little more than a breath. His face is so close that she can see the wound still healing on his mouth from the indentation of her teeth. By her feet, his tail flicks back and forth, never quite brushing her ankle.

His gaze trails over her face. "Learning every inch of each other. Every fluttering eyelash, every trembling lip, every hitching breath."

Only then does she realize her lips are parted, her heart thrumming in her throat. Everything around them fades as the light begins to glow through the cracks of Cav's scales.

"We don't stop when we come."

A white-hot image ignites in Lyx's mind. *We. You and me.* Like the two of them are as connected as she's always hoped and feared, her obsession roiling inside her and mirrored in him.

"We keep going," he murmurs. "We fuck through the mess. Ruin the sheets. Work ourselves past the point of breaking. We can't take any more, but we don't want to stop, so we just go so...fucking...*slow.*"

A sound blooms in the back of her throat. She clamps her mouth to keep it from escaping, legs shaking as her fingers curl into fists. The darts are trapped between them, stabbing into both of their hands in a reminder she doesn't want to let go of.

Then Cav retracts, leaving her body searing under his eyes. "That's what I dream about."

EIGHTEEN

Lyx

Slow. Deep. Languid.

Heat branches through Lyx's body. She doesn't know why the words get to her. For a moment, she lets herself imagine it. Cav's hips rolling against hers, their bodies pressed together, gasps hot against each other's mouths — but it's too simple. Too mild. Too tame. It's nothing compared to what she wants to do to him.

The thought splashes her face like ice cold water, her teeth digging into her cheek to taste the blood. No matter what Cav says, he doesn't understand the words he says. Not like she can. She is a creature born of extremity. She has seen how slowly the ocean devours a shipwreck, keeping it suspended in time. She has swum deeper than any land dweller can, until their lungs would collapse and their hearts would burst. Even then, she's never reached the bottom of the sea.

Cav cannot imagine her hunger. It would be too much for him.

Resolutely, she turns back to the board. She knew better than to entertain these thoughts. The darts dig into her palm, a reminder forcing her to focus. There is a purpose to this game, and it has nothing to do with Cav. Winning will give her the information she's after. Everything else is secondary.

The darts land exactly where she needs them, leaving her one spot behind Cav. His frivolity is gone. It's like he's still stuck on the words from before, images whirring behind the glassy look in his eyes.

Slow. Deep. Languid.

He moves toward the board and reaches for the highest dart. When his arm overextends, he winces but says nothing, rotating his shoulder as he settles into place beside her.

She doesn't look at him when she speaks. "If it's too much, you can forfeit now."

"Keeping an eye on me?"

"It's painfully obvious."

He adjusts his footing and lifts his wounded arm, lips pressed into a thin line. Still, he throws. "It never healed right." The dart lands low on the tree, missing the board entirely. He shakes his head and lifts his arm again. "And I've been putting it through the wringer lately."

The dart lands lopsided on the board, tilting the same way her mind does. She remembers the crow's nest. His tongue molded to her clit, her grinding against his face, her knee momentarily pressing into his shoulder.

"Don't get me wrong, it was well worth the strain." His tongue slides over his lips like he can still taste her. "I forget that I can't do things as freely as I used to." For the final dart, he shifts to his stronger hand. When he throws, the dart swings wide, but it lands with a certain *thwack* exactly where he wanted it. "I guess I don't really want to remember."

"Is that why —" She stops herself. There's no reason to ask him questions. She shouldn't remember these insignificant details, but they're trapped in her mind like seaweed tangled in a net. "Is that why you're not on a convoy anymore?"

While she takes her turn, Cav flicks a seed across the table. "After the grotto, things were different. The shipwreck took a toll on my body." He rolls another seed beneath his finger. "I tried other work, but no one would keep me onboard for long. I couldn't keep up. Couldn't pull my weight."

His usually-sunny face has become muddled, a dark cloud drifting across his expression. Lyx has the sudden urge to blow it away. He doesn't look at her, staring past the trees surrounding them. It's easier to watch him like this, when he isn't looking at her like he sees something she's hiding.

The game goes on. It takes a bit before he turns to her again. "I guess you wouldn't know anything about that. All those sentimental emotions."

She shakes her head.

"It is a bit strange you don't feel them, though," Cav wonders aloud, running a hand along one of his horns. "Because what's more chaotic than emotion?"

She's not sure where her dart lands. Her mind is too jarred by the question. It's staggering in its simplicity. Why *wouldn't* sirens feel the chaos of sentimentality? It's a thought that's never occurred to her, but now that it's here, her body feels hot and wrong.

She shakes the thoughts from her head. She doesn't need to question it. She *knows* it's true. It always has been. Every siren knows that. "We don't need to feel them. We need to *feed* on them."

The answer washes over her like a sudden tide, pulling her where she wants to go. She clings to it like it might carry her past Cav's inquisitive eyes, but he knows he's onto something, pushing off the table to step closer.

"What about your ex? You felt something for him. Enough that you were...together."

Lyx shrugs. "Passion."

"Is that all?"

"What else is there?" She can't help but laugh. "All 'relationships' are exchanges. You give something to get something. It's an agreement — not unlike the one we have."

Cav's gaze drifts over her face. His look is so soft that Lyx digs her nails into her palms to keep from reaching out. She doesn't need whatever that look is. It's too fragile. Too breakable. "What is passion to you?" he finally asks.

She scoffs. Isn't it obvious? "It's...desire and disgust." That's how she feels about Tidus. That's how she feels about every pirate who came before him. "Screaming. Fighting. Fucking." Memories play on a loop behind her eyes and stoke her anger. "It's want. It's hate. It's both."

It's exactly what she's always felt, exactly what she needs to survive, but Cav's expression hasn't changed. "What if it was something else?"

A strange feeling flounders in her gut, like a fish out of water. Passion is chaos. She, of all people, should understand that, but Cav's question flashes like a lure tempting her closer.

"What if passion wasn't a storm?" he murmurs. "What if it was the eye inside of it?"

Electricity crackles down her spine. What he says doesn't make any sense. Passion is unruly, uncontrollable, wild, yet the feeling he describes sounds just as strong. Just as fervent. Just as intense.

Like the way he looks at her, heart glowing through his chest. "The North Star guiding you. The moon pulling the tides. The thing you chase through everything else."

Her entire body is aflame, burning under Cav's attention. Is this what it's like to be set on fire?

She can't think like this. The questions Cav asks are…confusing. Unnecessary. She can't explain them away in this moment, but she knows he's wrong. He can't be right. Her mouth is dry. "I need another drink."

Cav pushes off of the table. "I can –"

"Play your turn." She steps back toward the bar, keeping her eyes on Cav until he returns to the dartboard. Only then does she veer away, slipping past the other patrons toward the entrance.

Foliage slaps her arms as she pushes toward the beach. She doesn't follow the path, bursting through the greenery to a spot where she can't see anyone. With one hand, she braces against a tree trunk and tries to steady her breathing.

What's happening to her? Her scales lift on end. Her mind is dizzy. There's no reason she should feel like this. It was a simple conversation, yet Cav's words thrum through her.

The thing you chase through everything else.

A hand clamps around her wrist. "Why the fuck are you off the *Indulgence*?" Tidus hisses.

She tries to pull away, but it grinds the bones in her arm together. Instinctively, she searches over his shoulder for — what? Someone to save her? That's foolish. The plants obscure everything, and Tidus makes sure of that when he pulls her deeper into the flora.

It grows darker around them, leaves dragging over her skin like a tide moving past her. She fights down the anxious fluttering in her stomach. "I'm working on *your* errand," she whispers. "Remember? The one you *insisted* on."

Tidus doesn't stop tugging until her skin is raw, until they're far away from anyone else. "Certainly looked like you're working on *something*." Despite his anger, his voice turns saccharine with mockery. "Cozying up to your little hero?" When Lyx shifts away, he ropes an arm around her waist to force her close, his breath hot and stale with ale. "Are you forgetting what you're here for?"

"*You* sent me here," she snaps. "You told me to do whatever I had to —"

She cuts off in a gasp when he bends her wrist backward. Her knees threaten to buckle, mind pinging with pain as she breathes through her nose. *Use your fucking head.* There is no reasoning with Tidus. She knows that; she's always known that. He enjoys tormenting her. No matter what she does, she'll be wrong until he's satisfied, and he won't be satisfied until he has what he wants.

She clamps her hand around her wrist to steady it. "I'm trying..." The shell in Tidus's chest flickers with distress. *Focus,* she reminds herself. *Focus on that.* "I'm trying to get what you want. But it's not like they'll just tell me; they don't trust me."

Tidus's grip scrapes against her. "And whose fault is that?"

She can't move. Can't escape. Chaos funnels into her throat, thick as smoke clogging her lungs. When he leans closer, her arm trembles from the effort to keep it in place. "They've seen your ship!"

She's not sure where the lie comes from, but it's desperate enough to be believed. Tidus doesn't loosen his hold, but he does pause.

"They think someone's following the *Indulgence,*" she pants. The story weaves together in a flurry. "You need to keep your distance. Avoid the next few islands. Stay out of sight."

He tightens his fingers. "*You* do not tell *me* what happens here." But his gaze darts toward the far end of the island where his flag waves at the top of the mast. Finally, he shoves her away. "Fine. Get back to your boytoy." He grabs her chin and jerks her eyes to his. "You have a week. You'd better bring me something, or our next conversation won't be so pleasant."

He thrusts her away and stalks off between the trees. The twinge in her throat grows with every step he takes, but it pales in comparison to the sharp pain of her wrist. She winces as she inspects it, tugging down her sleeve to cover the angry mark.

As always, Tidus has fed her well. Her skin is glowing, but her body is bloated and gorged to the point of sickness. She starts to move, but the nausea forces her to brace one hand on her knees while she heaves.

Once she's through, she wipes her mouth with the back of her sleeve and ignores the sour stench. As much as she despises Tidus, this is a wake-up call. She's been distracted. She's taking time she doesn't have to fall into silly caprices with Cav. That is not what she's here for.

By the end of the week, she *will* have something for Tidus. She'll have something to get her closer to her song.

Gritting her teeth, she makes her way back along the trail. Cav is exactly where she left him, balancing the tip of a dart on his finger. When he sees her, his face brightens. "Don't tell me you were trying to hide from losing. I got you another —"

"Forget it." She snatches up her darts and jerks her chin toward the board. "Is that where you landed?"

If it is, he's made it completely around the circle. He's won.

Something leaden settles in her stomach. She hadn't realized how close to the end they were, but Cav slides toward her. "Technically, I finished, but let's keep it interesting." The sweet scent of his breath wafts around her. "If you can catch me on this turn, the win is yours."

Lyx keeps her eyes ahead and digs her heels into the dirt. It's the only chance she has. She lines up her shot, exhaling slowly when she throws. The dart lands exactly where it needs it to. Impressed, Cav lifts a brow, but Lyx doesn't look toward him. She turns the second dart over in her hand before she sends it flying.

It lands perfectly.

Cav's posture straightens. "Damn."

The final dart is heavy between her fingers. Its red feathers tease her cheek as she lifts it toward her face. One shot, and she'll get what she's after. She'll have answers. She'll have what she needs.

But what would she have if she lost?

It's a traitorous thought. Her head jerks like that will shake it away, but it's still there. What is her fantasy? Nothing Cav can offer her is worth losing this game, but there is something she's always wondered. Something she could only pretend at. Something she'll never be able to experience.

It's impossible. There is no scene Cav could weave to fool her, no way that he could fuck her to make her feel a scrap of whatever he believes in…but she does wonder what it would be like, being loved by someone.

It has always eluded her. For most of her life, she never thought more of it. It never crossed her mind. She didn't want it, and she still doesn't, but she is curious. What would he say? How would he look at her? Would it feel different than every other time she's been touched?

It's a pointless notion, so puerile that it brings a smile to her lips. He's not capable of convincing her, and she's not capable of understanding it. It's trivial and inconsequential.

With a steadying breath, she throws the final dart. It sails to the board and lands directly next to Cav's – but hers is just outside the double ring.

Her arm falls back to her side. It can't be right. She crosses all the way to the tree before she's forced to admit it. Her dart has landed a centimeter off. She's outside the bounds of the board.

The throw doesn't score. She loses.

Her chest tightens. She hadn't *meant* to lose. It was a

fleeting thought, an inane contemplation, not something she'd actually considered.

When she turns, Cav looks equally surprised, but he clamps his mouth shut when he sees her face. "Hey, it's not so bad." His expression is encouraging, like he can sense her devastation. "You still get something out of it, right?"

Without a word, she brushes past him, flexing her wrist until it aches.

In the Grotto

Lyx

Quit playing with your food. Kill him.

That thought chases Lyx all the way back to the sirens' nest. She darts through coral and plants and hovers on the outskirts of the sunken ship.

It's the sirens' most impressive trophy, a massive hull covered in barnacles and lichens, tipping precariously on the continental shelf. Another prized possession bobs overhead; a metal buoy stolen from the nearest island, now stained with blood and rust.

Sirens do enjoy their toys.

Shrieks rise in the distance. Two of the other sirens are fighting. Lyx could sense it long before she could hear them, but their voices grow louder now, carried through the water until it's suffocating. She can't deal with them. Not today. Not when a pirate who should be long dead is hijacking her thoughts.

Ducking low, she follows the edge of the chasm. A jagged

hole in the shipwreck serves as the main entrance, but she searches instead for the crack that runs from bow to stern. There's barely enough room for her to squeeze through, but she does, fingers scraping moss as she wiggles her hips and pushes inside.

The ship blots out most of the sound. Lyx exhales and swims deeper, enveloped by groaning boards and slanting beams. When she reaches her room, she stops short. Something is off. The netting hanging from her walls are empty. Beneath it, her box of hooks has been strewn open. On the floor, a beam of sunlight glints off mutilated metal and broken glass.

Her collections have been tampered with. One of her siblings was here.

Rage boils inside her. The destruction is no surprise; it is the way of sirens, creating discord wherever they can. This disruption feeds her. Already, she can feel it in her throat, clogging her gills until she can do nothing but gasp. She should indulge in it, but instead, she gags.

Returning here was a mistake. She's felt the ominous churning for days: schools of fish fleeing, whales falling silent, pandemonium waiting to be unleashed. All of the sirens can sense it. It draws them together, conducting chaos like electricity. It's a vicious cycle; the more of them that gather, the quicker they combust. Sirens may share this transitory dwelling, but they share no affection or blood. The only thing they share is hunger.

A lone pirate in this territory won't stay alone for long. Once one siren gets a whiff of him, the others will be sure to follow. Lyx's tongue presses to her fangs to keep her mind sharp. That's why she's keeping Cav a secret. She's territorial. She doesn't want to share. That is the only reason.

Outside the wreckage, the feud has died away. It won't be long before it kicks up again. Lyx should seize the chance to flee — but not before swimming the length of the ship and smashing any trinkets she comes across.

Revenge is good. She's practically glowing when she wedges through the crack in the ship. It's freeing to escape this place. She's not the only one who thinks so. Below her, creatures scuttle toward the open ocean and disappear into its depths. She could be like them. She could dive deeper and vanish, away from her siblings. Away from this mess.

"If it isn't my favorite little sea jelly."

Lyx's head jerks toward the edge of the reef. There lies Sinoe, blue hair swaying as she lounges across a rock.

Her silver eyes glint. "What was all that racket in the ship? Surely you weren't getting into trouble all on your own."

Lyx doesn't speak, but she's not fool enough to think Sinoe doesn't know the answer. Sinoe always knows.

Sinoe pouts, releasing a stream of bubbles. "You know I hate the silent treatment, Lyxy. It's been a week since I last saw you. I was starting to think the last rip current swept you away."

Her barracuda tail flicks absently, but her fins are sharp and pointed. Turbulence ripples through the water, like something big is circling closer. Lyx wants to look behind her. Suddenly, the open ocean feels dangerous, but she knows it's just Sinoe making her uneasy. That's what Sinoe does best.

There's only one way to combat it. With a shrug, Lyx forces her tentacles to unfurl and floats closer to the reef. "I get tired of listening to you all bitching."

"No," Sinoe hums, a smirk settling on her lips. "It's not that."

Lyx's chest tightens. Sinoe scans over her, gaze flitting from her neck to her shoulders before her eyes latch onto Lyx's hip.

Sinoe's head tilts eerily. "What's that?"

Lyx doesn't look. She doesn't have to. She remembers the burning pain, the stick alight with Cav's fire in the grotto. The lie comes easily. "Shocked myself again. Always lose track of one tentacle or another."

Sinoe's nose twitches. "You haven't stung yourself since you were a child. Do you think I don't know my own sister?" She arches like a cat in the sun. "If I didn't know any better, I'd say you've been on land."

Lyx swallows roughly. The accusation isn't damning. It's not unheard of for sirens to hunt on land, but her voice is trapped in her throat.

Sinoe's scales shimmer. "Not that I can blame you, of course. I was just thinking what fun it would be to have a pirate as a pet. But where could I keep him?" She taps her chin with one long finger. "An island. A rowboat. Or perhaps you could lend me that grotto of yours."

Lyx's heart pulses in her gills. Sinoe knows. She's found Cav. She's been watching them.

Sinoe calls over her shoulder. "What do you think, Mollo? Should I go hunting for my next meal?"

A shape appears behind her, long tail swishing like a ribbon. Mollo's foggy green eyes land on Lyx. When she smiles, her branching teeth curve back into her mouth like a frilled shark's. A baby siren babbles in her arms.

Sinoe looks over the child. "Where'd you find this one?"

"When I was hopping islands." Mollo balances the baby on her hip, toying with the spiral shell hanging from her necklace. "It washed up right next to my other strange treasures."

Sinoe's nose wrinkles with distaste. "How come you always seem to find the little urchins first?"

Mollo sighs. "Maternal instinct." Then she deposits the hapless creature on the ground and settles onto a branch of coral. *"But we should go hunting. I'm starving for something fresh."*

Overhead, the sky suddenly rumbles with thunder. Lyx's skin crawls. A gathering of two sirens was bad enough, but four... She needs to get out of here. She needs to get back to Cav.

Sinoe rests on her stomach, tail swishing behind her like a pendulum. "Come sit with us, Lyxy." She extends her taloned hand. "Just for a minute. Just like old times."

Lyx's spinal fin grows tight and rigid. Even the urchin seems to sense something, its haunting eyes honed on Lyx's face. Panic claws at her throat. Does Mollo know about Cav, too? Has she had her way with him?

That is a threat far worse than Sinoe, but Lyx can't give anything away. She can't be sure how much they know. She has to put them at ease so she can slip away. Slowly, Lyx eases toward the reef, but Sinoe and Mollo both reach for her, pulling her onto the grooved coral between them.

"Was that so bad?" Sinoe teases. "You act like you have somewhere else to be."

"She's ready to go hunting," Mollo purrs, brushing a hand through Lyx's hair. Her fingers snag in the tentacles, but Lyx refuses to wince. "Those pirates really are so easy to catch. They still haven't realized we're both the lure and the net."

Sinoe winds a strand of Lyx's hair around her finger. "What do you think, sister?" Her scalp twinges like Sinoe is rooting around in her mind, playing with her secrets like a dolphin toying with dinner. "Or have they begun to bore you?"

Lyx's head radiates with pain. The baby begins to cry.

Mollo's tongue drags over her lips. "They're not so different from us, you know. That's why we go together. They don't love anything but themselves. They plunder. They pillage. They ravage."

The wailing baby crawls toward the drop-off, its tail fluttering as it tries to swim. There's no use saving it. In a week, this urchin will be lost to the tides or a passing shark. Sirens have to learn to fend for themselves.

"It's a perfect circle," Sinoe murmurs. "We hunt them, and they hunt us. We feed their appetites, and they feed ours."

"If you're lucky, you'll find a real pirate." Mollo tugs on Lyx's tentacles. "One whose cruelty matches yours. One that can capture and trap you. That's when you know. That's the pirate you want."

Lyx's head pounds.

The baby howls.

"Silence!" Mollo screeches. The baby's mouth opens and closes like a fish, but it doesn't make another sound. Mollo's necklace twinkles under her smug satisfaction.

"That's how you want to spend your life?" Lyx can't help herself. When she speaks, Mollo and Sinoe stare at her. Her voice is suddenly weak. "That's what you imagine?"

"A never-ending feast?" Mollo cackles, digging a fingernail between her teeth to dislodge something fleshy and pink. "Of course. Even if your body is captive, your song can set you free. That's our true power."

A shadow passes over Lyx's face. She tilts her head toward the surface of the water, watching ripples spread from the metal buoy.

"He must be awake now." Mollo stretches on her side, staring dreamily toward the surface. "My latest plaything tied me to the bow of his ship for a week...so I brought him back and took his leg."

Her grin widens, teeth flecked with chunks of skin and muscle. Overhead, there's a muffled scream. The water churns faster, turning red into foamy pink.

Lyx's mouth waters. Sinoe drifts toward the surface, forgetting everything but the wounded thrashing. Mollo snags her tail and jerks her back. "If I'm feeling generous, maybe I'll let you have a taste."

In the distance, a swarm of shadows appears. The other sirens are here, drawn by the promise of flesh and chaos. It is what they do, the one thing that draws them all in.

Mollo and Sinoe swim for the buoy, shoving and clawing each other as they fight toward the surface. Lyx starts to follow them, but an errant thought darts through her mind. The sirens will not be sated by one pirate. They will be ravenous, gluttonous, clamoring for another feast — and Sinoe knows exactly where to find one.

Lyx's stomach turns as she sinks back toward the reef, her body heavy with chaos. Sirens swarm the buoy. It's a mindless feeding frenzy, teeth gnashing as they devour their meal.

Her blood thrums. She has to get back to the grotto. She has to end this before the others catch Cav's scent. She has to do what she should have done the second he landed here.

She swims as fast as her fins will carry her. Behind her, the screams grow to a fever pitch.

NINETEEN

Cav

Maybe Cav got ahead of himself. As much as he enjoyed the crow's nest, it wasn't *enough*. He was so eager to touch Lyx's body again, but that's all he touched. Nothing deeper.

The night spent throwing darts was different. *Lyx* seemed different. Slowly, she unfurled, speaking without so much halting resistance. She asked him questions. She told him things. It felt like they were getting back to where they'd been before, synching into a familiar rhythm.

But it didn't last. When Lyx returned from wherever she'd been, there was a barbed look on her face. She wouldn't tell him anything else. She still hasn't.

Two days later, he lies in his hammock under the storm rolling overhead. It doesn't give him much warning. Within seconds, a massive cloud opens up and dumps rain over the deck. Everyone scrambles, steering the boat through roughened waves or scurrying below deck for cover. By the time Cav disassembles his soggy hammock, he's soaked to the bone. He splashes down the stairs, clothes steaming while his internal fire tries to warm him.

The ship groans and heaves. Cav braces against a wooden beam before he drapes his hammock over it to dry. All the cabin doors are shut tight, including his own. A strip of firelight flickers beneath it, taunting him from the end of the hall.

Fuck it. Lyx may want nothing to do with him, but at least he can get a fresh change of clothes. He wrings water from his shirt and moves down the corridor to knock at the door.

Lyx takes her time answering. He can see her shadow moving, but she's silent when she opens the door with a sullen look. Her curls are piled atop her head, the sleeves of her dress slung low on her shoulders. Her clothing may be dry, but it clings to her as if it isn't, hugging every curve of her body.

Cav tries not to stare. It takes a moment for him to remember why he's here. "I hate to be a bother —"

"No, you don't."

He bites back a smile. "The deck is inhospitable tonight." He gestures down his wet torso to the puddle forming at his feet. "May I come inside for some clothes?"

Her eyes narrow, but when the ship bucks, her fingers curl around the door frame. Her skin fades to almost white. It looks like she'll be sick.

"Are you alright?" he asks.

Water drips onto his lips. Her eyes flit to his mouth. For a moment, he wonders if she'll slam the door in his face, but then the boat pitches. He skids across the ground, claws scraping the wall as he collides with her.

They stagger into the room, nearly knocking the lantern from its perch. He catches her around the waist, planting his feet to keep from sliding when the boat rocks back in the opposite direction. The door slams closed, and he lands against it, his back to the wood with her body held tight against his chest.

Their breaths are as scattered as his thoughts. Her face hovers before him, her palms pressed to his chest. They drift downward as if they're separate from her mind, fingers curling in the fabric of his shirt, like it would tear open as easily as wet parchment...

Then the glassy look in her eyes is gone. She pries herself away. When the boat rocks again, her hand darts out to steady her.

She's as far from him as she can get. He sets his disappointment aside and unlaces the soggy ties of his vest. The room looks much the same as when he left it, although the odds and ends have been put away, no longer rolling across the floor.

Something about that makes him smile. "I hope the accommodations have been up to your standards."

Rain pelts the window behind him, but it's half as hostile as she looks. "It's obscenely quiet, *usually*."

"My apologies." He discards his vest. "I'm sure we can liven things up."

She scoffs, but it catches in her throat when he works his shirt off over his head. He drops it on the ground, body warm where her eyes rove the wet jumps covering his chest. No matter how he yearns to, he doesn't look at her, like her arousal is a fickle cat he doesn't want to scare away.

"If it helps," he says, "I talked to Heathen about your tour." Lyx perks up at that. It fills Cav with guilt. "She doesn't have time for it now. Maybe at the end of the season when things slow down."

It's foolish to imagine that Lyx will still be here then, but that doesn't stop him from hoping. Lyx looks none-too-pleased. "So that's why you're here."

His hands pause on his open belt buckle. "For my dry

clothes?”

"You're here to collect your dart winnings. And I'm past due for your experiment."

He waves the thought away. In truth, he'd forgotten both of those agreements — but clearly, Lyx hasn't. A thought spreads over his mind. "Have you been waiting for me to collect?"

The accusation makes her scoff. "Of course not."

"So you haven't been counting down the days?" Now that he thinks of it, she mentioned being "overdue" during their dart game as well. Why does she continue to remind him? Why not let him forget?

Her mouth twists sourly. "I just want to get it over with."

"There's a simple way of accomplishing that." He leans back against the wall, tucking his hands into the tops of his pockets. "Two birds, one stone. Tell me your wildest fantasy."

Her jaw sets. He's not sure any words could pass through if they wanted to, but then, her head tilts. She gets a distant look in her eyes, something close to a smile playing on her lips. "You, with your mouth shut."

He hums sweetly.

With every word, her expression grows more vicious. More beautiful. "You, with your head underwater. You, with air bubbles streaming from your nose."

"Do all your fantasies revolve around me?"

Her mouth hangs open for a moment before she clamps it shut.

It's an opportunity. Cav takes it. "Why *did* you agree to Heathen's offer? To doing this with me?"

Lyx's brow knits. Her arms fold across her chest. "I needed a spot on the ship."

His tongue clicks when he shakes the water from his hair, pants sinking lower on his hips. "I don't buy it. I think you agreed because you want to know just as badly as I do.

Because you're curious."

For a brief moment, her eyes dart to the trail of scales that lead down from his navel, but she snaps it up again. "And what would I be curious about?"

In this light, she looks almost pink, shadows dancing across her dogged expression. It's strange how her sharpened edges only make him speak more softly, his voice dipping low for just the two of them. "Have you wondered what it could have been like? If we'd had more time. If we'd had more of each other."

Maybe he shouldn't say it. Maybe he shouldn't dredge up the past, but it's less like ancient history and more like a dream he can't pull himself out of.

One he doesn't *want* to pull himself out of.

There's a waver in her face that's more than lanternlight. "No." Her voice crackles. A flush spreads up her neck before she clears her throat. "I don't think about you."

"Except for how much you hate me."

Her eyes darken, fierce as the storm roiling outside. "Great Abyss…" Her voice is little more than a hiss. "Have you never been denied *anything*?"

Cav stands straighter. This is not their usual back-and-forth. Something swarms beneath her surface, drawn up from deep inside her. *This* is what she's spent years thinking about.

It boils out of her, harsh and bitter. "You enter every room like it's happy to see you. You swagger through every problem. You smile at every adversity. You yearn for *nothing*."

The ship rolls again. He braces against the wall. "That's not true." His throat is thick when he shallows, always looking at her. "I *want*."

"There's nothing you need that you can't have." Her fingers curl into fists, irritation branching through her. "You couldn't begin to understand."

"Let me give it to you, then." It slips out of him as easily as breathing. When he licks his lips, he can still taste the words. "Let me show you what it's like to not be denied. To hear 'yes' to everything you want."

She blanches, like the thought of Cav giving her everything she wants is a threat. Her hand lifts to her throat before she drops it again. "I don't need that." It almost sounds like she's trying to convince herself. "I have my song."

Oh, he remembers her song. The reminder tightens hot and heavy in his gut. Under her thrall, he was delirious to please her, soaking in every delicious second of her control. He swears he can see the memory dancing behind her eyes, but that's not what he's after.

"I don't mean by force." When the ship tips, Cav finds his sea legs and rides the wave as he follows the thought. "Has no one ever done something just to see you enjoy it? Been desperate to know your desires, just because they're yours?" He steps toward her, his voice and body finding balance. "Has no one ached to fulfill them? To fulfill *you*?"

She fights the motion of the ship and clings to a hook on the wall. Her face goes pale when her legs hit the bed, forcing her to sit on the end of the mattress.

"You wouldn't need your song." Cav pushes off the wall and lets the motions carry him across the room until he's standing before her. "What if someone could read you? Learn you so well that they sense what you need?"

The boat jerks and knocks him off his feet. He stumbles forward, catching himself with a hand on either side of her hips. Both their breathing is heavy, chests rising and falling out of time. A droplet of water drips from his hair, skirting down the column of his neck and tracing between the scales on his shoulder. They both watch as the water beads on the tip of one scale, dropping and splashing onto her clavicle.

He's so caught up that he can't catch himself when the boat dips again, sending him sprawling backward. She lands on top of him, knocking the air from his lungs when his good shoulder collides with the door. Lyx groans and pushes up onto all fours. She holds her weight off of him, but her hips are caged by his thighs. Her hair has slipped from its bindings and falls like a curtain around them, blocking out everything else.

His heart drums in his ears. He knows what she wants. He doesn't have to think when the smoke coils in his throat and urges him to offer it.

"Slap me."

TWENTY

Lyx

Slap me.

Lyx feels like she's been electrocuted, but she can't focus when the sea tosses her like she's nothing. No matter how long it's been, she's never managed to get used to sailing through storms. With Tidus, no journey is smooth. Every single one is filled with choppy waves and angry skies as the ocean tries to drag him back to where he belongs.

Once upon a time, she relished rough seas. She basked in the turmoil. She sensed what the ocean would do. Now, she fears the unknown like any other land dweller. She can't trust she'll make it to the next port.

But the way Cav speaks to her is a distraction. He's warm and pliant beneath her, making her head swim far more than the motion does. "Why?" she croaks. His mouth is so close that she's not sure what she's asking. She tries again. "Why would you offer that?"

"Because I think you want to." His chest glows beneath the fabric. "Because I want to give you what you want. Because I like the fire in you."

"No, you don't." She knows better. She won't be fooled. Pirates do not want the sirens of legend or myth; they want a pretty woman to tame, to melt down and forge into something they can use. "You just want a toy you can break."

She'll show him. She reaches for his throat, prepared for him to flinch — but he doesn't. In fact, he tips his head back and arches into her palm. His voice vibrates under her hand. "I want you to break *me*."

His gaze looks so glassy under her touch. It's impossible for him to be under the thrall of her song, and still, he looks so...compliant. Subservient. Obedient.

She can't think with him this close. With him looking up at her like *that*. She pushes to her feet, but he eases up onto his knees. "You want to shut me up, right?"

It's as if the ocean is playing along, pitching Lyx back against the bed and sending Cav sliding toward her.

His hands dart out to catch himself. "You've thought about it, haven't you? Payback. Revenge."

Her mouth twitches.

That's answer enough. He shakes out the tension in his shoulders like a diver preparing for a plunge, presenting the untouched skin of his cheek. "So rough me up a little."

Her palm itches to make contact. She presses it against her thigh to will the feeling away, but the sight of him on his knees twists in her stomach. When was the last time she touched someone without duress? Because *she* wanted it, not because it was required. Not because it was the only way out.

Her nails dig into her palm, but the wild urge remains. She wants to do this. She wants the satisfaction, the retribution, the emotions that have plagued her to form into a handprint across his face.

Cav watches her hungrily. "You know the word to use if you want to stop? If *I* want to stop?"

Parley. Lyx nods once.

He releases his grip on the bed. "Then slap me."

Her skin flares hot. Foolish pirate, trusting a siren to obey his rules. It's so careless, so confusing, made worse by his fingers trailing up the back of her calf. She pushes to her feet to keep from shivering, her fist still clamped tight. Cav waits on the floor for a long moment before he carefully reaches for her hand.

Every instinct in her screams to jerk away...but she doesn't. Her throat bobs, eyes burning into his as he caresses the inside of her wrist. Slowly, his fingers drag against hers, unfurling them fully so that he can set her palm against his face.

It glows beneath her touch. A raindrop falls from his hair, sizzling when it slips between his cheek and her palm. He fits perfectly in her hand, his head tilting until she's cradling his jaw.

The sight of it is too much. She has to pull away, to put some space between them, but she doesn't go far. Her hand hovers next to his cheek, still soaking in the warmth.

A dreamy smirk drifts across his face. "Would it help if I mouthed off a little? Give you an excuse?"

Her mind is as splattered as the raindrops on the window, a mix of awe and unbridled appetite. She recognizes something in him, but she can't think past the craving buzzing through her. "What is wrong with you?" she whispers.

Cav shrugs. "I don't know. Why'd you let me bury my mouth in your pussy?"

Her hand meets his cheek.

"Better." He grins. "Now, can you come just from chaos, or do you need me to get you there?"

Another lackluster slap. Depths, why doesn't she just *hit him*? She wants to. She *knows* she does, but she fears how much she'll enjoy it. How much more she'll want.

Cav flexes his jaw. "Come on, I tail-fucked you harder than that."

Her hand lands with a satisfying sound, and she can finally see the outline on his skin.

With a laugh, Cav stretches out his jaw. "Now we're getting somewhere."

She's practically vibrating. "The more your mouth moves, the easier it gets."

"Yeah?" He settles back on his heels. "Maybe I should move it on your clit again."

This time, the sound is as sharp and sudden as lightning.

It's like a dream. She wonders if she's gone too far, but Cav's eyes are bright and vibrant, looking up at her like she's feeding him from her hand. "There you go."

Her palm tingles. She should stop this. She should deny him the pleasure...but she wants it just as badly. This is more than a game. This is more than revenge.

It's like he can see the hot hook tugging on her stomach. "Chaos feeds you, right?" He licks his lips. "This feeds me. Do it again."

Impossibly, it's true. With every slap, the tension melts from his body, leaving him open and easy. Her hand trembles to touch him again.

His pupils blow wide. "Now shut me up before I have you coming on my face again."

Her hand connects. *Hard.* The boat rocks beneath them, and slowly, he turns back to her. The outline of her palm is embedded in his skin.

"Fucking *perfect*," he rasps.

Her toes curl. He looks *alive*, the same way he did on the *Silver Spoon*. The same way he did when she first kissed him.

Was this the way he looked before the grotto, too, disheveled hair and wild eyes begging for adventure?

Fucking perfect.

Her legs lock as desire tunnels through her. Cav eases his knees further apart, sinking lower until his ass meets the ground. His pants sit so low on his hips, exposing the V of muscle there. He taunts her like a drunk in a barfight, begging for one last swing. "I think you've got one more in you."

Her breath comes faster now, fingers flexing at the promise. She's done denying herself; she wants the stinging pain in her hand, the relief of her flesh against his, the sight of her mark across his face. She craves more than the physical reward. Every slap draws arousal into Cav's eyes like water from a well, and she wants more of it. Wants to swallow his desire the way she swallows chaos, drinking from his yearning until his lust runs down her lips and chin and makes a mess of her.

She meets him harder than she ever has, knocking out a gasp when his head whips sideways. Smoke pours from his nose and mouth. Only once it clears does she see blood beading on his bottom lip.

Cav's forked tongue probes the wound with a groan. "That's fucking *it.*"

Her stomach knots like the ache between her legs, a volcanic eruption threatening to cover everything with molten *need.*

Cav spits on the floor, eyes sparking when he lays out the flat of his tongue toward her. "Give it back to me. Spit in my mouth."

This time, she can't blame the boat for the way she tilts. Cav finds the backs of her legs and guides her forward until her knees brush his chest. She steadies herself with a hand on the wall, but it does little to offset the delicate patterns Cav traces behind her knees.

Her legs tremble. She hates that. This cannot be what gets to her. This is nothing. She's fucked her way through countless pirates, feasting on storms and shipwrecks, but this…

Lightning flashes before the sky falls dark as night again. Lyx's mind whirls at a dizzying speed, but her voice is sharp with laughter. "You want me to — what? Degrade you? Humiliate you?"

Blood blooms when a smile stretches across his lips. "Yes, ma'am."

She tries not to shudder. She's never witnessed such a willingness to be powerless. No pirate has ever kneeled before her. Not without her song. Not without compulsion. She's in a daze, some parallel world that couldn't possibly exist.

"Beg." She doesn't know where the word comes from. All she knows is that she desperately needs to hear his pleading.

Cav's irises glow like two midday suns. "My vicious captor…"

Lyx's body pings like a tuning fork.

His voice is hoarse with want. "I am but your humble servant. I take only what you deign to give." He spreads his knees to sink lower, eyes wide and wanton and pathetic. "*Please.*"

A different hunger spreads its aching jaws inside her. This is a part of her that has never been fed, a part that has never been set loose. Her mouth waters at the sight of him, staring up at her and willing to do anything she demands. He would let her suck bruises onto his skin. He would let her rake her nails down his back. He would let her sink her teeth into his flesh.

Depths, what has he done to her? She can't remember to hate him. When she's standing over him like this, all she can think of is the tantalizing sway of his tail and how beautifully he yields to her.

She lifts her hand toward his face. His lips part eagerly to suck on two of her fingers like they were sweet nectar. She adds another finger and stretches the rim of his mouth. He doesn't resist. He doesn't bite. He just takes it, opening wider until three of her fingers are buried to the hilt.

Abyss, he looks pitiful and needy and *hot*. Saliva gathers in the corners of his mouth, eyes glassy and helpless while he lets her do whatever she pleases.

She's never known anything like this. She's never felt this power, not even when she used her song. It makes her gluttonous, soaking up every second of his submission. "Beg like *this*."

Cav whines in the back of his throat. A strand of spit slips down to his chest, sizzling when it hits the glowing skin. His hips rut like he can't help himself, mouth forming pathetically around muffled words. *Please. Fuck. Gods.*

Her cunt clenches. She presses her fingertips down into the soft flesh of his tongue, drawing a moan from deep inside him. It's hypnotic. It's intoxicating. She wants to lap up every debased sound, every look, every motion, but she finally, *finally* withdraws.

Even gasping for breath, Cav keeps his tongue presented to her. She grits her teeth to keep from groaning, cupping his chin to keep his eyes on hers. And then, she spits.

It lands on his tongue and splatters across his lips. His eyes slip shut as if she's blessed him, her saliva held reverently on his tongue. Depths, why does it make her *ache*? Toying with his desperation is better than any other penance he could offer.

She tightens her grip on him. "Don't waste it. Swallow."

Cav does exactly as he's told, curling his tongue back into his mouth. He savors her spit for another moment before his throat bobs, and his swollen lips part to reveal the clean length of his tongue.

Lyx's entire body sings. "You're a mess," she pants, like *she's* the one being slapped and gagged and spit on.

All he does is smile, his tail snaking across the floor and curling up around her leg to spur her on.

Her fingers curve around his neck. He doesn't fight back. When she increases the pressure on his throat, his head lolls permissively. Fuck, that does it. She lifts her hand, dragging him to his feet and crushing their mouths together.

The boat careens and sends them tumbling onto the bed. It's a mass of knees clanging, teeth clacking, and chests colliding, but it doesn't slow them. They claw at each other like they can't get enough, hips winding to bring them closer.

She pins him beneath her. The blue light from her skin reflects off of his, and she wants to drag her tongue over him just to taste. Her fingers work at the low-slung trousers on his hips, shoving the belts and buckles aside.

With a mirthful hum, he spreads his legs. His thigh presses between hers, making her bite back a sound, but his pants don't budge.

Frustration courses through her. She needs him. There's no denying the ache. She wants to feel his scales scraping against her, to roam the hills and valleys of his body, to ingest all the parts of him that she has been denied.

But when she reaches for him again, he catches her wrists. "Are you being honest?"

Lyx squirms. It takes a moment to remember what he means, his warning from the first day scorching back into her mind. *If you want me to give you everything, it has to be real. Show me more than the facade.*

What the fuck does that even mean? She can't think when the sight of him, dazed and pliant, vibrates through her very being. She is *hungry*. She wants to know every inch of him, to leave teeth marks and lap at his blood, to bite off pieces so that he is forced to stay with her always.

Her thoughts are a tempest, whirling and spattering against her skull. Her tongue burns with words she can't make sense of, things she cannot say, so she keeps her mouth shut and prays the rest of her will put the fire out.

When she reaches for him again, he doesn't push her away. He pulls her closer, trapping her wrists between their chests. Her hair spills around them. She pants against his mouth, fingers curling in his bodice. He doesn't let her do more than that. Doesn't let her tug the fabric free. Doesn't let her touch him anywhere else.

"You're a brat," she snarls.

"I'll give it to you," he whispers. "Trust me." It's so soft she can barely hear it over the blood pounding in her ears. "Just tell me something real."

It should be easy to lie. Pretend that she needs him desperately, that she's helpless to this feeling, that he occupies all of her thoughts — but the tremor in her voice would give her away. Because it isn't a lie. It isn't pretend. It's *real*.

For a moment, it looks like he can see it. Like he knows the truth she's trying to hide.

Her entire body tenses. He cannot see it; she cannot abide that. Fear hones her voice into something sharp and venomous. "I've given you more than enough."

Cav's face falls. She tries not to feel the crushing feeling inside her. His fingers brush over her hands and slowly retract. "If that's how you feel."

Carefully, he eases out from under her and gathers his wet clothes. Lyx clenches her jaw and fights the sting burrowing in her chest. It doesn't matter. She has nothing to give. Nothing she *wants* to give. Showing Cav whatever he believes she's hiding would just remind her how alone she is.

But when Cav leaves her with a lingering look, the solitude she chose rings hollower than before.

TWENTY-ONE

Lyx

If Lyx wasn't avoiding Cav before, she certainly is now.

Once Cav left the cabin, the storm subsided. It was a cruel joke, like the sea was rocking only to thrust the two of them together. Her mind was still whirling, though, leaving her tossing and turning on the mattress where Cav had been pressed moments before.

Who does he think he is, asking her to be honest? She *is* honest, but when has that ensured anything but her suffering? Asking her to trust him might as well be asking her to carve open her chest and expose the delicate muscle of her heart.

Her fists clench. Cav will never understand that; he's always been willing — *desperate* — to offer up his throat for something foolish. He may enjoy being taught a lesson, but Lyx has learned hers. She knows the price of it. She's still paying for it.

Who gives a shit what Cav expects from her? He can wait

for her "honesty" as long as he'd like, but he'll die holding his breath.

Her indignation lulls her to sleep. Aside from the night after the crow's nest, it's the first time in years that she doesn't dream, doesn't wake, doesn't move. By the time her eyes crack open, the sun is low outside the window. She's slept through nearly the entire day.

She hurries out of bed, ignoring the wet spots left on the floor by Cav's clothing. The *Indulgence* is making another stop tonight, and she needs to get a closer look at where those glass jars are going.

When she ascends the stairs, the crew is milling about the deck, finishing dinner and preparing for the next landing. Thankfully, there's no sign of Cypher. Lyx exhales her relief, leaning back against the railing and staring out across the sea.

It is a beauty artists struggle to replicate. Nothing truly captures its movement, a swirling surface that descends into darkness. That's where it hoards its greatest mysteries, the biggest shipwrecks to the smallest treasures. There was a time when Lyx knew the ocean's secrets. When she could ask it for anything. When she was its confidant, feeling its whims like an instinct, colluding against those who underestimated them. Even now, its power rolls beneath her, a barely-restrained force that can transform in an instant.

She yearns to reach for it, but when she unfurls the tendrils of her mind, there's...nothing. Silence. A drop in a pond that creates no ripples.

Her chest tightens. She turns away.

Cav hasn't noticed her from where he meanders across the deck. His clothes are slightly too tight, borrowed from someone else on the ship, like he'd rather chafe than visit his cabin again.

She wonders if his mind is stuck in the same place as hers. She curls her fingers around the taffrail, throbbing with the

sweet sting of the night before. It's imprinted in her mind —
the feel of her palm against his cheek, the obscene spread of
his knees, the blood and spit glistening on his lips.

The blood that she can see now. His wound has begun to
heal, but there's no mistaking the mark she left on him. It tugs
at the pit of her stomach. His sharp teeth worry that spot on
his lip when he notices her. He looks unsure if he should
approach. When he does, he leaves more space than usual
between them. "Thought you'd be holed up in the cabin
again."

"We're about to make port."

He shakes his head and leans on the railing beside her.
The back of his shirt is so low that she can see the spikes along
his spine, his skin completely covered in scales. "We're not
making port. We're picking people up."

It takes a moment for her to tear her gaze to where he's
pointing. In the water below, two barrels float on their sides.
Out of their holes sprout two upright broomsticks with a sun-
bleached sheet stretched between them. Painted words are
scrawled in red across the fabric.

No Whores!
No Drink!
No Sinners!

A commotion begins on the ship. Crew members call back
and forth, taking their positions and turning the vessel toward
a nearby island. They're 200 yards from land, but they don't
move any closer. It's like the *Indulgence* is curling in on itself,
sails retracting before all the frosted lanterns go out.

The air is so still and quiet that Lyx jumps when there's a
heavy splash into the ocean. "Anchor," Cav murmurs.

After a moment, the clanking chain grinds to a halt. The
Indulgence drifts in place.

Lyx peers through the dusk. On the island, there's no sign of a port. No houses along the beach. No torches in the town center. Not even a candle in a window. The island seems completely isolated, save for a line of barbed barriers along the coast. Tall wooden fencing wraps around the island, plastered with signs that match the one they passed.

Something moves on the coast. Lyx lifts a hand over her eyes to see better. A section of wooden boards breaks away from the fence. It slams to the ground, covered by a large shape that appears from the forest. It looks like a giant grab scuttling along the beach, but when the shell topples into the water, she realizes it's a rowboat carried by half a dozen people making their escape.

On the far side of the island, torches flare to life, casting light over a much bigger group. Even from this distance, Lyx can tell they're angry, shouting and sprinting toward the small boat.

Everyone is dressed in the same cultish robes, a bland shade of beige that stands out against the dark. The escapees clamber through the shallows, hoisting and shoving each other inside their dinghy. The second group descends, torches bobbing when they wade into the water. One man snags the collar of a rower, but the others kick him away, digging in their oars and paddling with all their might.

A round of cheers swells on the *Indulgence*. Music kicks up on the forecastle, and the lanterns flare to life again. The rowers shout and wave as they draw closer, tying their boat to the ship before they climb the ladder to come aboard.

It's a celebration. Everyone on the *Indulgence* welcomes them, but Lyx's mouth fills with a sour taste. Why does their triumph feel like her defeat? Her throat aches.

The ship begins to move again. The newcomers are sweaty and panting and smiling. They've made it. They've escaped their torment and found the open arms of the

Indulgence.

Lyx feels hot with an envy she can't explain. "Do they owe you something now? For aiding their escape?"

"No," Cav says carefully. "We just give them a ride to the next port. Give them a place to start over that isn't so...controlling."

Lyx's teeth scrape the inside of her cheek. Everything inside her is volatile, like a wick has been lit, but she doesn't know where it begins or ends. Why is she full of such resentment?

Maybe because all they had to do was wait for their rescuer to arrive, and now, they're free. No strings attached. She can't imagine that. When she needed help the most, who was there for her? Only Tidus, prepared to snap a lock around her throat. When she leaves this ship, he will still be the only one there. There is no savior. No one to wipe her slate clean.

For the briefest moment, her mind wanders into places it shouldn't. What would have happened if the *Indulgence* had found her instead? If Cav had returned to her? If she'd spent the last two years with him instead of trapped under Tidus's control?

There's no point in wondering. That understanding numbs her until she can breathe again. The *Indulgence* did not appear to her. Cav did not return. Tidus has her song. This is her reality.

When she surfaces from her thoughts, Cav is still watching her. His eyes pour into her like he wishes he could do the same, diving past the scales and scars until he reaches the bottom. She isn't sure what he'd find. She isn't sure what she'd want him to see.

The tension from last night still hangs between them. She shouldn't feel it. She shouldn't feel *anything*, but simply being in Cav's presence stirs up emotions she still doesn't know how to name. She tilts her chin toward the newcomers. "Do you entertain them? Now that they're free to do as they please?"

By now, the group is coming down from the thrill. A few of them are giddy with shock. Another looks sick, but all of them are being distracted by the crew passing out mugs and offering fresh clothing.

Cav settles back against the taffrail. "Usually, I do, but lately, I think I've lost my touch."

She can't help but laugh, despite herself. There is no world in which Cav is not infuriatingly, disarmingly charming. "Maybe you just need someone who can properly appreciate it."

The words feel strange in her mouth. Almost...complimentary. Her throat aches in a way wholly different than she's used to.

Cav's lip quirks, but the smile doesn't reach his eyes. "Is this your way of getting rid of me?"

His body is warm beside her. She would barely have to move to touch him. If she shifted closer and stretched her fingers, she could feel him under her like the night before. She could reach out and find him waiting there.

But that is not a thought she should entertain. She isn't here for him. She is here to ruin whatever peace he has. Maybe that's why her mouth gets so reckless. Who cares what she says? In a few days, none of this will matter. She'll have her song, and she'll be on her own again.

"I want to watch you work." When she meets his eyes, her stomach clenches. His gaze is so potent that she has to brace against the railing. "I want to see what it could be like. If someone let themself be captivated by you."

Their bodies are closer now, unable to resist whatever force pulls them together. This is dangerous territory. She's saying things she shouldn't, but her mind refuses the consequences. She won't be here for the aftermath. Chaos spills into her, but it's not as good as the way he looks at her.

When he speaks, she sees fire crackling in the back of his throat. "If you will it."

TWENTY-TWO

Lyx

It's like Cav is slipping into a different skin, the muscles in his back shifting as he sways through the crowd. There's something luminous about him. Even in the midst of distress, a wave of heads follows him. It's almost like *he's* the siren with a silent song to lure everyone toward him.

He sets his sights on a newcomer with hawkish features and brilliant green plumage. It's no surprise the guest is immediately hooked. Cav's smile is lazy, face softening with heat, and Lyx feels a pang of recognition. It's almost like the way Cav looks at her, if not quite the same. When Cav works, there's a wall behind his gaze, a practiced flow to his motions and a mask thin enough to separate him from his audience.

With Lyx, there's none of that.

That doesn't make it any less powerful. She's suddenly aware of the lack of him. Her ears ring without his rambling voice, and the air cools, like a cloud has passed over the sunny spot she was basking in. But it's night. There is no sun or warmth or light; there's only Cav's attention.

Even as he gives it to someone else, she knows she's in the corner of his eye. He keeps his body angled so that she can always see his face. She takes in the line of his jaw when he speaks, the curve of his lip when he smiles, the duck of his head when he leans in to listen.

Has no one ever done anything just to see you enjoy it?

It burns inside her the same way slapping him did. It wasn't the action itself that got to her; it was everything else. The certainty with which he read her, the complete submission, the wild look in his eyes growing with the more pain she inflicted.

It's in her nature to destroy, but never has someone enjoyed it. Never has someone asked for more. Never has there been a balance. Her victims always went down too easily or not at all, but Cav hangs in perfect equilibrium.

Someone knocks into her elbow. "Sorry," Colt mutters, jostling an armful of glass jars filled with clippings. "Excuse me." He continues through the crowd, his head bobbing down the stairs and descending below deck.

It's exactly what she's been looking for, but her feet don't follow right away. She's drawn back to Cav. He shines in the middle of the crowd, holding the back of one guest's head while he pours a drink into their mouth. The others cheer. When the creature stands up again, Lyx can practically see the hearts in their eyes.

What if she stayed here? It surprises her that she wasn't lying when she spoke to Cav. She does want to watch him work. She wants to watch *him* doing anything, but she has a job to do. Tidus's patience is wearing thin.

Tearing her eyes from Cav, she squeezes through the crew and down the stairs. Fortunately, the hatchway is empty. Sounds fall away as she slinks deeper into the ship, hurrying past the sleeping cabins to find Colt. The light from his lantern shows he's already halfway down the length of the ship, turning behind a stack of barrels and disappearing from sight.

Lyx ducks under beams to weave her way after him, but there's no sign of Colt, only curving stairs and echoing footsteps descending deeper. When she takes the first step, the boards creak under her. She freezes, but Colt's footfalls continue to fade away.

With one hand on the railing, Lyx follows the spiral. If someone comes down after her, if they round the corner, she'll be caught. Her pulse throbs in her ears. She holds her breath until she reaches the bottom.

A dank, musty scent hits her nose. There's only one lantern hanging on the wall, shedding only enough light that she can make out shelves and crates throughout the open space. She's been here before during her searches, inspecting sacks of beans and bags of salt to no avail.

She cranes her neck out of the staircase. Colt is nowhere in sight. Carefully, she steps down to the floor and picks her way through the supplies. Some of them have been used since she was last here, but that's not surprising. She walks the length of the room, scanning for something she must have missed. There is no other set of stairs, no doors along the wall, nowhere Colt could have reached before she followed him.

Where could he have gone?

Something shatters behind her. She whips toward the sound, ducking behind a nearby shelf. A muffled voice curses, but she can't see anyone. Footsteps grow louder, and she waits for someone to appear on the stairs, but instead, the wall next to them swings open.

Colt exits, taking the curved stairs two at a time toward the floor above. The door he'd come through swings shut. Lyx feels along the wall to make her way back and slams her shin against a crate. She bites her tongue, but she has to hurry.

Who knows how long Colt will be gone?

Back at the staircase, she nearly misses the hidden room again. It's tucked beneath the stairs, made of the same timber as the walls. There is no handle, only a tiny keyhole blended into the knot of the wood. Silently, she approaches, pressing her palm to the door and easing it open.

The bright light makes her squint. Another set of stairs leads down into a room full of lanterns, the ceiling so low that it blocks most of her sightline. From this angle, all she can really see is the nearest corner.

She sinks down to see more of the room. Shelves line the walls, full of glass jars holding their collections from the deck. Across the room is a square hole in the wall framing a rope that reaches up into the ship. When the ship rocks, a pile of shattered glass on the floor shifts closer to the table at the center.

A tattooed arm reaches across it. Lyx chokes on a gasp, but Cypher keeps her back to the door and bends over the workspace. Past Cypher's body, she can make out assorted metal instruments scattered across the table. Next to them is a singular glass jar and something else sitting directly in front of Cypher.

With a pair of long tweezers, Cypher reaches into the jar to pluck out a green feather and carries it delicately to the object in front of her. Lyx leans in closer, pressing one hand to the top of the stairs for balance.

Cypher doesn't notice. She adjusts the jagged, swooping shape in front of her, and when she shifts to the side, Lyx can tell she's working on an oyster. Its shell is a roughened gray, but Cypher is more interested in what's beneath. She opens the shell just enough to see inside before she tucks the feather into the oyster's flesh and seals the mollusk shut again.

The ship jostles, making the floorboards creak and groan. Cypher calls over her shoulder. "Did you find the broom?"

Lyx nearly slams her fingers in the door when she scrambles backwards. Overhead, Colt's footfalls begin to descend the spiral stairs. Lyx lets the door fall closed and clambers over the nearest supplies so she can sink deeper into the room.

Colt is whistling when he appears, using his broom to push open the door under the stairs. There's a brief conversation before Cypher appears in the hidden doorway. She takes a few steps into the room, scanning the staircase and shelves of supplies with narrowed eyes.

Lyx covers her mouth to hide her breathing. She swears she can feel Cypher's eyes on her, but she doesn't move.

After a long moment, Cypher ducks back into the room and clicks the lock behind her.

TWENTY-THREE

Cav

At some point while Cav worked, Lyx disappeared.

She can't have been gone long. Cav kept his attention on his clients, but Lyx was always in his periphery. When a burly man brushed his hand against Cav's tail, Cav smirked toward Lyx, but she wasn't there anymore.

Cav scans the rest of the deck, but there's no sign of her. His chest deflates. He should have known better; it's clear Lyx is bound and determined not to give him anything, but he thought things were shifting. He could have sworn they were *this close* tonight.

I want to see what it could be like. If someone let themself be captivated by you.

He tongues the wound on his lip. They were *this close* the night before, too, when she spit in his mouth and put her fingers down his throat until he gagged.

And Cav kept his word. He denied her. It's almost a

matter of pride, but Cav has never been attached to his ego. Hell, he was on his knees asking Lyx to slap him. If anything, what's holding him back is desire. Desire for more — to know more, to share more, to do more than fuck her through the glory hole in the wall she's built between them.

Most would call him foolish. *Lyx* would call him foolish, but he enjoys the journey as much as where he wants to end up. It's like his mind has finally been roused from a deep sleep. Every moment with Lyx is an adventure, and if nothing else comes from it, he can at least hold onto that.

He wanders past the hatchway and sees Lyx's cabin door ajar. Odd. Since she arrived, she's been keeping herself sealed away behind it. He descends and raps his knuckles against the wood, prepared for Lyx to run him off. There's no sound from within. After a moment, he presses against the door and opens the cabin...but there's no Lyx.

His brow furrows. He walks down the corridor to ask the other crew members if they've seen her, but no one has. That doesn't surprise him. Lyx isn't the type to congregate, but where could she be? It would be less concerning if Cypher wasn't missing, too. Cav prays they didn't finally come to blows, but before he can check the galley for Lyx, he's pulled back into preparing hammocks for the newcomers to sleep. By the time he turns in for the night, Lyx's cabin door is shut again.

The next day is a whirlwind. They settle their guests in the next port and put out some errant embers that jumped from the stove. Cav hikes his brows toward Cypher. *See?* But she just tugs down her bandana to show him her tattoo is still there.

At least there's sign of life from Lyx. Her washed clothing hangs on one of the clotheslines. Cav tries not to think about them, but his mind always circles back to the distraction. He gets halfway through three different tasks before he realizes he hasn't finished any of them.

Exhausted, he collapses into his hammock. The *Indulgence* has been at sea for hours. The sky has long gone dark, leaving only the necessary crew on deck. Cav lost track of time, as usual. He should be sleeping, but he's never been good at following the cycle of the sun. His mind keeps whirring long after the moon shows itself.

His hammock sways while he stares up at the pinpricks of stars. The symphony of the deck might lull him to sleep if he didn't notice every single instrument. He picks them out one by one: idle chatter, sloshing waves, metal bumping against wood...

And bare feet padding across the deck.

A shadow passes over his face. He pushes up to peer over the side of the hammock and finds Lyx lingering by the railing, smoothing her hand over one of the clam inlays. She traces the details, curling her fingernails beneath it to pry it out of the wood.

Cav's head tilts. "What are you doing?"

Surprise streaks across her face. She steps away from the taffrail, and the back of her knees collide with the hammock to send her stumbling. She lands ass-first in Cav's lap, her head swinging back until both of them nearly topple. He pulls her down to keep them from falling, tangling their legs in the fabric while they curse and jostle for space.

"Why are you so jumpy?" he grunts. Her elbow digs into his ribs. "You're allowed to be on the deck, you know. The only one keeping you confined to that room is you."

Lyx wriggles to put distance between them, but that forces her onto her back. Her long skirt wraps around her legs, and Cav rolls onto his side to settle the swell of her hips between his knees.

When Lyx looks at him, he realizes how close her face is. Her skin glows in the dark, casting faint bioluminescence across her cheeks. It shines onto him too, darkening his scales in the blue light. Now that the commotion has subsided, it's quiet. Only their labored breathing rises above everything else. The hammock envelopes them both and sways gently on the waves.

Cav doesn't want to move. This moment with Lyx feels like a butterfly has chosen him, and the slightest movement might scare her away, but he's never been good at stillness. His fingers twitch between them, brushing the skin of her thigh. Her scales prickle, but she doesn't pull away.

It's tempting to follow that reaction, to see how else her body responds to him, but he tries to keep his head on straight. "Thought you wanted to watch me work."

Her pupils are wide in the dark, so focused on the way his mouth moves that it takes a moment for her to realize he's waiting for her response.

"Last night," he murmurs. "You disappeared."

The proximity must be clouding her mind, too. It's like she can't remember what she's supposed to be doing, leaving her in a daze "You were watching me?"

"I'm always watching you." For a moment, he regrets the words. A sentiment like that will make her recoil; it's too much, too jarring, but her eyes lock onto his. It heats him from his very core, so powerful he forgets all subtlety. "What are you hiding?"

Lyx's expression sharpens like a switchblade. It's the same question he's been asking since she came aboard, but her reaction is different this time. Cav has the same awareness that he did in the grotto. Lyx could kill him anytime she chooses; she is more dangerous than he lets himself believe.

None of that makes him want her any less. In fact, walking this delicate tightrope flames his desire. He likes knowing Lyx could destroy him, but she hasn't. That fuels some twisted part of him, the same part that has been pining after her for years. A smarter person would resist, but why should Cav listen to his head? It's never been able to keep up with him. His impulses may get him into trouble, but they always get him out of it, too.

Lyx shifts closer in the hammock, one strap of her dress slipping off her shoulder. "It's almost been three days." Her lashes lower as she drags her skirt higher on her legs. "Maybe we should have another go at your experiment."

It's clear her sudden interest is a diversion, but that doesn't dampen the effect. Cav's gaze clings to her mouth, hand wandering the cool skin of her leg. "Does this usually work?" he breathes.

She's so close that he can feel her teeth digging into her lip, her coy fingers toying with the hem of his shirt. "Does what work?"

"Distraction," he murmurs. The movement brushes his mouth against hers. "Does that usually throw people off?"

When she blushes, her cheeks glow brighter. "*Yes.*" She draws the word out, her eyes narrowing, but knowing he's caught onto her doesn't stop her ministrations. The tips of her fingers dip beneath his waistband. She sounds almost thoughtful. "You're softer here."

His stomach tenses as she wanders his abdomen. Beneath his navel, the patch of scales is like leather, growing smoother the lower she goes. Lyx teases with her touch, watching his face before she slips her palm against him.

He makes a sound in the back of his throat. Lyx quirks a brow, taking her time outlining the shape of each scale, lost in exploration. A shaky breath escapes him. It's both thrilling and soothing to be under her control, like the night she had him on his knees in her cabin.

Then she takes the tip of one scale and rubs it gently between her fingers.

Cav shudders.

Her lips curl into a smile. "More sensitive, too."

He gives a wheezing laugh, tracing the curve of her hip. He draws his thumb across the burn scar before he moves onto the smattering of her scales, teasing beneath one with the tip of his claw.

Her nails scrape his stomach.

"Like yours?" he asks.

Their eyes lock, breathing heavy, hands roaming each other. He rocks against her hand every time she tugs one of his scales. When he touches hers, she shivers, and his chest glows through his shirt.

But his hand doesn't drift any lower. He doesn't push further, doesn't nestle between her legs, doesn't move this along at all.

Eventually, she catches on. He hasn't changed his mind. He still won't cross that line with her. Minutes of delicious torture leave them both with wet lips and glassy eyes. When she works her hand lower, he stops her, encircling her wrist and bringing it to his face.

Her hand fits perfectly against his cheek. Of course it does; they both remember, her fingers flexing like she's back in the cabin again. This time, there is no slapping, just the slow turn of his mouth into her palm.

She trembles when she pulls back. If she weren't a siren, maybe he could name the emotions on her face. Frustration. Fear. Something delicate enough to break.

She pushes past whatever it was, twirling the laces of his shirt. He may be standing his ground, but so is she. Her voice maintains its sultry sheen, but he can hear the spike of irritation beneath it. "You all but fucked me in the crow's nest already. Why bother holding back now?"

TWENTY-FOUR

Lyx

When Lyx pools her dress at the tops of her thighs, Cav doesn't look down. Even with her body pressed against him, he keeps watching her expression, like *that's* what he wants to disrobe. Conspiratorially, he leans closer and lowers his voice. "I could ask you the same thing. Why are *you* holding back?"

Something real. Something honest.

She hasn't forgotten what Cav insists on, but Great Abyss, she didn't think he'd actually cling to it. Why bother resisting her when she's baring herself right in front of him? It doesn't matter. She doesn't care. With a shrug, she lowers her hand between her legs. "Fine. If you don't want it..."

Her fingers are slick immediately. She would have gasped if she weren't so proud, the stinging sensation of her own desire a sour reminder that this is all because of him. She hates what he's done to her; she hates even more that he won't finish her off.

Of course, her motions don't inspire Cav. He doesn't move, but he does watch her. She tries her best to entice him, letting her lips part when she circles a finger against her clit. It's a relief from the ache, but the look in Cav's eyes is more potent, making her toes curl.

Damn him to the Depths.

What started as a way to distract him has taken on a life of its own. She can hardly remember why she came on the deck at all when his body is pressed against her, an invitation she refuses to accept. Why walk through the front door when you can break in the back? She knows exactly how to get what she wants; she just can't stand the thought of giving into him.

But Cav isn't playing by her rules. Lyx has set a smooth rhythm against her clit, but her hand stutters aside when Cav reaches between her legs. "I *do* want it," he whispers. She makes a shameful noise when he eases her skirt out of the way. "But if I've touched you nearly every way a person can, why wasn't that enough? Why are you here asking for more?"

It's pathetic how her hips buck, made worse when Cav doesn't touch her. He doesn't delve inside her. He doesn't even brush her clit. Instead, he flattens his palm and his fingers, making one solid plane.

His breath is warm against her cheek. "Might as well be driftwood. Isn't that what you said?"

The memory of the crow's nest sinks its teeth into her. Fuck him. Fuck this abstinence, like he's teaching her a lesson. Like he wants her hungry enough to give in. He's not starving every part of her, just one.

Her skin glows bright from it, casting blue light across his face. If someone looks into this hammock, they'll see exactly what the two of them are doing. That only makes it hotter. If he thinks she's too embarrassed to use him, he'd better think again. She presses his hand against her, swirling her hips until the motion is wet and slippery. She works her clit against the ridges of his fingers, gripping the front of his shirt while the hammock sways beneath them.

It's getting to him. No matter how he tries to hide, his eyes melt over her, but he won't give in that easily. Not when he has her right where he wants her. Just to be cruel, he pulls back his hand to make her chase it.

She glares at him.

A mocking pout graces his lips. "Do you need *me* to share something honest first? Is that what it is?"

His palm heats between her legs. The sudden warmth makes her curse and bury her teeth against his shoulder.

"Let's see, then…" With a smile, he rests his head against hers, completely unmoved by what they're doing. "I don't need the experiment as an excuse; I would do this with you no matter what. You already know that, don't you?" He hums. "But I don't just want more of this. I want more *than* this. More than just touching you. More than fucking."

Lyx keeps dragging against his hand, her fingernails digging into his arms for leverage. She can't think about what that means, but Cav leans down toward her ear to make sure she hears him.

"You want me to tell you the truth about you?" His nose traces the shell of her ear. "I think you're here because you know there's more. That there could *be* more."

She clutches his shirt and clenches her eyes shut. Her hips don't stop moving. All the memories come bubbling up, days and weeks and months she's spent thinking about him. Even when her fantasies were vengeful violence, it was always the two of them: bodies colliding, his throat in her hands, his pulse under hers.

"And you know what else?" His laughter is raspy with lust, like he can't quite believe he's saying this. "If you are hiding something, I don't think I'd care."

Lyx bites her lip to keep from groaning. It's not true. If he knew what she was doing on this ship, it would matter, but she can't stop the surge of arousal at his words.

His other hand curls in her hair. "Now tell me something real."

She scoffs, but it turns into a shiver that runs through her entire body. "You can't handle it."

"Try me."

Every part of her bares down, like her secrets might slip out if she doesn't hold onto them. Her teeth grit as she moves against him. Why is he so intent to get this from her? He doesn't know how dangerous it is. Anything she tells him would send him running. Her most mild thoughts involve a frantic, obsessive urge to consume him.

Maybe that's why she *should* tell him. So he'll stop asking for it. So it will kill his foolish infatuation. So she won't be tempted to show him everything else she's hiding.

His smile stretches against her forehead. "I knew I shouldn't ask." It's like he's speaking to himself, his voice tinged with sadness. His claws retract. "I know you don't want to give me anything, but I can't help myself."

Then he sinks a finger inside her, and she mewls in her throat. Finally, *finally*, he's given her more than the flat of his hand. His finger curls against that spot inside her, easing her into the deep pressure that threatens to unravel her.

She wants to sob. He adds another finger, never slowing the circle of his palm against her clit. Urgency builds in her gut. She tries to outrun it, to keep pace, but her movements are sloppy and hopeless. Her teeth drag against his neck, rewarded with pinpricks of blood that drive every other thought from her head. "I want to eat you alive."

Cav stills. It takes a moment for Lyx to realize she's spoken, that this is not one of the fantasies she consoled herself with. She hovers in this fuzzy place between lust and reality, the *need* in her so strong it overpowers everything else.

In a few days, none of this will matter.

Cav strokes deep inside her again. "What else?"

Her head spins. She's told him something that would horrify anyone else, and he's asking for more?

He doesn't believe her. That's what it is. He thinks it's a metaphor, an exaggeration, anything but the truth. He wouldn't continue this if he knew, but her desire has pulled as tight as a sail line in a hurricane. Now that she's started, she can't stop. She wants more. She wants *him*.

"I want to scrape off your skin with my teeth." Her mouth waters at the thought. "I want to pry your scales away and drag my tongue underneath."

She can practically taste it. She knows how his blood feels on her tongue, but she doesn't want just a drop. She wants to suck it from his wounds, to feel it flow over her tongue, to make her mouth messy with it. "I want to hold your head underwater. I want to guzzle every bubble that escapes from your mouth."

She wants to destroy him. She wants to eat him, drown him, *kill him*, because what else could these thoughts mean? What else could a siren want?

Cav's motions grow more deliberate between her legs, honed exactly where Lyx wants him. She rakes her fingernails down his chest and laves her tongue over the scratches she leaves behind. When she digs her heel into the back of his thigh, he moans.

"I want to hold you on my tongue," she pants. "I want to brand you with my teeth. I want to swallow you piece by piece."

Every word digs a trench through her. Her thighs clench around his hand, and when he slides a third finger inside, her vision blurs.

"Tell me more," he pleads.

"I want you to cry from how good it hurts." Her voice is so strung out that she barely recognizes it. The world spins around her. She presses her forehead to his, seeking something to hold onto before she breaks. "I want to devour you. I want to ruin you. I want to be the last thing you see."

Her white-hot desperation combusts. He drinks the sounds from her mouth, their lips smearing hot and wanton against each other. Her orgasm flutters around his fingers, but he doesn't withdraw, even when her acid has surely begun to rub him raw. Their glowing skin casts a haze around them, as hot and humid as the truth she's finally given him.

TWENTY-FIVE

Lyx

Lyx has to get her head on straight. She leaves Cav in the hammock, shuttering herself in the cabin and leaning back against the door. What was she thinking? She'd gone on the deck to search for more clues, yet one moment with Cav made her forget what she's meant to be doing. He leaves her mind warm and heady, clouded with seafoam, ready to drift away and dissolve.

One thought solidifies. She carries it to the bed and sinks down on the mattress before she can bear to look at it. Cav didn't run when she told him the truth. He didn't cower from the wicked desires she has. Her vision blurs until all she can see is Cav beneath her, groaning and arching against her mouth, letting her sink her teeth into his flesh again and again.

Heat coils between her legs. *No.* She clenches her eyes shut, but the images of Cav don't stop whirring past. She cannot be distracted by some meaningless fantasy. It is not the reason she's here.

The pain in her throat grows stronger than anything else. When she swallows, it's raw and chafed, squeezing in search of something that's no longer there. She clings to that feeling, the reminder of exactly what she's working toward. Exactly what she has to lose. *That* is the only truth that matters. It was easy for Cav to play along in the heat of the moment, but that doesn't make it real. He could not withstand her undivided attention. He could not stomach the reality of what she is.

It stings like a misplaced tentacle, but she refuses to dwell on it. The day after tomorrow, the *Indulgence* will arrive at the next island, and she has no doubt Tidus will be waiting. She has to find an answer for him, something better than the scattered puzzle pieces she has.

Fingernail clippings. Oyster shells. A secret room.

A room that Lyx tried breaking into. Before she'd fallen into Cav's hammock, she'd hidden in the belly of the ship, watching the door in the wall. Once Cypher locked the door and returned upstairs, Lyx tried her best to get in. She searched sacks of dried beans and tins of coffee for an extra key, but there was nothing. When she rammed her shoulder against the door, it didn't budge. She has to look somewhere else, and there's only one place she hasn't checked.

The next morning, she stays in her cabin, avoiding Cav and any further diversions he might create. It's not until night has fallen that she prepares to leave. The sound of footsteps dwindles as crew members retire to their cabins. She waits for the lantern light to fade, for the idle chatter to be replaced by snores, for the ruckus on the deck to settle. Only then does she slip out of her cabin.

It's hours after midnight, far later than the night before. She wears a hooded cloak and long trousers to dampen the glow of her skin. Carefully, she creeps through the dark toward the hatchway and starts up the stairs. On the third step, the wood creaks. She freezes, peering between the slats toward the dark cabins.

Something rustles. Her scales prickle when a shadow moves in one of the rooms, but it rolls onto its other side and settles. She counts a full sixty seconds before she climbs the rest of the stairs and peeks out onto the deck.

The first thing she sees is Cav's hammock. His tail dangles over the side, swaying and twitching dreamily. Memories pour into her, but she shoves them aside to focus on the rest of the deck. It's a good night for what she needs to do. The sound of the ocean swells, and the sky is thick with clouds that blot out the moon. A handful of crew members are stationed up here. Lyx scans their faces. She can hardly make out their features, save for the opals of Heathen's eyes gleaming from the helm.

They swivel toward Lyx. Her breath catches, and she fights the urge to shrink back, tensing until her muscles burn for reprieve. She gives them none. After a long moment, Heathen rotates in the other direction.

Lyx exhales before she crawls onto the deck. It gives her a better view, but she's exposed, slipping along the wall to duck behind a barrel.

The railing sits above her. It's carved like all the others, a mollusk set into swirling patterns. Last night, she'd thought perhaps Heathen's secrets were hidden there, but she could deduce nothing from it. It was wooden, like everything else. Stubbornly, Lyx reaches for it and tries to wedge the clam out again.

Someone shouts. Lyx jerks her hand back, bracing to be hauled into the open, but Heathen just calls back a reply. A round of chuckles rises from the group. Lyx peers over the top of the barrel, catching Heathen engrossed in conversation before Lyx darts for the next cover.

She makes her way from bow to stern, slinking through the shadows until she reaches the captain's quarters. From this angle, she's nearly hidden by the awning that hangs overhead. It provides perfect cover for her to slide along the ground, lifting on her knees to press her ear to the glass windows.

There's no sound from inside. She tries the locked handle, already reaching into her hair for two pins. Her time with pirates has given her this skill, if nothing else. She bends the pins with her teeth and cuts a fervent glance down the deck. When no one appears, she eases the bent pins into the lock and feels for every miniscule *click*.

The boat creaks. Her heart pounds, but she forces herself to steady, timing her movements with the roll of the ocean.

Finally, the lock clicks open. She doesn't waste any time, tucking the pins into her pocket and sliding through the open door.

Heathen's room looks exactly as Lyx remembers. Her bed is tucked into the port side wall, and on the other, bookshelves surround the ornamental ship wheel. It's a little on-the-nose, but Heathen doesn't seem the type to care for decoration. In fact, there's still nothing Lyx can see that give her any clues about the captain.

She crosses to the desk at the back of the room. In the drawers, she uncovers papers, books, and coins. There are ship logs, manifests, and professional documents in pristine condition, but underneath everything else is a crumpled piece of parchment.

Lyx pulls it out and flattens it against her knee. It's a letter addressed to Heathen, signed by some name Lyx doesn't recognize. The paper smells sweet with the faintest hint of perfume. Unlike the other documents, this one is well-worn with smudges along the edges, like someone has held it more often than not.

Lyx isn't sure why. The letter is short, so vague that it's cryptic.

The jewels are working exactly as intended. You continue to impress. I'll have more shells for you at the end of the month.

Lyx flips through the papers again, but there's no other mention of "jewels." She arranges everything back into the drawer and moves onto the others, but all of them are locked tight. Lyx huffs. No doubt there's something she could use in there, but Heathen would never be so careless to leave the key here. They probably keep it on them at all times. Maybe she could pick this lock, too.

The floor creaks near the doorway. Lyx sinks behind the desk, leaning out with one eye to scan the entranceway. Was that sound of the ship groaning, or is someone headed in here?

No shadows pass over the curtains. After a moment, Lyx pushes to her feet. She's been here too long already. She needs to wrap this up. She crosses to the bookshelf. This is where Heathen retrieved the jar for Lyx's scales, but all the glasses here are empty. She scans the titles of the books and pulls on the spines of the particularly mundane. Heathen seems like the type to have a secret passageway, but no matter what Lyx tries, nothing happens.

"*Dammit!*" Frustration rises in her. Something is happening on this ship. She *knows* it is. She will not leave empty-handed.

She shuts her eyes and tries to remember everything she saw in the room downstairs. Glass jars. Oysters. Metal tools. A table, shelves, and —

A hole in the wall.

Her eyes fly open. That hole looked empty, except for the

rope hanging down through it. A rope very similar to the one before Lyx now. She'd thought it was just a piece of décor, but what if it's more?

She scans the floor and retraces her steps through the belly of the ship. If she's correct, the hole in the wall should be a few levels below her, with a rope stretching upwards.

She follows the curving rope on the wall. It trails around the shelves, a decorative outline that leads back to the mounted wheel. Lyx presses close to the wall to peer behind it. There, the rope winds around the axle before it disappears through a small hole in the wall.

Her fingers close around one of the spokes. The wheel turns for a second before it catches. Furtively, she feels along the back for something keeping it in place. At the very top, she finds a metal hook. It takes a few tries, but she unlatches it and pulls on one of the handles.

The wheel begins to turn.

With some effort, Lyx rotates the wheel, watching more of the rope wind around the spindle. Eventually, something settles behind the wall. The wheel stops moving.

She latches the wheel back into place, but nothing reveals itself. No door opens. Something is right on the other side of this wall, but Lyx can't quite reach it. Biting the inside of her cheek, she presses her palms against the wheel and wallpaper until a section gives way.

She traces the outline. Something large and square has been cut out, with the wallpaper aligned to cover it. On one side, Lyx finds a divot so small she can barely curl her finger into it, but when she pulls, it slides open.

She squints against the light inside the dumbwaiter. It looks like a piece of the moon, but when Lyx's eyes adjust, she realizes it isn't one mass. It's a collection of pearls of all shapes and sizes emitting beautiful light.

Is this what the oysters are for? That seems...familiar. Lyx plumbs her memories until she lands on one of Mollo. Lyx's jaw clenches. She was pissed at Mollo that day, too, screaming at her for destroying Lyx's room again.

Mollo hadn't even cared, floating flippantly through the water. "You know, oysters have a way of dealing with that. If something sneaks inside that they don't want, they trap it forever. They roll it up inside a pearly prison." Mollo smirked. "Maybe you should try it."

Lyx plucks up one of the pearls. Despite its smooth luminance, it's easy to see the imperfections of its form. In fact, all of the pearls are misshapen, dented or oblong or grown together. The sheer amount of them is impressive, but they can't be worth any money like this.

So what is Heathen doing with them?

Lyx sets the pearl back into place, but another one tumbles off the pile. She scrambles to catch it before it hits the floor, clamping it between her palms and lifting it back toward the others. But this pearl catches her eye. The color is a milky blue, an iridescent sheen with hints of purple and pink. It's shaped like a bell, large and round like —

The light from the pearl reflects off of Lyx's scales. They shimmer in sync, like they're rippling into each other.

Lyx sucks in a breath. This pearl is from *her*.

Overhead, someone crosses the floor. Lyx nearly drops the pearl again, stuffing it into her pocket as she shoves the dumbwaiter closed.

Someone moves down the stairs outside. Lyx rushes to the door and pulls back the edge of a curtain. Two of the crew members pass in front of the captain's quarters, lingering while they chat.

Lyx tries to keep her breathing even. She has to get out of here. If Heathen comes down while the crew are outside, Lyx is absolutely fucked.

Mercifully, the crew members meander away. Lyx takes a

moment to steel herself before she slips out the door and ducks behind a cluster of barrels.

Her heart thuds. She needs to distance herself. If anything is amiss in the captain's quarters, she can't be nearby. Pressing her back to the wall, she edges down the ship, too high on adrenaline to stay in one place for long.

Thank the Abyss it doesn't backfire. She's not sure she even takes a full breath until she makes it back to Cav. Her legs wobble, forcing her to lean against the railing. She shouldn't stop here. The hatchway is a few yards away, and she can be back in her cabin, free of danger. But when she pushes back her hood, she can see over the edge of Cav's hammock.

He's still sleeping. His tail is still now, draped over his body and curled against his chin. His lips are parted above it, eyelashes so dark where they rest against his cheek.

Her chest tightens. This is how he looked in the grotto. Peaceful. Trusting. As if she couldn't kill him without a second thought. In the years since then, *this* is what she hated to remember most: his softness. When all she wanted to feel was anger and vengeance, this image would come back to her. It reminded her of all the other things he made her feel. It reminded her of the way he looked when she pushed him away in that boat.

"What are you doing up here?"

Lyx whirls toward the voice. Of course Cypher is prowling the deck, scanning Lyx for a punishable offense.

Lyx resists the urge to dig into her pocket. Cypher doesn't know anything. She *won't* know anything. Lyx swallows her uncertainty. "Didn't realize I was sequestered to my cabin."

"It's the dead of night."

They watch each other, waiting for the other to slip. The pearl is a weight in Lyx's pocket, and she prays the fabric of her cloak is enough to block out its light.

Cypher's eyes narrow, finally registering Lyx's attire. "What are you wearing?"

Lyx's nails dig into her palm. She needs an excuse. Her words spill clumsily. "I'm here to fuck Cav."

Cypher recoils. Lyx presses further.

"We discussed a certain — scene for his experiment. It kept me up all night. I was too impatient to wait for our next meeting." It's surprisingly easy to sink into this role. She tosses her hair off her shoulder and braces a hand on her hip. "Fortunately, he's asleep, or I would have made a desperate fool of myself."

Cypher looks like she wants to spit out a bad taste, but her mouth twists skeptically.

Lyx lifts a brow. "Would you like specifics of what we were planning, or may I go?"

Cypher's head jerks to shake the thought away. She makes no move to stop Lyx as she descends the stairs, and when she reaches the bottom, she gives Cypher a snarky wave.

TWENTY-SIX

Lyx

The pearl is heavy in Lyx's pocket. No matter how small it is, it weighs her down, like it could sink her and the rest of the *Indulgence* to the bottom of the ocean.

She's never felt guilt. She hardly knows what it means, but that word rises to the surface of her mind like a stream of bubbles. She pops them one by one. There's nothing to feel guilty about. Whatever Tidus does with this pearl is none of her business. All she knows is that it'll get her song back, and it's about time she gets to be selfish. Besides, maybe the pearl is nefarious. Maybe it's trapping people in servitude by collecting pieces of them. Maybe Heathen and Tidus aren't that different.

But they don't feel the same. The tug of Lyx's song stretches and strains across the distance, but with the pearl, Lyx feels nothing. No tie pulling her toward it, no relief at being near it. It has no control over her.

So what is it for?

The *Indulgence* reaches a new port at midday. It's larger than the others, bustling with activity that immediately occupies the crew. Cypher is nowhere to be seen, probably off tormenting someone else. And Cav…

Lyx almost hopes he'll spot her. Foolishly, she wishes that his gaze would land on her, and he would follow her and ruin her plans. It would be good for the chaos, but it isn't to be. Cav is engrossed with Angélique, going over the stock list while crew members pass back and forth in front of them.

Lyx turns her gaze out over the harbor and catches the tail of Tidus's flag fluttering at the far end of the docks. Her chest tightens, but this meeting will get worse the longer she puts it off. Still draped in her cloak from last night, she tugs the hood over her head and squeezes down the gangplank.

It's easy to melt into the disarray. People's eyes follow her until they're distracted by barkers selling tickets, confectioners waving treats, or tavern maids hoisting trays of drinks. The longer Lyx walks, the more the excitement wanes. Bright colors and delicious scents turn to faded paint and the stench of day-old fish. Out here, the only sounds are trollers bargaining for lures and deckhands grunting as they unload shipments. A bird flies overhead. She gets the sudden, uneasy sense that someone is watching her.

She stiffens at the sight of Tidus. He looks worse than a week ago, skin both oozing and flaking when it's ruffled by the breeze. When he catches sight of Lyx, he takes a puff of his cigarette and jerks his chin down an alleyway.

She scans the faces around her. No one pays her much mind, too busy calling to neighbors or pushing carts. Her stomach sinks. She didn't realize she was looking for an excuse. She never enjoys her time with Tidus, but today feels nearly impossible. Still, she straightens her shoulders and ducks down the passage after him.

She weaves through garbage, sidestepping rusted cans and crates of spoiled food. Her sandal splashes through a puddle of rotten juice, and she hikes her skirt to keep from gagging. At the end of the lane, Tidus grins through his smoke and turns another corner.

Lyx grits her teeth. This isn't about being subtle. It's about forcing her to follow him.

She slows her pace. It's the only control she has with Tidus, but when she rounds the corner, he doesn't look irritable. He looks...pleased. His eyes are bright as he flicks away the butt and pushes back an errant strand of her hair. "Look at you."

Her stomach curdles. A calm Tidus is more of a threat than anything, but at least she's close to her song again. That tiny glow in his chest is a small comfort. Lyx tries to steady her breathing, so aware of his finger curling in her hair.

"It's been a while, huh?" His lips turn down into a pout. "The longest I've been without you. I missed you."

She bites her tongue to keep from recoiling. There's an almost-guilty look on his face, one he only pulls out when he fears his normal tactics have gone too far. A week without contact from her must have made him nervous. He's right; she's never been out of his sight for that long, but she can still feel the mark from his hand on her wrist.

Bring me something, or our next conversation won't be so pleasant.

She isn't falling for whatever this is. Nose wrinkling, she eases back enough to slip out from his touch. "Was the piss-stained alleyway our only option?"

His hand hovers in the air before it drops. "Thought it would be good for the chaos...although, you look well-fed."

Her mouth opens, then shuts. What is usually an echoing void in her chest is filled to the brim. Her hunger hasn't gnawed at her in days. It's apparent on her body, too; even under the cover of clouds, her skin sparkles.

That can't be right. For years, she's gotten all her feedings from Tidus, and she even doesn't feel like she's eaten. There's no exhaustion or fatigue or bloating, just...buoyancy. No feeding has ever made her feel like that.

Not that it matters. Tidus is already leaning toward her again. "I know things were tense last time we spoke. You just get me so..." He trails a sharp finger down her jaw, tapping before he shakes his head. "And you know how important this is. For both of us. I need *something*."

There is no apology. Whatever this act is, he's only putting it on until she gives him what he *really* came for. She digs into her pocket and holds out the pearl between her fingers.

Tidus takes it from her. It's only the size of a button, but it gleams. "A pearl?"

"Dozens of them." Lyx's arm drops back to her side, but she doesn't feel lighter. "They're hidden in Heathen's quarters."

Tidus grins. "Clever girl."

It rakes up Lyx's spine. "They're all like that. Misshapen. Discolored."

"Ever heard of quality control?" Tidus scoffs. Still, he keeps turning it in the light. A blemished pearl is the most valuable thing he has — besides Lyx. "What does this have to do with collecting pleasure?"

When Tidus handles the pearl, Lyx feels like she's watching a child with something fragile, something she wants to snatch away before he ruins it. "I'm not sure. There's a hidden room below deck. It must happen there."

The words leave a strange feeling on her tongue. She itches to take them back, but this is what she's supposed to do. Give Tidus what he wants, and get her song. It's an exchange, like everything else.

Tidus rolls the pearl between his fingers before he tucks it greedily away. "See? This is exactly what we need." He wraps a proud arm around her waist to pull her closer. "And all *you* needed was a little encouragement."

Her skin crawls. She braces her palms against his chest. Depths, she'd rather be anywhere but here. Her mind reaches for an escape and fills with soot and cinnamon.

"Listen…" Tidus's voice softens. "I know I pushed you last time, but you can't argue with results. We're *this close* to getting what we need. What *you* need." She wants to pull out of his grip, but he holds her fast and tugs on the neck of his shirt. "And to show you I'm serious…"

Urchins and coral sprout through his skin. Her shell is still embedded, but the area around it is raw and angry. Warily, she leans closer, until she can see the edge of the shell has started to lift. There's a gap between the mess of his chest and the surface of the shell, sticky with pieces of Tidus's skin.

In the midst of it all, her song glows. It knows she's there. It knows they're almost at the end of it. She reaches out her hand —

But Tidus tugs his shirt back into place, grabbing Lyx's hand in his. "It hurts like a bitch to pry it out, but I want you to know I'm serious. I mean it." He squeezes, and she grits her teeth when his shells dig into her. "Help me finish Heathen off, and your song is free. *You're* free."

Free.

Her heart stirs. The word she's dreamed of for years is finally within her grasp, but it doesn't feel the way she thought it would. It's not like shedding scales or unfurling tentacles; it's more like an anchor pulling her down.

Tidus grips her elbows. "Don't get distracted. Ok? Don't lose sight of it."

The sinking feeling doesn't release her. Neither does Tidus. He watches her closely, but she hardens her jaw to keep his prying eyes out. Eventually, he drops her arms and pulls out another cigarette.

"You know, I've been thinking..." Tidus cups a hand around his mouth. When he pulls it away, the end of his cigarette glows bright red. "I bet that cabin boy could get us what we need. What was his name again? Cav?"

Lyx's mouth goes dry. Tidus's eyes cling to her, watching the little flickers on her face while he waits to pounce. She forces a laugh. "Trust me, he doesn't know anything."

Tidus's smile glints like a blade. "He knows his way around your cunt."

A ringing starts in her ears. The alley is suddenly cramped, her skin clammy when the wind whistles past.

Tidus takes a long drag, voice singing with mockery. "Bet he'd fall over himself to give you anything you want — given the right motivation."

Her fingernails dig into her palm. She wants to tell him to stay away. She wants to wrap her hands around his throat and slam his head into the wall — but she can't do anything. A reaction will stoke Tidus's interest. It'll prove him right.

She swallows and prays it leeches the tension from her body. "*Don't bother with him,*" she murmurs. Her throat is like a balled fist desperately trying to unfurl. "*He's of no interest to you.*"

Beneath Tidus's shirt, the shell burns with light. It's so bright that they both squint before Tidus scowls. "It's been doing that since you joined that ship. Like it wants something."

He looks at her expectantly, but she doesn't have an answer. She has no idea what that radiance means. All she knows is she has to get away from here. "It wants the same thing I do — to finish this and get off that ship."

Smoke coils from his lips like a snake. "Good. You do that."

In the Grotto

Lyx

Cav has started to sense Lyx. His body has adjusted to a new rhythm, forgoing the cycle of the sun in exchange for the comings and goings of the siren. He has a feeling she's coming back, and when he pushes up onto his elbows, he glimpses something in the water.

"Close your eyes!" Lyx shouts.

He's tempted to disobey. Now that his strength is returning, he could sit up completely and crawl toward the water. He could see Lyx in all her glory.

But her voice comes sharply again. "I said, close your fucking eyes!"

There's an edge of panic in her voice. He does as he's told, but he can't deny the easy grin when he hears her emerge. Water taps against the rocks, dripping from her body into her footsteps. He waits for her to drop supplies, or chastise him, or grumble about his presence, but she doesn't do any of that.

Instead, her fingers brush his jaw. Only then does he open his eyes, as surprised by the touch as he is by the softness. He drinks in the sight of her, watching her gaze dart over him like she's expecting new injuries. If he didn't know any better, he'd say she looked worried. "What's wrong?" he asks.

Her body stiffens. She doesn't answer, but her aura changes as she rifles through the bag on her shoulder. "It's time to be rid of you."

By now, her threats have become a comfort, but there's something different today. A renewed purpose. A furious intention. A resolute rod through her spine.

"If you will it," Cav murmurs absently, but his eyes are drawn to the fading mark on her hip. "How's the burn?"

She stops moving. When she turns to face him, her teeth are grit, gaze murky with something Cav can't quite reach. "Do you not think I'll do it?" Lyx hisses. "You don't think I can kill you?"

His mouth hangs open. "I believe you can."

"But you don't believe I will." Her glare stays on him when she stands. She closes the space, wrapping her fingers around his throat to push him back against the wall. His airway tightens, hips bracketed by her knees digging into the dirt on either side. Lyx is panting, but Cav's breathing keeps a steady pace, even when she clenches her fist around his throat. "Why don't you fight back?" she snarls.

He wets his lips. "I don't want to."

She watches his mouth, her grip wavering before she tightens it again. Her fingers press against his pulse. His head swims, and he shakes — but it's not him at all. It's her arms trembling before she jerks them away.

The two of them stay like that, chests rising and falling against each other. Cav has a strange urge to comfort her, to guide her hands back to his neck, but then, she roots inside her bag and shoves a bottle against his chest. "Drink."

A dark purple liquid sloshes inside. Cav reaches for it, but he doesn't take it, brushing the inside of her wrist with his fingertips instead. "Pour it for me."

Her hand skitters away from his. "You're well enough to hold the bottle."

"And I'm weak enough to want it from your hand."

Waves crash behind her. Neither of them moves, and he relishes her weight against him, a reminder that she's real. She's here.

It's not like him to be patient, but he wants nothing more than to look at her, to note every detail of her face. Her finned ears flushing, throat swallowing, fingers curling...

After some time, she jerks the cork from the bottle and lifts it into the air. It's a game of chicken she knows she'll win, until Cav opens his mouth and lays out the flat of his tongue. Her breathing falters. "It could be poison."

Cav grins. "You wouldn't give away the opportunity to kill me yourself."

Her eyes widen, and he's not sure if it's a look of shock, or disgust, or awe. "What is wrong with you?" she whispers. Her eyes are on his mouth again, and he's not sure what she wants to do with it.

Whatever it is, he'll take it. Maybe he likes the thrill too much. Maybe any outcome is worth the chance to get closer to her. He inches forward, eyelids heavy. "I dare you to do it."

Her fingers flex around the bottle. He doesn't look at it, too consumed with every minute shift on her face. When she tilts the bottle, he opens his mouth, swallowing eagerly until errant rivulets of liquid streak down his chin. He drinks until she decides it's enough.

It doesn't matter what it is. All that matters is Lyx collecting the spills in droplets on her nails and knuckles.

Gently, Cav takes her wrist and laves his forked tongue over every finger until they're clean.

The bottle clatters down the rocky shore, but he can't hear it when Lyx grips his shirt and tugs him toward her. He follows eagerly, but she doesn't let him any closer with her hand pressing on his chest. "You..."

The word grinds out of her, like she's holding herself back. Like she doesn't want to want this. Like this is out of her control. His lips part like a flower unfurling. "Use your song. Use it on me." He's a fool to ask, but he can't shake the thought, desperately clawing to have one more piece of her.

Her pupils blow wide and hungry. "No one hears it and lives."

"Then kill me."

He is a fool, but he doesn't care. For a week, all he's done is imagine this moment — her luscious curves under his touch, her hands digging into him, her emotions boiling over between them. Perhaps tonight is his last, so he won't waste it. He wants everything he can get. Everything she'll give him.

Her fingers tangle in his hair, her mouth against his cheek while she rolls her hips in his lap. All he can do is groan, bucking when her teeth graze the shell of his ear, and her voice sounds like a melody. "Kiss me the way you've been dreaming about."

A haze settles over him. It's so easy to give into. He doesn't realize an invisible hand has reached into his chest and taken over. His heart no longer needs to beat. There is only her control pumping through him, sending her song through his veins to encourage his body to move for her.

All he wants is to follow her command. All he wants is to obey.

It's intoxicating, molding his free will into the shape of hers. He has no desires outside of her. He wants only what she does. He would give up any drug, any drink, any religion to fulfill her. This is why pirates jump from their ships. This is why sailors sink to their death.

And it's all worth it.

He kisses her. He has dreamt of this in every way there is. Ravenous, teeth and tongue desperate to have her. Slow and steady, indulging in every inch of her mouth. Sensually, cradling the back of her neck and trailing down her throat.

She matches him every time. The two of them are like waves colliding, seafoam fizzing, water splashing over them. She kisses like they're running out of time. Like this will never be enough.

He could kiss her for hours, but she finally pulls away, lips swollen and cheeks flushed. Already, he misses the sour taste of her mouth, the feel of her song wrapping around him. He doesn't want this to end. His grip tightens on her thighs, and she shivers when he brushes her scales. Between them, there's only the fabric of his pants doing nothing to disguise the slick marks she leaves behind.

Lyx's eyes are glassy and bright, watching where they meet. "You shouldn't ask for more," she says, but her hips keep moving, making him hiss when he hardens. "Any pirate who knows the depths of a siren's cunt soon knows the depths of the sea as well."

With one hand, he grabs the full flesh of her ass to rock her against him. "I'm willing to die for it. For yours."

Her tongue clicks, but her hips don't stop moving. "So ready to risk it all." When he tries to watch her work, she tugs on the back of his hair to force his eyes up. "But you couldn't handle the way I'd fuck you. The things I'd do to you."

When her hips swivel, his pants inch lower, dragging through the patch of scales that leads between his legs. His body glows from within, leaking molten desire through the cracks in his nether scales. Lyx drags against the sliver of

Cav's exposed skin, gasping when her wet desire sizzles against his heat. The lips of her pussy curve around one of his scales and hug tight when she grinds against it.

"You sure it's me who couldn't handle it?" Cav rasps.

Her cheeks flush darker. She presses her palms to his chest, forcing his back to the wall. "This'll give you something else to dream about." Each word is drawn out by the winding of her hips. "How you got so close. How you almost *fucked a siren.*"

Gods, she could move his pants lower. She could tug them down and ride him the way they both want, but she doesn't. She keeps rocking over his clothes, smearing a mess between them. Her clit is sloppy and swollen and begging for attention. When he reaches for it, she pins his wrists above his head. It traps him, forcing him to watch her take her pleasure. He groans under the delicious pressure, the leverage she uses to fuck herself against him.

His chest glows brighter. Her hungry eyes cling to it, one hand lowering to tug on the ties of his shirt. When she molds his bare breast in her palm, he bites his lip to keep from moaning, but there's no stopping the sound when she teases his nipple until it hardens.

He arches into her. There is no hesitancy in her touch, equally hungry for every part of him, like she would brand her teeth into his breasts and thighs and neck just to remind him who he's captive to.

He wishes she would. Gods, he wants her so badly, he might burn out of his skin. He wants more of this. He wants it again and again. He doesn't care how foolish it is.

There is something wild within her, spurring her on, sending her hair spilling over her shoulder. Her mouth scrapes his with a fervor he hasn't felt before. "You can never come back," she gasps. Her motions grow stronger along with her voice. "Swear it."

Nothing comes out of him. He can hardly think with the heat burrowing in his gut. All he can see are her hips rocking, her wet cunt clenching around his scales, her lips parting when she whines. "Say it."

They can't stop, frantically spiraling while their desperate desires clash and climb and race toward the peak.

"Swear you'll never return here," she grits. "Swear you'll never even try."

His teeth clamp together. Of all the things she's done to him, this is the worst. It doesn't matter that she's setting him free. He won't say it. It's the one thought he can't bear. It's a denial of the only thing he wants.

A furious look sparks in her eyes. "Swear it, pirate!"

It almost sounds like a plea, but Cav knows better. Why would she beg when she could command it? There's no use fighting. He is helpless to deny her, with or without her song. Mournfully, he breathes out. "I swear."

She meets him like waves crashing against rocks, overtaking him and dragging him down into his release. Her teeth dig into his lip to hide her sounds. It draws blood to the surface, and all he can do is whimper when she rakes her tongue against it. Lava swells between his scales and leaves a sticky mess between them.

Her head drops to his shoulder. She catches her breath in the crook of his neck, and he has the irresistible urge to hold her, to fit their mouths together, to convince her to keep him here...but darkness seeps in from the rims of his eyes.

Lyx lifts her head like she knows it's coming. She eases him onto his back and hovers over him. When sleep overtakes him, she fades from his vision and into his dreams.

TWENTY-SEVEN

Lyx

Lyx doesn't look back when she escapes the alleyway. She keeps a steady pace toward the *Indulgence*, her limbs buzzing to take off sprinting.

Bet he'd fall over himself to give you anything you want — given the right motivation.

She forces her feet to slow. If Tidus is watching, she can't prove him right. She cannot give away anything else. She cannot give him more reason to take interest in Cav.

There's no reason to run. She saw Cav not an hour ago, and Tidus couldn't possibly have gotten to him since then. Yet she can't deny the strange urge pushing her forward, an insistence to lay eyes on Cav, to see for herself that he's alive and well.

Along the dock, the crowd thickens. Lyx presses through the sea of bodies, but they jostle her off course until she can't make out the *Indulgence's* sails any longer. Her chest tightens. She'd almost call it panic, but panic is for people who can't appreciate chaos.

Not her.

This is not the first time she's raced to reach Cav before someone else. She remembers the last time with dizzying clarity, swimming from the feeding frenzy of sirens until her gills burned. She had to get to Cav before any of the others. She has to get to him before Tidus has a chance.

She shoves through the crowd. If anyone complains, she doesn't hear them, honed on the tip of the *Indulgence* like a black marlin. It takes too long before she breaks through the throng of people. Her heart pounds until she sees him.

He's fine. He's *fine*, his eyes rolling at some comment from Lace. Lyx can finally take a breath, bracing her hand against a nearby pole.

She's seen him. It should be enough to satisfy her, yet she can't pull herself away. Strange how she never noticed the restless charm in his movements before — or at least, never put words to it. His smile twitches, thumb pressed to his canine, tail curling around his ankle. It's a relief to see him in motion. No one could replicate this, not when every movement is undoubtedly Cavalier.

Yet when Lyx slapped him, he was completely calm. All the thoughts drained from his head, and he melted at her feet, all that energy funneled into desire. She didn't know he could be that still. She didn't know she could bring him to that.

She didn't know she'd crave both parts of him so eagerly.

The thought is so sudden and shocking that she jolts. That's when Cav looks at her. It's like he hears her thoughts and knows some part of her is reaching toward him. He wastes no time moving in her direction, and she knows she should move away, that she should get back on the ship and finish what she came here for...but she doesn't.

Cav stops in front of her, his lips parted like there's

something he wants to say. It takes a moment before he does. "I've been thinking about what you told me."

Scales lift on her arms. Depths, she'd forgotten everything she said in that damn hammock. It still feels like a fever dream. She wasn't thinking straight. How could she with his mouth against her ear, his fingers inside her, him begging for more?

Weakly, she clears her throat. "That was a mistake."

"It was honest. And I want to show you something." He turns and makes his way into the crowd, the opposite direction from where Lyx came. Lyx can't help but follow, but he doesn't slow for her to catch up, instead slipping lithely through the mob of people.

Her brows knit. She catches glimpses of his bobbing horns before they disappear, and a familiar tingling spreads through her limbs. Old instinct rushes back. Her breathing slows, senses sharpening until her attention fixates on the back of Cav's head. His auburn hair is secured behind him like a beacon calling to her.

No longer does the mass of bodies move Lyx; she moves with them, weaving as fluidly as water. She's hunting Cav. It's like it used to be, the thrill of the chase building in her chest. Her fingers flex, body primed and ready to track him down.

Ahead, Cav scans the crowd for her.

Lyx freezes. One of her eyes peeks out from behind a man's hat, her gaze sharp and unblinking. She circles toward Cav, slow and smooth, until she's almost close enough to touch him. If she reaches out, she could —

His eyes finally land on hers. She can only imagine what he sees: her pupils blown, fins twitching, face half obscured by someone else.

Whatever it is, he *smiles*.

Then he's off again. His movements are faster now, and she picks up speed, scanning every blur of red for a sign of him. She loses him for an entire minute, searching frantically until his earrings glint in the corner of her vision.

Her mouth waters. He's *running* from her.

Heat brands in her stomach. She darts through the crowd, eyes only for him. The wooden slats of the dock give way to sand beneath her feet. When the mass of people thins, there's no sign of Cav. She's lost him. Swiveling, she scans the foliage until she catches the end of a red tail disappearing down the hill.

Her heart kicks up again. She follows him down, pushing plants aside and letting the leaves snap back into place. The sounds and smells of the dock fade in the distance, replaced by crashing waves and sea air. At the bottom of the hill is an oasis. Palm trees sway overhead, shading the natural pool carved into the smooth rocks. Beside it, the tide comes in, almost close enough to touch. Vibrant flowers sprout from the bushes, keeping the clearing hidden from the bustle of the pier.

Cav appears beside her. "Glad to see your prey drive is still intact."

His presence is heady. All her synapses fire, still high from chasing him. She wants to finish it, to reach out and drag him down with her, but she stops herself. She pretends she can think of anything else. "So you admit I could destroy you."

She swears the ground quakes when he looks at her. "I don't think that was ever in doubt."

Her skin glows brighter. She doesn't understand it. She should be missing the tumult of the dock, yet she has no desire to go back. How can being alone with Cav make her feel more alive than the clamor of a hundred people?

She tears her gaze away from him and back to the pool. It's twice her size and wide enough that she couldn't reach both sides. "What is this? Your next experiment?"

Cav kneels to trail his hand through the pool. "No. This is

for you." He rises to his feet and flicks water from his fingertips. "I know you've been avoiding the ocean." She opens her mouth to argue, but he doesn't give her a chance. "You don't have to tell me why. But I thought this might be a way to dip your toes back in, if you're not ready for the sea itself."

Her skin prickles. This saltwater must have flooded in during high tide. Now that she looks closer, she can see the trenches dug through the rocks. Water is like that, wearing down solid stone to get back to the sea. It's like the ocean knows every drop of water, missing them whenever they're gone, and always calling them home.

Her toes curl in the sand. She's spent so long imagining this that it became impossible, something that happened only in the safety of her mind. There, she could prepare for anything, torturing herself with the thoughts again and again. What if the ocean refuses to accept her? What if her body transforms into something unfamiliar? Or what if nothing happens at all? What if the sea doesn't even recognize her anymore?

Shit. What if she's forgotten how to swim?

That was how she paid her penance, running through those thoughts and making empty promises. *I'll get my song, and then I'll return to the ocean.* But she never got her song. And she never returned.

Leaves rustle behind her. When she turns, Cav is moving back up the pathway. "You're leaving?" she asks, more desperate than she means to.

He pauses. "I thought you'd want me to."

Her heart trips. She does want him to leave; she *needs* him to, because she knows what happens if he doesn't. It's one thing when it's just talk, but it's quite another to bear witness to exactly what she is.

"It's for your benefit." She rolls her shoulders back to

steady herself. "You'd lose your appetite once you see what mine can do."

Cav scoffs. "Like you could scare me off."

She shakes her head, staring down through the clear water. "You act like you can handle anything. Like nothing in the world can make you flinch."

"Nothing about *you* can." He doesn't take his time coming back down the hill; he slides through the sand, letting the momentum carry him. When he slows in front of her, his cheeks are flushed. "I asked for what's real," he murmurs. "I asked for *you*. I'm still asking."

Her entire body heats. Foolish. He's always been foolish, and this will be the time he finally learns. She turns away and works her dress up to her waist. This is what she needs. This will cut the ties between them, and he will finally abandon whatever threads of fate he believes are tying them together.

She tosses her clothing aside and steps into the pool. Water laps at her ankles, and it's like the rivulets defy gravity, flowing up her legs to pull her in.

Her heart beats in her throat. Half of her wants to turn back, but there's only one way to know. She wades in until the water meets her calves, her thighs, her hips. Her feet slip on the smooth rock, and it sends her under with a splash. She can't touch the bottom. The scare has turned her body against her, arms flailing as she sinks.

Aerated water swirls around her. She closes her mouth and shuts her eyes to brace for — what? Only when she stops moving does the water grow calm. Her ears ring with a noise that sounds like singing, and she swears she can feel every grain of salt prickling her skin.

Her lungs burn for air. She knows she has to breathe through her gills, but it's been so long; the flaps on her neck refuse to open, clenched in fear.

Then the growing pains begin. It's been years since her

body stretched out of her human shape, but this cage has grown too small for her. Pained groans and bubbles seep past her sharpening fangs. Vicious spikes jut out from her forehead, a crown encircling the mass of tentacles her hair has become. Her nose flattens to two slits for nostrils. A large fin sprouts along her spine with webbing weaving between her taloned fingers.

Her legs are the biggest change, ballooning and fusing into a billowing dome with dozens of tendrils beneath. With this tail, she moves like a jellyfish, contracting muscles to propel herself through the water.

Hesitantly, she cracks one eye open. No longer is her vision blurry. Everything beneath the water appears with keen accuracy, though she knows her new eyes are foggy and glowing.

She can't put it off any longer; she has to breathe. At long last, she flares her gills, and water rushes over them. She nearly chokes. It's been so long since she felt this, something that was once so familiar now strange and unusual. It comes back to her quickly. No matter how long she's been away, *this* is what she knows best. It is what she has always been.

She is finally home.

She soaks in the feeling. It's tempting to stay under forever, ignoring all the reasons why she can't. When the tide comes back in, she could slip out of the pool and back into the sea. She'd never have to surface and see the look on Cav's face. She'd never have to watch his uncertainty spreading into horror when he recognizes that the truth of her is more than he can handle.

But she wants to see him break. She needs that finality to push her back on track. She wants the image of Cav's revulsion branded in her mind for when it tries to wander back to thoughts of him.

With a final breath, she pushes upward. Without the

insulation of the water, everything is louder. She can't be sure Cav's still behind her. Maybe he's gone. Maybe he reconsidered and fled.

Slowly, she turns. From this distance, she can make out only a blurry image of the land. Pops of colorful flowers sit on a backdrop of greens and beige with a molten red figure in the middle.

Lyx can't read his expression. She keeps still, the bell of her tail undulating beneath the water.

Cav doesn't move. A sour taste rises in Lyx's mouth, and her lip curls to remind him he asked for this, that he thought he wanted it *so badly* — but then, he speaks. He sounds like he did the first day in the grotto, like she's his savior, a myth brought to life, a legend and fantasy all at once.

"You look *just* like the ocean feels."

TWENTY-EIGHT

Cav

This is the moment Cav has dreamt about.

He's always known there was more to Lyx, and now, he finally sees it. No matter how her features have changed, she is unmistakably the same. Same scowl, same plush body, same threatening aura, same emotions stirring in Cav's chest.

He steps closer. If he wasn't looking for her, it'd be difficult to tell where she ends and the water begins. Beneath the surface, her tentacles sway, a calm under the storm of her teeth and talons. She is otherworldly. Ethereal. Powerful enough to enchant and consume him in the same breath.

You look just like the ocean feels.

Her arms spread against the water. "That's easy to say from dry land."

It could be an invitation or a threat; either way, it doesn't matter. Cav strips out of his clothes and steps into the pool. It's like she expects him to turn back, but he wades up to his waist before the rocks drop off. Her tendrils twitch out of his path, but he doesn't grapple for something to hold onto. He treads water, leaving himself completely at her mercy.

Her fins lift on end. There are more of them now. No doubt she thought he'd stay safe on shore, but that has never been Cavalier. She bares her teeth like a cornered animal, but her voice is beautifully breathless. "Reckless pirate."

He eases forward, and water drips from her cheek onto the corner of his lips. He finds the droplet with his tongue. "What do you do to reckless pirates?"

A hiss builds in her throat, but her eyes follow his mouth — and then, she surges toward him. By the time he gasps for breath, he's pressed against the opposite wall. Her strength and speed are thrilling. She presses her body to his, her tentacles streaming behind her. "I could drown you."

"Do it," he chokes out.

She falters only a moment before she pulls him under.

Water swirls around them. Her face hovers over him, blocking out the light. He lets his arms fall to his sides. There is no fear, no scramble to the surface, no desire for anything but what she gives.

Bubbles spill from his mouth. Lyx watches them before she opens her mouth. She swallows each of them, following them to the source until her lips crush against his. It starts as a collision, tongues rough against fangs. Her kiss is halting and sloppy, torn between uncertainty and diving deeper. This version of her isn't used to this. Cav realizes it in the scrape of her claws, all her sharp parts meeting his flesh and jerking back in surprise. Her siren form has only been used to fight, to destroy, to create a barbed defense against the rest of the world.

Cav doesn't swim away. He wraps his arms around her waist to pull her in, and she freezes. He half-expects her to pry out of his grasp, but she doesn't; instead, her frenzied movements ease. She stops gnashing her teeth. The tension in her jaw melts. Slowly, her mouth molds against his and gives into the slide of his tongue. Her sharpened teeth prick his lip, drawing out his moan when she sucks the wound into her mouth.

His lungs burn. He needs to breathe, but he doesn't want to pull away, even when his brain flickers. He doesn't want to escape. He doesn't want the safety of the shoreline. He wants to be *here*, in the grips of a siren, swirling in this feeling. He could drown like this and be completely happy.

Before he can succumb, Lyx drags them both to the surface.

He gasps when she eases him back against the sloping rock. Their breathing entwines, and he swears she's tugging his soul out between his lips, their mouths still sliding against each other. Underwater, a tentacle curls coyly around his wrist. He spreads his fingers to reach for her, exploring the nubs and ridges of her tendrils. She takes a shaky breath.

"Sensitive?" he whispers.

Hot electricity jolts through him, leaving a tingling trail between his scales. It pulses and crackles long after she stops stinging. Cav shudders, lifting his hand to his weakened shoulder and draping her tentacle down his neck.

It's wet and sticky, like the churning low in his gut. Her tendril curls around his bicep, and he understands how easily sailors could get trapped in this, their arms and legs entangled and numb.

He can't think of anything better. With both hands freed, he pulls her closer by the waist. "Show off for me."

Her gills flutter anxiously when he lowers his mouth to her neck, but he takes his time, gently brushing them with his lips. Her breathing picks up, talons scraping his chest. When he teases the edge of one slit with his tongue, a moan vibrates through her throat.

"Show me what you can do," he breathes. He laves his tongue over the swell of her breasts. She is cool and smooth and salty, and he holds her in the heat of his mouth, watching her face when he drags his lips over her hardening nipple. She tightens a fist in his hair. It spurs him on to tease his teeth against her nipple, flicking both tips of his tongue against it.

Tentacles flutter on his shoulder, and delicious pain whizzes through him again. It steals his breath. His tongue spasms, and her whimper binds up with his in a chain reaction. If he thought her slap was divine, he can't put words to what this is. She is otherworldly, dipping him into delectable pain and showing him her power. Cav has never been afraid, even when he should be. He has never favored the certainty of land. He has always craved the depths and everything that waits there.

He wants to sink into Lyx. He wants to drown in her. She is an oasis, and he is dying of thirst. He will drink every drop of her before she vanishes.

He carries her toward the sloping ramp into the pool, licking saltwater from her body. His shoulders crest the water, and he lies back against the smooth bank to keep his lower half submerged.

Now he can truly see her. Sunlight shines on the large tentacles of her hair slipping off her shoulder. Her skin is brighter than he's seen it. When he pulls her toward him, she eases onto his lap, the dome of her tail spreading like a ballgown over his hips.

Her translucent skin lets him see through her, the warm red of his body pressed against the translucent blue of hers. She's watching it, too. Her tentacles splay around them, draped over his chest and trailing in the water.

It drips from her and lands with a sizzle on his glowing chest. His body is made up of layers, scales over skin with pockets of magma between. That magma has grown hot and viscous, rising up between his scales like it's breaking through the crust of the earth. It's hottest between his legs, beaming nearly white where Lyx grinds down against him.

His back arches. He feels the burn of her acid, but he's not sure where it's coming from. She no longer has the sex organs he's come to expect. He remembers what she told him in the crow's nest. *They're only there on land to fool pirates.*

He wants to know this new part of her, but before he can, Lyx makes his head spin. She reaches under her skirt to stroke the soft scales between his legs. All Cav can do is shiver while the light from his body follows her touch. His pelvis looks much like the rest of him, a patch of scales gathered between his legs. The difference is, everything is heightened here. His scales are softer and more responsive, the molten rock beneath rising faster than anywhere else.

Experimentally, Lyx slides the pad of her finger between two scales. "What do you call this part of you?"

It's so fucking *sensitive*. Cav's hips rut. "*Fuck.*"

"That's not it," she chides, and he would laugh if he could catch his breath. She keeps teasing him, trailing her talons through the mess of building magma. Every touch brings more to the surface until her fingers are sticky with it. She lifts them to her mouth, and he could die at the sight of it. Lyx, terrifying and beautiful, licking remnants of him from her hand. When she sucks her fingers between her lips, her eyes close for a long moment before they open again. "It tastes *just* like you."

He wants to ask what that means, how she knows, but she's moving against him now. Beneath the umbrella of her tail, he can see where the tentacles sprout from her body. They're a mass of ruffles and ribbons, but they part around him until his scales are settled against her delicate core.

"What do you call it, Cav?" she asks again.

It's all he can do to get the words out. "Vent. Shaft. Cunt.

Anything, just —"

Satisfied, she winds her hips. They both draw in a breath, and Lyx nearly loses her balance. Cav can't blame her. It's unlike anything else, like there's a gelatinous clover between her tentacles, and he's pressing into the very center. Her viscid core fits itself around him, drawing him into her with suction that seals over every inch of his scales.

He can feel her *everywhere*. His eyes roll back, chest heaving under the tentacles draped across his shoulder. "Yes," he rasps. "Sting me — while you —"

It zaps through him, delectable pain and sweet relief soothing the deepest strain of his wounded shoulder. He doesn't know how it works. All he knows is he's gasping for breath when another tentacle drapes across his chest.

This sting cascades over him like a wave. Everywhere, he burns for her. Each shock pumps more desire through him, threatening to make his heart spill out of his mouth. He knows what he wants to tell her. He knows why he can't. Only a fool would fall for a siren, but he'd rather drown in this feeling than be adrift without her.

He can't help but want more of her. He knows what her tentacles are capable of; he wants to feel it for himself. Carefully, he traces the scars on her torso. "Please leave a mark."

Her head tilts. "Why?"

She's taunting him. Gods, he wants to wear her stripes tomorrow. Wants her embedded in his skin. Wants a permanent reminder of how close they are.

His voice strains through his teeth. "Because I'm fucking *begging* you."

TWENTY-NINE

Lyx

If Cav wants a mark, she'll give him one.

Lyx's tentacles wrap around his wounded shoulder, clinging to his sides and the crevices between his scales. It's like she's a vine scaling a stone wall, finding the cracks inside of Cav where she can burrow in deep.

He pants beneath her, but she makes him wait. His eyes are glassy, a whine building in his throat while he bucks. It's too good to stop him. She wonders if he would look like this if she dug her teeth in, if she peeled back his scales and licked at his blood, but that's too much. She's shown him enough for one day, and his words have stirred a new hunger in her.

She wants to mark him.

A sting is not enough to satisfy her, but it's close. It's almost perfection when Cav spasms at the pain, head tipping back, throat exposed, breasts arching into the air. He clenches his teeth, but it doesn't stop the moan that escapes.

She stings him again. He makes a needy sound she's never heard, and through the dome of her tail, she can see lava pushing up through the cracks of his vent. It clings to both of them, a sticky mess as hot as her arousal.

She stirs her hips. "What does that mean?"

A blissful smile seeps across his face. "Means you're fucking *perfect*."

She wants to kiss the words right out of his mouth, to swallow them down so they can never be heard by anyone else. When she withdraws her tendrils, they drag between his scales, and he groans and shudders. Already, she can see welts forming on his body. They're not as deep as her scars, but they're the same shape, lightning bolts across one of his shoulders. Each mark is indented with details, the beads and ruffles of her tentacles embedded in him.

Like he's *hers*.

Heat sizzles beneath her. When she grinds against him, water splashes onto the lava between his legs, cooling and hardening it to the same color of his scales. The dome nudges inside her, pressing deeper until she gasps.

"It keeps growing like that," he murmurs. "As much as you want. The more you work me up, the more it builds."

He lays on the sloping rock, wet hair tousled and slipping out around his crooked smile. Lyx's stomach clenches. No one has ever looked at her like this. Not really. Not after she dropped her facade. Not without her song. She has manufactured this look a hundred times, convinced dozens of pirates to adore her, but she used nothing on Cav.

Her pulse trips. She closes her hands around his throat just for something to hold onto, teeth scraping her lip when she moves against him. "So if I keep doing this, you'll keep spilling."

Cav follows the pace she sets. More lava leaks out of him, firming up beneath her, molding to the tender flesh of her cunt. She tries not to shudder, but the sight of Cav coils and strikes her. He's losing himself to lust, rolling up into her and watching where they meet.

"Is it more sensitive like this?" There's a cruel lilt in her voice, heightened when she drags against him.

Cav whimpers and writhes, and that's all the answer Lyx needs. Every motion draws them together, her cunt suctioned to his like it can't get enough. When Lyx shifts, their bodies fight to stay together, the delicious friction pulling them right back into place.

No one has dared to brave what lies beneath her tail — except for Cav. It's like their bodies were made for this, molding together until she swears she can feel him against every inch of her.

He claws at her hips, his eyes rolling back. "You're fucking gripping —"

It's addictive seeing him like this, all minced thoughts and breathless words, so good she can almost taste it. "What if I don't stop? If I keep riding until you're a pitiful, writhing wreck? Would it keep growing?"

Cav's curses when their foreheads brush. Neither of them can look away from where they meet, watching the ridges of his hardened shaft drag between her tentacles. It's a *mess*, her slickness and his heat binding them closer together.

Her skin sparkles brilliantly. It doesn't make sense. Gorging herself on chaos is the only way she knows, but Cav has never given her that. With him, it's like he's feeding morsels from his hand, placing them into her mouth so gently that she hadn't realized she was eating.

And still, she's hungrier than ever. All her instincts scream to destroy Cav, to tear him apart, but something isn't right. Her heart thuds behind her eyes. For so long, she has craved his destruction. She has dreamt of prying him apart and scraping the marrow from his bones. She has imagined fucking the soul out of his body so she could swallow it down.

All she knows is ruination, but what if something's buried beneath it? What if her need to devour all the pieces of Cav is something more? What if she's longing for the whole of him?

Her world tilts on its axis. The thought is so impossible and foreign that she can't grasp it. Her arms wobble, tugging her back into her body and reminding her where she is. Cav looks up at her, but Lyx can't face him. She can't face any of it. With renewed vengeance, she bares her teeth and tightens the circles of her hips.

"You're hopeless," she pants. Her voice is too shaky. She grips him tighter to keep from trembling. "I bet I could get you to say anything like this. I wouldn't even need my song." The idea spreads like wildfire. With one hand, she drags her talons down Cav's chest and pricks his nipple. "Tell me all of this is mine."

"You fucking own it."

No hesitation. Wanton desire surges through her, and her tail billows as she takes him deeper with every thrust. That hungry feeling brims dangerously inside her. She wants more. She wants to push the limits of what she knows, teasing the edges of her containment. "Tell me you're my bitch."

Cav laughs. "I'm your *bitch*," he rasps, hotter than his skin. "I'll do anything you want. Anything you let me."

This is going to her head. She can't stop herself, words spilling out of control. "Tell me you love me."

"I'm in love with you."

It's so easy, it steals her breath. A thousand others have said those same words, but this is nothing like that. Cav is not under her spell, but that's not all. This time, *she* feels different. When he says it, her heart stops. Her thoughts vanish. There is nothing but him.

Water drips back into the pool and ripples across its surface. Cav's chest rises and falls beneath her palm. His pulse thrums, as strong and certain as the way he looks at her. Her fingers flex. This has gone too far. She's gotten all she needs. She has tormented both of them enough, and yet...

"Show me what it's like," she whispers. It is the fantasy she's never allowed herself, something she would only say to be cruel, but there's nothing vicious about it. Nothing except the way her lungs burn, like the words have been trapped inside and desperate to come up for air.

When he kisses her, it's a relief. Her body moves without thinking, tentacles winding around him to pull him closer. His lips leave her dizzy, heady, intoxicated, until terrifying pleasure jolts through her. Her mind and body are at odds. She asked for this, but the unknown makes her shiver above him.

With an arm around her waist, he eases her back into the pool. Water laps at her shoulders, but it can't disguise her trembling. Frantically, she reaches for him, coiling tendrils around his breasts and hips before she stings again. She shouldn't have asked for this. She's running from something — running *to* something. Escaping it. Chasing it. She doesn't know where she's headed, but if she stops, she'll have to acknowledge it. She'll have to look it straight in the face.

The look in Cav's eyes calms her. "I want to take my time," he murmurs. He takes in the details of her face like he's memorizing every feature, standing at the cliff's edge of her being and diving into her depths.

Only then does he close the space between them. Her back meets the rock wall, and he holds onto it to keep himself afloat. With his other hand, he runs along her tail, brushing the lining before he reaches beneath it.

There are dozens of tentacles, but Cav finds the center. His fingers trace her core, still sticky with the mix of their desire. When she gasps, her tentacles sting, but Cav barely winces. The touch of his hand is so different. She loved the solid press of his hardened scales, but his fingers are so delicate. So vulnerable. He gives them to her freely, no matter how her tendrils jitter. There is no fear on his face, only sincerity. Certainty. An offering. It's decadent and tender and intimate, and she doesn't know how to repay it.

"Slow," he breathes.

She remembers what Cav said at the dartboard. *Slow. Deep. Languid.* Their chests press together, bodies intertwined, her back against the wall. This is both her fantasy and his bound into one.

Yet all she can see are their differences. Lyx's heart trips over itself, but Cav's pulse remains steady. Her breathing is short and sharp through her nose, but he opens his mouth to inhale deeply. "Slow."

She stares at his lips forming a circle, her eyes slipping closed when she takes a ragged breath. Their bodies fall into sync, and every feeling heightens. The pads of his fingers dip into the rings between her tentacles. He explores her, watching the flutter of her eyelashes and the part of her lips. Her talons rake down his arm. His mouth brushes hers and hovers out of reach.

Her teeth grit. "Cav —"

"I want you here with me," he murmurs. "I want you to feel everything."

He delves deeper. When she gasps, his nose brushes her cheek, and it pulls on her like a riptide sucking her away. Her tentacles curl around his forearm. When she stings, he groans and palms the expanse of her cunt, grinding the heel of his hand into her core. She makes a pathetic sound and tries to hide it against his neck, but Cav keeps her pinned open.

A wave crests in the pit of her stomach. "What does it feel like?" she gasps. It's foolish. She shouldn't ask, but the need builds to a fever pitch inside her. "What does it feel like — when you love me?"

His chest glows, and the water around them warms. "It feels like..." His pupils blow wide and focused on her. "The sun on the horizon." The scales of his chest tease hers. "The first sight of land in the middle of the sea." His smile brushes her mouth. "The first step into the ocean after years of dry land."

White heat drips down her spine and melts into her limbs. She can't look away from him. He's given her the answer, but her craving grows. How can she be satisfied just hearing the words? She wants to taste it. She wants to hold love on her tongue until she can name every flavor, every tang, every hint of what he means.

The wave builds inside her, drawing her hopelessly toward the peak. Her tentacles wrap around his legs and weave between his scales until they're locked together. She digs her claws into his back, but nothing is close enough. She wants to bury herself in his skin. She wants to sear her being into his.

"There you go," he pants. "There you go..."

His hand keeps moving against her. This pleasure is so *different*. It is not the climax she's used to; it submerges her, engulfs her, swallows her whole. It sucks her in until she can see only Cav, her mind swirling around him. She's drawn to him like he's the center of a whirlpool, and she doesn't want to escape. She doesn't want to come up for air. She wants to follow him all the way down.

She cries out when she comes. Her tentacles sting uncontrollably, and Cav bucks and shivers, but his rhythm never wanes. He follows the rise and fall of her body, dragging their open mouths together so he can drink in every drop of her.

"Do you feel it?" he asks. His forehead rests against hers when he presses kisses to her fangs. "This is what it's like. This is what it feels like."

For the first time, Lyx understands what it means to drown.

In the Grotto

Lyx

Lyx could have killed Cav. She could have rutted in his lap and taken the last thing she wanted. She could have ended him. She could have, if the bottle had been poisoned. If she'd held him underwater. If her malicious instincts took over.

But they never did. Instead, she retrieved a dinghy and hoisted him inside. The sleeping draught worked wonders. He didn't stir when she nudged the boat out of the cave and into the night. She pushed that boat for miles, arms burning and teeth grit, until she found an island dotted with houses. Candles glowed in the windows with smoking chimneys rising toward the dawn, signs of life that Lyx typically avoided. Today, though, she swam closer until the water grew shallow. Her fingers curled around the edge of the boat. She should have loosened her grip. She should have let go, but she allowed herself one final look.

Cav's body was tucked against the wood, eyelashes

resting on his cheeks. For the first time, his mouth was slack, haunted by the ghost of a grin. Lyx traced his lips, following the curved bridge of his nose into the hollows under his eyes.

Just a look, hm?

Saltwater dripped from her onto his face. His pointed ears twitched, and she jerked back, shoving the boat with all her might. It drifted aimlessly, carried sideways by the current. Lyx lowered until only her eyes peered above the water.

Take him to shore. Please, *she thought.*

Slowly, the ocean shifted. Waves moved past her shoulders and rushed beneath the dinghy. It rocked out of her reach, floating toward the island until the hull dug into the sand. Further down the beach, someone began their morning walk. They leaned against their cane, head tilting toward the strange boat washed ashore.

Since then, Lyx hasn't stopped swimming. Her muscles ache, but she relishes the pain, putting distance between herself and that foolish pirate. She doesn't even think his name anymore. She skirts schools of fish and scours underwater volcanoes. She watches ships pass overhead. She dives as deep as she can, until her body is compressed and there's no light left to see by.

Anything to keep her mind off him.

She doesn't surface for weeks. When she does, she avoids the island where she left him. There are plenty of others to choose from. They're all the same, anyway. She can't find a single stretch of beach that isn't splattered with lovers wrapped in each other's arms for all the world to see. They giggle and whisper, eyes for only their paramours.

Lyx blows bubbles from her mouth. She bets they all think they're in love. One word of her song, and those sweethearts would tear each other apart. What do they know about anything?

A storm rolls in. That's why she returns to the grotto. There is no sentimental reason. When she rises out of the water, she ignores the swelling in her throat. She knows what she'll find here: charred sticks and barren bottles gathered on the shore. If she stares at them hard enough, she can forget why they're here. She can forget everything that happened. She can forget that she is alone.

Waves echo against the cave walls. It's louder than before, no longer dampened by another body. On the bank, the plants wither and wilt, like the life has been sucked out of this place. Lyx pads beside them. It's been weeks since she used her legs, but she finds a familiar indentation in the dirt. The ground is no longer warm from his body, but she can almost pretend. She sinks down, curling her knees beneath her and reaching for the bottle of sleeping draught. His mouth was here. If she shuts her eyes, the image dances across her mind, his golden eyes staring up at her when offered his tongue. Her cheeks burn, but she curls her fingers around the neck of the bottle and brings it to her lips —

"I was wondering when you'd show back up."

Lyx splutters. Beyond the rocky ledge, Mollo's glowing eyes drift on the water's surface.

Lyx shoves the bottle into the weeds. "Haven't you found someone else to torture?"

"I was gonna ask you the same thing." Mollo's sleek tail weaves back and forth. Thunder rumbles in the distance. "You swam off so fast the other day, I don't think you got a bite of the treat I brought."

"I don't need your sloppy seconds."

"You like 'em fresh, don't you?" Mollo flashes her frilled teeth. "Keep 'em alive like a lobster in a cage, waiting for you to get hungry."

Lyx pushes to her feet. She may have the high ground, but there's something strange about another siren watching her on land. She feels naked, missing all the parts that make her dangerous. When Lyx moves down the shore, Mollo follows like a shadow.

"Are you just here to bother me?" Lyx asks. Chaos dribbles down her throat, but she keeps her eyes on the overgrowth of vines overhead.

"You've been gone a while. No one knew where you swam off to — except Sinoe. But she wouldn't tell me anything." Mollo hides her smile in the water. "You can't blame me for being curious."

"Be curious somewhere else."

"Perhaps you're right." Mollo sighs, floating on her back. "Maybe I'll visit one of the islands. There's always something new to play with. Some new pirate washed up on the shore."

Lyx's scales prickle. She tugs at one of the leaves, but she can't stay focused, always watching Mollo in her periphery.

Mollo stretches her arms behind her head. "In fact, I heard someone's looking for us. Handsome, witless...the best kind." Chuckling, she shakes her head. "A dragon. What are the odds?"

The vine snaps. Lyx's pulse pounds through her mind. Mollo knows. Mollo has been watching her. Mollo has seen Cav.

"It'd be perfectly ruinous." Mollo clicks her tongue. "Fire, water, star-crossed lovers destined for tragedy. I heard he's been roaming the beaches, wading out into the waves and searching for a siren to sing to him. And you know what?" The slits of her nostrils flare. "He just might find me."

Lyx doesn't realize how close she's gotten to the ledge. Rocks dig into her bare feet, her fingernails imprinting on her palm. Lightning rips across the sky. It scatters over Mollo's face, the corners of her smile sharp as two daggers while her tail weaves like a snake.

Lyx can take her on. Mollo may be faster with vicious

teeth, but Lyx sees red. She braces to dive into the water, knees bent and arms outstretched –

But something appears outside the cave. It's a massive shape against the fog, a dark mass floating atop the water.

A ship, headed straight toward the grotto.

Lyx's chest tightens. Only one person knows about this place. Only one person would be foolish enough to return here.

Cav.

She should be furious. She told him to stay away, but when her teeth dig into her lip, she realizes she's smiling. Her body feels light when she lifts onto her toes, opening her mouth to shout a warning —

But this ship is bigger than she expected. Surely this is too much for one person to handle. Figures appear on the deck. Lyx's eyes dart from one face to another, but Cav is not among them. She swallows thickly. This isn't right. All the men on the ship look gleeful and hungry, staring directly at her.

Mollo ducks beneath the waves, and Lyx's feet slice on shells as she dives. She breaks into the water, body straining back into its siren form. Her flailing legs unravel into tentacles. She swims with all her might and plunges deeper.

The ship hull looms beneath the water. Something splashes down beside her, stretching wider until she recognizes the crisscross of netting. Her gills flutter as she scrambles toward the ocean floor. One of her tentacles tangles in the net, wrapped as tightly as the panic in her throat. She claws to free herself, but the rope surrounds her on all sides, cinching shut and rushing toward the surface.

The muffle of the ocean is shattered when she breaks through to the air. Thunder rolls into cheers from the men. Both Lyx's gills and lungs splutter for breath, body contorting to find the proper form.

Beside her, Mollo swings in her own net. "Release us!" she screeches, lunging toward the deck. Her siren song permeates the air. She searches wildly for Lyx. "Lend me your song, sister."

She's right. The persuasion will be more powerful with the two of them. Lyx hisses. "Release us!"

The words dry up in Lyx's mouth. Light glints off Mollo's necklace, but she looks just as disturbed as Lyx. There are no glassy eyes or desperation. Their songs have no effect. Twenty pirates sneer back at them, inspecting their catch.

The mob parts to allow their captain through. His eyes are calculating beneath the clean brim of his hat, bringing out the barest hint of blue to his pale skin. He saunters toward the railing with a rolled parchment and sets a ruffled blade of grass between his teeth. "Do you think this is our first day on the water?"

Lyx's heart plummets. Siren's tongue. These pirates are immune to their magic. Terror fills her throat, like her very song has been ripped away. She tries to steady her breathing. This is what happens to sirens. They're captured. They feed. They fight their way back to the sea.

But Lyx has never been trapped like this.

The captain unrolls the parchment and spreads it against the railing. It's a map covered in scribbled question marks and scratched out islands, references and page numbers jotted near the key at the bottom. The captain walks his fingers through the printed water toward a frantic circle around the rocky grotto near the map's edge. "That chatty dragon knew exactly where you'd be."

The betrayal leaves her entire body cold. Cav told them? He drew them a map? Any hope she'd felt for his return now sickens her, leaving her stomach churning in its wake.

And she'd thought he was a foolish one.

Mollo jerks at her netting. "You don't want us."

The captain tips back his head and laughs. It's a howl that spreads through the rest of the crew, and Lyx wants to scream, to tear out their vocal cords, to slash them down to the quick.

"You know what they say about a siren on a ship," Mollo interrupts and licks her lips. "Angers the ocean. Brings nothing but treachery and misery."

The captain's gaze follows her tongue. "I'll take my chances."

This time, the crew's chuckles are driven away by Mollo's lazy smirk. "Of course. Who wouldn't want to risk their ship? Their crew? Their life?"

The captain's eyes narrow. Behind him, a hush falls over the other men.

Lyx's body buzzes. It's chilling how at ease Mollo looks lounging back in her net when she speaks. "Surely two sirens in close quarters wouldn't conspire. Surely they wouldn't escape, or worse...return for revenge."

Lightning strikes behind her. The air sizzles. The crew tries to hide the way they shift toward each other, but the captain doesn't move.

"Sirens are vengeful creatures," Mollo purrs. "There are depths to the sea you've never imagined. There is cold you couldn't fathom. A pain your mind could never comprehend — and that's just what we save for our favorite captors."

The captain's eyes give nothing away, but his teeth grind together, hands flexing at his sides. Lyx clutches the net and holds her breath.

Mollo toys with the shell around her neck. "You could never convince a siren to obey you...but you could force her."

Lyx's brows knit. That's not right. That won't get them out of here, but Mollo doesn't look at her. She keeps her eyes on the captain.

"Free me." Mollo jerks her chin toward Lyx. "And I'll

hand you her song. She'll do whatever you demand. She'll be trapped in your service forever."

A sickening feeling branches through Lyx. Mollo is not bargaining for their escape; she's bargaining for hers alone. Lyx lifts onto her knees and tugs at the netting. "She's lying! That's not possible! Release —"

But when she tries to use her song, there's nothing. Any sound she makes is lost to the emptiness. She clamps a hand around her throat and feels the hollowness. Chaos pours into her like sand, filling her body until she can hardly move under the weight of it.

The captain's eyes reflect the glow from Mollo's shell. When he looks at Lyx, she swears his hunger could swallow her whole. "Looks like we have a deal."

THIRTY

Cav

They take their time leaving the pool. Once the sun has set, Cav helps Lyx onto the sand. He sits behind her while she transforms, his chest pressed to her back. Her entire body tenses. If changing in front of him was difficult, he can only imagine what it's like to have him this close during the transformation. She grits her teeth at the growing pains, but he stays with her, massaging the muscles in her newly-formed legs.

Her knees wobble when she dresses, so he loops an arm around her waist to support her back to the ship. Once they hear the buzz of activity on the docks, she slips out of his grip to walk on her own, but her pace is different. She idles closer than before, the backs of her knuckles brushing his wrist.

By the time they reach the *Indulgence*, the party is in full swing. It's easy to slip into the crowd and weave toward the hatchway, but he senses a change in Lyx's demeanor. She puts space between them. Her shoulders are tight, eyes darting toward everyone else onboard, like they might somehow see how exposed she's been.

He'd like nothing more than to follow her, but the gravity of what they shared is not lost on him. She looks skittish and raw and desperate for breathing room. He slows his pace and catches her hand until she turns to face him. "I'll see you tomorrow?" he asks.

Relief washes over her, followed by a mix of emotions that seem to confound her. She retreats below deck, but not before giving him a lingering look that leaves his entire body tingling.

With a dopey smile, he floats across the deck and into the hammock. He can't be bothered to entertain tonight. The sounds of the ship fade into a hum that matches the honeysweet drizzle of his memories.

He never expected what happened today. At the beginning of this, his time with Lyx felt like a tug of war where he would gain ground just to lose it, but as the days pass, he thinks she's starting to let him win. When he tugs her closer, she doesn't pull as far away. When he asks for the truth, she is finally giving it to him. He gave her something real, too.

I'm in love with you.

Remembering it makes him flush, the weight of his words settling into him. He could pretend he said it to play along with her, to give her what she demanded, but that's a lie. He *is* in love with her. He doesn't remember what it's like not to be. He doesn't *want* to remember.

Sirens can't fall in love, the voice of reason tries to remind him, but that voice has always been weak for him. Now, it can barely get a word out before his other thoughts come rushing in. When Cav confessed, Lyx didn't run away. She didn't toy with him. She asked questions. She was curious. When he described it, she looked him in the eyes and fell apart in his arms.

That feels like the furthest thing from impossible.

Cav falls asleep drunk on that hope, dreaming of Lyx's siren form. He pricks his fingers on her fangs and watches her lick the blood away. He traces the ridge of her finned ears with his tongue. He drifts tangled in her tentacles until someone shakes him awake.

Cav can barely make out Colt rubbing his tired eyes. It's not quite daylight, but he can see the tops of stone buildings beside the ship. Scowling, Cav tries to roll over back into his dreams, but Colt nudges him again and grumbles, "Restock."

Cav exhales. Right. That's what he gets for agreeing to help with early morning cargo. Reluctantly, he hoists himself out of the hammock and winces at the twinge in his shoulder. By the time he walks down the gangplank, Heathen and Cypher are bent over a piece of parchment, checking off inventory. Cav lifts one of the boxes and turns back to the ship, but Heathen picks up a barrel and falls into step beside him.

They move back and forth between the dock and the deck, working in silence. Well, *Heathen* works in silence, listening to any topic Cav meanders into. While his thoughts feel like a stream attached to his mouth, the act of speaking requires much more effort from Heathen. It's a comfortable understanding between them.

After countless trips up and down the gangplank, Heathen leans against the ship's railing to catch her breath. "You haven't mentioned your experiment lately."

Cav scrounges up two cups of water and hands one to her. Heathen tilts her mug back, and the two of them stay like that for a minute. "You're right," Cav pants. "I haven't."

He doesn't know why he's nervous, like he's done something wrong. He knows Heathen will ask what they want to know, yet a flood of thoughts threaten to spill out of him. He forces his lips shut.

Heathen takes another drink. "Is it going well?"

Cav sets his cup aside. It would be easy to give a throwaway answer, but he's anything but indifferent. There's something inside him that he's beginning to understand, pieces of a puzzle he didn't realize he was putting together. "We have been experimenting," he assures her. "We've tried new things. We've explored...desires we've never shared with anyone else." He's falling into distraction, but he can't help it. With Lyx, he feels *alive* again, blazing trails he's imagined for so long.

"And you've been safe?" Heathen continues.

Cav's mouth twists. "I've taken more time preparing. I've slowed things down. It's not perfect, but it's better."

"That's an improvement," Heathen says, but she's watching him like she knows there's something more he wants to say.

Maybe he shouldn't. He could get away with this conversation and refocus on the experiment, but that doesn't hold his attention. His heart's not in it; it's in something else.

"But you were right," he sighs. "I'm not as dedicated as I should be. I'm doing it selfishly. I'm not trying to gain insight or make changes to the *Indulgence*. I'm doing it for me."

Heathen looks concerned, but she doesn't speak. Cav leans back against the railing and lets the weight of recognition settle over him.

"Even after I joined this crew, I've always been missing *something*. Something that keeps me on my toes. Something to captivate me. Something that makes me feel the way Lyx does."

That's what it really comes down to. Cav has never found his role on this ship because he's been searching for Lyx in everything he does. That thrilling feeling she gives, the challenges she presents, the way she captivates him. She is the place his flighty mind can land and pour into. He may have been moving forward the past two years, but he was always looking back at her.

"I *do* need something to guide me." He braces his hands against the railing. "A beacon. A purpose. Lyx is that for me." Heathen's mouth opens, but he cuts them off. "I know that's not what you want to hear. I told you I could keep my feelings out of it, but I can't. I've never been able to keep that wall up like you can. I'm sorry."

Cav can't face the disappointment in her eyes. He searches the shore for anything else to look at. Merchants unlock their doors and wave to each other in the dawn light. Chickens peck at worms in the dirt. On a nearby ship, a blue flag snaps in the wind.

Eventually, Heathen sidles up beside Cav. She stares out across the same scene, but from the corner of Cav's eyes, he can tell she's not really looking at it. "It's harder than it seems," Heathen says slowly, "maintaining lines when there are emotions involved. I do understand that. I should have approached this differently."

The way they say it, he could almost believe they know what he means. Heathen has always appeared unflappable, led by facts and figures. Cav can't imagine a world where she'd allow herself to be led by her heart instead of her head.

"I still think the experiment is worthwhile," he murmurs. "It's the kind of change we need. It opens people up. Lets them try things they never have before." His mouth twists. "Maybe we were both wrong about the *Indulgence*."

Heathen lifts a brow.

Cav continues uncertainly. "People don't come here because they know what to expect — at least, not with sex. They don't come here for monotony, but they don't come here for the risk, either. They come here because it's safe. Because whatever happens, they know they'll be taken care of. That's the real beauty of this ship."

The words stir in Cav's chest before they foam out of him.

"It's a comfort. It's a place where people can try things. Test their limits. *Be* themselves. That's why there's always a crowd to come aboard. That's why we still stop at the islands that refuse us. Because there are people who need an escape, and the *Indulgence* gives them that. It gives *us* that."

Heathen's expression changes, looking over the deck like they're seeing it with new eyes.

Cav's voice softens. "This was the first ship that didn't want me to hide some part of myself. Where I didn't have to worry about how I dressed or what people noticed first. I could just exist."

Heathen's fingers flex. Cav may not be privy to the details of her history, but he's always sensed a kinship between them. There's a reason why a banshee would set out on their own, forgoing their religious order and all the rules that come with it.

After a moment, Heathen lets out a long breath. "I have not appreciated your wisdom enough, Cav."

He scoffs. "Let's not get carried away. I still failed this experiment."

"Yes, but..." Heathen drums her fingers on the railing. "You've unearthed something that I hadn't given enough thought to." When she turns to him again, there's a meaningful look in her eyes. "Let's get to the end of our route, and we'll figure out what happens next. Your venture still has merit."

Cav leaves Heathen behind when he descends the gangplank. There's no hiding the spring in his step, a brightness so light that it carries him easily toward the remaining crates...and Cypher. In his joyful mood, Cav hardly notices her. He picks up two crates and lugs them under each arm. Even his shoulder twinge can't get to him now, but Cypher doesn't let him get far. "We need to talk."

"I'll finish these up!" he calls over his shoulder. "There, see? You don't even have to yell at me."

He takes the supplies onboard, but when he makes his way back, Cypher's still watching him with a somber expression. The crow perched on her shoulder looks even more grave.

"Gods, what?" Cav picks up another crate. "You're looking at me like I'm dying."

Cypher's mouth sets into a thin line. "You're not going to want to hear it."

"So don't tell me." Cav carries another load onto the ship, an uneasy feeling creeping up his spine. The pain in his shoulder grows more insistent. He doesn't know what Cypher has to say, but something is going on. Something real.

He hates that. No matter how fraught things are between them, Cypher would not bring something to him if she wasn't certain of it. It's clear his resistance is wearing on her. When he returns to the dock, she is primed to follow. "I do not enjoy this, ok? I know we have our differences, but we're…"

She cuts herself short. That stops Cav. She doesn't have to say it; he knows. They have been crammed onto the same ship for the last two years, spending nearly every day in each other's orbit. When Cypher was knocked overboard, Cav jumped in without a second thought. When Cav's healing wounds got infected, Cypher scoured three islands to find the medicine he needed. They are not two strangers in the same vicinity; they share a life, a bond forged on the *Indulgence*. Difficult as it may be, they care for each other.

He straightens slowly. "What is it?"

Cypher tugs at her bandana. "I know you have feelings for Lyx, but they're clouding your judgment."

His eyes roll, but anxiety creeps through him. "This again?"

"I'm serious, Cav. She's been sneaking around since she

got here. I caught her on the deck in the dead of night."

"That makes someone guilty?"

"She met someone yesterday morning." Her eyes glint like she's forcing herself not to look away, the inkblot sharpening on her cheekbone. "I followed her all the way down the dock with my crow. I couldn't tell who it was, but she disappeared with him. She's hiding something."

Cav's heart lurches. Yesterday morning, before Lyx showed him everything. His heart thuds. Who was she meeting? Her ex? Was the pool just a distraction? Was any of it real?

He shakes his head. It *was* real. He *knows* it was, even if what Cypher says is true. Thoughts cloud his mind, but he pushes through them. "It doesn't matter."

"Of course it matters!"

"Heathen doesn't know, does she?"

Cypher's jaw tenses. Of course she doesn't. While this might be enough for Cypher to come to Cav, they both remember what happened with Heathen last time. Cypher won't risk her pride again without solid proof. "I'm telling *you* so you can spare yourself the heartache. Lyx is only here to get what she needs before she makes a fool of you. Of all of us"

Smoke coils from Cav's nostrils. "Have you considered maybe there's a reason?"

Cypher scoffs cruelly.

"It's not like you've asked!" Cav's tail jerks behind him. "If she did meet with someone, maybe there's a purpose. Maybe she's ashamed of something. Maybe she needs help instead of your constant accusations."

"She's leading you on, Cav!" Cypher laughs humorlessly. "If you want to play hypotheticals, let's do it. Maybe she's setting us up. Maybe she's calling her siren friends to run us aground. Maybe she's leeching off of you until there's nothing left."

"I trust her."

It comes to him so easily. He means it. Lyx saved his life in the grotto. She healed him. She sent him back to shore. Since the *Silver Spoon*, she could have killed him half a dozen times, but she hasn't. She showed him more than she ever did before. She opened up to him.

Cypher's head shakes back and forth. There's the disappointment he expected from Heathen, her anger boiling over. "No wonder she let you live," she spits. "You're such an easy mark. She knew she could come back years later, and you'd still be a fucking sucker. How does that feel?"

"What is your problem?" he growls. She knows exactly what to say to hurt him...and so does he. The words seep out before he thinks better of it, before he can stop himself. "Are you just mad because I have what you can't? Is that it?"

The crow's feathers ruffle. Cypher's inkblot shifts.

An icy chill wraps around Cav's spine. He swallows, like that will take the words back. "I'm sorry." His gaze drops to the ground. "I shouldn't have —"

She doesn't look at him when she shoves the parchment to his chest. "Handle the rest yourself, then, since you know every-fucking-thing."

He calls after, but she doesn't stop. She storms back onto the ship, leaving Cav clutching the supply list and his apology. No matter what front Cypher puts up, her curse is a delicate subject. He knows that. He knows better than to touch it.

Dejected, he leans back against the dock piling and flattens out the parchment. There's one last produce drop to pick up. The least he could do is finish it. Scrubbing a hand down his face, he makes his way between two storefronts to the fruit vendor's stand.

The marketplace begins to grow crowded, customers running morning errands or searching for breakfast. Cav loads the full basket onto his strong shoulder and starts back toward the ship, weaving into an alleyway to let a group of children pass.

A hand closes over his arm. When he turns toward the interruption, a voice flows between his ears and drowns out his thoughts.

"You're coming with me, pretty boy."

THIRTY-ONE

Lyx

Lyx still feels like she's floating in that pool.

Her body is more buoyant than it has been in years, splayed on her back and drifting. She's carried through thoughts of Cav, but she's no longer stuck on the memories of before. Now she remembers his warmth when she pinned him beneath her, his shiver under her tentacles, his mouth forming certainly around the words.

I'm in love with you.

Her skin tingles. She turns the word over in her mind again and again, as if she can sand down its meaning, strip it of its power, reduce it to nothing but ash.

Love.

Love.

Love.

No matter how much she handles it, the meaning remains.

It lingers when she wakes in her cabin to light creeping across the sky. Upstairs, the *Indulgence* rustles to life. She lies on her back and listens to the creak of the ship, the sleepy mumbles of the crew, the gentle jostling of the tankards. If she weren't so used to the agitation of Tidus, the mellow chaos here might almost be...nice.

Her nose wrinkles. She pulls herself out of bed and ascends the stairs to Cav's hammock, but it's already flat and empty. She scans the faces on deck, but Cav is not among them.

Lace sidles up beside her with a piece of hardtack. "Looking for Cavalier?" He points past the railing, and Lyx follows his finger to one of the shops where Cav hoists a basket of fruit onto his shoulder. Lace dunks the bread into his coffee. "Why don't you two share a room? Or is the distance part of the foreplay?" His eyes sparkle. "Pretending you're strangers. That you couldn't *possibly* spend the night together."

"Don't give them ideas," Briar grumbles, nursing a steaming mug. "Cav doesn't need more reason to hoard her away."

Their banter is familiar, a mischief that would fit right in among the sirens. The comparison surprises Lyx. How long has it been since she thought fondly of her siblings? Of anyone? It's a strange, homesick feeling that hits her in the center of her chest.

Briar misreads her. "Don't worry. You won't be cooped up on the ship for much longer. We're almost at the end of our route."

"A week off. *Unsupervised.*" Lace nudges his hip against Lyx's. "You know what that means..."

She lifts her brow, but a blue fluttering catches in the corner of her eye, and the flag of Tidus's ship waves like a set of gnarled fingers.

Her heart seizes. He's never gotten so close to the *Indulgence*, but today, he's tied only a few spots away. Has he grown tired of waiting on her? Has he struck out on his own? Has he done something to Cav?

She leans over the railing until it digs into her abdomen, but she strains further. There's no sign of Tidus, but when she looks back at Cav, he's vanished.

Lyx breaks away from the railing, pushing through the disgruntled crew until she reaches the bottom of the gangplank. It's like swimming upstream, shoving her way through bodies toward Tidus's ship. Standing on her toes, she can't make out anything. There's no sign of movement on his ship, but she needs to get closer. When she lowers to elbow through the throng of people, someone knocks her into the shops.

Her feet skid on something sticky. A pulp of berries clings to her sandals. When she steps back to inspect it, she nearly trips on an apple. There are more abandoned fruits along the side of the building. Lyx follows the trail, passing trampled bananas and scuffed oranges until she finds the basket discarded. It sits half-empty beside the mouth of the alley, obscured by an overhang of vines that swings gently, like someone has just passed through them.

She ducks into the alley to find a maze of paths, worn trails that wind through stone and flora and jut off in different directions. Lyx turns right, but she stops short and doubles back. She has no clue where to go until she spots the purple smear of berries sloping down the hill.

She dives after them. The clamor of the dock fades away. The trail grows more faint, but she pins her hopes to it until the berries fade completely.

Her chest heaves. She spins in the intersection, searching desperately for a sign. Down one of the forks, sunlight glints off something silver. She sprints after it, ducking under archways and scraping the walls until she reaches the courtyard hidden in the trees.

A blue hand clamps around Cav's throat and pins him to the wall. He doesn't look at Lyx. He's focused on the woman before him, his eyes covered in a film that Lyx hasn't seen in so long.

She flings herself forward and knocks the woman to the ground. They are a mass of scraping nails, gnashing teeth, and swinging fists. Lyx rolls herself on top, but the woman squirms out from under her. It's instinctual how their hands tangle in the other's hair, jerking back to root each other in place while they catch their breath.

Only now does Lyx recognize her sister. So rarely has she seen Sinoe on land, her features tempting but sharp. She moves fluidly, adapted to this environment like any other. There's the barest widening of her barracuda pupils before she wipes away the shock and shoves out of Lyx's grip.

They both rise to their feet. Cav rushes toward Lyx, no longer trapped under Sinoe's spell. He handles her gently. Sinoe's gaze flicks over them until Lyx speaks. "Sinoe."

Sinoe's lips curl into a smirk. "I see we're all lining up to kill this one."

A typhoon of emotions courses through Lyx, but she knows better than to take her eyes off Sinoe. Lyx eases Cav behind her, but it doesn't go unnoticed. Subtly, Sinoe maneuvers two steps to the left, eyes sparking when Lyx mirrors her.

Lyx has to turn Sinoe's attention elsewhere. She settles onto the balls of her feet, toeing the line between bracing herself and inciting this further. "How did you find me?"

"I didn't." Sinoe jerks her chin toward Cav, who rubs the mark on his throat. "I was looking for *him*. Something was pulling me here." Her focus hones on Lyx. "I guess that was you."

Lyx swallows around emptiness. It couldn't have been her. She doesn't have her song, the only thing that connects her to other sirens. She's been cut off from it for years, but...could it do this on its own? Could it be reaching for people that Lyx isn't aware of, crying out for things outside of Lyx's control?

She can't give anything away. Encountering another siren isn't simple. It's a deadly game, and Lyx is at a disadvantage. Her body tunes to Sinoe's. The tide of Sinoe's being laps at her ankles, and Lyx wants to step deeper into it.

Sinoe senses it. She keeps her eyes on Lyx when she speaks to Cav. "You're the pirate who ran your mouth, aren't you? The one who sent the hunters our way. Couldn't stop bragging about the siren you found, huh?"

"I wasn't bragging."

Sinoe's gaze scrapes to his like a fork across a plate. "Then how did your *friends* know exactly where to find us?"

"They weren't –" He exhales, eyes slipping shut under an invisible weight. "I made a map. It took days figuring out where I'd been, looking through all the books we had on board. I kept the map on me, because I didn't want anyone else to find it, but in the end..." He swallows. "I wasn't careful enough. I didn't realize it was missing until I'd spent a full day in port making trades. It must have slipped out of my pocket, or —"

"A *map*?" Sinoe seethes. "Why the fuck would you do that?" She edges viciously toward him. "You wanted the hive all to yourself, is that it? You thought you'd make a killing?"

"Of course not!"

"What, then?"

His gaze is soft and warm on the back of Lyx's neck. Her skin prickles with goosebumps. Deep down, she always knew. She always *hoped*, even when she knew she shouldn't. No matter how foolish, she wanted Cav to return to her. *For* her.

That was her wish when she saw the ship sailing toward her grotto. That was her dream when she was trapped with Tidus and had nothing else to hold onto.

But it doesn't matter. Even if Cav had been trying to get back to her, nothing has changed. Lyx was still captured. The sirens were still scattered. She still lost her song.

Sinoe's cruel laugh cuts through the air. "Oh, you poor thing; you're not the first to be left unrequited."

She pouts at Cav, but an unchecked emotion crosses Lyx's face. Sinoe latches onto it, and Lyx tries to reel it back, but it's too late.

"He *is* spoken for." Sinoe's head tilts in disbelief. Her finned ears twitch. "Not just a plaything?"

Lyx's mouth clamps shut. She can't look at Cav. She wants to lock him away in some tower out of Sinoe's grasp, but Sinoe's scales brighten when she taps this new vein of chaos.

Lyx tries to deflect. "Where are the others?"

Sinoe's teeth snap around the turbulence, like a snake about to unhinge its jaw. "Who cares?"

Lyx clenches. She can't leave Sinoe's attention on Cav. Who knows what she'll find. What she'll do to him. What Lyx will have to face? She grapples for something else, *anything* else. "What about Mollo?"

That steals Sinoe's attention, drawing her gaze back to Lyx. "She's been missing since you left. I thought *you* might've killed her."

It's strange to hear. All this time, Lyx has imagined destroying Mollo, but what if she's already gone? Lyx never considered that. Something unsettles in her chest, and she's not sure if it's grief or rage or relief.

Curiosity peaks on Sinoe's face. "Why would *you* be looking for her?"

Dammit. Lyx has shown her hand. She worries the inside of her cheek, but she refuses to be cowed. There's a way to give

Sinoe something without revealing everything, a way to satisfy her appetite without giving her a feast. "She stole something from me."

"Stole what?"

She's brazen to hope Lyx would divulge so easily when every word between them is a snare, but Lyx moves deftly around them. "She sold it to the highest bidder. Now I'm going to take it back."

Sinoe's fingernails clack together. There's no telling if she believes it. No doubt Sinoe wants more, but this is a dance they both learned the steps to long ago. Sinoe twists her mouth, mulling over Lyx's words and trying to pick out the lie between her teeth.

Lyx doesn't flinch.

Eventually, Sinoe's eyes narrow. "Well. I certainly hope no one else gets there first."

Is it a threat? A warning? Lyx can't begin to guess which, because Sinoe steps forward. Lyx moves in front of Cav, but Sinoe doesn't go for him. Instead, she reaches out to twirl a strand of Lyx's hair around her finger.

"Ditch the pirate," Sinoe purrs. "There's more out there than ships and islands. There's an entire world you've never seen." She leans closer, whispering like when the two of them were children. "Buildings as tall as the continental drop-off. A kingdom in the clouds. Everything you could want in the palm of your hand."

Lyx can't picture it. She's lost in some strange feeling, a sandbar stretched between opposing currents. One side crashes and roils with waves, but the other is bright with memories. Both sides are Sinoe.

"None of them are prepared for what sirens can do. All that chaos ripe for the taking." Sinoe presses their foreheads together, their eyes locked in a vicious embrace. Her voice lowers to an almost-desperate whisper. "Come with me."

Lyx holds her breath to imagine it. The two of them swimming off together, hunting side by side, exploring a new world without any of the anchors that keep Lyx tethered here.

But it isn't real. Who knows if the world Sinoe describes exists? Either way, Lyx is stuck here. She can't escape the pull of her song, and she doesn't want to escape the pull of something else.

Some*one* else.

The revelation startles her, tightening the muscles in her body. Sinoe senses it. The corners of her mouth turn down, but she masks her disappointment the same way she does everything else. "You have to hide it better, Lyxy." Her finger winds tighter in Lyx's hair. "You know a siren's favorite toy never lasts. We get bored. Someone gets jealous." She releases Lyx's curl and lets it spring back into place. "Or someone else wants to share it. To play with it. To tear it apart." Sinoe lifts her hand toward Lyx's cheek. Lyx sucks in a breath, but the touch never lands. It hangs in the air like the indiscernible look in Sinoe's eyes. "And it's not just other sirens you have to worry about."

Dread sinks in Lyx's stomach. No matter what games Sinoe's playing, she's right. Any attachment Lyx has to Cav is a danger. Another siren would come after him just for a taste. If Tidus had any idea of her affection, he wouldn't stop until he drained Cav of life. Until he devoured every bit of joy and hope and spit it back out.

Things are worse than she imagined. Her song has become a beacon out of her control, and without it, she is helpless. She can't protect Cav. Every moment they spend together draws a larger target on his back, and Sinoe is the first of many headed straight toward it.

Whatever emotion Sinoe shared is gone. When she reaches for Cav, only delighted spite remains. "Word of advice, pirate," she coos. "Give up your siren fantasies. Find someone nice and boring to settle down with. Someone who wouldn't trade you in at the first offer. Who can share your fragile affection."

Her fingers dance dangerously close to the mark she left on him. Cav doesn't flinch, but Sinoe's made her point. Her hips sway as she saunters down the alley.

"Otherwise..." She shoots Lyx one last, pointed look over her shoulder. "You'll only get hurt. Isn't that right, sister?"

THIRTY-TWO

Cav

While Sinoe disappears, Cav rubs at his neck, still twinging from the indentations left by her fingers. There was no hesitation when she snatched him off the street. It's haunting how mercurial she was, fluid but unpredictable. His life meant nothing to her; he was barely an obstacle. In the blink of an eye, she controlled him with her song and forced him to walk happily to his doom. He could do nothing while his free will slipped away.

Sinoe is an apex predator on land. What could she have done to him in the water?

His scales lift on end. No wonder Lyx called him a fool. During his time in the grotto, they were surrounded by a horde of sirens. What if the others had found him first? Where would he be now? Dead at the bottom of the sea?

It's only because of Lyx that he survived. It's not that he forgets she's as powerful as Sinoe, but their power feels different. Under Sinoe's control, his mind sent up emergency flares; with Lyx, he craves the vulnerability. He loves to leave his fate in her hands. It's been that way since the moment he washed up on her shore. As certain as he was that Sinoe would kill him, he's always been equally certain that Lyx will not.

When he turns to her, she's scowling with a far-off look in her eyes. Whatever Sinoe said took a toll on her, riddles that only Lyx can comprehend, but Cav wants to understand.

"What did your other sister take from you? Mollo?" He tries to make sense of it with what he knows. "Did she give it to your ex? Is that why you've been meeting with someone?"

That brings Lyx back. Her head whips toward him. "You followed me? Did he see you?"

"Of course not. Cypher —" He shakes the thought away. "It doesn't matter. What matters is getting back what you lost."

Lyx gnaws at her lip for a long moment before she starts back down the path.

Cav jogs to keep up. "What is it? What did Sinoe mean?" When Lyx doesn't respond, Cav swings in front of her to catch her by her arms. "Lyx, please, talk to me. I can help you. *Let me* help you."

There is something so distant about her now. Something desperately out of reach, like Sinoe's appearance put her into a boat and cast her out on her own. When Lyx finally speaks, it's slow and punctuated, so that Cav grasps every word. "I lied to get on the *Indulgence*. I lied to *you*."

"About looking for your ex?" The ghost of a smile crosses Cav's face. "I told you I wouldn't care if you were hiding something. Whatever it is, we can fix it."

"No, *we* can't!" she grits when she pulls free of his grasp, but it almost sounds like she's pleading with him. "Do you *never* think about yourself? You toss yourself into danger without any idea what it entails. You risk your life for nothing."

"It's not for nothing," he murmurs. "It's for you."

"*Why*?!"

His face softens. "Something you don't believe in."

Her eyes slip shut. She remembers what he confessed in the pool. He's not afraid of it. He doesn't regret it, but she keeps her eyes closed, like she's in pain. Like she can't look at him. "Sinoe was right." Her words are heavy. "You should do what she says. You should find someone nice —"

"I don't want *nice*." Cav recoils. "And I don't care what she says. I want to hear it from you."

Her head shakes sharply. "Sirens can't —"

"Don't tell me about sirens. Tell me about *you*."

He can't take watching her suffer for some rule she's been told to follow. He reaches for her hands, smoothing his fingers over the pulse in her wrist.

"It's always 'sirens can't,' but never '*I* can't.'" He cups her face and holds it between his hands. "Tell me what *you* feel. Tell me what's real for *you*."

Her lip trembles, and Cav swears there's a storm brewing in her eyes. Bewildering and wild, threatening the certainty she's always clung to, the laws of nature she's built her life around. Maybe it's all in his head. Maybe it's wishful thinking, but her voice does crack. "You're wasting your time with me."

"Then let me waste it." His thumbs brush her cheeks. "Let me help you. Even if you can't feel the same, I do. I'm still here."

She lets out a shaky breath. Her gaze flicks over his face like she's standing at a cliff's edge – and then, she jumps, grabbing ahold of him and rushing to meet his mouth. It's as all-consuming as the rest of her. Fire roars up his throat and heats his mouth when she presses him back against the wall. This time, she doesn't kiss like she needs to claw her way inside. She kisses like she's already there, entwined with his body and soul. She kisses like they're being swept away, fingers clutching his shirt, knee hiking over his hip, doing everything she can to keep him close.

He leans into her, clings to her, molds his mouth against her neck to suck a bruise under her jaw. It doesn't satisfy her. She tugs at his shirt and fumbles with the laces, sliding her hand down to the waist of his trousers. He doesn't want to deny her, but something isn't right. There's a frantic insistence that vibrates off of her, a panic running out of time, like she might vanish into thin air if he lets go of her.

"We need to get back," he breathes against her mouth. "The ship's going to leave."

When he pulls back, her eyes are wet. He thumbs at the tears.

"What's wrong? What is it?"

He's not sure he's seen her like this. She looks over his face like she's memorizing every detail. "Stay with me tonight. Please." It's the first time she's asked him to come closer. The first time she hasn't disguised her want with barbs or sharp edges.

"Of course," he murmurs.

She pries her fingers out of his shirt, and he takes her hand to lead her back through the winding stone walls. She keeps a tight grip on him when they reemerge, scanning the nearby ships until they reach the *Indulgence*. Colt is loading the last of the supplies and frowns when he catches sight of Cav.

"Hey, what happened to —" Colt spots the hold Lyx has on Cav, the mark blooming on her neck, the disheveled look of both of them. He smirks. "Shit, never mind."

They push past him and descend to the cabin. Cav's heart thuds. He has always wanted Lyx *so badly*, and now, they're racing toward a place they've never reached before, one he's only been able to find in his dreams.

He wants to go there with her.

As soon as the door swings shut, she tears at his shirt. It rips down the center, and Cav jerks the rest of the fabric apart so he can touch her again. She gasps into his mouth, her hands roaming his breasts, his waist, his hips, and leaving a scorching trail behind. He wishes her palms could burn him. He wishes he could have a map of everywhere she's touched him, scar tissue rising from his skin and reminding him that she was here.

They land on the bed, cursing when it keeps them from freeing their clothes. Lyx tugs at his belt, but her shaking hands can't finish the job, urgent and clumsy.

His hands close over hers and guide the buckle open. "It's ok."

"It's not enough," she pants. Her nails rake his stomach. "It's not *enough*."

"*What's* not enough?"

"You're not *close* enough."

He works his trousers down his legs before he tugs off her dress in one motion. The full lengths of their naked bodies press against each other. It's the first time they've been together like this. Nothing between them. Not even water.

His fingers skate over her body. He finds the scars that rope her torso, the iridescent scales at her clavicle, the juncture of her thighs where her tentacles formed. She wanders over him with the same reverence, her cool skin against the heat of his.

He understands what she meant. Even with their naked bodies wrapped together, there is a desperation to be closer, a longing to be entwined in something deeper than skin. He feels that same hunger to be consumed, to be devoured, to become part of each other.

He drags his mouth against hers. She molds against him, gasping when he drags his teeth into her bottom lip before he speaks. "What if we could be closer?"

Her eyes open, heavy and wanton. She kisses him again, her tongue curling into his mouth until his brain sparks. It's so hard to pull away, but he wants more. He *needs* it.

He forms the words against her lips. "What if you ate me?"

THIRTY-THREE

Cav

Lyx's pupils blow wide, two black holes drowning out the violet of her iris. It's a hunger unlike anything Cav's seen, seeping through her until she trembles. "I — can't." Even denying it, she trails her tongue over her lips. "You would die."

"You could take pieces." He guides her hand toward his chest and sets her fingers against one of his scales. The tip of her fingernail eases beneath it. "You could pry it off."

Intently, her gaze follows him, a predator tracking prey. He moves her nail under the edge, hissing when the scale barely lifts away from the skin. It stirs magma between his legs.

Lyx watches the heat of his vent. "Why would you offer that?"

Laughter strains out of him, his chest arching into her palm. The reckless part of him wants to provoke her, pushing and pushing until she closes the space between them.

"Because I want to be inside you."

Her finger flexes.

"I want you to know my flavor." He sucks in a breath. "I want to plague your dreams."

It's only fair. Cav has spent the last two years looking for Lyx in everything, searching for something to move him as strongly as she does. If he made her give him something real, he can do the same. When she came aboard, he was kidding himself. The experiment would never have been enough to satisfy him. He wanted Lyx's obsession. He wanted her to hunt him down and make him pay for his mistakes. He wanted her to take as much of him as she desired.

When Lyx digs deeper, Cav's head tips back. He groans and grits his teeth, but he refuses to look away. "I want you to savor me. *Do it*."

She pushes him onto his back and lowers her mouth to his chest. She meets his eyes, easing her tongue under the scale and tormenting him with the slow spread of pain.

It's a game of nerves. Cav refuses to lose. Not when he's waited so long for this, when he wants to be engulfed by her in every way, when all his baser instincts cry out to know her carnally.

She doesn't push further. She's still holding back, teasing the tender flesh under his scale. She's trying to scare him, to make him reconsider what this means, but he wants it as badly as she does.

More.

He pushes up onto his elbows. "You think I'm a fool. That I'm doing this just to please you. You think this will leave a mark on me, but what about you?"

Her brows knit when his head tilts toward her. He fights the urge to moan when her teeth graze him.

"You want to devour me," he pants, "because it's all you can think about."

He knows it's true the same way he knows where north is, an instinct worn into the core of his being. He is pulled to Lyx like the magnetic needle of a compass. He always has been, and he always will be.

"And once you do..." His lips brush her ear. "You'll never get the taste of me out of your mouth. You'll crave me the same way I've craved you. You'll be hungry for me, until nothing and no one else can sate you."

Lyx surges toward him, pinning his hands beside his head. Her teeth dig under his scale until he's writhing, gasping, throbbing with need. No longer does Lyx taunt him. She uses her teeth to work under his scale, scraping the raw skin beneath.

He moans out a cloud of smoke. Lyx laves at his blood, smearing her lips until her eyes sink closed and her hand moves between his legs. His eyes roll back when she finds his wet, hot center. His scale is still in place, but Lyx laps her tongue under it. She works her fingers and mouth in the same rhythm, fucking his cunt and wound in time.

"Please don't stop," he begs.

She sinks blunt teeth into his scale and tugs. His head swims, torn between pain, pleasure, and the sight of her looking up at him. "I've never done this without fangs." The words come streaming out of her while her fingers work deeper inside him. "I've never taken my time. I've never wanted to."

She looks as dazed as he is, her skin glowing beside the vibrant ember in his chest. It's hypnotizing to watch her slowly pulling him apart, staining her mouth with him, getting drunk on his taste. She doesn't rush through any of it. She keeps them both suspended, soaking in every sight and scent and sound.

Slow. Languid. Deep.

He doesn't know how much time passes. All he knows is

the exquisite scrape of her teeth bound up with the stroke of her fingers. Every time he gets too close to the peak, she eases back, making him moan and plead for more. He loses track of how many orgasms she steals away from him, leaving him shivering while she soothes her tongue over his growing wound.

"Not yet," she murmurs. "Not until I've had my fill of you."

He nearly comes right then. With her fingers inside him, the lava never cools, dripping over her hand and the sheets. Tears streak Cav's cheeks, and she licks them away, kissing his own blood back into his mouth. It's divine. It's ecstasy, the two of them mixed together, a clash of hot and cold melting on his tongue.

She could have ended it far sooner. She could have ripped the scale away, but she draws it out, letting blood dribble toward his collarbone. It keeps him hanging in this rarefied state, brushing back her hair to get a better look at where she mouths at him.

Finally, the scale hangs loose. Pressure builds deep in his gut, but Lyx still doesn't allow him to find release. She keeps fucking him over three fingers, stretching him while she licks at the bloody mark. She presses her teeth into his weakened shoulder, leaving behind an indentation that she kisses tenderly. He wants it to scar. Gods, if he could spend the rest of his life being picked apart by her, he would.

She picks up the pace between his legs. He whines and grasps at her, but he doesn't want her to stop. His hips keep working against her until he shudders, muscles tensing in his legs as his toes curl.

Lyx meets Cav's eyes when she closes her teeth around the base of the scale and pulls. He arches and bites his lip, panting and blurry-eyed when he stares at the rough, triangular patch missing from his body.

Lyx turns the scale over in her mouth. Her eyes slip closed, and a hum rises from her throat, so deep and wanton that Cav's vent clenches around her fingers.

He touches her lips. She opens her eyes again — possessive, like an animal guarding a meal — but she doesn't hold back from him. She parts her lips and extends her tongue to show off her prize. There, amidst the cool colors of her mouth, sits his burnt red scale awash in blood.

The sight of her holding him so reverently sends heat scorching through him. He digs his heels into the sheets, urging her to move faster, but her strokes are slow and deep. She curls her fingers and lowers to him, kissing him open-mouthed and filthy. Every ridge and divot of the scale slides across his tongue. His mouth is a forge, molding the taste of both of them into one molten flavor. Her tongue rolls against his and matches the pace of her slick fingers. Every touch heats him beyond his melting point, drawing out his desire and shaping it into something thick and heavy.

Lyx doesn't stop until he comes. His claws tangle in her hair, his mouth dragging helplessly against hers when lava spurts over her wrist. She fucks him all the way through it, and only once he's a writhing, pitiful mess does she lick the scale out of his mouth. Gently, she presses it to the roof of her mouth, holding onto it like she doesn't want to lose it, like she doesn't want this to end...until finally, she swallows.

Cav traces a hand down the column of her throat to follow the scale's path. He can't describe the feeling. Part of him is inside her. It *belongs* to her. Impossible as it seems, he's still connected to it. No matter what becomes of the scale now, Cav will still be there. He and Lyx are entwined. Nothing can unravel that.

With weakened fingers, he traces the curve of her cheek. "What do I taste like?"

Every emotion has been wrung from the depths of his

body. He can barely move in the midst of the blissful cool of her. No matter how he tries to keep his eyes open, exhaustion creeps in so easily. He remembers this feeling, drowsiness pouring over him like the last night in her grotto. But this time, there is no potion. This time, she can't send him away.

Lyx's fingers trail hesitantly through his hair, brushing tendrils behind his horns, unsure if she should touch him so softly. Sleep wraps its arms around him to pull him under, but he tries to stay afloat. He wants to hear her, even as exhaustion threatens to overtake him.

Lyx's voice is barely a whisper, precarious and halting. "You taste like…a rogue fruit splashing into the ocean. A bed of seagrass in the sun."

It's not a taste, but Cav understands. He imagines that warmth, the sway of the waves, the tickle of grass against his skin. Slowly, he drifts, until he can barely hear her. Until he can't be sure she's speaking at all.

"The first step into the ocean after years of dry land."

THIRTY-FOUR

Lyx

She has to settle for a piece of him.

Lyx has dreamt of destroying Cav for so long, of tearing him apart, but maybe it was never about that. Maybe she was always looking for an excuse to consume him. A way to keep him with her always.

Never has she eaten someone because she wanted them closer. Only because she wanted them gone.

But Cav has found a way to satisfy all her hungers. With him, the need for discord is quelled. It doesn't claw and scratch and leave her itching to fight; it sates her without sickening her, something she'd long believed was impossible.

For hours, Cav and Lyx are in a haze, drifting in and out of sleep until they can't help but touch each other again. Cav buries his face between her legs while his tail wraps around her mouth, and she groans and pries one of his scales off with her teeth. Lyx rides his vent until it's a hot and sticky mess, both of them panting and shivering when they come again and again. She drags her tongue over his body, soaking in every sight and smell and sound.

This is what it's like to drown.

Pale morning light glints into the cabin. Overhead, footsteps move across the deck as the *Indulgence* jostles into a new dock. Cav's sleeping breath teases Lyx's neck. Her mouth is still warm from the taste of him, a smoky, coppery cinnamon. She trails her tongue over her lips. Now, she'll have a part of Cav forever, but it isn't enough to ease the aching hole inside her. The hollow place left behind by her song is nothing compared to lying next to Cav and knowing she has to leave.

For a moment, she pretends that she can stay here. That no one else controls her. That Cav is not endangered by her presence.

Then she slips out from beneath his arm.

Her head spins when she stands. She braces against the hanging desk and silently tugs on her clothing, stuffing a few other pieces into a bag. Everything is unfinished. Instinct prickles her scales. *You dreamt of killing him for years, yet you leave him intact? You take a bite, but not all of him? Did you learn nothing when you spared him the first time?*

Lyx squeezes her eyes shut. She has to set Cav free. It was the kindest thing she did in the grotto, and she must do it again. If she tells him how she's trapped, he'll endanger himself. He'll put himself close to Tidus, and that is one of the most dangerous places he can be.

And if Lyx's song has begun calling out on its own, she needs to take it far away from Cav. She knows what will happen if other sirens emerge. Like Sinoe, they will see the way she looks at Cav. They will watch with covetous eyes. They will sense Lyx's weakness. If she stays, she will lose Cav in a worse way than she's ever imagined.

She fumbles for a scrap of parchment on the desk. Cav stirs and rolls toward the place Lyx left behind. She watches him for a long moment, tracing the lines of his body with her eyes before she finds a quill and dips it into the inkwell.

If love is real, then I have to leave.

She writes the word slowly. *Love.* It's unfamiliar, a notion she never desired, and an abstraction always out of reach. It never had a place among sirens. Love could never satisfy her the way chaos did. There was no reason to seek it.

But what if love is what she's been chasing all along? What if that's why she's been looking for Cav? Not hate, not revenge, but something else that devoured her completely. A desperate obsession. A bottomless longing. A reckless indulgence.

Her chest is tight. She can't consider that now, so she leaves the note on the desk and eases the cabin door shut behind her. When she creeps onto the deck, the morning crew is sluggishly huddled around the coffee pot. The gangplank hasn't yet been lowered, but Lyx finds the ladder attached to the side of the ship and descends.

She feels like she's getting away with something awful, turning her back on Cav and walking across the dock. Water laps at the posts by her feet, and in the distance, a bell clangs. There is no bustle of activity. No eager visitors. No mellow disarray. It's such a stark change from the *Indulgence* with its hum of conversation. Behind her, a round of laughter carries on the wind.

Before her, there is nothing but Tidus's ship sailing into port.

The dock feels endless. Lyx almost wishes it was, the dread mounting inside her with every plank she crosses. Her mind tries to latch on some other possibility. *You could run.*

You could swim. You could turn around.

But she knows how each of them ends: with her song crying out for her, and Tidus hunting her down.

Ahead, Tidus's ship comes to a stop behind a larger one. Waves rush past her beneath the dock. Her tentacles yearn to break free. She can almost feel them wrapping around the trees and stones to hold her in place, but her feet don't stop. She knows where she must go. She knows what she must do.

She climbs aboard Tidus's ship.

He pushes out of the galley, eyes darting wildly behind her. "What the fuck are you doing here?"

"Heathen kicked me off."

Tidus grips the doorframe so hard it squeaks. His jaw twitches. When he points behind him through the doorway, his finger shakes with rage.

Lyx doesn't move. She should revel in the tumult, but it makes her sick. Going below deck will give Tidus license to take out his fury however he sees fit.

He knows it too. Baring his teeth, he clamps a hand around her arm and yanks her into the galley.

He storms and paces like a caged animal past the pot heating on the stove. Lyx doesn't take her eyes off it. "I told you she was suspicious," she says. "Her quartermaster followed me to our last meeting. They saw how close your ship was docked yesterday. They figured it out."

A reasonable explanation won't calm Tidus, but it's the only thing she has. He keeps pacing, running fingers through his hair until he grabs the pot and flings it across the room. Liquid splatters against the wall and across the table. Lyx forces herself not to flinch.

"How could you fuck this up?!" he screams. "We were *this close!*"

Lyx waves the thought away with a trembling hand. "You can do better than the *Indulgence*. That's a small fish. We'll find a different target. A better one."

Depths, she prays it strokes his ego. The room is suffocating with chaos spiraling out of her control, and she doesn't know how to calm it.

"What about that disappearing treasure island?" She grasps for anything to distract him. "Chart a course for that. You can get rich. Buy all the followers you want."

It's like he doesn't hear her. His eyes are rabid, chest heaving, filling her with an endless pool of nausea.

Then he takes a steadying breath.

It's alarming how the tension seeps out of his body. His shoulders settle, and her heart thuds. All she can see are the empty, hollow depths of his pupils.

His voice is terrifyingly even. "What did your little hero think of this?"

A sour taste etches into her mouth. She wants to scream. "Who?"

It's a pitiful excuse for a lie, but it's the only hope she has. Maybe Tidus will forget Cav's name again. Maybe he'll forget Cav exists at all. Maybe he won't see the panic rising inside Lyx like a tidal wave.

Tidus's gaze catches on her like a hook. "Bet he hated to see you leave. Bet he thinks Heathen got it all wrong."

Bet he'd give you anything you want — given the right motivation.

A chill crackles up Lyx's spine. "*Do not touch him.*"

Beneath Tidus's shirt, the shell glows until it vibrates. The light casts across Tidus's face from below, leaving haunting shadows behind.

"You're right, Lyx." He eases in front of her and drags his pointer finger across the table. Only now does she realize he's blocking the door. He smears through the liquid, pressing the pad of his finger down against the wood. "I don't need you on the *Indulgence.* I need you right...here."

The bell in the distance stops clanging.

The second Lyx lunges, Tidus slams her to the ground. The wind escapes her lungs, but she tries her best to scream. Tidus catches every sound in his palm.

The boat rocks beneath them. She scratches and kicks, but he locks his other hand around her throat. Pain lances through her. Her eyes are wide and wild as Tidus's trembles above her from the effort.

"If you won't get me what I want..." His rough hands dig in deeper, slicing the delicate skin of her gills. "I know someone who will."

THIRTY-FIVE

Cav

Never has Cav slept so soundly. The afternoon sun on his eyelids is enough to keep him drowsy. His muscles ache, sated and heavy. A smile flits across his lips. When he shifts, the raw skin on his chest twinges. Last night felt like a dream, but the pain is a reminder that it was real. It happened. He and Lyx have seen each other in a way unmatched by anyone else.

Groggily, he reaches out for her. The sheets beside him have no hint of Lyx's cool body.

He cracks one eye open against the light, but he can tell there's no sign of Lyx. Maybe she got hungry. Despite the events of last night, she can't sustain herself on pieces of Cav alone.

With a stretch, he swings his legs over the side of the bed. Overhead, there are only two sets of footsteps. It must be later than he realized. Most of the crew will have already disembarked, so Cav needs to get a move-on. He'd rather not get stuck taking the *Indulgence* for maintenance when he has a week-long holiday ahead of him.

He tugs on the clothing tossed across his desk, and a scrap of parchment flutters to the ground. He crouches to retrieve it. The handwriting is unfamiliar. His fingers trace the jagged, unpracticed letters with fondness. They're Lyx's.

If love is real, then I have to leave.

He could float to the ceiling. *Love.* Does she love him? Is it possible?

Then the bubble bursts, sending him crashing back to the ground. *Leave.* What does that mean? Why would she go? *Where* would she go?

He yanks open the door and bounds up the stairs, nearly knocking Heathen over. She steadies herself on the banister. "I was starting to worry. You're the last —"

"Where's Lyx?" he pants. "Have you seen her?"

Heathen blinks. Cypher appears behind her. "She's not with you?"

Cav's stomach sinks. He hurries across the deck with Heathen calling after him. "Cav, we already swept the ship. There's no one else on board."

He can't accept it. How can Lyx be gone, *again*? It's like he's reliving a nightmare where he's always too late to change the ending.

There's no sign of her. Of course there isn't. He moves back to his cabin, passing Heathen and Cypher in the doorway. Heathen speaks softly. "Cav..."

"She left." The words echo through him, hollow and heavy at once. Gods, why does she always leave him like this? Because she knows he'd try to stop her? Because she knows it would work? Why will she never let him *help her*?

Heathen takes the crumpled parchment from his hand

and scans it. Cav's raw skin throbs. Lyx truly has taken a piece of him, and he wants that to mean something. He *knows* they crossed a threshold last night. It was more than an experiment or revenge or thrill.

When Cypher takes the parchment from Heathen, Cav wants to snatch it back. "Are you happy?" It's not her fault, he knows, but the hurt swirls inside him like steam looking for any crack to escape from. "At least you can finally take off that fucking bandana."

Cypher scratches at the edge of the fabric. The outline of the fiery *Indulgence* is still imprinted in black.

Of course. For all of Cypher's suspicion, Lyx isn't to blame for the mark, just like he said.

He grabs the parchment and pushes past them. The deck is completely empty now, but music and chatter rise from the island below. It's the largest port in the archipelago, bustling with shops and food and entertainment. Cav was supposed to be enjoying himself. He was supposed to be with Lyx, showing off his favorite spots and feeding her delicacies.

Now, he's just here. Alone.

Heathen emerges from below. "I'm sorry, Cav." She scans the crowd like she might see Lyx's face. "We checked everyone off when they disembarked. She must have left hours ago. Maybe she's on the island somewhere."

Cypher lingers behind them at the hatchway. "Do you..." She shifts her weight and maintains the space between them. "Do you want help looking?" Her voice is gruff with uncertainty. "Maybe another tattoo will show up, or —"

"Don't bother." When Cav walks down the gangplank, it's like wading through mud. He tries to keep his head above it. Around him, the crowd ebbs and flows and moves him along with it. Vendors shout and wave sizzling legs of meat. Music stampedes from different stalls and crashes into itself. Through it all, he searches for Lyx. He has no idea where to start, but he traverses the length of the dock and peers into every ship he passes. He retraces his steps, ducking into every shop and stand. Every flash of blue draws his eye, but it's never Lyx, just a fluttering flag or some other creature at the edge of the crowd.

She's nowhere to be found. He knew she wouldn't be, but it crushes him all the same. He trudges back down the port. The *Indulgence* has long since pulled away, and he can just make out its sails disappearing behind the furthest island.

Someone slings an arm around his shoulder. "Where's your girl?"

Cav winces, and Briar's grip loosens.

Lace nudges Cav from the other side. "We want to play with her."

A knot forms in Cav's throat. "She left."

Briar and Lace exchange a look over his head. "...Let's get you drunk."

"I don't want to drink," he mumbles, but the two of them are already tugging him toward a familiar pub, one he would have taken Lyx to if she were still here.

"Three of your strongest," Lace calls to the barkeep.

Briar sits Cav down at the bar. He's exhausted from searching. It's not the satisfying feeling of the night before; this fatigue makes his scales dry, eyes itchy, tail heavy behind him. He curls it around the stool legs to keep it from dragging on the floor.

Lace slides a shot in front of him. Cav doesn't reach for it, even when Briar and Lace tip theirs back. They're still watching Cav when they set their empty glasses on the counter. "You sure you don't want it?" Briar asks.

Their typically flippancy has been replaced by concern, and that makes Cav feel worse. He pushes away from the bar and wanders out onto the wooden deck. As far as the eye can see, there are places to explore and things to do. Cav is drawn to none of it. Nothing drives him. Nothing excites him.

Usually, he adores the hustle and bustle, but right now, he wants nothing more than to curl up in his sheets and smell Lyx embedded there. It'll be days before he can do that again. Until then, he'll have to settle for the hammocks strung up between trees at the edge of the deck.

He finds one hanging on its own. The fabric is almost the same color as his hammock on the ship. The place where Lyx laid next to him. Where he slept until she asked him to stay with her.

He climbs inside and finally lets his eyes slip shut. Every gentle breeze, every ripple, every sway reminds him of where he is. Where Lyx isn't. Where he could be instead. If he closes his eyes, he can still feel Lyx's body aligned with his, her breath against his neck, her whispered words weaving through his bloodstream.

He reminisces until he dozes off. It's a small mercy for his aching heart, sending him to a dream world where he can pretend Lyx is still with him. When he wakes with his legs tangled in the fabric, he reaches out for Lyx before he remembers she isn't here. His heart plummets again, stopped only by something crinkling in his hand.

It's too dark to make out in the setting sun. Cav sits up in hammock to use the light of the torches. In his hand is a different piece of parchment, hastily folded and tied with twine. The knot is sturdy, more suitable for a boat than a letter. Cav slides the tip of his claw to cut the twine in two before he moves to a nearby table. He flattens out the parchment with his palms.

Northern boathouse. Alone. Come get your prize.

His heart trips. How does he recognize that handwriting? It's not the scrawl of Lyx from before, but he can't quite place it. Where did this come from? What does it mean?

Torchlight dances across one of the parchment's creases. Cav cups his hand to pour out what's inside. The objects are small and iridescent, so feather-light they might blow away in the wind. Around their edges is a darker rim of flesh, like they're tiny scales plucked from a fish.

A chill spreads through Cav's body. Not a fish.

Lyx.

His head snaps up. On the deck, clusters of people laugh and dance, playing games and drinking in the fading light. There is no sign of Lyx. No sign of anyone who'd leave this note. There's not even anyone glancing in Cav's direction, except for Briar and Lace.

"Look who's finally awake." Briar holds up a shot from their table. "Ready to make bad decisions?"

Cav lifts the letter. "What is this?"

Lace cups a hand to his ear against the ruckus. When Cav moves closer, Briar and Lace both look at the parchment in confusion. "Where'd you get that?"

"I don't know," Cav answers. "Did someone give it to me?"

Briar leans out to look toward the hammock, then back to Lace. "Was it that crusty guy?"

Cav's ears perk. "Who?"

"Some man hovering around you while you slept. We ran him off." Lace gestures along the side of his face. "He was covered in crustaceans or something."

Fear latches onto Cav's chest. Who could that be? What do they want? And *what is happening to Lyx?*

Who knows how long Cav's been holding that letter — and Lyx's life — in his hands. He stuffs the scales into his pocket and moves to the wooden stairs off the side of the deck.

"Wait! Cav!" Briar leans back in her chair to shout after him. "What does it say? Where are you going?"

But Cav is already gone.

THIRTY-SIX

Cav

Cav shoves through the marketplace. People grunt and shout, but he finally breaks through the crowd and takes off toward the north of the island. A worn path meanders through sand dunes, dotted with stragglers wandering the outskirts of the port.

The further he goes, the more everything dwindles. Twilight has fully settled. The path fades into rough terrain, covered in beachgrass and rocks that Cav's feet catch on. Crickets chirp near his ankles, no longer dampened by the throng of people. For a while, there's nothing but insects and frogs until the sound of waves returns.

He's getting closer. Wind ruffles the grass, but he pushes through it to find the abandoned boathouse on the shoreline. It's a dark blot against the horizon with no torches in the broken, rotted windows. Nothing stirs inside.

Cav's pace slows. He tries to take a full breath, but

standing in the dark so far from everyone else makes his chest tight. Maybe he should have thought this through. He could have told Briar and Lace what was happening, or at least warned them to come after him. What if this is a setup? What if Lyx isn't here at all?

Foolish pirate.

Her voice stirs in his head. That's the only thing that gives him hope. She has to be here. She has to be alive. If there's even a chance she's in trouble, he's going after her.

Clenching his jaw, Cav slinks toward the boathouse. It's a strange sensation to be cautious and feel that inkling of uncertainty. His scales prickle as his gaze darts around the structure. Something moves in the window – or is it just the shadows playing tricks on him? He freezes. Is someone watching him from inside?

He forces himself to keep moving. For once, he hates the glow his body gives off, a muted beacon through his clothing. He grips his collar to keep it closed, wincing when the weathered stairs creak beneath him. There is no hiding his arrival. Whomever is waiting for him knows he's here.

The boathouse door hangs off its hinges and blocks the entrance. Beyond it, there is nothing but darkness and the skitter of dead leaves across the floor.

If love is real, then I have to keep going.

Teeth bared, he lowers his shoulder to the door and breaks his way inside. It scrapes the floor, leaving a gap barely big enough to squeeze through. Cav tilts his ear toward the opening and strains to hear. Besides the low thrum of waves, there are no other sounds. He tries to wedge past the door, but his shirt catches on a rusty nail, ripping a strip of fabric off the bottom. He curses, heart pounding before he tears himself free and squeezes inside.

Stars blink through the holes of the dilapidated roof. The floor is rough with sand and salt, and the ember inside him sheds light on moldy ropes and water-logged buckets. A few feet in front of him is an open boat bay where the ocean sloshes against its walls.

But no sign of Lyx.

"I was beginning to think you didn't care for her after all."

Cav tenses for an attack. To his right, a match strikes against the wall and catches on the tip of a cigar. It glows red on the face of a man behind it.

There's no telling what type of creature he is. His face is crusted with barnacles and anemones, gray skin pulled brittle and taut over his bones. Every movement he makes looks like a struggle. His chest rises shallowly, crushed beneath the small crustaceans embedded there. Tiny organisms cling to his body, twitching and stretching and draining the very life from him.

This must be the man who left the note, but seeing him doesn't help Cav understand. Who is he? What does he want? "Where's Lyx?"

The man takes a slow drag before he points his cigar at Cav. "Cavalier. *That's* what your name is." Smoke slips between his lips when he coughs. "You'd think I would have remembered something that fucking stupid, but you'll forgive me. It's been years."

Cav's brows knit. What does he mean? Cav doesn't know that face. He can hardly make it out, but then the man presses his cigar to the wick of a candle until it shines on his malicious smile.

An eerie familiarity skitters up Cav's spine. He knows that smile. He saw it the last day on the convoy. "Prodeus?"

Ash falls from the cigar while the man hacks and spits on the floor. "That name's so tired. 'Tidus' has more of a Captain ring to it, don't you think?" He grins. "I have you to thank for that."

He reaches into his coat and pulls out a frayed roll of

parchment. When he opens it to the light, Cav sees it's covered in jotted images and scribbled notes.

Cav's notes.

His heart lurches. Those are all his references, his shoddy illustrations, his damning circle around Lyx's grotto. A sickly feeling swirls in his stomach. "How did you get that?"

"Once you washed back up, you kept saying a siren saved you. *I* never believed you. No one did...but I kept an eye on you." Prodeus — *Tidus* takes another puff of his cigar and waves the map between his fingers. "Plucked it right out of your pocket that last day. You never even noticed."

Shame burns through Cav. He remembers Prodeus's hand on his back as he sent him off the ship. It was all a distraction. Cav spent two years regretting his carelessness, but he never lost the map in port. He never lost the map at all.

Tidus stole it.

"Don't be sad, kid." Tidus lifts the map to the flame and lets it catch. "All your hard work paid off. She was right where you said she'd be."

Cav grits his teeth to fight his panic. "*Where is she?* What did you do to her?"

"Easy..." Tidus clicks his tongue. "So impatient for someone who took their sweet time getting here." He carries the candle to a work table along the wall without any hurry in his movements.

"Look," Cav tries, "I don't know what you want, but whatever it is, I'll get it. I just need to see her —"

Tidus lifts two pinched fingers in the air. "What's this?"

Even when Cav squints, he can't make out what Tidus is holding. Only when Tidus lowers it near the candle does the light catch on it. It's a small object, milky white reflecting the flame in its glossy sheen.

"A — pearl?" Cav guesses. "What does that have to do —"

"Good," Tidus hums. "Now, what does it do?"

Cav scoffs helplessly. What the fuck does that *mean*? He tries to think of an answer, any answer, but his mind is blank.

Tidus crouches to set the candle on the floor. He's closer to the open boat bays than Cav realized. Docking loops line the platform, and sodden ropes trail off of them into the dark patch of water.

One of the ropes looks fresh. It's knotted around a metal loop, but it stretches toward the ceiling and disappears into the dark, like it's hoisting something off the ground.

Tidus nudges the candle beneath the rope.

Cav's claws dig into his palms. "I don't know what you're asking. Where is Lyx? Where —"

Unhurried, Tidus tilts the candle. Flames lap around the knot.

Cav's eyes jerk toward the rafters, but he can't make out anything. No movement. No motion. Nothing but an overwhelming dark that saturates everything.

His stomach roils. "What do you want?"

"The answer."

"I don't know!" Cav shouts. Blood pulses through him. His body itches to move, to knock Tidus into the water, to do *something*. His weight shifts onto the balls of his feet —

Tidus yanks a pistol from the back of his waistband. "*Stay right fucking there.*"

Cav's body jerks to a halt. His calves spasm, but his feet root in place like he's nailed to the floor. He doesn't want to stop. He wants to *move*, he wants to —

Light glows beneath Tidus's shirt. For a merciful moment, Cav thinks the fire has sparked onto his clothing, but the flame is still eating away at the rope. One of the strands snaps, springing apart and jolting something near the ceiling.

Cav strains to make it out. When the shape sinks lower, he sees Lyx trapped in a fishing net. It digs into her legs, pulling tight around her body to keep her arms trapped. She struggles to move, eyes wide and screams muffled by the rag bound around her head. It pulls tight across her neck and gills. Attached to her feet is a bag filled with rocks swaying threateningly over the ten-foot drop.

Fear sinks its teeth into Cav. When the candle burns through the rope, Lyx will plummet into the water. Her body will transform and tangle in the netting while her gills are smothered by the wet rag. The rocks will drag her to the bottom of the sea and keep her there.

She'll drown.

"Got your attention now, huh?" Tidus smirks, but it's short-lived. Impatience fills his eyes again. "Heathen has a stash of these pearls on the *Indulgence*." He leans down to blow on the fire lapping at the rope. "They must be for something."

"I don't know!" Cav's breath notches in his chest. He has to save Lyx, but it's like he can't move. He can't answer Tidus's impossible questions. He can't do *anything*. "I don't know what the pearls are for!"

Tidus lifts the candle. "Time's ticking."

"I don't!" Cav's heart lodges in his throat until it's suffocating. There has to be a way to save her. To stop this. He scrambles for anything. "But I know where Heathen's taking them!"

Tidus's pupils spread like ink. "Tell me."

Another strand of the rope snaps. Lyx's body jolts closer to the water.

Cav doesn't take his eyes off her. "Put out the fire."

"*Tell me!*"

"She took them somewhere!" Cav grapples for anything to satisfy him. "An island on the outer reaches, the one with the old slipway. They say they're taking it for maintenance, but Heathen only takes a skeleton crew. Always the same people. The rest of us don't see her for days."

The answer hangs in the air. Tidus gives nothing in response, mulling over the words until Cav wants to scream.

Finally, Tidus moves the candle away from the rope. "See?" he coos. "Was that so hard?"

Cav lets out a shaky breath.

"You could learn a thing or two from him," Tidus calls to Lyx before he grins at Cav. "See, Lyx *almost* finished her job for me. She used you to get a spot on the ship. She snuck around behind your back. But she couldn't wrap things up in a nice little bow."

It doesn't matter what Tidus says. What Lyx did. Relief washes over Cav, and he looks at Lyx to reassure her.

Her eyes stay wide with fear.

Tidus curls his hand around the rope and drags the broken shells of his hand against it. "So I will."

The final strand snaps, and Lyx plunges into the water.

THIRTY-SEVEN

Lyx

Drowning is nothing like Lyx imagined.

Everything is quiet. She can't hear Tidus's voice or Cav's scream, everything drowned out by the flounder of her pulse. The light from the surface grows faint until it's barely a pinprick overhead. Darkness seeps in. The water grows colder and colder.

Wet fabric clogs her mouth. She tears at it with her teeth, but that wedges it deeper. Netting grips raw lines into her flesh and tangles hopelessly with her tentacles. Her body fights to transform. There's not enough room. The ropes dig into the bell of her tail.

Something brushes her back. Her body jerks, but her eyes haven't adjusted yet. She doesn't know what else is down here with her.

She can't swim. Can't move. Can't *breathe*. Her thoughts scatter. Her lungs burn.

Above her, something splashes into the water.

Mucky fabric clings to her gills, and bubbles rise up around her as if the ocean itself is in distress.

A shadow passes over her, and two clawed hands find her face. In her panic, she yanks away, but the hands don't release her. They tug on the rag around her neck, backlit by the glow of the person behind them.

Cav.

He slices through the fabric and tugs it free. Lyx's gills expand, and Cav grabs onto the net and swims lower. Lyx can hardly make him out any longer, but something pulls taut and begins to vibrate near her feet. Cav's arm saws back and forth through the rope connecting the bag of rocks. Finally, something snaps, and Cav wraps his arms around her waist and kicks off of the sea floor.

They surface with a gasp, and he kicks toward the stone staircase. "I've got you."

Lyx keeps her head above water, gritting her teeth when the netting twists tighter. Her body is impossibly heavy, weighed down with chaos, but Cav settles her onto the bottom step to keep her lower half submerged.

His hands smooth over her face. "Can you breathe?"

"Where's Tidus?" she croaks.

Cav sighs his relief before he cuts away at the net with his claws.

"You have to go after him," Lyx rasps. "He wants the pearls, he —"

"I'm not leaving you here."

He keeps cutting her free, but the air between them sizzles with what's left unfinished.

After a long moment, his voice comes low and pointed. "What part of it was real?"

Shame and guilt curdle in her throat. They're strange emotions she barely knows how to name. If she were smart, she would say none of it. She would say it was all an act, that everything she did was in service to her mission. If she were Mollo, or Sinoe, she would laugh at Cav's pain and lap it up to feed herself.

Even if she did, Cav would keep freeing her from the net. He would still help her. He would not abandon her.

"He was telling the truth." She watches the waves rolling in. "I lied to get onto the ship. I spied on Heathen's work. I was working for him."

"And the rest of it?" Water slips off Cav's nose and drips into the water. "Did you show me yourself in that pool because he told you to? Did you save me from Sinoe because you had to?" His eyes dip to her mouth where her fangs are still receding. "Did you eat from me because of someone else?"

She trembles, but not from cold. It's a truth she's avoided for so long, but...what's the fucking point of it? She's tired of fighting it. Tired of running from it. She doesn't try to lie; there's no longer a part of her that would believe it. "No."

Cav's breath gusts across her lips, but he doesn't close the space. "Why did you *leave* again?"

That seems to wound him more than anything else. She exhales sharply. "I'm – sorry. I thought...it would protect you. I didn't want you to be in danger, but you ended up here, anyway."

"I can't help it." He smiles tenderly. She wants to see that smile again, a hundred times over.

All her life, she has believed she had nothing and no one to answer to, but she was never truly free. Tidus is not the only thing to have control over her. The most obvious, maybe, but not the first. Long ago, she learned the ways of sirens. She followed those rules as if they were laws of nature, unchangeable and innate. She sought the things she was supposed to want. She never questioned it. She did what she was supposed to do.

Until Cav arrived in her grotto.

That was the first time she wondered if there could be something else. Something she wasn't supposed to be able to feel. Something more powerful than the desires she'd been taught to have.

She sent him away so she wouldn't have to face it, but it couldn't kill her curiosity. She just found other names for it. Ones that were acceptable. Ones she could deal with. Loathing. Hatred. Revenge. If those were the reasons she looked for Cav in every port, she could understand that. If that was why she boarded the *Indulgence*, then so be it. If it allowed her to get closer to him, then she would dedicate herself to it.

But it was never the truth.

And then she left Cav again. Not because she wanted to, but because something else still controlled her. Her fingers curl into fists. She is tired of watching her choices be stripped away. She is tired of being ordered around by things outside of her control.

Under Cav's hands, the final piece of netting falls away. He eases her tentacles free and curls one gently around his finger. "What does Tidus have on you? What did he take?"

She presses her lips together. She's never said it aloud. That would mean admitting it's not temporary, but devastatingly real. She's never told anyone, but then again, she's never had anyone to tell. The words are fragile in her mouth. "My song."

He kneels on the step below her, a knight swearing his fealty. "Then we'll get it back."

Arms around her waist, he lifts onto a higher step. She grits her teeth while her legs knit back together and her other markers fade until Cav can help her to her feet.

They look out across the sea from the edge of the platform. The moon is high, but even without it, the lights of the marketplace are bright. It almost makes it hard to see the blue-flagged sloop headed for the overgrown island in the distance.

Her body aches. It's not used to these sudden changes, tentacles spreading and sewing back together. She's been confined to her land form for so long that she doesn't have the strength to swim after Tidus.

There's no way to stop him.

She sags against the wall, but Cav moves back into the boathouse. He maneuvers through the dark, grunting and pushing until a sailboat splashes into the bay. The wooden ship is rough and worn, a sail hanging feebly from the mast, but Cav hops inside and offers his hand. "It's not much, but it's all we have."

They've been here before. It's déjà vu, but this time, she doesn't hesitate when she takes his hand and climbs down beside him. He casts them off into the water and tugs at the sails until they billow.

It's not a rapid pace, but they're moving. They glide along the island and nearly reach the southern port when something tears above them, and the weakened sail flutters with a massive rip down the middle.

Cav curses and tries to adjust, but their boat slows to a glacial pace. Tidus's ship has disappeared from sight.

"Fuck!" Lyx slams her fist against the side of the ship and splashes into the water.

Cool water clings to her skin. It's familiar. She peers over the edge of the boat and down at her reflection. Her shadow blurs the edges, and her face ripples until she and the ocean become indistinguishable.

Hesitantly, she lowers her fingers. They dip into the water, and she swears something holds onto her. With a steadying breath, she shuts her eyes and tries to sense every droplet that flows between her fingers.

Please.

She doesn't know what she's asking. It's been years since she reached out to the sea. Her cheeks burn. Maybe this is foolish — or maybe Cav's audacity has finally rubbed off on her. Her fingers drift through the water in search of something. A connection. A response. She isn't sure any longer. No matter how she hopes, there's nothing. She almost withdraws, but instead, she sinks her hand in deeper and submerges up to her elbow.

Around her, the water fizzes. Hope lodges in her throat.

Take us to the island. Please. I'll come back to you. I'll send Tidus back, too.

Behind her, Cav sighs. "I can't fix it. It's —"

The boat jerks and sends Cav toppling. Lyx braces against the side, holding Cav in place when the boat takes off across the water. It sprays up around them as they bounce along the waves. The worn boat creaks with effort. Cav and Lyx cling to whatever they can, and behind them, a wake churns. Cav laughs above the sound of the water. It's rough and choppy, jostling them as the boat moves faster than should be possible. In minutes, the overgrown island in the distance becomes a stretch of beach before them.

The boat gives out when they reach the shallows. The vessel slows, stutters, and falls apart at the seams.

Cav lifts Lyx onto his strong shoulder and wades toward the shore. She trails her fingers into the water behind him.

Thank you. Thank you. Thank you.

The waves rush up after them and urge them forward.

THIRTY-EIGHT

Lyx

Sand kicks up behind Cav and Lyx as they run. The island is covered in wild shrubbery, vines and brambles that stretch out along the beach. They maneuver the coastline, pushing through bushes and branches until they come across a clearing.

It hosts a slipway hidden from view of the other islands. A metal rail slopes out of the water and up to a cradle that holds the *Indulgence* aloft. Its hull is exposed, already scraped free of barnacles and seaweed. Otherwise, the ship is dark and empty.

On the ramp below are half a dozen nets, full of oysters and clams and scallops. It looks like a haul fresh from the ocean, but Lyx knows better. These are no ordinary mussels. These mollusks are coming *off* the ship. The shells look almost natural, but when she creeps closer, the undertones ripple with magic. Fiery red, aquatic blue, deathly white, like the pearls she found on board.

Something shatters next to the ship. Lyx and Cav move through the shadows until they find a clam smashed on the ground. Tidus kneels over it and curses when he slices his finger on the jagged shell, but the pain is soon forgotten. With one hand, he lifts a shimmering pearl from the wreckage.

He wastes no time pocketing it and moving onto the next shell. His greedy, roughened fingers force their way between the oyster's lips and pry it apart. The shell flickers, but when Tidus wrenches the pearl free, the oyster's hue fades in a dying gasp.

Only now does Tidus notice Cav and Lyx. He jerks the gun from his waistband and points it toward each of them. "How the fuck did you get here?"

Lyx tries to keep Cav behind her, but he has the same idea. When Cav steps forward, Tidus hones the gun on him.

"You left me to drown!" Lyx shouts.

Tidus jerks the gun back to her. "That's chaos, baby!" With his empty hand, he lifts a bag of mollusks and slams it onto the ground. Every swing makes Lyx flinch as the air fills with a chorus of *cracks*, stirring a sickly feeling in her stomach.

Pearls roll and bounce at Tidus's feet. His movements are loose and easy now, but it won't last. It never does.

"Is this your plan?" she calls. "Destroy the shells to get back at Heathen?" If Tidus starts talking, maybe they can slip away. Maybe they can find Heathen and the others. With one hand on Cav's shirt, Lyx takes a step back.

Tidus cocks the gun.

Lyx's heart thuds. She knows what's coming from the sharpness of his smile. His temper is a tidal wave, rising inside him and sucking the life from everything else. With his boot, he kicks the mollusks aside and steps over them.

Cav presses Lyx behind him, but Tidus keeps prowling

toward them. They back up into the bushes, Lyx's nails digging into Cav's arm to shove him aside. He doesn't move.

"I'm not going to destroy them," Tidus murmurs.

He lifts the barrel of the gun to Lyx's head, and a nauseous tide rises inside her.

Then Tidus turns the gun on Cav. "Because you are."

Lyx's mind stutters, repeating the phrase to make some sense of it.

"You won't do it for *me*, of course," Tidus admits. When he lowers his chin to his shoulder, there's a vicious glint in his eyes. "*Kiss her goodbye.*"

The shell glows. Ice seeps through Lyx's blood. The shell has never glowed for anyone else. She doesn't know what that means, what Tidus expects to happen...

Until Cav turns to face her.

Something is wrong. His eyes are panicked, but then clouds drift across his gaze like fog over the sea. There is no emotion any longer. He grabs her waist and presses his mouth to hers like it's the last time.

Her head swims. "What are you doing?" she hisses and clutches at him, but it's no use. He has one thought on his mind.

Tidus laughs in surprise, uncocking the gun and stuffing it back into his waistband. "Now, Cavalier: *burn the Indulgence to the ground.*"

Unblinking, Cav releases Lyx and moves toward the ship.

She struggles to hold onto him. "Cav! *Stop!*" She rushes in front of him, but it's like fighting a rip current, the dead weight of his goal pushing him forward. He doesn't hear her. He doesn't see her. He's possessed, a pirate locked inside her song.

"That's not how it works," she pants. She whirls back to Tidus. "You can't use my song. It's impossible. You tried it before —"

"We just weren't doing it right."

We. Like the two of them are in this together. Like she wanted this. Her feet are filled with lead. She moves toward the ship, but it's too late. Cav is already there. All she can do is watch when his lips part, fire billowing from his throat and spreading across the hull.

Tidus settles beside her. "I couldn't be sure. The shell's been acting strange since you saw him again. But in the boathouse, I knew." Firelight bounces off his smile. "When I told him to stop, and the shell lit up, and he couldn't move..." He whistles. "The song works. We just needed someone who wanted to hear it. Someone who's in love with you."

The fire spreads, eating up the sides of the ships and lighting the ropes.

Tidus cups his hands around his mouth. *"Climb aboard, Cav!"*

Mindlessly, Cav walks through the smoke toward the ladder. Lyx scrambles after him, but it doesn't matter. Nothing will keep him from his goal. Wincing, she hangs all her weight on his wounded shoulder, but he barely flinches.

"Stop him!" she begs. "Call him back!" Desperately, she pries his fingers from the rungs, but he's so determined. He has only one thought. One desire. One purpose.

A flaming rope falls and singes her shoulder. She jumps back, watching the fire spread onto a bag of mollusks. It slowly consumes the shells, making them hiss and scream until the fire catches onto the next net.

"We can do so much with this!" Tidus calls.

Chaos clogs Lyx's throat, followed by smoke billowing so thick she can no longer see Cav. She feels for the ladder hanging from the ship, but it crumples at her feet and burns through the last of her hope.

Her stomach heaves. She stumbles away from the ship and falls to her knees and tries not to retch. Her eyes burn, but she can't wipe away the tears. Behind the ship, flames dance dangerously close to the brush. At this rate, the *Indulgence* will burn to ash, and then the fire will eat across the rest of the island. Everyone will die. *Cav* will die, if he hasn't already.

Tidus watches it like it's a beautiful sunset. With a sigh, he crouches beside her and offers his hand. "Come on. Let's celebrate."

Rage boils inside her. It lifts her onto her feet, slamming her into Tidus and knocking them both to the ground. They tumble over each other until he wrestles on top of her and strains to keep her pinned. "Do not fucking waste this! Think of what we could do. Look at what we've already done!"

Behind him, the *Indulgence* burns. Heat wafts over her body. It's powerful, so much more powerful than one siren without her song.

"You could make a hundred people fall for you," Tidus shouts. "A thousand. A whole *fleet* of pirates, desperate to serve. You'd never be hungry again!"

Her teeth grit. She knows where this is headed. She can't go there again. She *can't.* "Give me my song!"

Foolish, desperate hope lodges in her chest. Tidus got what he wanted. The *Indulgence* is burning and turning everything Heathen built to ash. The job is done. If she has her song, she can still save Cav. She can still —

Tidus gives her a pitying smile. "You know I can't do that."

Her body goes numb. She sinks out of herself and into a hole inside the earth. Deep down, she knew this was coming. She was foolish to believe anything else, but it was all she had. With her song, she could be free. She could be whole again. She could get back to the life she had before all of this. Back to the person she used to be.

But her song is not hers any longer. It hasn't been for a

long time. It never will be again.

The resistance leeches out of her. Finally, Tidus rolls off her. He sits in the sand and watches the world burn. This feels like drowning, too.

Her hand brushes something cold and rough. She spreads her fingers over the weathered stone. In the corner of her eye, something glows.

Tidus doesn't notice the shell flickering in his chest. Lyx's throat aches to be reunited, but her song is different this time. It no longer reaches out to pull her toward it; instead, it seems to be pushing her away.

Her heart breaks. Sadness threatens to consume her, but she understands. No matter what else Tidus took from her, he could never take that.

She can't keep looking behind her. She can't keep fighting to return to a life she isn't sure she ever wanted. She can't go back. The person she used to be is gone.

Slowly, she pushes off the ground. Her fingers curl around the rock, heavy and solid amongst the fire and smoke.

Tidus doesn't look away from the ship. "You'll come around, Lyx. You'll see."

She swings. Pain jolts up her arm. The rock connects with the shell, and Tidus sprawls back and clutches at his chest.

The shell is still intact. He breathes a sigh of relief, snarling and raring back his arm to lunge for her —

The crack in the shell spreads. It splits like ice over water, a shrill scream building in the air. The light inside it glows so bright that Lyx has to cover her eyes and turn her face away before the shell bursts.

Shrapnel pelts her skin. Her throat grasps and tightens, reaching for the final trail of her song, but it's gone. It slips away, fading further and further until she can no longer feel its pull.

Her song is free.

The husk of the shell topples from Tidus's shoulder. He grapples to reassemble the broken pieces, but they fall apart in his hands. "Fucking *bitch!*"

He collides with her. It takes all her strength to jam her knee into his stomach and knock the wind from him. Even then, he keeps coming. She gets her feet under her and scrambles toward the blazing ship, searching desperately for Cav. Her song is gone. He should be free. He should be —

A bullet whizzes past her. She ducks behind a barrel, and through the smoke, she can make out a body lying limply on the boat ramp. Cav is blackened with soot, facedown and arms outstretched.

More shots fire. One pierces the barrel. Liquid leaks onto her feet, and when it becomes red and muddy, she realizes her cheek is bleeding.

Tidus circles in front of her and aims straight for her head — but the gun clicks. He squeezes the trigger again, but the chamber is empty. With a scream, he drags Lyx to her feet and flings her backward. Something jams into her side, a metal switch creaking out of place as she slides to the ground. The pain is dizzying. She tries to stand, but Tidus is on top of her, falling to his knees on either side of her. "You threw this away. For *what*?!"

Beneath the ship, its wooden supports begin to burn. They char and crack as the full weight of the hull settles onto them.

Tidus's fingers dig into her throat. "For *him*? He's nothing! He's dead!"

Gravity takes its toll. The metal carriage holding the *Indulgence* shifts inch by inch.

Tidus's face distorts. "You can't even love him! You can't love anything!"

Darkness creeps in from the edge of Lyx's vision. *This is drowning*, she remembers. Her fingers fumble for something, anything, but all she finds is a pile of rope.

Beside them, the ship picks up speed. The rope slips through her hands as the coil unravels. Her mind is cloudy. She doesn't fight Tidus's hold. She grabs the rope, entangling and knotting it hopelessly around Tidus's thigh.

He bears down harder. He never looks at where she's scrabbling at his leg, where the pile of rope is growing smaller, where it finally pulls taut.

Tidus is yanked off her, dragged behind the ship while he shouts and claws at his leg. His fingernails scrape the ramp for purchase, but there's no stopping it. He can't free himself.

The *Indulgence* crashes into the water and sends up a massive spray. Waves pour over the ship's railing and roll to the other side. It's like the ocean is stirring the water back and forth, rocking the ship side to side until the entire blaze is extinguished.

There's nothing left of Tidus. Not even a struggle.

The sea always claims its due.

THIRTY-NINE

Cav

Cav can't open his eyes. Raw pain scratches up his throat, branching into his shoulder until it throbs. His skin is tight and dry. His body is too heavy, or too weak, to move. There's a crackling in his ears, but past that, he hears waves crashing.

He smiles. He remembers this. For years, he's dreamt of returning to this moment. Back to his shipwreck, when his eyelashes were crusted with salt, and his nose was scraped out by seawater. He knows what comes next. He lies on his back and sinks into the feeling of her fingers brushing hair from his face.

But something's wrong. The ocean sounds too far away. When he inhales, he breaks into a fit of coughing. The scent of fire burns away everything else.

He fights to open his eyes. Around him, the world is blurry and streaked with shadows. This is not the grotto. There is no rock formation overhead, no waves lapping at his feet, no water dripping onto his face. Above him, stars blink in the hazy sky. Flames dance on the debris around him. His scales are gritty with ash.

His neck creaks in protest when he turns toward the ocean. There bobs the *Indulgence*, looking almost peaceful, aside from the burnt sails and charred hull.

Cav's brow knits. That small movement makes him groan, but cool hands cradle his face. There she is. Lyx. *Beautiful* Lyx, looking down on him where his head rests in her lap.

"I think we've — been here before," he rasps.

Her lip quivers, and her body glows, but her eyes look wearier than he's seen. She keeps moving her hands down his body. He arches into them until he realizes she's checking for something. Wounds. Tenderness.

Her cheek is bleeding. He reaches toward it. "What's wrong?" Clearly *something* is, but his mind is too thick with muck to remember how they got here.

Her hands rest on his chest. "You don't remember," she murmurs, like she's to blame for the state he's in.

Cav reaches through the cloud of his memories. There was a sailboat, nets of oysters, a gun... Tidus was here. Cav tries to sit up, but his shoulder spasms. "Is he still here? Is he —"

Lyx lowers him back to her lap. "Gone."

He sighs with relief, but that stirs up another round of coughing. "Did he — start a fire?"

Lyx's gaze flicks to Cav's mouth. Every breath he takes is a struggle, his lungs chafed with smoke. It's strange; his body can withstand more fire than most, but this is different. This feels like he was standing in the middle of it.

A dream unravels in his mind. It's so distant he can hardly remember it. Lyx's voice in his ear. A respite, drawing him out of his body to watch from above. Someone set fire to the ship.

Someone stepped into the blaze. Someone stoked the heat that he can still feel on his skin.

Not someone. *Cav.* It was his hands curling around the ship's ladder. It was his eyes staring up at the wooden beams. It was his mouth spilling flames.

This destruction is all Cav's doing.

From deeper in the island, a stampede of footsteps grows. Heathen and Cypher emerge from the brush, followed by the remaining crew. Their chests are heaving, eyes rimmed with sleep, trying to make sense of the ruin around them.

"Cav?" Heathen pants. "How are you..." They blink blearily toward the empty ramp. "Where's the fire? We saw it. We saw..."

Shame spreads up the back of Cav's neck. With a wince, he tries to push to his feet, but Lyx bears the brunt of his weight. Heathen rushes toward them, reaching to support him before she catches sight of his singed flesh. "You're burned."

Behind her, the rest of the crew sprints toward the water, piling into dinghies and rowing to secure the *Indulgence*. Cypher stays behind. Already, the flaming ship tattoo is fading. The mark has served its purpose.

Guilt and soot clog Cav's throat. "It was — Prodeus," he chokes. He has to place a hand on his knees to catch his breath. "He's been watching — following us."

"He did this? After all this time?" Heathen scans the beach. "Where is he?"

Lyx looks out across the water. "Returned to the sea."

Cypher crouches next to a pile of scorched netting, searching the debris before she rubs the sooty tips of her fingers. "Something doesn't add up." She rises to her feet, gaze flicking over both of them. "How did he know where to find the *Indulgence*?"

Cav schools his expression. "I told you — he's been

following us." He takes a few ragged breaths. "He must have been — watching you today." He wants to tell the truth, but that means giving up Lyx, and he refuses to do that.

"Today." Cypher gestures toward Lyx. "After *she* disappears and magically returns?"

Cav huffs. "I'm sure his boat is — somewhere close. Look for it."

"Who *really* set the fire?"

"I did." Cav's admission stuns Cypher and Heathen. Lyx's fingers curl around his wrist, but he doesn't take it back.

Cypher's head shakes slowly. "You wouldn't do that." Her eyes dart toward Lyx. "Not without someone else pulling the strings."

"I told you — it was me!" Cav limps in front of Lyx. "She didn't do this. She didn't cause it."

"She's the only one with that kind of power!"

"Cypher..." Heathen warns.

Cypher throws up her hands. "If she used her song on you, you'd do anything she wanted. Anything!" A wild thought crosses her mind. "Was she — was she *working* with him? Is that who she's been meeting?"

The beach falls silent. Heathen opens her mouth, but when she looks at Lyx, it snaps shut again.

Cav steps forward. "N-"

"Yes." Lyx's voice is certain and strong. Cav didn't expect her to admit it amidst all the hostility. Clearly, neither did Cypher, whose eyes are wide as dinner plates. "I knew him as Tidus." Lyx glances at Heathen. "He captured me after he broke off from you. Within a couple of years, his crew fell apart, and he wanted revenge. That's why I needed a spot on your ship. To spy on your business. To find out how you collected pleasure."

"I fucking knew it," Cypher spits.

"He was — blackmailing her!" Cav's lip curls, the spikes

along his spine flaring. "He tried — to kill her!"

Lyx smooths a hand down his back. "I admit, I told Tidus about the pearls, but I tried to turn his attention elsewhere. That's why I left your ship this morning."

Cypher scoffs. "Clearly, it didn't work."

"He wanted to — destroy everything!" Cav growls, but his voice gives out. It takes a long moment before he can speak again. Slowly. "He was...going to burn...the whole island down. Lyx...brought us here. She saved everything."

Cypher's mouth twists. Heathen's voice is slow and methodical. "How did Tidus control you? With your song, couldn't you force him to do whatever you please?"

Lyx's hand flutters toward her throat, but it drops quickly. She wets her lips before she speaks. "He had my song. That's why I couldn't leave him." She gestures toward the still-smoldering nets. "That's why Cav started the fire. He had no choice. Tidus used my song to command him."

The memories of it become more familiar. Cav's mind was trapped in his body like a puppet on a string, nothing like the time Lyx used her song on him in the grotto. That felt like divine guidance; tonight felt like a parasite taking over.

Cypher's eyes narrow. "How did you stop him?"

Lyx searches the ground, moving a few paces away and returning with fragments of a spiral shell. It's large and crusted with barnacles, much like Tidus had been. Lyx holds the pieces out, but her fingers curl like she wants to cradle them. "I destroyed it."

Cav sucks in a breath. He knew she'd stopped Tidus, but he didn't know how.

Heathen reaches for the shell. "That's where he kept it? Your song?" She looks at the shells scattered around them, burnt and broken husks. Heathen clears their throat and averts their eyes. "I'm afraid...I may have played a part in your capture."

Lyx stiffens.

"I'm not sure how, exactly," Heathen explains. "But that shell looks like one of mine. We tried different containers for collecting pleasure: bottles, dice, barrels. Seashells were the first breakthrough. Once the mollusks produced pearls, we set the other shells aside."

Lyx's glare is hot. "Who's 'we'?"

Heathen's mouth presses into a thin line. "It doesn't matter."

"Is that who the letter in your desk was from?"

Heathen blanches. Cypher looks surprised. Cav can't help but be a little impressed, leaning toward her to whisper. "You were in — Heathen's office?"

"The shells," Heathen interjects, "reside on a small island. It's remote. I assure you, no one would have willingly provided the shells to Tidus. To anyone."

"But could someone have stolen them?" Lyx asks. "If someone swam up to shore, could they take what they wanted?"

"They would need a ship to get there." Heathen's eyes narrow on a strange, new thought. "*Most* people would need a ship. And that would surely be spotted."

Lyx's eyes darken on some distant memory. Her fingers curl around the shell in her hand. "How careless to leave something so powerful out in the open."

"It was only meant to collect pleasure. We didn't —" Heathen bites their tongue with a remorseful shake of their head. "You're right. I'm sorry. It shouldn't have happened. It *won't* happen again."

Lyx's scales are still raised, but she eases back next to Cav.

Heathen pushes the hair out of their eyes and watches the *Indulgence* slowly being towed back to shore. "You two should rest. There's a cottage down the path through the trees. We can finish this in the morning."

The thought of a bed makes Cav's entire body throb. The weight of the night settles over him, churning through his aching muscles and tired limbs. Lyx takes some of his weight, and the two begin to make their way toward the forest.

"And Lyx?" Heathen calls after them. When they turn, she's kneeling to take an oyster in her hand. There's an almost sadness to her motions as she traces what remains of its shape. "I can't change what happened, but I would like to try to make it right. If you'll take it, there's a place for you on our ship." She swipes a line of soot with her finger. "Whatever's left of it."

Behind her, Cypher folds her arms across her chest. A smirk flickers on Lyx's lips. "Because I know about the pearls. About how you collect pleasure. *Keep your enemies close.*"

Heathen's lip quirks. "I do not consider you my enemy, but I would be foolish not to keep that information under wraps...but that's not the only reason." They look past Lyx to Cav. "Someone told me that the beauty of the *Indulgence* is that it's safe. If you're looking for that, I hope we can provide it." After a long moment, Heathen bows their head. "The offer's on the table. Think it over."

FORTY

Lyx

Lyx helps Cav through the woods. Around them, the forest slowly returns to life, whirring and calling without the threat of fire. They come across an outdoor shower, and Lyx sits Cav on the wooden bench and washes the soot from both of them until the water runs clear.

The nearby cottage is quaint, one large room strewn with clothing and alcove beds carved around the windows. Lyx finds a bed that's undisturbed and eases Cav up against the pillows before she rifles through the others' bags.

Cav's lip quirks. "Stealing from our hosts?"

Lyx gathers fresh clothing and potion bottles, summoning the words through the painful vice of her throat. "I'd say we've earned it." She returns to the bed and dresses them both, plying Cav with medicine and water. He makes her pour all of it from her hand.

By the time she's done, his breathing is still shallow, but

his cough has calmed from violent to sporadic bursts. His eyelids are heavy where his head lolls against the pillows. Even after treatment, the burns on his body are still vicious beneath the bandages, raw skin surrounded by crusted blood.

Lyx digs her nails into her palm. She wishes it was Tidus's neck. Her hatred has amplified. It doesn't matter that he's gone, that he's gotten what he deserves. She wants to give him *more*. It's a cruel twist of fate that when Tidus had the shell, he held all her power. She felt useless without it. Hopeless. Weak. Yet now that her song is gone for good, just seeing Cav's wounds makes her feel deadly. Suddenly, she could kill Tidus with her bare hands. Maybe she could bring him back just to make him suffer. Maybe the ocean would help. Maybe —

"Are you going to leave again?" Cav's voice is little more than a whisper, his eyes barely cracked in their war against exhaustion. There is no doubt in his expression. He already knows the answer, body braced for the familiar feeling of falling asleep together and waking up alone.

That breaks something in Lyx's chest. It's a crack she's long ignored, but the chisel of Cav's eyes finds the seam and taps it gently. When that fissure opens, the hate boiling inside her begins to leak and leave room for something else. She sinks down on the end of the bed. "Yes."

Cav doesn't flinch, but a deep-seated hurt blooms behind his eyes.

Lyx's heart trips. She has to say the rest. She has to speak the words she's wanted to say since the last night in the grotto. Roughly, she swallows. "And I want you to come with me."

Cav tries to sit up, wincing and coughing, but she reaches out to still him.

"I don't want to rejoin the *Indulgence*," she says. "Right now, I want..." Hesitantly, she rests the heel of her hand on the mattress. Without thinking, she reaches toward his, and he mirrors her to slot their fingers between each other. Her chest flutters. "I want to decide where I go. What I do. I want to be *free*. I know that ship is your home —"

"It's not my home if you aren't there." He presses their palms together, lowering his head to catch her eyes. "I mean it. Take me with you. I wouldn't miss it for anything." He winces when his wounds shift. "I may be slower now, but —"

"I'll wait." She flushes at her own eagerness. It surprises her, almost as much as his. No one would follow a siren without some convincing...no one, except for Cav.

He lifts a hand to run his thumb down the column of her throat. His face is etched with regret, like she's not the only one holding her pain. "I'm sorry we didn't get your song back. That was the only thing you wanted."

For the first time, she faces it fully. Her eyes close. She swallows again, breathing deep and sinking into the loss. This pain is different. It's not the separation she spent years accepting; it is a void, a chasm, an emptiness that cannot be filled. When she reaches outside of herself, there is no painful response. There is nothing. Nothing to call to. Nothing to answer her.

Her throat aches like she screamed it raw, like a hand reached into her mouth and dragged out her vocal cords. Every breath gets caught on the gaping wound, but when she opens her eyes, Cav sits in front of her. When she looks at him, a balm smooths over the pain. The sight of him alone dulls the ache until it's easier to bear. "I'm not sorry."

It's blasphemy coming from a siren, but somehow, that feels good. It's *freeing*. She's never found these words before, but they rise to the surface like the empty space in her is desperate to be filled.

"I spent my whole life seeking misery, because I was supposed to. I was made to create turmoil. To fight — my siblings, the hunters...my emotions." Her eyes dip. "I was like the tide, moved by these forces out of my control. My song was just another thing to pull on me. But I needed it, because it was the only way to get what I wanted — but *what* did I want? *Why* did I want it?"

The words feel like they're spilling out of her now, possessed by the effusive spirit that always has a hold on Cav.

"I never thought about that. It didn't matter. I was only allowed to hunger for one thing." She looks at Cav again — at the vibrant heat pooling in his golden eyes — and her body thrums. "But I see now that it didn't dampen my other appetites. It only made them stronger."

Cav's chest glows. He doesn't look away from her, that same hunger spreading across his face. "What other appetites?"

The glint in his eye says he knows the answer. He's always known it, even when she swore it was impossible. But knowing is not enough. He wants to hear her say it. Her body flushes with nerves, apprehension, and the thrill of finally speaking it aloud. "Something I don't believe in."

A smile tugs at his lips.

The sight of it fills her so completely that the hollow place inside her no longer aches as strongly. "I do have sentimental feelings...for you." Each word sits on her tongue so that she can savor the taste, the weight, the feeling. "I do...love you."

Her mouth tingles around the words when Cav reaches to pull her closer.

All her life, she thought love was weak and fragile. It couldn't be what she felt for Cav. Love wasn't powerful enough to captivate her thoughts and drive her every motion. To keep her going for days while she dreamt of finding him again. To fill her with feeling so compelling that she needed to eat him alive. She thought only hatred could do that. Now, she understands. It was always this. It has always been this.

Love.

His lips find her cheek, and her head swims. How can one

emotion be so potent and delicate all at once? He kisses her temple. "You love me," he teases, but he says it again with a reverence she's never heard before. "You love me."

Her heart swells, and she groans when she realizes she wants this dragon to antagonize her for the rest of time. It's overwhelming. It's strange. It's *embarrassing*.

She presses her forehead into the side of his neck. "I swore I'd never crave you." She mouths at his pulse to make her voice sound weary, but her affection gets in the way. "Those roaming hands. That cocksure smile. The never-ending stream of your voice."

Depths, she wants them all. Her grip tightens in his shirt, and his fingers curl in her hair until the curved bridge of his nose brushes hers. Her body illuminates the window.

"My most vicious captor..." His breath is warm against her lips. "You haven't had your song since you found me again, yet you still have me ensnared."

Her chest fills with bubbles. She rolls her eyes, but he cups her jaw to keep her attention.

"I can't imagine what it's like to lose that, but you're still just as powerful. Just as captivating. Just as strong. You're not lacking in anything. You did all of this without it."

Her head tilts into his hand. She never recognized it before. Even without her power, she survived Tidus. She got a place on the *Indulgence*. She discovered the pearls. Above everything else, she kept Cav alive, when days ago, she thought she was incapable. What once felt like the only worthwhile part of her now seems like a relic from another time. She does not need her song to be whole.

"And you have me without it." Cav's voice grows softer. "I want to give you everything you crave. You don't need command or persuasion." His thumb brushes her cheek. "You don't need magic to have my devotion. It's always been yours. It always will be."

She molds their mouths together, and he meets her with the same need. He always does. Somehow, this pirate has found a way to match a siren's intensity. It's never scared him off; if anything, it draws him closer. When they stand on the precipice of what this could be, he doesn't back away. He puts his arm around her waist and cuts the lifeboat free, sending them plunging into the unknown together.

For so long, she thought only pain and suffering could sustain her, but perhaps chaos is more than that. Perhaps it's the unexpected. Like Cav, crashing in her grotto. Offering his cheek to her hand. Feeding her his scales.

Like her, falling impossibly in love with him.

EPILOGUE

Lyx

It's still dark out when Cav's tail curls around the back of Lyx's neck, his lips soft against her hairline. "Want to watch the sunrise?"

Even half-asleep, her skin glows at the promise of the unexpected.

Cav's smile spreads against her jaw, and that's nearly enough to change her answer and keep her tucked against him. It'll be cold outside. If she listens closely, she can already hear tiny flakes *pinging* against the window. She'd never seen snow before — not until Cav charted a course for the Winter Isles. It's one of many places he was happy to show her, one of many things he encouraged her to experience for herself.

He takes her everywhere in this old sloop. It's weathered and worn, but it never lets them down, as if the ocean itself blesses all their journeys. Unlike Tidus's ship, this one never feels cramped or suffocating. Instead, it's as warm and bright as the stove crackling in the corner of the room.

Cozy. A word Lyx had never understood before. A word that feels right now.

Almost as right as being next to Cav. When they set off on their own after the fire, she tried to resist him. Just a little. Just enough to prove to herself that she wasn't being controlled by someone else. She tried to make decisions without being distracted by the pools of his eyes, the tilt of his smile, and the heat of his hands.

Cav obliged her everything. He laid out maps for her to wander, setting new courses without question, happy to be guided by her whims.

They returned to the grotto once. It was overrun with broken crates and empty bottles from the slew of hunters that followed in Tidus's wake. Those pirates were long gone now, but Lyx felt fury rising inside her. Of course they'd invaded siren territory, but to tarnish the only place where she had memories of Cav? The place where they'd first been together?

Cav saw the change in her eyes. Softly, he touched her cheek before he started to clean up the bank. After a couple of hours, the two of them had the cave looking just the way it used to. It was like being transported back in time. Before Tidus. Before the *Indulgence.* Before Lyx knew what love was. As the sun set, she laid Cav out on the shoreline and showed him everything she wished she had the first time they were there.

They haven't stopped sailing together. Cav looks perfect behind the wheel of this ship, like he was born to be there, wind tousling his hair while he scans the horizon for the next adventure...and his eyes always land on her.

It makes her stomach flip. At first, she feared that her hunger would slip out of control. What if happiness wasn't enough? What if she truly needed the misery she'd always forced herself to digest?

She should never have worried. Since she's been alone with Cav, her skin has become smooth and bright. She's forgotten what it's like to be hungry. In fact, she's put on more weight, because Cav never passes up a chance to feed *all* her appetites.

Like now, when he pushes the quilt down her legs. She makes a sound of protest, but she allows herself to be guided out of their tousled bed and onto the snowy deck. The sudden cold is biting, but Cav's laughter is warm, and he pulls her into his chest when he strips her of her clothing.

She returns the favor, their hands wandering each other until they're both completely bare. There's only moonlight between them when he steps up onto the railing and offers her his hand.

It's familiar. They've been here more than once. She soaks in the memories before she slips her palm into his and steps up beside him.

Steam rises from the water below. She shivers against the wind, but Cav keeps her close and murmurs against her ear. "You looked like you were sleeping well. Must have been a good dream."

A hum crackles through the sleep in her voice. "The image of bubbles streaming from your mouth has never lost its touch."

His breath teases her lips. "Do all your fantasies still revolve around me?"

They do. They all do. There is not a dream she has that does not involve him. Teeth digging into her lip, she nudges him overboard, and he tugs her right after, sending them both splashing into the hot spring bay.

Salt tingles against her skin. She's still getting used to this — returning to the ocean whenever she chooses. The water embraces her immediately, and no longer does she hide when she transforms. Now, she shows herself off for Cav's eager eyes, surfacing as the changes overtake her.

He looks at her for a long moment, still as awe-struck as the first time. Then he pulls her into him and kisses where her fangs protrude. His hands curve around the billow of her tail while his own sways to keep him afloat. It's second-nature when his legs tangle with her tentacles before he drapes a few tendrils over his shoulder.

Lyx holds her breath at the sight of him, water dripping from his eyelashes like the ice melting around her heart. Some days, she's tempted to return to her old ways. To hunt Mollo down and exact revenge. To begin another endless cycle of suffering for the sake of chaos. But her time with Cav quiets those urges until Lyx can hear *herself* past them. Until she remembers she is not beholden to misery. Until she allows herself to feel every swell of emotion that Cav inspires in her.

Drifting in the water, Lyx plucks a scale from the base of her neck. Its edges are paper-thin and bloodied, but Cav's pupils widen. He opens his mouth eagerly. With one finger, she presses the scale to the flat of his tongue. Their gazes stay locked, her sharp talon teasing his delicate muscle until she speaks. "Take it."

His mouth closes over her, his cheeks hollowing, as warm and wet and inviting as the rest of him.

Arousal twists inside her like a key into a lock. Cav knows it, too, looking up beneath his lashes while he rolls the forks of his tongue against her.

A stinging zap shoots through her tentacles. Cav shudders, leaning into her touch when he swallows her down. Behind him, pink light seeps across the horizon. The waves rock the two of them together, and Cav curls his fingers in the tentacles draped across his shoulder.

"Do you ever wonder if the sea brought us together?" he asks. He leaves her no time to doubt it. "Of all the places I could have landed, I ended up in your grotto. Of all the fancy ships I could have trespassed onto, I wound up on the same one as you."

A smile flits across her face.

Cav turns up his palm to admire the way they weave together, her cool, slick strands against the red heat of his skin. "I think it did." He says it certainly, lifting his hand to kiss her tentacles one by one. "And I think we owe it for all it's done."

Her gaze stays on his lips. "And how do you plan to repay it?"

He grins with sharpened teeth. "By worshipping its finest creation, of course…" Then his kisses reach a boiling point, the forks of his tongue dragging tight on either side of one tentacle.

Electricity crackles through her, forcing her to bite back a whine. No one has ever done *that*. It's delicate and sensual and unpredictable…just like Cav. He is the most unexpected thing she knows, surprising her in ways she never imagined. Just when she thinks he's discovered the last way to astonish her, he touches her for the first time all over again.

He lifts his mouth to her jaw and finds the leftover wound in her neck. His wicked tongue delves into it, licking her clean until her claws drag down his back. It spurs him on, his tongue pressing into the shape of her missing scale, like he can fill the gap.

She moans against his skin, tentacles spasming, wrapping around his thighs and slotting into the heat of his vent.

His laugh is low and breathless, and she chases the sound, hungrier for his happiness than she ever has been for anything else.

When she pulls him under, he needs no song to follow her.

* * * * *

THANK YOU for reading *A Reckless Indulgence*! **Want more Cav & Lyx as well as Sinoe, Heathen, and Cypher's stories?** Sign up for my NEWSLETTER to get an exclusive extended epilogue, and join my PATREON for extra scenes.

AVEDAVICE.COM/NEWSLETTER
AVEDAVICE.COM/DISCORD
PATREON.COM/AVEDAVICE

About the Author

Aveda Vice is an author of unconventional kink and monstrous romances. In their books, you'll find a fondness for queer creatures, polyamorous love, and grumpy girls. She falls down rabbit holes, decorates every day like it's Halloween, and is going to hell.

AVEDAVICE.COM

Sign up for Aveda Vice's NEWSLETTER and PATREON to stay up-to-date on new releases, special offers, and bonus content.

Follow @AVEDAVICE on social media for sneak peaks and promotions.

Join the DISCORD READER GROUP for community chats and posts.

Leave a review for this book on RETAIL and REVIEW sites.

Acknowledgements

Burnout is a bitch. I wasn't sure I'd ever finish this book, but I'm so glad that I finally did.

Thank you to my wonderful beta readers, Steph, May, and Gabbi, for helping guide and shape this story. Your feedback was just the breath of fresh air that I needed.

Rabbit, no matter how much time passes, you are always a wonderful sounding board.